ROMANCE

W9-BUH-423

43055

Large Print Bal
Balogh, Mary.
One night for love /

WITHDRAWN

DEC 1999
STACKS

NEWARK PUBLIC LIBRARY
NEWARK, OHIO

GAYLORD M

One Night
for Love

Mary Balogh

One Night
for Love

WHEELER
PUBLISHING, INC.
ROCKLAND, MA

★ AN AMERICAN COMPANY ★

Copyright © 1999 by Mary Balogh
All rights reserved.

Published in Large Print by arrangement with Dell Publishing, a division of Random House, Inc. in the United States and Canada

Wheeler Large Print Book Series.

Set in 16 pt Plantin.

Library of Congress Cataloging-in-Publication Data

Balogh, Mary.
   One night for love / Mary Balogh.
     p. (large print) cm.(Wheeler large print book series)
   ISBN 1-56895-795-5 (softcover)
   1. Napoleonic Wars, 1800-1815—Participation, British—Fiction. 2. Large type books. I. Title. II. Series
[PR6052.A465O54   1999]
813'.54—dc21   99-048206
                                         CIP

To Gayle Knutson,
a former student and present friend,
who designed and created my Web site
in time for the promotion of this book.
With thanks.

www.marybalogh.com

NEWARK PUBLIC LIBRARY
NEWARK, OHIO 43055-5087

Large Print Bal
Balogh, Mary.
One night for love /

5692604

PART I

The Return

1

Despite the early hour and the chilly weather, the yard of the White Horse Inn in Fetter Lane, London, was crowded and noisy. The stagecoach for the West Country was preparing to make its daily run. Few passengers had yet boarded; most were milling about anxiously to see that their luggage had been properly stowed. Hawkers attempted to sell their wares to passengers for whom the day would be long and tedious. Grooms bustled about their business. Ragged children, when they were not being shooed back into the street, darted about, feeding on the excitement.

The guard blew his horn, a deafening warning that the coach would be departing within a few minutes and anyone with a ticket would be well advised to climb aboard.

Captain Gordon Harris, looking smart in the green regimentals of the Ninety-fifth Rifles, and his young wife, who was warmly and modishly dressed, looked somewhat out of place in such inelegant surroundings. But they were not themselves passengers. They had accompanied a woman to the White Horse in order to see her on her way.

Her appearance was in marked contrast to theirs. While she was clean and tidy, she was

3

undeniably shabby. She wore a simple high-waisted cotton dress with a shawl for warmth. Both garments looked well worn and well washed. Her bonnet, which had perhaps once been pretty even if never quite modish, had clearly shielded its wearer from one too many rainstorms. Its wide brim was limp and misshapen. She was a young woman—indeed, she was so small and so slight of frame that she might at first glance have been mistaken for a mere girl. But there was something about her that drew second, more lingering glances from several of the men who were busy about their various tasks. There were beauty and grace and some indefinable air of femininity about her to proclaim that she was indeed a woman.

"I must be getting into the coach," she said with a smile for the captain and his wife. "You need not stay here any longer. It is too cold to be standing about." She held out both her slim hands to Mrs. Harris, though she looked alternately at both of them. "How will I ever be able to thank you sufficiently for all you have done for me?"

Tears sprang to Mrs. Harris's eyes, and she enfolded the young woman tightly in her arms. "We have done nothing of any great significance," she said. "And now we are abandoning you to travel on the stage, the very cheapest form of transportation, when you might have gone more respectably by post chaise or at the very worst by the mailcoach."

"I have borrowed enough from you," the young woman said, "without indulging in needless extravagances."

"*Borrowed.*" Mrs. Harris removed a lace-edged handkerchief from her reticule and dabbed at her eyes with it.

"It is still not too late to alter your plans, you know." Captain Harris took one of the young woman's hands in both of his own. "Come back to our hotel with us for breakfast and I shall write that letter even before I eat, and send it on its way. I daresay there will be an answer within the week."

"No, sir," she told him quite firmly, though she smiled. "I cannot wait. I must go."

He did not argue further but sighed, patted her hand, and then impulsively pulled her into a hug as his wife had done. By that time she was in danger of losing the inside seat he had quite adamantly insisted upon. He had even slipped the coachman a tip to ensure her a window seat for the long journey to the village of Upper Newbury in Dorsetshire. But a large woman, who looked as if she might be ready to take on any coachman or any army captain who dared cross her, or indeed both at once, was already settling herself into the only window seat still available.

The young woman had to squeeze herself into a middle seat. But she did not appear to share the captain's wrath. She smiled and lifted a hand in farewell. As she did so, the guard's horn blew again as a warning to everyone nearby that the stage was about to begin its journey.

Mrs. Harris's gloved hand was still raised in an answering farewell wave after the stagecoach had rumbled out of the yard, turned onto the street, and disappeared from sight.

"I have never in my life known anyone so stubborn," she said, using her handkerchief again. "Or anyone so dear. What will become of her, Gordon?"

The captain sighed once more. "I fear she is doing the wrong thing," he said. "Almost a year and a half has passed, and what seemed like madness even at the time will doubtless be a total impossibility now. But she does not understand."

"Her sudden appearance is going to come as a dreadful shock," Mrs. Harris said. "Oh, foolish girl to have refused to delay even a few days while you wrote a letter. How will she *manage*, Gordon? She is so small and so frail and so—so *innocent*. I fear for her."

"For as long as I have known Lily," Captain Harris replied, "she has looked much the same, though admittedly she is thinner than she used to be. The appearance of fragility and innocence are largely illusory, though. We know that she has been through a great deal that would severely test the roughest and toughest of my men. But she must have experienced worse things that we can only imagine."

"I prefer not even to try," his wife said fervently.

"She has survived, Maisie," he reminded her, "with her pride and her courage intact. And her sweetness too—she seems not to have been embittered. Despite everything there still appears to be more than a touch of innocence about her."

"What will he do when she arrives?" she

6

asked as they began to walk back to their hotel for breakfast. "Oh dear, he really ought to have been warned."

⌇

Newbury Abbey, the country seat and principal estate of the Earl of Kilbourne in Dorsetshire, was an imposing mansion in a large, carefully tended park that included a secluded, fern-laden valley and a private golden beach. Beyond the gates of the park, Upper Newbury was a picturesque village of thatched, whitewashed houses clustered about a green with the tall-spired Church of All Souls and an inn with its taproom belowstairs and its assembly room and guest rooms abovestairs. The village of Lower Newbury, a fishing community built about the sheltered cove on which fishing boats bobbed at rest when not in use, was connected to the upper village by a steep lane, lined with houses and a few shops.

The inhabitants of both villages and the surrounding countryside were, on the whole, content with the quiet obscurity of their lives. But, when all was said and done, they were only human. They liked a spot of excitement as well as the next man or woman. Newbury Abbey supplied it on occasion.

The last grand spectacle had been the funeral of the old earl more than a year before. The new earl, his son, had been in Portugal at the time with Lord Wellington's armies and had been unable to return in time for the somber event. He had sold his commission and come home later to take up his responsibilities.

And now—in early May of 1813—the people of the Newburys were about to experience something far more joyful, far more splendid than a funeral. Neville Wyatt, the new Earl of Kilbourne, a young man of seven-and-twenty years, was to be married to his cousin by marriage, who had been brought up at the abbey with him and his sister, Lady Gwendoline. His father, the late earl, and Baron Galton, the bride's maternal grandfather, had planned the match many years before.

It was a popular match. There could be no more handsome couple, the villagers were generally agreed, than the Earl of Kilbourne and Miss Lauren Edgeworth. His lordship had gone away to the wars—much against his father's wishes, it had been rumored—as a tall, slender, blond, and handsome boy. He had returned six years later improved almost beyond recognition. He was broad where a man should be broad, slim where a man should be slim, and fit and strong and rugged. Even the scar of an old saber wound that slashed his face from right temple to chin, only narrowly missing both his eye and the corner of his mouth, seemed somehow to enhance rather than mar his good looks. As for Miss Edgeworth, she was tall and slim and elegant and as pretty as any picture with her dark shiny curls and eyes that some described as smoky and others as violet, though all were agreed that they were uncommonly lovely. And she had waited patiently for her earl to an almost dangerously advanced age—she was all of four-and-twenty.

It was all very proper and very romantic, everyone agreed.

For two days a steady stream of grand carriages had passed through the village and been duly gawked at by the more vulgar and peered at from behind parlor curtains by the more genteel. Half the quality of England was coming for the occasion, it was said, and more titled persons than some of them had known existed in all of England, Scotland, and Wales combined. Rumor had it—though it was surely more fact than rumor since it had come directly from the first cousin of the brother-in-law of the aunt of one of the kitchen maids at Newbury—that there was not a bedchamber at the abbey that was not to be filled with guests. And that was a prodigious number of rooms.

A number of local families had received invitations—to the wedding itself and the breakfast that would follow it at the abbey, and to the grand ball that was to take place on the evening prior to the wedding. Indeed, no one could remember more elaborate plans. Even the humbler folk were not doomed to being mere spectators. While the wedding guests were partaking of their breakfast, the villagers would be enjoying a sumptuous repast of their own, to be served inside the inn at the earl's behest and expense. There was to be dancing afterward about the maypole on the green.

The wedding eve was a time of heightened activity in the village. Tantalizing aromas of cooking wafted from the inn all day long in promise of the next day's feast. Some of the women set the tables in the assembly room while their men hung colored streamers from the maypole and children tried them out and were scolded for tangling them and getting under everyone's feet. Miss Taylor, spinster daughter of a former vicar, and her younger sister, Miss Amelia, helped the vicar's wife decorate the church with white bows and spring flowers while the vicar set new candles in the holders and dreamed of the glory the morrow would bring him.

The next morning would see the convergence of all the illustrious guests and their carriages on the upper village. And there would be the earl to admire in his wedding finery, and the bride in hers. And—bliss of all blisses—there would be the newly married couple to cheer as they emerged from the church doors with the church bells pealing out the glad tidings that there was a new young countess for the abbey. And then the feasting and frolicking would begin.

Everyone kept a wary eye on the western horizon, from which direction most weather approached. But there was nothing ominous to see. Today was a clear, sunny, really quite warm day. There was no sign of clouds building in the west. Tomorrow looked to be a fair day— as was only right and proper. Nothing was to be allowed to spoil the day.

No one thought to look east.

The stagecoach from London set Lily down outside the inn in the village of Upper Newbury. It was certainly a pretty place, she thought, breathing in the cool, slightly salty evening air and feeling somewhat restored despite her weariness and the stiffness of her limbs. It all looked very English to her—very pretty and very peaceful and rather alien.

But the dusk of evening was falling already and she still might have a way to go on foot. She had neither the time nor the energy to explore. Besides, her heart had begun thumping in her chest, making her slightly breathless. She had realized that she was very close now—at last. But the closer she came, the more uncertain she was of her welcome and of the wisdom of having made this journey at all—except that there had seemed to be no real alternative.

Lily turned and walked into the inn.

"Is Newbury Abbey far?" she asked the innkeeper, ignoring the near silence that fell over the taproom as she entered it. The room was full to overflowing with men, who all appeared to be in a festive mood, but Lily was not unaccustomed to such situations. Large numbers of men did not embarrass or frighten her.

"Two miles if it is anything to you," the innkeeper said, leaning massive elbows on the counter and looking her up and down with open curiosity.

"In which direction?" she asked.

"Past the church and through the gates," he said, pointing, "and follow the driveway."

"Thank you," Lily said politely, and turned away.

"If I was you, my pretty wench," a man seated at one of the tables called to her, not unkindly, "I would knock on the vicarage door. Next to the church this side. They will give you a crust and a mug of water."

"If you cares to sit down between me and Mitch 'ere," someone else called with rough jocularity, "I'll see that you 'as your crust and a mug of cider to go with it, my lovely."

A hearty guffaw of laughter greeted his words as well as a few whistles and the sound of tables being pounded with the flat of the hand.

Lily smiled, unoffended. She was accustomed to rough men and rough ways. They rarely meant any harm or even any great disrespect.

"Thank you," she said, "but not tonight."

She stepped outside. Two miles. And it was very nearly dark. But she could not wait until morning. Where would she stay? She had enough money to buy herself a glass of lemonade and perhaps a small loaf of bread, but not enough to buy lodging for the night. Besides, she was very close.

Only two miles.

The ballroom at Newbury Abbey, magnificent even when empty, was laden with yellow, orange, and white flowers from the gardens and hothouses and decked with white satin ribbons and bows. It was ablaze with the lights of hundreds of candles set into the crystal chandeliers overhead and by their myriad reflections in the long mirrors that covered two facing walls. It was crowded with the cream of the *ton* as well as with members of the local gentry, all dressed in their finest for the wedding eve ball. Satins and silks shimmered and lace and white linen glowed. Costly gems glittered. The most expensive of perfumes vied with the scents of a thousand flowers. Voices were raised in an effort to be heard above others and above the strains of the music, provided by an entire orchestra.

Beyond the ballroom, guests strolled on the wide landing and ascended or descended the twin curved staircases to the domed and pillared great hall below. They strolled outdoors—on the balcony beyond the ballroom, on the terrace before the house, about the stone fountain below the terrace, along the graveled walks of the rock and flower garden to the east of the house. Colored lanterns had been strung about the fountain and hung from trees though the moonlight would have offered illumination even without them.

It was a perfect May evening. One could only

hope, as several of the guests did aloud to Lauren and Neville as they passed along the receiving line, that tomorrow would be half as lovely a day.

"Tomorrow will be *twice* as lovely," Neville replied each time, smiling warmly at his betrothed, "even if the wind howls and the rain pours and the thunder rolls."

Lauren's smile was unmistakably radiant. It seemed strange to Neville as he led her eventually into the first set of country dances that he had ever hesitated about making her his bride, that he had kept her waiting for six years while he worked off the restless rebellion of youth as an officer with the Ninety-fifth Rifles. He had advised her not to wait, of course—he had been far too fond of her to keep her dangling when he had been quite uncertain of his intentions toward her. But she *had* waited. He was glad of it now, humbled by her patience and fidelity. There was a rightness about their impending marriage. And his affection for her had not dimmed. It had grown along with his admiration for her character and his appreciation of her beauty.

"And so it begins," he murmured to her as the orchestra began to play. "Our nuptials, Lauren. Are you happy?"

"Yes."

But even the single word was unnecessary. She glowed with happiness. She looked like the quintessential bride. She was *his* bride. It felt right.

Neville danced first with Lauren, then with his sister. Then he danced with a series of young ladies who looked as if they expected to be wallflowers while Lauren danced with a succession of different partners.

After taking a turn upon the balcony with one of his partners, Neville entered the ballroom through the French doors and joined a group of young gentlemen who, as always at balls, seemed to need one another's collective company in order to summon the courage to ask a young lady to dance. He had the misfortune to remark on the fact that none of them appeared to be dancing.

"Well, you have done the pretty every set, Nev," his cousin Ralph Milne, Viscount Sterne, said, "though only once with your betrothed. Hard luck, old chap, but I suppose you are not allowed to dance with her more than once, are you?"

"Alas, no," Neville agreed, gazing across the ballroom to where Lauren was standing with his mother, his paternal aunt, Lady Elizabeth Wyatt, and his maternal uncle and aunt, the Duke and Duchess of Anburey.

Sir Paul Longford, a childhood neighbor and friend, could not resist such a perfect opportunity for bawdiness. "Well, you know, Sterne," he said with his best drawl, "it is only for tonight, old chap. Nev is to dance alone with his bride all night tomorrow, though not necessarily on a dance floor. I have it on the best authority."

The whole group exploded with raucous male laughter, drawing considerable attention their way.

"A hit, Nev, you must confess," said his

cousin and tomorrow's best man, the Marquess of Attingsborough.

Neville grinned after pursing his lips and handling the ribbon of his quizzing glass. "Let those words fall on any female ears, Paul," he said, "and I might feel obliged to call you out. Enjoy yourselves, gentlemen, but do not neglect the ladies, if you please."

He strolled off in the direction of his betrothed. She was wearing a high-waisted gown of blond net over daffodil-yellow sarcenet and looked as fresh and lovely as the springtime. It really was too bad that he was not to dance with her again for the rest of the evening. But then it would be strange indeed if he could not maneuver matters more to his liking.

It was not i mmediately possible. There was the necessity of conversing politely with Mr. Calvin Dorsey, a middle-aged, mild-mannered acquaintance of Lauren's grandfather, who had come to solicit Lauren's hand for the dance after supper and who stayed for a few minutes to make himself agreeable. And then the Duke of Portfrey arrived on Dorsey's heels to lead Elizabeth away for the next set. He was her longtime friend and beau. But finally Neville saw his chance.

"It is more like summer than spring outside," he remarked to no one in particular. "The rock garden must look quite enchanting in the lantern light." He smiled with deliberate wistfulness at Lauren.

"Mmm," she said. "And the fountain too."

"I suppose," he said, "you have reserved the next set with Lauren, Uncle Webster?"

16

"Indeed I have," the Duke of Anburey replied, but he winked at his nephew over Lauren's head. He had not missed his cue. "But all this talk of lanterns and summer evenings has given me a hankering to see the gardens with Sadie on my arm." He looked at his wife and waggled his eyebrows. "Now if someone could just be persuaded to take young Lauren off my hands..."

"If you were to twist my arm hard enough," Neville said, while his mother smiled in enjoyment of the conspiracy, "I might be persuaded to take on the task myself."

And so one minute later he was on his way downstairs, his betrothed on his arm. It was true that they were stopped at least half a dozen times by guests desiring to compliment them on the ball and wish them well during the coming day and the years ahead, but finally they were outside and descending the wide marble steps to feast their eyes on the rainbows created by lantern light on the spraying water of the fountain. They strolled onward toward the rock garden.

"You are a quite shameless maneuverer, Neville," Lauren told him.

"Are you glad of it?" He moved his head closer to hers.

She thought for a moment, her head tipped to one side, the telltale dimple denting her left cheek. "Yes," she said quite decisively. "Very."

"We are going to remember this night," he said, "as one of the happiest of our lives." He breathed in the freshness of the air with its faint tang of saltiness from the sea. He squinted his eyes so that the lights of individual lanterns in the rock garden ahead all blurred into one kaleidoscope of color.

"Oh, Neville," she said, her hand tightening on his arm. "Does anyone have a right to so much happiness?"

"Yes," he told her, his voice low against her ear. "You do."

"Just look at the garden," she said. "The lanterns make it seem like a fairyland."

He set himself to enjoying the unexpected half hour with her.

∽ 2 ∽

Lily found the driveway beyond the massive gates to the park—a wide and winding road so darkened by huge trees that grew on either side and whose branches met overhead that only the occasional gleam of moonlight kept her from wandering off the path and becoming hopelessly lost. It was a driveway that seemed more like four miles long than two. Crickets chirped off to either side and a bird that might have been an owl hooted close by. Once there was the crackling of movement off in the forest to her right—some wild animal that she had disturbed, perhaps. But the sounds only succeeded in intensifying the pervading silence and darkness. Night had fallen with almost indecent haste.

And then finally she turned a bend and

was startled by light in the near distance. She found herself staring at a brightly lighted mansion with another large building to one side of it also lighted up. There was light outside too—colored lanterns that must be hanging from tree branches.

Lily paused and gazed in amazement and awe. She had not expected anything of near this magnitude. The house appeared to be built of gray granite, but there was nothing heavy about its design. It was all pillars and pointed pediments and tall windows and perfect symmetry. She did not have the knowledge of architecture with which to recognize the Palladian design that had been superimposed upon the original medieval abbey with remarkably pleasing effect, but she felt the grandeur of the building and was overwhelmed by it. If she had imagined anything at all, it was a large cottage with a well-sized garden. But the name itself might have alerted her if she had ever really considered it. *This* was Newbury Abbey? Frankly it terrified her. And what was going on inside? Surely it did not look like this every night.

She would have turned back, but where would she go? She could only go forward. At least the lights—and the sounds of music that reached her ears as she drew closer—assured her that he must be at home.

Somehow she didn't find that a particularly comforting thought.

The great double doors at the front of Newbury Abbey stood open. There was light spilling out onto marble steps leading up to them, and the sounds of voices and laughter and music echoed behind them. There was the sound of voices outside too, though Lily saw only distant shadows in the darkness and no one noticed her approach.

She climbed the marble steps—she counted eight of them—and stepped into a hall so brightly lighted and so vast that she felt suddenly dwarfed and quite robbed of breath and coherent thought. There were people everywhere, milling about in the hall, moving up and down the great staircases. They were all dressed in rich fabrics and sparkled with jewels and gems. Lily had foolishly expected to walk up to a closed door and knock on it, and he would answer it.

She wished suddenly that she had allowed Captain Harris to write his letter and had awaited a reply. What she had done instead no longer seemed a wise course at all.

Several liveried, white-wigged servants stood about on duty. One of them was hurrying toward her, she saw in some relief. She had been feeling invisible and conspicuous all at the same time.

"Out of here immediately!" he commanded, keeping his voice low, attempting to move her back toward the doors without actually pushing her. He was clearly trying not to draw attention to himself or to her. "If you have business here, I will direct you to the servants' entrance. But I doubt you do, especially at this time of night."

"I wish to speak with the Earl of Kilbourne," Lily said. She never thought of him by that name. She felt as if she were asking for a stranger.

"Oh, do you now?" The servant looked at her with withering scorn. "If you have come here to beg, be off with you before I summon a constable."

"I wish to speak with the Earl of Kilbourne," she said again, standing her ground.

The servant set his white-gloved hands on her shoulders, obviously intending to move her backward by force after all. But another man had glided into place beside him, a man dressed all in black and white, though he did not have the same sort of splendor as other gentlemen who were in the hall and on the stairs. He must be a servant too, Lily guessed, though superior to the first one.

"What is it, Jones?" he asked coldly. "Is she refusing to leave quietly?"

"I wish to speak to the Earl of Kilbourne," Lily told him.

"You may leave of your own volition *now*," the man in black told her with quiet emphasis, "or be taken up for vagrancy five minutes from now and thrown in jail. The choice is yours, woman. It makes no difference to me. Which is it to be?"

Lily opened her mouth again and drew breath. She had come at the wrong time, of course. Some grand sort of entertainment was in progress. He would not thank her for appearing now. Indeed, he might not thank her for coming at all. Now that she had seen all this, she began to understand the impossibility of it all. But what else could she do?

Where else could she go? She closed her mouth.

"Well?" the superior servant asked.

"Trouble, Forbes?" another, far more cultured voice asked, and Lily turned her head to see an older gentleman with silver hair and a lady in purple satin with matching plumed turban on his arm. The lady had a ring on each finger, worn over her glove.

"Not at all, your grace," the servant called Forbes answered with a deferential bow. "She is just a beggar woman who has had the impudence to wander in here. She will be gone in a moment."

"Well, give her sixpence," the gentleman said, looking with a measure of kindness at Lily. "You will be able to buy bread for a couple of days with it, girl."

With a sinking heart Lily decided it was the wrong moment in which to stand her ground. She was so close to the end of her journey and yet seemingly as far away as ever. The servant in black was fishing in a pocket, probably for a sixpenny piece.

"Thank you," she said with quiet dignity, "but I did not come here for charity."

She turned even as the superior servant and the gentleman with the cultured voice spoke simultaneously and hurried from the hall, down the steps, along the terrace, and across a downward sloping lawn. She could not face that dark driveway again.

The light of the moon led her onward to a narrow path that sloped downward at a sharper angle through more trees though

22

these did not completely hide the light. She would go down far enough, Lily decided, that she was out of sight of the house.

The path steepened still more and the trees thinned out until the pathway was flanked only by the dense and luxuriant growth of ferns. She could hear water now—the faint elemental surging of the sea and the rush of running water closer at hand. It was a waterfall, she guessed, and then she could see it gleaming in the moonlight away to her right—a steep ribbon of water falling almost sheer down a cliff face to the valley below and the stream that flowed toward the sea. And at the foot of the waterfall, what appeared to be a small cottage.

Lily did not turn up the valley toward it. There was no light inside and she would not have approached it even if there had been. To her left she could see a wide, sandy beach and the moonlight in a sparkling band across the sea.

She would spend the night just above the beach, she decided. And tomorrow she would return to Newbury Abbey.

When Lily awoke early the following morning, she washed her face and hands in the cold water of the stream and tidied herself as best she could before climbing the path back up over the fern-draped slope and through the trees to the bottom of the cultivated lawn.

She stood looking up at what appeared to be stables with the house beyond. Both looked even more massive and forbidding in the morning light than they had appeared last night. And there was a great deal of activity going on. There were numerous carriages on the driveway close to the stables, and grooms and coachmen bustled about everywhere. Last night's party guests must have stayed overnight and were preparing to leave, Lily guessed. It was clearly still not the right time to make her call. She must wait until later.

She was hungry, she discovered after she had returned to the beach, and decided to fill in some time by walking into the village, where perhaps she could buy a small loaf of bread. But when she arrived there, she found that it was by no means the quiet, deserted place it had been the evening before. The square was almost surrounded by grand carriages—perhaps some of the very ones she had seen earlier by the stables of the abbey. The green itself was crowded with people. The doors of the inn were wide open, and a great bustling in and out discouraged Lily from approaching. She could see that the gateway to the church was tightly packed with an even denser throng than the green held.

"What is happening?" she asked a couple of women who stood on the edge of the green close to the inn, both staring in the direction of the church, one of them on tiptoe.

They turned their heads to stare at her. One looked her up and down, recognized her as a stranger, and frowned. The other was more friendly.

"A wedding," she said. "Half the quality of England is here for the wedding of Miss Edgeworth to the Earl of Kilbourne. I don't know how they squeezed them all inside the church."

The Earl of Kilbourne! Again the name sounded like that of a stranger. But he was *not* a stranger. And the meaning of what the woman had just said struck home. He was getting married? Now? Inside that church? The Earl of Kilbourne was *getting married*?

"The bride just arrived," the second woman added, having thawed to the idea of having a stranger for an audience. "You missed her, more's the pity. All in white satin, she is, with a scalloped train and a bonnet and netting that covers her face. But if you stand here a spell, you will see them coming out as soon as the church bells start to ring. The carriage will come around this way before going back around and through the gates, I daresay, so that we can all wave and get a good look at them. Leastways that is what Mr. Wesley says—the innkeeper, you know."

But Lily did not wait for further explanations. She was hurrying across the green, threading her way among the people standing there. She was half running by the time she reached the church gateway.

Neville could tell by the flurry of movement at the back of the church that Lauren had arrived with Baron Galton, her grandfather. There was a stirring of heightened expectation from the pews, which held all the flower of the *ton* as well as a number of the more prominent local families. Several heads turned to look back, though there was nothing to see yet.

Neville felt as if someone had tightened his cravat at the neck and dropped a handful of frisky butterflies into his stomach, both of which afflictions had been with him to varying degrees since before the early breakfast he had been unable to consume, but he turned eagerly enough for his first sight of his bride. He caught a glimpse of Gwen, who was stooping apparently to straighten the train of Lauren's gown. The bride herself stood tantalizingly just out of sight.

The vicar, splendidly robed for the occasion, stood just behind Neville's shoulder. Joseph Fawcitt, Marquess of Attingsborough, the male cousin closest to him in age and always a close friend, cleared his throat from his other side. Every head, Neville was aware, had turned now to look toward the back entrance in expectation of the appearance of the bride. Of what importance was a mere bridegroom, after all, when the bride was about to appear? Lauren was exactly on time, he guessed with a private half smile. It would be unlike her to be late by even a single minute.

He shifted his feet as the movements at the back of the church became more pronounced and there was even the sound of voices inappropriately loud for the interior of a church. Someone was telling someone else with sharp urgency that he or she could not go in there.

And then she stepped through the doorway into the view of those gathered inside the church. Except that she was alone. And not dressed as a bride but as beggar woman. And she was not Lauren. She took a few hurried steps forward along the nave before stopping.

It was a hallucination brought on by the occasion, some remote part of his mind told Neville. She looked startlingly, achingly familiar. But she was not Lauren. His vision darkened about the edges and sharpened down the center. He looked along the nave of the church as down a long tunnel—or as through the eyepiece of a telescope—at the illusion standing there. His mind refused to function normally.

Someone—two men actually, he observed almost dispassionately—grabbed her arms and would have dragged her back out of sight. But the sudden terror that she would disappear, never to be seen again, released him from the paralysis that had held him in its grip. He held up one staying arm. He did not hear himself speak, but everyone turned sharply to look at him and he was aware of the echo of someone's voice saying something.

He took two steps forward.

"Lily?" he whispered. He tried to restore reality and passed a hand swiftly over his eyes, but she was still there, a man holding to each of her arms and looking his way as if for instructions. There was a coldness in his head, in his nostrils.

"*Lily?*" he said again, louder this time.

"Yes," she said in the soft, melodic voice that had haunted his dreams and his conscience for many months after her—

"Lily," he said, and he felt curiously detached from the scene. He heard his words over the buzzing in his ears as if someone else were speaking them. "Lily, *you are dead!*"

"No," she said, "I did not die."

He was still seeing her down the tunnel of his hallucination. Only her. Only Lily. He was unaware of the church, unaware of the people stirring uneasily in the pews, of the vicar clearing his throat, of Joseph setting a hand on his sleeve, of Lauren standing in the doorway behind Lily, her eyes wide with the dawning premonition of disaster. He clung to the vision. He would not let it go. Not again. He would not let her go again. He took another step forward.

The vicar cleared his throat once more and Neville finally comprehended that he was in All Souls Church, Upper Newbury, on his wedding day. With *Lily* standing in the aisle between him and his bride.

"My lord," the vicar said, addressing him, "do you know this woman? Is it your wish that she be removed so that we may proceed with the wedding service?"

Did he know her?

Did he know her?

"Yes, I know her," he said, his voice quiet, though he was fully aware now that every single wedding guest hung upon his words and heard him clearly. "She is my wife."

The silence, though total, lasted only a very few seconds.

"My lord?" The vicar was the first to break it.

There was a swell of sound as half the people present, it seemed, tried to talk at once while the other half tried just as loudly to shush them so that they would not miss anything of significance. The Countess of Kilbourne was on her feet in the front pew. Her brother, the Duke of Anburey, rose too and set a hand on her arm.

"Neville?" the countess said in a shaking voice, which nevertheless was distinctly audible above the general buzz of sound. "What *is* this? Who *is* this woman?"

"I should have had her taken up for vagrancy last night," the duke said in his usual authoritative voice, trying to take charge of the situation. "Calm yourself, Clara. Gentlemen, remove the woman, if you please. Neville, return to your place so that this wedding may proceed."

But no one paid his grace any heed, except the vicar. Everyone had heard what Neville

29

had said. There had been no ambiguity in his words.

"With all due respect, your grace," the Reverend Beckford said, "this wedding may not proceed when his lordship has just acknowledged this woman as his wife."

"I married Lily Doyle in Portugal," Neville said, never taking his eyes from the beggar woman. The shushing voices became more insistent and a hush so total that it was almost loud fell again on the congregation. "I watched her die less than twenty-four hours later. I reached her side no more than a few minutes after that. I stood over her dead body—you were *dead*, Lily. And then I was shot in the head."

Everyone knew that for over a month before his return to England Neville had lain in a hospital in Lisbon, suffering from a head wound sustained during an ambush among the hills of central Portugal when he had been leading a winter scouting party. Amnesia and persistent dizziness and headaches had prevented his return to his regiment even after the wound itself had healed. And then news of his father's death had reached him and brought him home.

But no one had heard of any marriage.

Until now.

And clearly the woman he had married was *not* dead.

Someone in the church had already realized the full implications of the fact. There was a strangled cry from the back of the church, and those who looked back saw Lauren standing there, her face as pale now as the veil that covered it, her hands clawing at the sides of her gown and sweeping up the train behind it before she turned and fled, followed closely by Gwendoline. The church doors opened and then closed again rather noisily.

"I am sorry," Lily said. "I am so very sorry. I was not dead."

"Neville!" Lady Kilbourne was clinging with both gloved hands to the back of the pew.

Sound swelled again.

But Neville held up both hands, palm out.

"I beg your pardon, all of you," he said, "but clearly this is not a matter for public airing. Not yet at least. I hope to offer a full explanation before the day is out. In the meantime, it is obvious that there is to be no wedding here this morning. I invite you all to return to the abbey for breakfast."

He lowered his arms and strode down the aisle, his right hand reaching out toward Lily. His eyes were on hers.

"Lily?" he said. "Come."

His hand closed on hers and clamped hard about it. He scarcely broke stride, but continued on his way toward the outer door, Lily at his side.

❦

Neville threw the doors wide, and they stepped out into blinding sunshine and were met by a sea of faces and a chorus of excited, curious voices.

31

He ignored them. Indeed, he did not even see or hear them. He strode down the church-yard path, through the gateway, between crowds of people who opened a way for him by hastily stepping back upon one another, and around to the gates into the park of Newbury Abbey.

He said nothing to the woman at his side. He could not yet trust the reality of what had happened, of what was happening, even though he held tightly to the apparition and could *feel* her small hand in his own.

He was remembering...

❦ PART II ❦

Memory: One Night for Love

～ 3 ～

Lily Doyle is sitting alone on a small rocky promontory jutting out over a deep valley high in the barren hills of central Portugal. It is December and chilly.

She is wrapped in a shabby old army cloak that she has cut down to size. But it cannot hide the fact that she has been transformed over the past year or so from a lithe, coltish girl into a heart-stoppingly beautiful woman. Her dark-blond hair waves loose down her back to below her waist. The wind is blowing it out behind her and hopelessly tangling it. Her slender arms, covered by the sleeves of her faded blue cotton dress, clasp her updrawn knees. Her feet, despite the cold, are bare. How can she feel the earth, how can she feel *life*, she once explained, if she is always shod?

Neville Wyatt, Major Lord Newbury, is reclining at his ease on the ground some distance behind her, a tin mug of hot tea cupped in both hands. He is watching her. He cannot see her face, but he can imagine its expression as she gazes down over the valley below, up at the cloud-dotted sky and the lone bird wheeling there. It will be dreamy, serene. No, those descriptions are too passive. There will be a glow in her face, a light in her eyes.

Lily sees beauty wherever she goes. While the men of the Ninety-fifth and the women who follow in its train curse the Iberian landscape, the weather, the endless marches, the dreary camps, the food, one another, Lily can always find something of beauty. But she is not resented for her eternal cheerfulness. She is a favorite with all who know her.

Until recently she has been a girl. She is a girl no longer.

Neville tosses the dregs of his tea onto the grass beside him and gets to his feet. He looks about, first at the company of men he has brought with him on a winter scouting expedition to make sure that the French are observing the unwritten truce of the season and are keeping behind their lines in Spain or else inside the border fortress of Ciudad Rodrigo, which the British forces will besiege as soon as spring comes.

He squints across to the hills opposite and down into the valley. All is quiet. He has not expected otherwise. If there had been any real danger, he would never have allowed Corporal Geary to bring his wife or Sergeant Doyle to bring his daughter. It is a routine mission and has been unexpectedly pleasant—this is normally the rainy season. Tomorrow they will return to base camp. But tonight they will camp where they are.

He can no longer resist. He strolls toward the promontory on which Lily sits and makes a show when he is standing beside her of shielding his eyes and sweeping his gaze over the valley again. She looks up and smiles. He is not quite sure when her looks and smiles started to make his heart skip a beat. He has tried to continue seeing her as the young daughter—the *too*-young daughter—of his sergeant. But he has been failing miserably of late. She is eighteen, after all.

"You have observed no French regiment tip-toeing stealthily along the valley floor, Lily?" he asks without looking down at her.

She laughs. "Two of them actually, sir," she says. "One cavalry and one infantry. Was I supposed to have *said* something?"

"No, no." He grins down at her, and there—it happens again. His heart turns over when he sees the eager delight in her face. "It is not important. Not unless old Boney was with them."

She laughs again. He wonders as he seats himself beside her, one leg stretched out, one arm draped over the raised knee of the other, if she knows the effect she has on men—on him. He is not by any means the only one who has noticed that she has become a woman.

"I suppose, Lily," Neville says, "you can see some beauty in this godforsaken place?"

"Oh, not godforsaken," she says earnestly, as he knew she would. "Even bare rocks have a certain majesty that inspires awe. But see?" She lifts one slender arm and points. "There is grass. There are even a few trees. Nature cannot be repressed. It *will* burst through."

"They are sorry apologies for trees." He looks to where she is pointing. "And the gardener at Newbury Abbey would consign that grass to the rubbish heap without a second thought."

When she turns toward him and her eyes focus on his, he finds himself drawing a slow breath, half of him wanting to edge farther back away from her, the other half wanting to close the distance until...

"What is the garden *like* there?" she asks him, an unmistakable wistfulness in her voice. "Papa says there is nothing so lovely as an English garden."

"Green," he says. "A lush, vibrant green that cannot be adequately described in words, Lily. Grass and trees and flowers of every color and description. Masses of them. Especially roses. The air is heavy with their perfume in summer."

He rarely feels nostalgia for home. Sometimes the realization makes him feel guilty. It is not that he does not love his mother and father. He does. But he was brought up to take over his father's role as earl one day, and he was brought up to marry Lauren, his stepcousin, who was raised at Newbury Abbey with him and was as dear to him as his sister Gwen was. The time came when he was stifled by his father's loving plans for him, desperate for a life of his own, for action, adventure, freedom...

He has hurt his parents by becoming a military man. He suspects he has done more than hurt Lauren, having informed her as tactfully as he could when he left that he would not promise to be back soon, that he would not expect her to wait for him.

"How I would love to see them and smell them." Lily has closed her eyes and is inhaling slowly as if she actually can smell the roses at Newbury.

"You will one day." Without thinking, he

reaches out to draw free with one finger a strand of her hair that has blown into the corner of her mouth. Her skin is smooth—and warm. The hair is wet. He feels raw desire stab into his groin and withdraws the finger hastily.

She smiles at him. But then she does something Lily rarely does. She blushes and her eyes waver and then look away rather jerkily to the valley again.

She knows.

He is saddened by the thought. Lily has always been his friend, ever since Doyle became his sergeant four years ago. She has a lively mind and a delightful sense of humor and a natural refinement of manner despite the fact that she is illiterate. She has talked to him about her life, especially her years in India, where her mother died, and about people and experiences they have in common. She once argued with him when he found her on a battlefield after the fighting was over and scolded her for tending a wounded and dying French soldier. A man is simply a man, a *person*, she told him. She has always been uncowed by his rank even though, like her father and all the men, she calls him "sir." He knelt beside her and gave the Frenchman a drink from his own canteen.

But things have changed. Lily has grown up. And he desires her. She knows it. He will have to withdraw from the friendship because Lily is off limits to him as anything more than a friend. She is Sergeant Doyle's daughter, and he respects Doyle even though they are from different social classes. But besides that, Lily is an innocent, and it is his duty to protect her honor, not take it. And she too, of course, is of a different class from his own. Such things do matter in the real world, unfortunately. Rebel as he still is, he has nevertheless not broken with his own world and never will. He has too much of a sense of duty for that. He is a gentleman, an officer, a viscount, a future earl.

He can never be Lily's lover.

"Lily," he asks, trying to cling to the friendship, to suppress the other, unwelcome feelings, "what do you look forward to? What will you do with your life? What are your dreams?"

She cannot stay with her father forever. What *does* the future hold for her? Marriage to a soldier chosen carefully for her by her father? No. He wishes he has not thought it.

She does not immediately answer. But when he turns his head to look at her again, he sees that she is gazing upward and that her wonderful dreamy smile is lighting her face again.

"Do you see that bird, sir?" He turns his head and glances at it. "I want to be like that. Soaring high. Strong. Free. Borne by the wind and friend of the sky. I do not know what will become of me. One day you will be gone, and one day..."

But her words trail off and her smile fades and what she has just said hangs in the air before them like a tangible thing.

Then the silence is broken by the crack of a single gunshot.

One of the pickets has caught sight of a rabbit out of the corner of his eye and has imagined a ravenous French host. That is Neville's first thought. But he cannot take a chance. His years as an officer have trained him to act from instinct as much as from reason. It works faster, and sometimes it saves lives.

He jumps to his feet and hauls Lily to hers. They are running back to the company, Neville protectively hunched over her from behind, even as Sergeant Doyle bellows to her and everyone else is grabbing rifles and ammunition. Neville checks for his sword at his side even as he runs. He yells orders to his men, Lily forgotten as soon as he has her back in the relative safety of the makeshift camp.

He has misjudged the picket. It is not a rabbit that has caught his attention; it is a French scouting party. But the warning shot was a mistake. Without it, the French probably would have gone peacefully on their way even if they had spotted the British soldiers. Nothing can be gained for either side by engaging in a fight. But the shot has been fired.

The ensuing skirmish is short and sharp but relatively harmless. It would have been entirely so if a new recruit in Neville's company had not frozen with terror on the bare hillside, a motionless, open target for the French. Sergeant Doyle, cursing foully, goes to his assistance and takes the bullet intended for the boy through his own chest.

The fighting is all over five minutes after it has started. With a derisive cheer the French go on their way.

"Leave him where he is!" Neville shouts, racing across the slope of the hill toward his felled sergeant. "Fetch the first-aid box."

But it will be useless. He sees that as soon as he is close. There is only a small spot of blood on the dark-green fabric of his sergeant's coat, but there is death in his face. Neville has seen it in too many faces to be mistaken. And Doyle knows it too.

"I am done for, sir," he says faintly.

"Fetch the damned first-aid box!" Neville goes down on one knee beside the dying man. "We will have you patched up in no time at all, Sergeant."

"No, sir." Doyle clutches at his hand with fingers that are already cold and feeble. "Lily."

"She is safe. She is unhurt," Neville assures him.

"I should not have brought her out here." The man's eyes are losing focus. His breath is coming in rasping gasps. "If they attack again..."

"They will not." Neville's fingers close about those of his sergeant. He gives up the pretense. "I will see Lily safely back to camp tomorrow."

"If she is taken prisoner..."

It is highly unlikely even on the remote chance that there will be another encounter, another skirmish. The French will surely be as little eager for a confrontation at this time of year as the British. But if she is, of course, her fate will be dreadful indeed. Rape...

"I will see that she is safe." Neville leans over the man who has been his respected comrade, even his friend, despite the differences in their rank. His heart is involved in this death more than his head. "She will not be harmed even if she *is* taken prisoner. You have my word as a gentleman on it. I will marry her today."

As the wife of an officer and a gentleman, Lily will be treated with honor and courtesy even by the French. And the Reverend Parker-Rowe, the regimental chaplain, who finds life in camp as tedious as the most restless soldier, has come with the scouting party.

"She will be my wife, Sergeant. She will be safe." He is not quite sure the dying man understands. The cold fingers still pluck weakly at his own.

"My pack back at the base," Sergeant Doyle says. "Inside my pack..."

"It will be given to Lily," Neville promises. "Tomorrow, when we arrive safely back at camp."

"I should have told her long ago." The voice is becoming fainter, less distinct. Neville leans over him. "I should have told *him*. My wife... God forgive me. She loved her. We both did. We loved her too much to..."

"God forgives you, Sergeant." *Where the devil is the chaplain?* "And no one could ever have doubted your devotion to Lily."

Parker-Rowe and Lily arrive at the same moment, the latter hurtling down the hill at reckless speed. Neville gets to his feet and stands to one side as Lily takes his place beside her father, gathering his hand into both her own, bending low over him, her hair a curtain about his face and her own.

"Papa," she says. She whispers his name over and over again and remains as she is for several minutes while the chaplain murmurs prayers and the company stands about, helpless in the presence of death and grief.

After they have buried Sergeant Doyle on the hillside where he died, Neville orders the camp moved two or three miles farther on. He walks on one side of a silent, frozen-faced Lily while Parker-Rowe walks on the other side. He has already spoken with the chaplain.

Lily has not wept. She has not spoken a word since Neville took her by the shoulders and raised her to her feet and told her gently what she already knew—that her father was gone. She is accustomed to death, of course. But one is never prepared for the death of a loved one.

"Lily," Neville says in the same gentle voice he used earlier, "I want you to know that your father's last thoughts were of you and your safety and your future."

She does not answer him.

44

"I made him a promise," he tells her. "A gentleman's promise. Because he was my friend, Lily, and because it was something that I wanted to do anyway. I promised him that I would marry you today so that you will have the protection of my name and rank for the rest of this journey and for the rest of your life."

There is still no response. Has he really made such a promise? A *gentleman's* promise? Because it was what he wanted? Has he wanted to be forced into doing something impossible so that it can be made possible after all? It is impossible for him, an officer, an aristocrat, a future earl, to marry an enlisted man's humble and illiterate daughter. But doing so has now become an obligation, a *gentleman's* obligation. He feels a strange welling of exultation.

"Lily," he asks her, bending his head to look into her pale, expressionless face—so unlike her usual self, "do you understand what I am saying to you?"

"Yes, sir." Her voice is flat, toneless.

"You will marry me, then? You will be my wife?" The moment seems unreal, as do all the events of the past two hours. But there is a sense of breathless panic. Because she might refuse? Because she might accept?

"Yes," she says.

"We will do it as soon as we have made camp again then," he says.

It is unlike Lily to be so passive, so meek. Is it fair to her...

But what is the alternative? A return to

England, to relatives he knows she has never met? Marriage to an enlisted soldier of her own social rank? No, that is an unbearable thought. But it is Lily's life.

"Look at me, Lily," he commands, no longer gently, using the voice that she, as well as all the men under his command, obeys instinctively. She looks. "You will be my wife within the hour. Is it what you want?"

"Yes, sir." Her eyes stare dully back into his before he looks over her head and locks eyes with the chaplain.

It will be so, then. Within the hour. The great impossibility. The obligation.

Again the panic.

Again the exultation.

⌒

The marriage service is conducted before the whole company and is officially witnessed by Lieutenant Harris and the newly promoted Sergeant Rieder. The gathered men seem not to know whether to cheer or to maintain the subdued solemnity they have carried from Sergeant Doyle's funeral three hours ago. Led by the lieutenant, they applaud politely and give three cheers for their newly married major and for the new Viscountess Newbury.

The new viscountess herself appears totally detached from the proceedings. She goes quietly off to help Mrs. Geary prepare the evening meal. Neville does not stop her or mention the fact that a viscountess must expect to be waited upon. He has duties of his own to attend to.

⤳

It is dark. Neville has checked on the pickets and the schedule for the night watch.

He will remain in the army, he has decided. He will make a permanent career of it. In the army he and Lily can be equals. They can share a world with which they are both familiar and comfortable. He will no longer feel pulled in two directions as he has since he left Newbury. They would not want him back there now anyway. Not with Lily. She is beautiful. She is everything that is grace and light and joy. He is in love with her. More than that, he *loves* her. But she can never be the Countess of Kilbourne, except perhaps in name. Cinderellas are fine in the pages of a fairy tale and might expect to live happily ever after with their princes. In real life things do not work that way.

He is glad he has married Lily. He feels as if a load has been lifted from his soul. She will be his world, his future, his happiness. His all.

His tent, he notices, has been set up a tactful distance away from the rest of the camp. She is standing alone outside it, looking off into the moonlit valley.

"Lily," he says softly as he approaches.

She turns her head to look at him. She says nothing, but even in the dim moonlight he can see that the glazed look of shock has

47

gone from her eyes. She looks at him with awareness and understanding.

"Lily." Everything they say now is in whispers so that they will not be overheard. "I am so sorry. About your father."

He lifts one hand and touches the tips of his fingers lightly to one of her cheeks. He has thought about this. He will not force himself on her tonight. She must be allowed time to grieve for her father, to adjust to the new conditions of her life. She still says nothing, but she raises one hand and sets it against the back of his, drawing his palm fully against her cheek.

"I ought to have said no," she says. "I *did* know what you were asking of me. I pretended even to myself that I did not so that I would not have to refuse you and face an empty future. I am sorry."

"Lily," he says, "I did it because I wanted to."

She turns her head and sets her lips against his palm. She closes her eyes and says nothing.

Lily. Ah, Lily, is it possible...

"You take the tent," he tells her. "I will sleep on the ground here. You must not worry. I will keep you quite safe."

But she opens her eyes and gazes at him in the moonlight. "Did you really want to?" she asks him. "Did you really want to marry me?"

"Yes." He wishes he could retrieve his hand. He is not made of stone.

"You asked me what my dream was," she tells him. "How could I tell you then? But I

48

can tell you now. It was this. Just this. My dream."

He touches his mouth to hers and wonders while he still can if they have an audience.

"Lily," he says against her mouth. "Lily."

"Yes, sir."

"Neville," he tells her. "Say it. Say my name. I want to hear you saying it."

"Neville," she says, and it sounds like the most tender, the most erotic of endearments. "Neville. Neville."

"Will I share the tent with you, then?" he asks her.

"Yes." There can be no mistaking that she means it, that she wants him. "Neville. My beloved."

Surely only Lily could utter such a word without sounding theatrical.

It seems strange to him that they are about to consummate a marriage when they buried his comrade, her father, a mere few hours ago. But he has had enough experience with death to know that life must reaffirm itself immediately after in the survivors, that living on is an integral part of the grieving process.

"Come then," he says, stooping to open the flap of the small tent. "Come, Lily. Come, my love."

~

They make love in near silence since there undoubtedly are listeners enough eager to hear grunts of pleasure, cries of pain. And they make love slowly so as not to cause any undue shaking of the tent's flimsy structure. And they make love fully clothed except in essential places, and covered by their two cloaks so that they will not be chilled by the December night.

She is innocent and ignorant.

He is eager and experienced and desperate to give her pleasure, terrified of giving her pain.

He kisses her, touches her with gentle, exploring, worshipful hands, first through her clothing, then beneath it, feathering touches over her warm, silken flesh, cupping her small, firm breasts, teasing his thumb across their stiffening crests, sliding gentle, caressing fingers down into the moist heat between her thighs, touching, parting, arousing.

She holds him. She does no caressing of her own. She makes no sound except for quickened breathing. But he knows that she is one with his desire. He knows that even in this she is finding beauty.

"Lily..."

She opens to him at the prodding of his knees and wraps herself about him at the bidding of her own instincts. She croons soft endearments to him—mostly his own name—as he mounts her, surprising himself with his own sobs as he does so. She is small and tight and very virgin. The barrier seems unbreakable and he knows he is hurting her. And then it is gone and he eases inward to his full length. Into soft, wet heat and the involuntary contraction of her muscles.

She speaks to him in a soft whisper against his ear.

"I always knew," she tells him, "that this would be the most beautiful moment of my life. This. With you. But I never expected it to happen."

Ah, Lily. I never knew.

"My sweet life," he tells her. "Ah, my dear love."

But he can no longer think only of not hurting his bride. His desire, his need, pulses like a drumbeat through every blood vessel in his body and focuses as exquisite pain in his groin and the part of himself that is sheathed in her. He withdraws to the brink of her and presses deep again, hears her gasp of surprise and surely of pleasure too, and withdraws and presses deep.

He holds the rhythm steady for as long as he is able both for her sake and his own, resisting the urge to release into pleasure too soon, before she can learn that intimacy consists of more than simple penetration.

She lies relaxed beneath him. Not out of distaste or shock or passive submission. He would know. Even if she were not making quiet sounds of satisfaction to the rhythm, he would know. She is enjoying what is happening. He finds her mouth with his own and it is warm, open, responsive.

"My love," he tells her. "This is what happens. Ah, you are beautiful, Lily. So very beautiful."

He can hold back no longer. He slows the rhythm, pressing deeper, pausing longer. He

51

is enclosed by her, engulfed by her, part of her. Lily. My love. My wife. Flesh of my flesh, bone of my bone, heart of my heart.

He withdraws and delves deep again. Deeper. Beyond barriers. Beyond time or place. He releases deep into the eternity that is himself and Lily united.

He hears her whisper his name.

⌒

They have only a few miles to go before reaching the base camp. But there is a narrow pass to be negotiated before they get there. There can be no real danger of any French force being this far in front of its winter lines, but Neville is cautious. He sends men ahead to scout the hills. He arranges the line of his company so that he has the most dangerous position in front while Lieutenant Harris is at the rear and the rawest of his men as well as the chaplain and the two women are in the middle.

Lily is quiet today though no longer dazed. The reality of her father's death has begun to sink in. She has begun to grieve. But she made love with him for a second time in the early-morning darkness before he got up, and she twined her arms about his neck and told him that she loved him, that she had always loved him from the first moment she saw him, perhaps even before that, before her birth, before time and creation. He had laughed softly and told her that he adored her.

She is wearing a package on a cord about

her neck. In the package is a copy of their marriage papers—the other copy will be duly registered by Parker-Rowe when they return to camp. Lily's package is a final precaution. Anyone opening it will see that she is the wife of a British officer and will treat her with the appropriate chivalry.

The French are clever. At least this particular company is. They have evaded detection by the advance British party. They allow the front of the British line to march through the pass and emerge on the other side before they attack the weak center.

Neville whips around at the sound of the first volley of shots from the hills. It seems to him that the world slows and his vision becomes a dark tunnel through which he observes Lily in the middle of the pass, throwing up her hands and tipping backward out of sight amid the smoke and the milling bodies of his trapped men.

She has been hit.

He calls her name.

"L-i-l-y! L-I-L-Y!"

Instinctively he acts like the officer he is, drawing his sword, bellowing out orders, fighting his way back into the killing field of the pass. Back to Lily.

Lieutenant Harris meanwhile has led his men from the rear up onto the hill. Within minutes the French are put at least to temporary flight. But during those minutes Neville has reached the middle of the pass and found Lily, who has blood on her chest. More blood than was on her father's yesterday.

She is dead.

He looks down at her slain body and falls to his knees beside her, his duty forgotten. His arms reach for her.

Lily. My love. My life. So briefly my life. For one night.

Only one night for love.

Lily!

He feels no pain from the bullet that grazes his head. The world blacks out for him as he falls senseless across Lily's dead body.

PART III

An Impossible Dream

4

They did not proceed up the driveway as Lily had expected. They turned just inside the gates and were soon walking along an unpaved, wooded path. Neville neither spoke to her nor looked at her. His grip on her hand was painful. She had to half run to keep up with his long strides.

He was dazed, she knew, not quite conscious of where he was going or with whom. She did not try to break the silence.

In truth she was hardly less in shock herself. He had been about to get married. He had thought her dead—she knew that from Captain Harris. But it had been less than two years ago. He had been about to marry again. So soon after.

Lily had caught sight of his bride when she had burst into the church in a panic. She was tall and elegant and beautiful in white satin and lace. *His bride.* Someone from his own world. Someone whom perhaps he loved.

And then Lily had hurried past his bride and into the nave of the church. It had been like last night, like stepping into a different universe. But worse than last night. The church had been filled with splendidly, richly clad ladies and gentlemen, and they had all been looking back at her. She had felt their eyes on her even as her own had focused on the man who stood at the front of the church like a prince of fairy tales.

He was clothed in pale blue and silver and white. Lily had scarcely recognized him. The height, the breadth of shoulder, the strong, muscular physique were the same. But this man was the Earl of Kilbourne, a remote English aristocrat. The man she remembered was Major Lord Newbury, a rugged officer with the Ninety-fifth Rifles.

Her husband.

The Major Newbury she remembered—*Neville*, as he had become to her on that last day—had always been careless of his appearance and impossibly attractive in his green and black regimentals, which were often shabby, often dusty or mud-spattered. His blond hair had always been close cropped. Today he was all immaculate elegance.

And he had been about to marry that beautiful woman from his own world.

He had thought Lily dead. He had forgotten about her. He had never spoken of her—*that* had been clear from everyone's reaction in the church. He had perhaps been ashamed to do so. Or she had meant so little to him that he had not thought to do so. His marriage to her had been contracted in haste because he had felt he owed it to her father. It had been dismissed as an incident not worth talking about.

Today was his wedding day—to someone else.

And she had come to put a stop to it.

"Lily." He spoke suddenly and his hand tightened even more painfully about hers. "It really is you. You really are alive." He was still looking straight ahead. His pace had not slackened.

"Yes." She stopped herself only just in time from apologizing, as she had done in the church. It would be so much better for him if she had died. Not that he was an unkind man. Never that. But—

"You were dead," he said, and she realized suddenly that the path was a short route to the beach where she had spent the night. They had left the trees behind them and were descending the hillside, brushing through the ferns at reckless speed. "I saw you die, Lily. I saw you dead with a bullet through your heart. Harris reported to me afterward that you had died. You and eleven others."

"The bullet missed my heart," she told him. "I recovered."

He stopped when they reached the valley floor and looked toward the waterfall, which knifed downward in a spectacular ribbon of bright foam over a fern-clad cliff to the pool below and the stream that flowed to the sea. The tiny thatched cottage that Lily had noticed the night before overlooked the pool. There was a pathway leading to its door, though there was no sign that the house was inhabited.

He turned in the opposite direction and strode toward the beach, taking her with him. Lily, who was feeling overwarm at the length and speed of their walk, pulled loose the ribbons of her bonnet with her free hand

and let it fall to the sand behind her. She had lost hairpins during the night. The few that remained were not sufficient to the task of keeping her mane of curly, unruly hair confined on her head. It fell about her shoulders and down her back. She shook her head and allowed the breeze to blow it back from her face.

"Lily," he said, looking down at her for the first time since they had left the church. "Lily. Lily."

They were walking, not along the hard level sand of the beach, but down it. They stopped at the water's edge. If only they were still separated by the ocean's expanse, Lily thought. If only she had stayed in Portugal. It would have been better for both their sakes.

He would have married the other woman.

She would not have known that he had forgotten her so soon, that she had meant so little to him.

"You are alive." He had dropped her hand at last, but he turned to her now, gazed into her face with searching eyes, and lifted one hand. He hesitated before touching his fingertips to her cheek. "Lily. Oh, my dear, you are alive!"

"Yes." She had reached her journey's end. Or perhaps merely the beginning of another. He stood there in all the splendor of the Earl of Kilbourne.

Neville realized suddenly that he was standing on the beach, at the water's edge. He had no idea why he had come here of all places. Except that the house would soon be filled with guests again. And this was where he always came to be alone. To think.

But he was not alone now. Lily was with him. He was *touching* her. She was warm and alive. She was small and thin and pretty and shabby, her long hair blowing wildly in the wind.

She was—oh, God, she was *Lily*.

"Lily," he asked, and he squinted out to sea, though he did not really see either the water or the infinity beyond it, "what happened?"

He had been carried off unconscious from that pass. Lieutenant Harris had told him in the hospital that Lily and eleven of the men, including the chaplain, the Reverend Parker-Rowe, had died. But the company had been forced to make their escape carrying only their packs and their wounded with them. They had had to leave the dead and their belongings for the returning French to plunder and bury.

Guilt had gnawed at Neville in the year and a half since then. He had failed to protect his men from harm. He had failed Sergeant Doyle. He had failed Lily—his wife.

"They took me to Ciudad Rodrigo," she said, "and a surgeon dug the bullet out of me. It missed my heart by a whisker, he told me—

61

it was the word he used. He spoke English. A few of them did. They were kind to me."

"Were they?" He turned his head and looked sharply down at her. "They found your papers, Lily? They treated you well? With respect?"

"Oh, yes," she said, looking up at him. He remembered then the large, guileless eyes as blue as a summer sky. They had not changed. "They were very kind. They called me 'my lady.' " She smiled fleetingly.

Relief made him feel slightly weak at the knees. The shock was beginning to wear off, he realized. He should be married now and on his way back to the abbey for breakfast— with Lauren, his wife. Instead he was standing on the beach in his wedding finery with—his wife. He felt a renewed wave of dizziness.

"They kept you in captivity and treated you well?" he said. "When and where did they release you, Lily? Why was I not informed? Or did you escape?"

Her gaze lowered to his chin. "They were attacked soon after we left Ciudad Rodrigo," she said. "By Spanish partisans. I was taken captive."

He felt further relief. He even smiled. "Then you were safe," he said. "The partisans are our allies. They escorted you back to the regiment? But that must have been months ago, Lily. *Why* did no one notify me?"

She was turning, he noticed, to look back up the beach toward the valley. Her hair blew forward over her shoulders, hiding her face from his gaze.

"They knew I was English," she said. "But they would not believe I was a prisoner. I was not confined, you see. And they would not believe that I was an officer's wife. I was not dressed like one. They thought I was with the French as a—as a concubine."

He felt as if his heart had performed a complete somersault in his chest. He opened his mouth to speak, but he could scarcely get the words out.

"But your papers, Lily..."

"The French had taken them and not returned them to me," she said.

He closed his eyes tightly and kept them closed. The Spanish partisans were notorious for the savagery with which they treated their French captives. How would they have treated a French concubine, even if she was English? How had she escaped horrible torture and execution?

He knew how.

He gasped air into his lungs. "You were with them...for a long time?" he asked. He did not wait for her answer. "Lily, did they..."

Had all of Doyle's worst fears been realized? And his own? But he did not need to hear the answer. It was pitifully obvious. *There was no other possible answer.*

"Yes," she said softly.

Silence stretched before she continued speaking. Somewhere a seagull was crying, and it was easy to imagine that the sound was mournful.

"After many months—seven—an English agent joined them for a few days and convinced them to let me go. I walked back to Lisbon. Nobody there would believe my story until by chance Captain Harris came to Lisbon on some business. He and Mrs. Harris were returning to London. They brought me with them. The captain wanted to write to you, but I would not wait. I came. I had to come. I needed to tell you that I was still alive. I tried last night when there was a p-party at the house, but they thought I was a beggar and wanted to give me sixpence. I am sorry it had to be this morning. I—I will not stay now that I have told you. If you will...pay my way on the stage, I will go...somewhere else. I think there is a way of ending a marriage for what I have done. If you have money and influence, that is, and I daresay you do. You must do it and then you can...continue with your plans."

To marry someone else. Lauren. She suddenly seemed like someone from another lifetime.

Lily was referring to divorce. For adultery. Because she had allowed herself to be raped as an alternative to torture and execution—if she had even been given the choice. Because she had set her face toward survival. And had survived.

Lily raped.

Lily an adulteress.

His sweet, lovely innocent.

"Lily." It was not his imagination that she was thinner. Her slender frame had used to have a lithe grace. Now it looked gaunt. "When did you last eat?"

It took her awhile to answer. "Yesterday,"

she said. "At noon. I have a little money. Perhaps I can buy a loaf of bread in the village."

"Come." He took her hand in his again. Hers was cold now and limp. "You need a warm bath and a change of clothes and a good meal and a long sleep. Do you have no belongings with you?"

"My bag," she said, looking down as if she expected it to appear suddenly in her empty hand. "I think I must have dropped it somewhere. I had it when I went into the village this morning. I was going to buy breakfast. And then they told me about—about your wedding."

"It will be found," he assured her. "It does not matter. I am going to take you home."

Into complications his mind could not even begin to contemplate.

"It is not that I think of you as a servant, Lily," Neville explained—the first words either of them had spoken since they left the beach, "but this way we may avoid the worst of the crowds."

The door through which they entered Newbury Abbey was not at the front. It was, Lily gathered, a servants' entrance. And the bare stone steps they ascended inside must be servants' stairs. They were deserted. The rest of the house certainly was not, if all the carriages that were before the stables and coach house and on the terrace were any indication. And there were people on the terrace too, standing together in small groups—some of those richly clad wedding guests who had been in the church.

Neville opened a door onto a wide corridor. It was carpeted and lined with paintings and sculptures and doors. They were in the main part of the house now, then. And there were three people there in conversation with one another, who stopped talking and gazed curiously at her and looked embarrassed and greeted Neville uncertainly. He nodded curtly to them but said not a word. Neither did Lily, whose hand was still in his firm clasp.

And then he opened one of the doors and released her hand in order to set his at the back of her waist to move her into the room beyond the door. It was a large, square, high-ceilinged room. There were gilded moldings all about the edges of the ceiling, she saw in one glance upward, and a painting on the ceiling that included fat, naked little babies with wings. Two long windows showed her that the room faced over the front of the house. It was a bedchamber, richly carpeted and sumptuously furnished. The bed was canopied and draped in heavy silk. The dusky pink and moss-green colors of the room's furnishings and draperies blended pleasingly together.

Lily had never seen anything half so grand in her life—except perhaps the great hall she had glimpsed the evening before.

"I shall have food and drink brought up immediately," Neville said, striding across the room to pull on a tasseled strip of silk beside the bed, "and then I shall have hot water carried up to the dressing room for a bath. It should be possible to retrieve your bag, but for now I am sure a nightgown and a dressing gown can be found for you. You must sleep then, Lily. You look weary."

Yes, she was tired, she supposed. But weariness had been a condition of her life for so long that she hardly recognized it for what it was. She knew she was hungry, though she was not at all sure she would be able to eat. His tone was brisk and formal. It was not at all the joyful homecoming she had imagined—or the horrified rejection she had feared. He knew what had happened to her, yet he had brought her to the house, to this grand apartment.

"Is this your room?" she asked him. She did not know what to call him. "Neville" seemed too familiar, even though she was his wife. She would have felt comfortable calling him "sir," but he was no longer an officer and she was no longer a part of his regiment. She could not bring herself to call him "my lord." And so she called him nothing.

"It is the countess's room," he said. He nodded toward a door in the room she had not yet seen beyond. "You will find the dressing room through there."

The countess? The countess would be his wife or his mother. He would hardly have put her in his mother's room. That tall lady at the church was to have been his wife, his countess. But he had been unable to marry her because he was already married to herself, to Lily. That made her…the countess. Did it? She really had not thought of it before. She had been startled when her French captors had called her "my lady" and she had realized that she was Viscountess Newbury. But that had been a long, long time ago.

"It is to be my room?" she asked. "I am to stay, then?" She had never really thought beyond the end of the journey. She had known deep down that an earl would surely rid himself of a sergeant's daughter at the slightest excuse—and the Earl of Kilbourne would have an excuse that was hardly slight. But she had tried to focus on the fact that the Earl of Kilbourne was also Major Lord Newbury. *Her* Major Newbury, the man she had always admired, trusted, adored. Neville. Her husband. Her lover. Her love. But she knew, standing in the countess's room, that she had never really expected a happily ever after. Only some sort of completion.

"Lily." He stepped toward her, and she could see that he was as uncertain and bewildered as she. More so, perhaps. He had had no warning of what was to happen to him this morning. "Let us not look beyond the moment. You are alive. You are here. And you are in the countess's room. To eat and to rest. Do both before we speak further."

"Yes. All right." Yes, she wanted oblivion more than anything else in this world. She did not know how to stay on her feet any longer, how to keep her eyes open, how to focus her mind on anything more than its need for sleep.

The door opened behind Lily and she turned to see a young girl in crisp black dress and white apron and mob cap, saucer-eyed and curtsying. Neville gave her instructions while Lily walked over to the window and gazed out with heavy-lidded eyes. He was ordering enough food to feed an army. And a hot bath—what an unbelievable luxury!

He came to stand behind her after the maid had left. "I will stay until the tray arrives," he said. "I shall leave you alone then while you eat. There will be water and night clothes awaiting you in the dressing room by the time you have finished. Then you must lie down and sleep. I shall come back for you later. We will talk then."

"Thank you, sir," she said, and immediately felt foolish.

She wondered suddenly if she had merely imagined that once upon a time, for one brief night, there had been a glorious flowering of love—strangely mingled with deep grief for her father. Both emotions had been shared with this man, this stranger who was her husband. Love—or what sometimes went by the name of love—had been so very ugly since that night that it was hard to believe it ever could be beautiful. But it had been. Once. Once in her life. With him—with Major Lord Newbury. With Neville.

It had been the most beautiful experience of her life. All the love she had stored secretly in her heart since she first knew him had culminated in that night of carnal passion. And she had believed—she had *felt*—that it was a shared love, though she had learned since that men were capable of passion without feeling one iota of love. They could even murmur endearments.

Had she imagined that Neville had felt both that night? In her naïveté had she imagined it—or in the need she had felt during the months following that night to believe that once, for one short night, she had loved a man who had loved her in return?

The tray arrived while she was lost in memory and was set down on an elegant little table. Neville drew back a chair, and when Lily went toward it, he seated her and pushed the chair closer. There really *was* enough food for an army. She looked hungrily at a couple of boiled eggs while he poured her a cup of tea.

"I will leave you in privacy now," he said then, taking her right hand in both of his. "I can't express to you how glad I am that you did not die, Lily. I am glad you survived everything else." He raised her hand to his lips and kissed the backs of her fingers before turning and leaving the room and closing the door quietly behind him.

Was he glad? she wondered, staring after him. Apart from the fact that he was not a cruel man and would not wish for her death, was he *glad*? That she had survived, yes, perhaps. But that she had come back into his life to complicate it? Was he glad that it had happened through some ghastly coincidence on his wedding day to another woman?

How could he possibly be glad? Especially

knowing the truth of what had happened to her.

Who was his intended bride? Lily wondered. She was beautiful. Lily had not had a good look at her, and her face had been covered by the veil of her bonnet, but she had given an impression of grace and elegance and beauty. Did he love her? Did she love him? Were they perfect for each other? Had they been minutes away from a happily ever after?

But such thoughts were pointless. And it was impossible to think when every thought was like a leaden weight pressing down on her eyelids. Lily picked up the cup of tea and sipped the warm liquid. She closed her eyes in sheer bliss.

If only, she thought, she had been able to recover her father's pack after she had returned to Lisbon. But far too much time had elapsed. It had probably been sent back to England, she was told eventually, to some surviving relative, unless it had been simply lost or destroyed. Papa had had a father and brother living somewhere—was it in Leicestershire? Lily did not know for sure, and she had never met them. Her father had been estranged from them. But he had told her over and over again as she grew up that if he were to die suddenly she must take his pack to a senior officer and have him look at the package inside. It was her key to a secure future, he had always said, just as the gold locket she had always worn was her talisman.

She supposed her father had been saving some of his wages for her all his life. She had no idea how much money there might have been in the packet. It probably would not have been enough to last long, but it might at least have got her back to England and into some decent employment. If she had been able to find it, she need not have come here to New-bury Abbey. Though she would have done so anyway. The only thought that had sustained her through her two captivities had been the thought of *him* and the hope of seeing him again. She had not really thought of the impossibility of it all until recently, after her arrival in England. And especially last evening, when she had seen and then entered his home and his world.

She was his wife—but she was also by strict definition an adulteress.

If she had found the pack and the money, she would have had an alternative now...

But just as she had finished eating one of the eggs and was biting into her second piece of toast, Lily closed her eyes tightly and fought a wave of panic. Her locket! It was in her missing bag. She had not worn it for a long time, as the chain had broken when Manuel ripped it from her neck. But by some miracle he had returned it to her when he released her. She had not let it out of her possession since—until this morning.

Would Neville find her bag? She would have rushed out herself in search of it, but she did not know that she would be able to find her way out of the house. And she might meet people on her way. No, she would have to trust him to find it for her.

But the thought of losing the last link with her father brought on a wave of nausea, and she could eat no more.

She got to her feet and crossed to the dressing room door, swaying with exhaustion as she did so. She turned the ornate handle gingerly.

ᕽ 5 ᕽ

The Countess of Kilbourne had taken charge of a very embarrassing situation, having recovered somewhat from her shock at the church. The house guests would be coming for breakfast. She had given directions that it was to be served in the ballroom, as planned. As many obvious signs as possible that it had been intended as a *wedding* breakfast were to be removed—the white bows and the wedding cake, for example.

The ballroom was by no means full, but it was full enough for all that. Several of the guests, the countess included, had changed out of their wedding finery and wore clothes more suited to early afternoon. Despite what they might have talked about in and outside the church and during their return to the abbey, good manners prevailed at breakfast. Polite conversation was the order of the day. Any stranger wandering into the ballroom would scarcely have guessed that the meal in progress was to have been a wedding breakfast but the wedding itself had met with catastrophic disaster—or that both family members and guests were close to bursting with curiosity to know more.

The countess was composed and gracious. She set herself to conversing with her neighbors at table on a variety of topics and showed no outer sign of the acute distress she was feeling. Private and personal concerns must wait. She was not the Countess of Kilbourne for nothing.

This was the scene that greeted Neville's eyes when he entered the ballroom. But the artificiality of it all became apparent when an immediate hush fell on the gathering and all eyes turned his way. He became horribly aware of the fact that he had not changed *his* clothes—he had not thought of doing so. He was a bridegroom without a bride. He stood where he was just inside the ballroom doors and clasped his hands at his back.

"I am delighted to see that the meal is proceeding," he said. He looked about him, meeting the eyes of friends and relatives, and noting without surprise that there was no sign of either Lauren or Gwen. "I shall not disturb you for long. But naturally I owe you all a little more explanation than I was able to give at the church this morning. Indeed, I cannot recall what I said there."

The Marquess of Attingsborough, who had risen from his seat, perhaps to indicate to Neville the empty chair at his side, sat down again without saying anything.

Neville had not planned the speech. He did not know quite how much or how little to tell.

But there was really no point in withholding anything. His mother was staring at him with blank-faced dignity. His uncle at her side was frowning. There were several servants present, including Forbes, the butler. But the servants had a right to know too, Neville supposed. He would not wait to dismiss them before speaking.

"I married Lily Doyle a few hours after her father, my sergeant, was killed," he said. "I married her to fulfill a dying promise to him to give her the protection of my name and rank in the event that she was captured by the French. The following day the company I led was indeed ambushed. My...wife was killed, or so both I and the lieutenant who reported to me afterward believed. I was carried back behind British lines with a severe head wound. But Lily survived as a French captive." Her captivity by the Spanish partisans he had no intention of sharing with anyone. "She was treated honorably as my wife and finally released. She returned to England with Captain and Mrs. Harris and came on alone to Newbury Abbey to be reunited with me."

No one, it seemed to Neville, had moved a muscle since he had begun to speak. He wondered if any of those gathered here had seen Lily last night or knew that she had been turned away from the abbey with the offer of sixpence because she had been mistaken for a beggar. He wondered how many were telling themselves that she was in reality the Countess of Kilbourne. It needed to be said.

"I will be honored to present my wife, *my*

countess, to you all later," he said. "But understandably this would be somewhat overwhelming to her at present. Many of you know...Lauren as a friend and relative. Most of you—*all* of you—will be imagining her pain today. It is my hope that you will lay none of the blame for her suffering at—at my wife's door. She is innocent of any intention to cause either disruption or pain. I—Well." There was really no more to say.

"Of course she is, Nev," the Marquess of Attingsborough said briskly, but he was the only one to break the silence.

"I beg that you will excuse me now," Neville said. "Enjoy the meal, please. Does anyone know where Lauren is?" He closed his eyes briefly.

"She is at the dower house with Gwendoline, Neville," Lady Elizabeth told him. The dower house was where they had lived with the countess ever since the betrothal last Christmas. "Neither of them would admit me when I stopped there on my way back from church. Perhaps—"

But Neville merely bowed to her and left the room. This was not the time for thought or consultation or common sense. He had to go with the momentum of the moment or collapse altogether.

Neville was on his way downstairs when his uncle's voice called to him from the landing above. He looked up to see not only the duke, but his mother too, and Elizabeth.

"A private word with you, Kilbourne," his uncle said with stiff formality. "You owe it to your mother."

Yes, he did, Neville thought wearily. Perhaps he ought to have spoken with her first, before making a public appearance and a public statement in the ballroom. He just did not know the proper etiquette for a situation like this. He was not amused by the grim humor of the thought. He turned with a curt nod and led the way down to the library. He crossed the room and stood looking down at the unlit coals in the fireplace until he heard the door close and turned to face them.

"I suppose it did not occur to you, Neville," his mother said, some of the usual gracious dignity gone from her manner to be replaced by bitterness, "to inform your own mother of a previous marriage? Or to inform Lauren? This morning's intense humiliation might have been avoided."

"Calm yourself, Clara," the Duke of Anburey said, patting her shoulder. "I doubt it could have been, though the whole thing might have been somewhat less of a shock to you if Neville had been more honest about the past."

"The marriage was very sudden and very brief," Neville said. "I thought her dead and...well, I decided to keep that brief interlude in my life to myself."

Because he had been ashamed to admit that he had married the unlettered daughter of a sergeant even if she *was* already dead? It was a nasty possibility and one he hoped was not true. But how could he have explained the impulse that had made him do it? How could he have described Lily to them? How could he have explained that sometimes a woman could be so very special that it simply did not matter who she was or—more important—who she was not? He would have given the bare facts and they would have been secretly glad, *relieved,* that she had died before she could become an embarrassment to them.

"I have been able to think only of somehow handling the dreadful disaster of this morning," the countess said, sinking down into the nearest chair and raising a lace-edged handkerchief to her lips, "and of what is to become of poor Lauren. I have not been able to think beyond. Neville, tell me she is not as dreadful a creature as she appeared to be this morning. Tell me it is only the clothes..."

"You heard the boy say she is a sergeant's daughter, Clara," the duke reminded her, taking up his stand at the window, his back to the room. "I daresay that fact speaks for itself. Who was her mother, Neville?"

"I did not know Mrs. Doyle," Neville replied. "She died in India when Lily was very young. There is no blue blood there, though, Uncle, if that is what you are asking. Lily is a commoner. But she is also my wife. She has my name and my protection."

"Yes, yes, that is all very well, Neville." His mother spoke impatiently. "But... Oh dear, I cannot think straight. How *could* you do this to us? How could you do it to *your-self*? Surely your upbringing and education meant more to you than to—to marry a woman who looks for all the world like a vulgar beggar and is indeed a product of the lower classes." She stood up abruptly and swayed noticeably on her feet. "I have guests I am neglecting."

"Poor Lily," Elizabeth said, speaking for the first time. She was Neville's aunt, his father's sister, but she was only nine years his senior and he had never called her aunt. She was unmarried, not because she had never had offers, but because she had declared long ago that she would never marry unless she could find the gentleman who could convince her that the loss of her independence was preferable to keeping it—and she did not expect that ever to happen. She was beautiful, intelligent, and accomplished—and no one quite knew whether the Duke of Portfrey was more friend or beau to her. "We are forgetting *her* distress in a selfish concern for our own. Where is she, Neville?"

"Yes, where *is* she?" his mother repeated, her voice unusually petulant. "Not *here*, I suppose. There is not a single spare room at the abbey."

"There *is* one unoccupied room, Mama," Neville said stiffly. "She is in the countess's room—where she belongs. I left her there to have a meal and a bath and a sleep. I have given instructions that she is to be left undisturbed until I go up for her."

His mother closed her eyes and pressed

the handkerchief to her lips again. The countess's room, formerly hers, was part of the suite of rooms that included the earl's bedchamber—Neville's own. He could almost see her coming to grips with the reality of the fact that Lily belonged there.

"Yes," Elizabeth said. "I am sure it is best for her to rest for a while. I look forward to making her acquaintance, Neville."

It was like Elizabeth, he thought, to be gracious, to take a situation as it was and somehow make something bearable of it.

"Thank you," he said.

His mother had pulled herself together again. "You will bring her down to tea later this afternoon, Neville," she told him. "There is no point in keeping her hidden, is there? I will meet her at the same time as the rest of the family. We will all behave as we ought toward your—your wife, you may rest assured."

Neville bowed to his mother. "I would expect no less of you, Mama," he said. "But excuse me now. I must go and see Lauren."

"You will be fortunate if she does not throw things at your head, Neville," Elizabeth warned him.

He nodded. "Nevertheless," he told her.

He left the house a couple of minutes later and set out on foot in the direction of the dower house, which was close to the gates into the park, set back from the driveway in the seclusion of the trees and its own private garden. He was well on his way before he realized that he was *still* wearing his wedding finery. But he would not go back to change. Perhaps he would never regain his courage if he did that.

He was about to face, he realized, one of the most difficult encounters of his life.

～

Lauren was not inside the dower house. She was out behind it, sitting on the tree swing, idly propelling herself back and forth with one foot. She was staring unseeingly at the ground ahead of her. Gwendoline was seated on the grass to one side of the swing. Both of them were still dressed for the wedding.

He would rather be anywhere else on earth, Neville thought just before his sister spotted him. They were two of the dearest people on earth to him, and he had done this to them. And there was no comfort to bring. Only a totally inadequate explanation.

Gwendoline jumped to her feet at sight of him and glared. "I hate you, Neville," she cried. "If you have come here to make her unhappier still, you may go away again—*now!* What do you mean by it? That is what you can explain to me. What did you *mean* by saying that dreadful woman is your wife?" She burst into noisy, undignified tears and turned her face sharply away.

Lauren had stopped swinging, but she did not turn around.

"Lauren?" Neville said. "Lauren, my dear?" He still did not know what he could say to her.

Her voice was steady when she spoke, but it was without tone too. "It is quite all right," she said. "It is perfectly all right. It was just a convenient arrangement after all, was it not, our marrying? Because we grew up together and were fond of each other and it was what Uncle and Grandpapa had always wanted. And you *did* tell me not to wait when you went away. You were quite fair and honest with me. You were not betrothed to me or even promised to me. You were quite free to marry her. I do not blame you at all."

He was appalled. He would have far preferred to have her rush at him, teeth bared, fingers curled into claws.

"Lauren," he said, "let me explain, if I may."

"There is nothing *to* explain," Gwendoline said angrily, having mastered her tears. "Is she or is she not your wife, Neville? That is all that matters. But you would not have lied in church for all to hear. She is your wife."

"Yes," Neville said.

"I hate her!" Gwendoline cried. "Shabby, ugly, *low* creature."

But Lauren would not participate. "We do not know her, Gwen," she said. "Yes, Neville. Tell me. Tell us. There must be a perfectly good explanation, I am sure. Once I understand, I will be able to accept it. Everything will be perfectly all right."

She was in shock, of course. In denial. Trying to convince herself that what had happened was not so disastrous after all but merely something bewildering that would be perfectly acceptable once she understood. The exquisitely scalloped and embroidered train of her wedding gown, Neville noticed, was trailing in the dust.

It was so typical of Lauren to react rationally rather than emotionally, even when there *was* no rational way to act. She had always been thus, always the good one among the three of them, the one to think of consequences, the one to be concerned about upsetting the adults. Her story partly explained her, of course. She had come to Newbury Abbey at the age of three when her mother, the widowed Viscountess Whitleaf, married the late earl's younger brother. She had stayed at the abbey when the newlyweds left on a wedding trip—from which they had never returned. There had been letters and a few parcels from various parts of the world for a number of years and then nothing. Not even word of their deaths.

Lauren's paternal relatives had made no move to take her back. Indeed, when she had written to them on her eighteenth birthday, she had had a curt response from the viscount's secretary to the effect that her acquaintance was not something his lordship sought. Lauren, Neville suspected, had never quite trusted her lovableness. And now there were these circumstances to confirm her in her low opinion of herself.

"I do not want to understand," Gwendoline said crossly. "And how can you *sit* there, Lauren, sounding so calm and forbearing and forgiving? You should be scratching Neville's eyes out." She began to sob again.

"Neville?" Lauren said, motionless once

more. "I need to understand. Tell me about—about L-Lily."

"Lily!" Gwendoline said scornfully. "I *hate* that name. It is despicable."

"She was a sergeant's daughter," Neville explained. "She grew up with the regiment, living with it, moving about with it. She always did her share of the work and she was everyone's friend. The toughest of the men and the roughest of the women loved her. But she was her own person. There was something dreamlike, fairylike about her—I do not know quite how to describe that quality in her. She had been untouched by the ugliness of the life by which she was surrounded. She was eighteen when I—when I married her." He went on to give brief details of the circumstances of their marriage.

"And you loved her too," Lauren added when he had finished.

For her sake he wished he could deny it. Not that it would make any difference to essentials. He said nothing.

"That is no excuse," Gwendoline said. "*You* were not eighteen, Neville. You were a man. You should have known better. You should have had more of a sense of duty to your family and position than to marry a sergeant's daughter for such a stupid reason. Marriage is for *life*."

"I will have to learn to love her too," Lauren said as if Gwendoline had not spoken. "I am sure it will be possible. If *you* love her, Neville, then I…" But her words trailed away. She set the swing in motion with one foot.

Neville wondered if it would help her if he strode all the way to the swing, hauled her off it by both shoulders, and shook her soundly. But he remembered his own shock of a few hours before. He had walked all the way from the church to the water's edge on the beach without knowing he had even moved from the altar. He could not take the alternative to shaking her of lifting her off the swing into the sheltering comfort of his arms.

"Lauren," he said, "I am so very sorry, my dear. I wish there were more to say, something to comfort you, something to make you feel less...abandoned. I could say all sorts of meaningless things to assure you that eventually this will be in the past and... But they would not comfort now and would be presumptuous in me. Know, though, that you are loved by this family, which is yours as much as it is mine or Gwen's." Pompous, empty words despite their truth. He did not belive he had ever felt more helpless in his life.

"But nothing is ever going to be the *same*," Gwendoline cried. "When Vernon died and I came home a widow and then Papa died, I thought the world was at an end. But then you came back and we three were together again and I could see that you would marry Lauren and... But now everything is ended, shattered beyond repair."

Neville ran a hand through his hair. Lauren swung gently.

Gwendoline had married for love while he was away in the Peninsula. He had never met Viscount Muir. But it had been a short, tragic marriage, over in two years. First Gwen had had a dreadful riding accident that had caused a miscarriage and left her with a permanent limp after her broken leg had healed, and then just a year later, Muir had died in a fall through a broken banister from the balcony of his own home to the marble hall below. Gwen had fled to the familiar comfort of home rather than remain at her husband's house.

"And how I despise my own selfishness," Gwendoline said when no one responded to her words. "I am thinking of my own unhappiness when it is *nothing* to poor Lauren's. Oh, what a brute I am." She gathered up her skirts and dashed toward the house, avoiding Neville's outstretched arm as she passed him.

"Poor Gwen," Lauren said. "She wanted so very much to go back in time after Lord Muir's death, Neville. She wanted life to be as it was when we were children, and it seemed to her that her dream was coming true. But we can never go back. Only forward. We cannot go back to yesterday or early this morning. There is Lily now."

"Yes."

"I have been selfish too," she told him. "I have been preoccupied by my own disappointment. But you must be so very happy, Neville, even though in your kindness you are sad for me and have taken time to come and talk with me. Lily is alive and she has come to you. How wonderful for you."

"Lauren," he said softly. "My dear, don't do this. Please don't."

"You want me to tell you how much I hate her, then?" she said. "How much I wish she had died and stayed dead? How much I wish even now that she would die? You want me to tell you how much I resent your going away after telling me not to wait and then marrying a sergeant's daughter on mere impulse? You want me to tell you how much I hate you for not telling me? For caring so little for me that you did not mention the fact that this would be your second marriage? For causing me such humiliation this morning?"

He drew a slow breath. "Yes," he said. "This is what I want to hear, Lauren. Let it out. Yell at me. Throw things at me. Hit me. Don't just sit there." He ran his fingers through his hair again. "Oh, dear God, Lauren. I am so wretchedly *sorry*. If I could only—"

"But you cannot," she said quietly, though there was an edge to her voice at last. "You cannot, Neville. And hatred is pointless. As are violent emotions. Will you go now, please? I wish to be alone."

"Of course," he said. It was the only thing he could do for her. To take himself out of her sight.

She was still pushing the swing with one foot when he turned to leave. Nursing her shock. Her conviction that if she just stayed calm and rational, everything would be all right. Her intense hatred for the sergeant's daughter who had destroyed her hopes and her dreams, her very life, in one stroke. And for the man she had loved all her life.

It did not help Neville to know beyond all doubt that she had always loved him with a far deeper intensity than he had ever loved her.

He thought suddenly, as he made his way back up the drive, of Lauren as she had been the night before—radiant, glowing with happiness, asking him if anyone could possible deserve to be so happy.

She could, as he had told her then. But life did not always give what one deserved.

What had he done to deserve Lily's return? His footsteps quickened as he thought of her even then asleep, *alive*, in the countess's bed.

ᕲ 6 ᕲ

The food and the tea had satisfied Lily; the deep, hot bath with perfumed soap and large, fluffy towel had soothed and lulled her; she had slept long and deep and had woken refreshed but bewildered. For several moments she was unable to remember where she was or how she had got there. She could not recall when she had last slept so well.

It did not take long for everything to come back to her, of course. She had arrived. She had reached the end of a journey that had begun she did not know how long ago when Manuel had come to her and told her she could go. Just like that—after seven months of captivity and enslavement. She had been somewhere in Spain. All she had known to do was set her face for the west, where Portugal lay, to search for him—for Neville, Major Lord Newbury, her husband. She had not even known if he was still alive. He might have died in the ambush that had wounded and made a prisoner of her. But she had begun the journey anyway. There had been nothing else to do. Her father was dead.

She had arrived, she thought, flinging back the bedcovers and stepping out onto the soft pile of the pink and green carpet. She had to hold up the hem of her nightgown in order not to trip over it. It was at least six inches too long, or she was six inches too short—probably the latter. She had arrived in spectacularly embarrassing circumstances, and distressing ones too. But she had not yet been turned away even though she had admitted the essential truth that might have caused him to dismiss her without further ado.

He might still do it, of course. But he had treated her kindly despite the fact that she had ruined his future plans. Surely he would at least give, or lend, her enough money to get her back to London. Perhaps Mrs. Harris would be good enough to help her find some employment, though she did not know what she was capable of doing.

She turned the handle of the dressing room door as gingerly as she had done earlier. But this time she was not so fortunate. There was someone else in there.

"Oh, I am sorry," she said, closing the door quickly.

But it opened again almost immediately and

the startled face of a young girl about Lily's own age looked in at her. The girl was wearing one of those pretty mob caps the servant who had brought the food had worn.

"I beg your pardon, I am sure, my lady," the girl said. "I just come up with your clothes, and Mrs. Ailsham told me to stay to help you dress and do your hair. She said his lordship is to come for you in half an hour, my lady, to take you to tea."

"Oh." Lily smiled and held out her right hand. "You are a *maid*. What a relief to learn that. How do you do? I am Lily."

The maid eyed her outstretched hand askance. She did not take it but curtsied instead. "I am pleased to make your acquaintance, my lady," she said. "I am Dolly. My mum and dad had me christened Dorothy, but everyone has always called me just Dolly. I am to be your personal maid, Mrs. Ailsham says, until your own arrives."

"Mrs. Ailsham?" Lily stepped into the dressing room and looked about her. The bathtub had been removed, she saw.

"The housekeeper, my lady," Dolly explained.

And then Lily saw her bag lying on the stool before the dressing table. She rushed toward it and searched anxiously inside. But all was well. Her hand closed about her locket at the bottom of the bag. She drew it out and clasped it comfortingly in her hand. She would have felt she had lost part of herself if she had lost the locket. Some other things were missing, though. She looked about the room.

"I took the liberty of taking a dress and shift out of your bag, my lady," Dolly said. "I ironed them. They was creased bad."

There they were laid carefully over the back of a chair, her cotton shift and the precious, pretty pale-green muslin dress Mrs. Harris had insisted on buying for her in Lisbon.

"You *ironed* them?" she said, smiling warmly at the maid. "How very kind of you, Dolly. I could have done it myself. But I am glad not to have to do so. However would I find my way to the kitchen?" She laughed.

Dolly laughed too, a little uncertainly. "You are funny, my lady," she said. "How everyone would *look* if you was to walk into the kitchen with your dress over your arm, asking for the iron." The idea seemed to tickle her enormously.

"Especially dressed as I am now," Lily said, grasping her nightgown at the sides and raising it until her bare toes showed. "Tripping all over my hem."

They laughed together like a pair of children.

"I'll help you dress, my lady," Dolly told her.

"Help me? Whatever for?" Lily asked her.

Dolly did not answer. She pointed to Lily's rather battered shoes, the only pair she owned. Mrs. Harris had bought those for her too, but she had told Lily that the army was paying for them. The army, in Mrs. Harris's opinion, owed Lily something. The army had bought her bag too and her passage on the ship that had brought them to England.

"I had them polished, my lady," Dolly said. "But you need new ones, if you was to ask me."

"I do not believe I need to ask," Lily said as she dressed quickly. She was feeling curiously lighthearted. "One day soon I am going to take a step forward and my shoes are going to decide to remain where they are, and that will be the end of them."

Lily could not remember laughing with such merriment for a long, long time—until now as she did so yet again with Dolly.

"You have a pretty figure, my lady," Dolly said, looking critically at her when she was dressed. "Small and dainty, not all arms and legs and elbows like me. You will dress up nice when all your trunks have arrived."

"But I wish I had some of your height," Lily said with a sigh. "Is there a ribbon anywhere, Dolly, with which to tie back my hair? I do believe I have lost all my hairpins."

"Oh, a ribbon will not be enough, my lady." Dolly sounded shocked. "Not to go down to *tea*. You sit down on the stool now—here, I will move the bag to this chair—and I will dress your hair for you. You need not worry that I will make a mess of it. I dressed Lady Gwendoline's hair sometimes before she moved to the dower house, and I even patched up Lady Elizabeth's hair last night when some of it fell down during the ball and her own maid was nowhere to be found. She said I done a nice job. I want to be a lady's maid all the time instead of just a chambermaid. That's what my big ambition is, my lady. You got lovely hair."

Lily sat. "I do not know what you can do with it, though, Dolly," she said dubiously. "It curls hopelessly and is like a *bush*. It is more than usually unruly today because I washed it. Oh, how novel—I have never had anyone do my hair for me."

Dolly laughed. "What funny jokes you make, my lady," she said. "There are some I know as would kill for the curl in your hair. Look how it piles nice and stays high without falling like a loaf of bread when the oven door is opened too soon. And ooh, look, my lady, how it twists into ringlets without any rags or curling tongs. *I* would kill for this hair."

Lily looked at the developing style in the looking glass, her eyes wide with astonishment. "How extraordinarily clever you are," she said. "You have amazing skill, Dolly. I would not have thought it possible for my hair to look *tame*."

Dolly flushed with pleasure and pushed the final pin into place. She picked up a small hand mirror from the dressing table and held it up at various angles behind Lily so that she could see the back of her head and the sides.

"That will do for tea, my lady," she said. "For this evening we will need something more special. I will think of what to do. I hope your own maid does not arrive too soon, though I ought not to say so, ought I?" She was fluffing the short puffed sleeves of Lily's dress as she talked, watching the effect in the looking glass. "There you are, my lady. You are ready whenever his lordship comes."

It was not a comforting prospect. He was

going to take her *to tea*. What did that mean exactly? But there was no time for reflection. Almost immediately there was a tap on one of the three doors of the dressing room and Dolly went to answer it—she seemed to know unerringly which one to open. Lily got to her feet.

He had changed out of his pale wedding clothes. He looked more familiar wearing a dark-green coat, though it was far more carefully tailored and form-fitting than his Rifleman's jacket had been. He looked her over quickly from head to toe and bowed to her.

"You are looking better," he said. "I trust you slept well?"

"Yes, thank you, sir," she said, and grimaced. She *must* remember not to call him that.

"You were fast asleep when I looked in on you earlier," he told her. "You are looking very pretty."

"Thanks to Dolly," she said, smiling at the maid. "She ironed my dress and tamed my hair. Was that not kind of her?"

"Indeed." He raised his eyebrows. "You may leave us...Dolly."

"Yes, my lord." The maid curtsied deeply without raising her eyes to him and scurried from the room.

Well, Lily could understand *that* reaction. She had seen soldiers leave his presence in similar fashion—though they had not curtsied, of course—after he had turned his eyes on them. His men had always worshiped him— and been terrified of his displeasure. Lily had never felt the terror.

"My name is Neville, Lily," he said. "You may use it, if you please. I am going to take you to the drawing room for tea. You must not mind. Several of my guests have already left so the numbers will not be quite overwhelming. They are mostly members of my family. I will stay close to you. Just be yourself."

But *some* of those grand people she had seen last night and this morning would be there, gathered in the drawing room? And he was going to take her there to join them? How could she possibly meet them? What would she say? Or do? And what would they think of her? Not very much, she guessed. She had lived most of her life with the army and was well aware of the huge gap that had separated the men— her father included—from the officers. And here she was, an earl's wife, making her first appearance at his home on the very day he was to have married someone else—a lady from his own class, she did not doubt. It would be difficult to imagine a less desirable situation.

But all her life Lily had been led into difficult situations, none of them of her own choosing. She had grown up with an army at war. She had adjusted to all sorts of places and situations and people. She had even lived through seven months of what many women would have considered a fate worse than death.

And so she stepped forward and took Neville's offered arm without showing any of her inward qualms, and they stepped out into the wide corridor she remembered from earlier. They descended one of the grand curved staircases. She looked down over the banister to the marble, tiled hall below and up to the gilded, windowed dome above. She had that feeling again of being dwarfed, overwhelmed.

"I expected a large cottage," she said.

"I beg your pardon?"

"Your home," she said. "I expected a large cottage in a large garden."

"Did you, Lily?" He looked gravely down at her. "And you found this instead? I am sorry."

"I thought only kings lived in houses like this," she said, and felt very foolish indeed, especially when his eyes crinkled at the corners and she realized she had said something to amuse him.

Then they were approaching two huge double doors and one of those liveried footmen waited to open them. He was the footman she'd encountered last evening, Lily saw. She could even remember what the superior servant had called him. Her life with the army had made her skilled in remembering faces and the names that went with them. She smiled warmly.

"How do you do, Mr. Jones?" she asked.

The footman looked startled, blushed noticeably beneath his white wig, bobbed his head, and opened the doors. Lily glanced upward to see that Neville's eyes were crinkled at the corners again. He was also pursing his lips to keep from laughing.

But she had no chance to consider the

matter further because as soon as they stepped inside the drawing room, she was assaulted by so many impressions at once that she was struck quite dumb and breathless. There was the hugeness and magnificence of the room itself—four of her imagined cottages would surely have fit inside it with ease. But more daunting than the room was the number of people who occupied it. Was it possible that any of the wedding guests had already left for home? Everyone was dressed with somewhat less magnificence than either last evening or this morning, but even so Lily suddenly realized that her own prized muslin dress was quite ordinary and her wonderful coiffure very plain. Not to mention her *shoes*!

Neville took her, in the hush that followed their entrance, toward an older lady of regal bearing and attractively graying dark hair. She was seated, a delicate saucer in one hand, a cup in the other. She looked as if she had frozen in position. Her eyebrows were arched finely upward.

"Mama," Neville said, bowing to her, "may I present Lily, my wife? This is my mother, Lily, the Countess of Kilbourne." He drew breath audibly and spoke more quietly. "Pardon me—the *dowager* Countess of Kilbourne."

She was the lady who had stood up at the front of the church during the morning and spoken his name, Lily realized. She was his mother—she set down her cup and saucer and got to her feet. She was tall.

"Lily," she said, smiling, "welcome to Newbury Abbey, my dear, and to our family." And she took one of Lily's hands from her side and leaned forward to kiss her on the cheek.

Lily smelled a whiff of some expensive and exquisite perfume. "I am pleased to meet you," she said, not at all sure that either of them spoke with any degree of sincerity.

"Let me present you to everyone else, Lily," Neville said. The room was remarkably silent. "Or perhaps not. It might prove too overwhelming for you. Perhaps a general introduction for now?" He turned and smiled about him.

But the dowager countess had other ideas and told him so. "Of course Lily must be presented to everyone, Neville," she said, drawing Lily's arm through her own. "She is your countess. Come, Lily, and meet our family and friends."

There followed a bewildering spell that felt hours long to Lily though it was doubtful it exceeded a quarter of an hour. She was presented to the silver-haired gentleman and the lady with all the rings she had seen downstairs last evening and understood that they were the Duke and Duchess of Anburey, the dowager countess's brother and sister-in-law. She was presented to their son, the Marquess of something impossibly long. And then she was aware only of faces, all of which belonged to persons with first names and last names and—all too often—titles too. Some were aunts or uncles. Some were cousins—either first or second or at some remove. Some were family friends or her husband's particular friends or someone else's friends. Some of them inclined their heads to her. Several of the younger people bowed or curtsied to her. Most smiled; some did not. All too many of them spoke to her; she could think of nothing to say in reply except that she was pleased to meet them all.

"Poor Lily. You look thoroughly bewildered," the lady behind the tea tray said when Lily and the dowager countess finally reached her. "Enough for now, Clara. Come and sit on this empty chair, Lily, and have a cup of tea and a sandwich. I am Elizabeth. I daresay you did not hear it the first time, and really it does not matter if you forget it the next time you see me. We have only one name to remember while you have a whole host. Eventually you will sort us all out. Here, my dear."

She had been pouring a cup of tea as she spoke and handed it to Lily now with a plate of tiny sandwiches with the crusts cut off. Lily was not hungry, but she did not want to refuse. She took a sandwich and then discovered that if she was to drink, as she dearly wished to do, she must eat the sandwich first so that she might have a hand free with which to lift the cup. The china was so very delicate and pretty that she felt a sudden terror of dropping some of it and smashing it.

Neville's hand came to rest on her shoulder.

The room was no longer silent, Lily noticed in some relief, and all attention was no longer focused on her. Everyone was being polite, she gathered. She listened to the conversation that flowed around her as she ate her sandwich and succeeded in sipping her tea without mishap. But she was not being ignored either. People whose names she could not remember—what a time for her usual skill of memory to have deserted her!—kept trying to draw her into the conversation. A few of the ladies had been having a spirited discussion on the relative merits of two types of bonnet.

"What do *you* think, Lily?" one of them, a dashingly dressed red-haired lady, asked graciously. Was she one of the cousins?

"I do not know," said Lily, to whom a bonnet was simply something to keep off the sun.

Then they talked about a certain theater in London and had differing opinions on whether its audiences preferred comedies or tragedies. Lily found herself remembering with pleased nostalgia the farces the soldiers had sometimes put on for the merriment of the regiment.

"What do you think, Lily?" one gentleman asked, a pleasant-faced youngish man with receding fair hair. Was he a relative or one of the friends?

"I do not know," Lily replied.

They talked about a concert several of them had attended in London a few weeks before. The Duchess of Anburey thought Mozart the greatest musical genius ever to have lived. A portly, florid-faced gentleman disagreed and put forward the claims of Beethoven. There were firm supporters of both sides.

"What do you think, Lily?" the duchess asked.

"I do not know," Lily said, not having heard of either gentleman.

She began to wonder if they asked her opinion deliberately, knowing that she knew *nothing*, that she was almost as ignorant now as she had been on the day she was born. But perhaps not. They did not appear to be looking at her with malicious intent.

They were discussing books, the gentlemen speaking in favor of political and philosophical treatises, some of the ladies defending the novel as a legitimate art form.

"Which novels have you read, Lily?" an extremely elegantly dressed and coiffed young lady asked.

"I cannot read," Lily admitted.

Everyone looked suddenly embarrassed on her behalf. There was an awkward little silence that no one seemed in a hurry to fill. Lily had always wanted to read. Her parents had told her stories when she was a child, and she had always thought it would be wonderful to be able to pick up a book and escape into those magical worlds of the imagination whenever she wished—or acquire knowledge of matters on which she was ignorant. She was so *very* ignorant. But there had never been the chance to go to school, and her father, who had been able to read a very little and to write his name, had always declared himself incompetent to teach her himself.

Neville half bent over her from behind her chair. He was going to rescue her and take her from the room, she thought in some relief. But

101

before he could do so, the lady behind the tea tray spoke up—Elizabeth. She was very beautiful, Lily had noticed earlier, though she was not young. She had a grace and elegance that Lily envied and a face full of character and hair as blond as Neville's. She was his aunt.

"I daresay Lily is a *living* book," she said, smiling kindly. "I have never been able to travel beyond these shores, Lily, because the wretched wars have been raging for almost the whole of my adult life. I would dearly love to travel and see all the countries and cultures I have only been able to read about. You must have seen several. Where have you been?"

"To India," Lily said. "To Spain and Portugal. And now England."

"India!" Elizabeth exclaimed, gazing admiringly at Lily. "Men come home from such places, you know, and tell us about this battle and that skirmish. How fortunate we are to have a *woman* who can tell us more interesting and important things. Do talk about India. No, that is too broad a question and will doubtless tie your tongue in knots. What about the people, Lily? Are they very different from us in any essential ways? Tell us about the women. How do they dress? What do they do? What are they *like*?"

"I *loved* India," Lily said, memory bringing an instant glow to her face and a light to her eyes. "And the people were so very sensible. Far more so than our own people."

"How so?" one of the young gentlemen asked her.

"They dressed so sensibly," Lily said. "Both

102

men and women wore light, loose clothes for the heat. The men did not have to wear tight coats buttoned to the throat all day long and leather stocks to choke their windpipes and tight breeches and high leather boots to burn their legs and feet off. Not that it was the fault of our poor soldiers—they were merely following orders. But so often they looked like boiled beets."

There was a burst of laughter—mainly from the gentlemen. Most of the ladies looked rather shocked, though a few of the younger ones tittered. Elizabeth smiled.

"And the women were not foolish enough to wear stays," Lily added. "I daresay *our* women would not have had the vapors so frequently if they had followed the example of the Indian women. Women can be very silly—and all in the name of fashion."

One of the older ladies—Lily had no memory of her name or relationship to the rest of the family—had clapped a hand to her mouth and muffled a sound of distress at the public mention of stays.

"Very silly indeed," Elizabeth agreed.

"Oh, but the women's dresses." Lily closed her eyes for a moment and felt herself almost back in the land she had loved—she could almost smell the heat and the spices. "Their *saris*. They did not need jewels to brighten those garments. But they wore glass bangles that jingled on their wrists and rings in their noses and red dots here"—she pressed a middle finger to her forehead above the bridge of her nose and drew a circle with it—"to show that they were married. Their men do not have to steal sly glances at their fingers, I daresay, as *our* men do, to see if they may freely pay court to them. All they have to do is look into their eyes."

"They have no excuse, then, to pretend that they did not *know*?" the young gentleman with the long name—the marquess— asked, his eyes twinkling. "It does not seem sporting somehow."

Several of the younger people laughed.

"Did you *know*," Lily asked, leaning forward slightly in her chair and looking eagerly about her, "that saris are really just very long strips of cloth that are draped to look like the most exquisite of dresses? There is no stitching, no tapes, no pins, no buttons. One of the women who was a friend of my mama taught me how to do it. I was *so* proud of myself the first time I tried donning one without help. I thought I looked like a princess. But when I had taken no more than three steps forward, it fell off and I was left standing there in my shift. I felt very foolish, I do assure you." She laughed merrily, as did the bulk of her audience.

"Goodness, child." That was the countess, who had laughed but who also looked somewhat embarrassed.

Lily smiled at her. "I believe I was six or seven years old at the time," she said. "And everyone thought it was very funny—everyone except me. I seem to recall that I burst into tears. Later I learned how to wear a sari properly. I believe I still remember how. There is no lovelier form of dress, I do assure you. And no lovelier country than India. Always when my mother and father told me stories, I pictured them happening there, in India, beyond the British camp. There, where life was brighter and more colorful and mysterious and romantic than life with the regiment ever was."

"If you had gone to school, Lily," the gentleman with the receding fair hair told her, "you would have been taught that every other country and every other people are inferior to Britain and the British." But his eyes laughed as he spoke.

"Perhaps it is as well that I did not go to school, then," Lily replied.

He winked at her.

"Indeed, Lily," Elizabeth said, "there is a school of experience in which those with intelligence and open, questioning minds and acute powers of observation may learn valuable lessons. It seems to me that you have been a diligent pupil."

Lily beamed at her. For a few minutes she had forgotten her ignorance and her inferiority to all these grand people. She had forgotten that she was frightened.

"But we have kept you talking too long and have caused your tea to grow cold," Elizabeth said. "Come. Let me empty out what remains and pour you a fresh cup."

One of the young ladies—the one with the red hair—was asked then to play the pianoforte in the adjoining music room, and several people followed her in there, leaving the double doors open. Neville took the seat beside Lily that had just been vacated.

"Bravo!" he said softly. "You have done very well."

But Lily was listening to the music. It enthralled her. How could so much rich and harmonious sound come from one instrument and be produced with just ten human fingers? How wonderful it must feel to be able to *do* that. She would give almost anything in the world, she thought suddenly, to be able to play the pianoforte—and to be able to read and to discuss bonnets and tragedy and to know the difference between Mozart and Beethoven.

She was so terribly, *dreadfully* ignorant.

❧ 7 ❧

Neville stood on the marble steps outside the house watching Lily stroll in the direction of the rock garden with Elizabeth and the Duke of Portfrey. He made no attempt to join them. Somehow, he realized, if Lily was to function as his countess, she was going to have to do so without his hovering over her at every moment, ready to rescue her whenever she seemed in distress—as he had been about to do at tea when she had admitted to being illiterate. He had felt everyone's shock and her embarrassment and had been instantly intent on taking her out of the way of more humiliation. But Elizabeth had come magnificently to her rescue with her questions about India, and Lily had been suddenly transformed into a warm and relaxed and knowledgeable student of the world. She had shocked a few of his aunts and cousins with her candid references to breeches and stays and such, it was true. But more than one or two of his relatives had seemed charmed by her.

Unfortunately his mother was not one of them. She had waited for Lily to leave and for all but an intimate few of the family to withdraw after tea.

"Neville," she had said, "I cannot imagine *what* you were thinking of. She is quite impossible. She has no conversation, no education, no accomplishments, no—no *presence*. And does she have nothing more suitable to wear for afternoon tea than that sad muslin garment?" But his mother was not one to wallow in a sense of defeat. She straightened her shoulders and changed her tone. "But there is little to be gained by lamenting the impossibility, is there? She must simply be made possible."

"I think her deuced pretty, Nev," Hal Wollston, his cousin, had said.

"You would, Hal." Lady Wilma Fawcitt, the Duke of Anburey's red-haired daughter, had sounded scornful. "As if pretty looks have anything to say to anything. I agree with Aunt Clara. She is impossible!"

"Perhaps," Neville had said with quiet emphasis, "you would care to remember, Wilma, that you are speaking of my wife."

She had tutted, but she had said no more. His mother had got to her feet to leave the

107

room. "I must return to the dower house and see what is to be done for poor Lauren," she had said. "But tomorrow I shall move back into the abbey, Neville. It is going to need a mistress, and clearly Lily will be quite unable to assume that role for some time to come. I shall undertake her training."

"We will discuss the matter some other time, Mama," he had said, "though I agree it would be best if you moved back here. I will not have Lily made unhappy, however. This is all very difficult for her. Far more difficult than for any of us."

He had left the room before anyone could say anything more and had come to stand on the steps. There were some days, he reflected, that were so unremarkable that a week afterward one could not recall a single thing that had happened in them. And then there were days that seemed packed full of a lifetime of experiences. This was definitely one such day.

He had written several letters after returning from the dower house and then checking on Lily, who had been fast asleep. He had sent the letters on their way. It would not be easy to be patient in awaiting the replies.

The fact was that for all his solicitude, for all his apparent calm, *he simply was not sure Lily really was his wife*.

They had married without a license and without the customary banns. The regimental chaplain had assured him that the wedding was quite legal, and he had drawn up the proper papers to which Neville had put his signature and Lily her mark and which had been witnessed by Harris and Rieder. But Parker-Rowe had been killed in that ambush the following day. Harris had reported that the belongings of the dead had been left with them in the pass.

That would seem to mean that the marriage had never been registered. Was it therefore not a marriage at all? Was it void? Neville supposed that his mind must have touched upon the possibility before today. But he had never pursued the question. It had been unimportant. Lily had been dead.

But now she was alive and at Newbury Abbey. He had acknowledged her as his wife and his countess. Lauren had been made to suffer. All their lives had been turned upside down. But perhaps there was no legality to the marriage. He had written to Harris—now *Captain* Harris, it seemed—and to several civil and ecclesiastical authorities to try to find out.

What if he and Lily were not legally married after all?

Should he mention his doubts to her now before he knew the answer? Should he mention them to anyone else? The question had been weighing on his mind ever since it had struck him as he stood on the beach with her, gazing out across the sea. But he had decided to keep his doubts to himself until he had the answer. He was not sure it would make a great deal of difference anyway. He had married Lily in good faith. He had made vows to her that he had had every intention of keeping. He had consummated the marriage with her.

And he had loved her.

But he could not rid his mind of the image of Lauren, swinging gently back and forth on the tree swing in her wedding gown, listless and quietly accepting of her disappointment—and surely about to explode with the anger she had told him was pointless. A bride rejected and humiliated.

This was the devil of a coil, he thought. He felt weighed down by guilt even though common sense told him that he could not possibly have foreseen the day's events.

⁓

Lily was thankful to be out of doors again—away from that great daunting mansion and the bewildering crowds of people.

Elizabeth had suggested a stroll to the rock garden, which was strangely named as it had far more flowers and ornamental trees than rocks. Graveled walkways meandered through it and a few well-placed wrought-iron seats allowed the stroller to sit and appreciate the cultivated beauty. Lily was more accustomed to wild beauty, but a garden lovingly created and tended by gardeners had its charm, she decided.

Elizabeth walked with her arm drawn through the Duke of Portfrey's. Lily had to be told his name again, but she had noticed him in the drawing room, partly because he was a very distinguished-looking gentleman. She guessed his age to be about forty, but he was still handsome. He was not very tall, but his slim, proud bearing made him appear taller than he was. He had prominent, aristocratic features and dark hair, which had turned silver at the temples. Mainly, though, she had noticed him because he had watched her more intently than anyone else had. He had scarcely taken his eyes off her, in fact. There had been a strange expression on his face—almost of puzzlement.

He asked some pointed questions as they walked.

"Who was your father, Lily?" he asked.

"Sergeant Thomas Doyle of the Ninety-fifth, sir," she told him.

"And where did he live before he took the king's shilling?" he asked.

"I think Leicestershire, sir."

"Ah," he said. "And where exactly in Leicestershire?"

"I do not know, sir." Papa had never talked a great deal about his past. Something he had once said, though, had led Lily to believe that he had left home and joined the army because he had been unhappy.

"And his family?" the duke asked. "What do you know of them?"

"Very little, sir," she replied. "Papa had a father and a brother, I believe."

"But you never visited them?"

"No, sir." She shook her head.

"And your mother," he asked her. "Who was she?"

"Her name was Beatrice, sir," she said. "She died in India when I was seven years old. She had a fever."

"And her maiden name, Lily?"

Elizabeth laughed. "Are you planning to write a biography, Lyndon?" she asked. "Pray do not feel obliged to answer, Lily. We are all curious about you because you have suddenly been presented to us as Neville's wife and your life has been so fascinatingly different from our own. You must forgive us if we seem almost ill-bred in our inquisitiveness."

The duke asked no more questions, Lily was relieved to discover. She found his blue eyes rather disconcerting. He gave the impression of being able to see right into another person's mind.

"Do you know the names of all these flowers?" she asked Elizabeth. "They are very lovely. But they are different from flowers I know."

They sat on one of the seats while Elizabeth named every flower and tree and Lily set herself to memorizing their names—lupins, hollyhocks, wallflowers, lilies, irises, sweet briar, lilacs, cherry trees, pear trees. Would she ever remember them all? The Duke of Portfrey strolled along the paths while they talked, though he did pause for a while at the lower end of the rock garden to gaze back at Lily.

Lady Elizabeth stood beside the fountain watching Lily return to the house. She looked small and rather lost, but she had declined Elizabeth's offer to accompany her to her room. She thought she could remember the way, she had said.

"She has courage," Elizabeth said more to herself than to the Duke of Portfrey, who was standing behind her.

"I must thank you, Elizabeth," he said stiffly, "for pointing out how ill-bred and excessively inquisitive my questions were."

She swung around to face him. "Oh, dear," she said, smiling ruefully, "I have offended you."

"Not at all." He made her a slight bow. "I am sure you were quite right."

"Poor child," she said. "One feels she is a child, though if Neville married her well over a year ago she cannot be so very young, can she? She is so small and looks so fragile, yet she has lived in India and Portugal and Spain with the *armies*. That cannot have been easy. And she was a captive of the French for almost a year. What is your particular interest in her?"

The duke lifted his brows. "Have you not just stated it?" he asked her. "She is a curiosity. And she has appeared at a moment that could not have been better chosen if it had been done for deliberate effect."

"But you surely do not believe that it was?" she said, laughing.

"Not at all." He was gazing broodingly at the door through which Lily had disappeared. "She is very beautiful. Even now. When Kilbourne has spent money on clothes and jewels for her and has brought her into fashion..." He did not complete the thought—he did not need to do so.

Elizabeth said nothing. She was never able to explain even to herself the nature of her relationship with the Duke of Portfrey. They had been friends for several years. There was an ease and a closeness between them that was rare for a single man and a single woman. And yet there was a distance too. Perhaps it was a distance that was inevitable when they were of different genders but were not also lovers.

Elizabeth had sometimes asked herself whether she would become his lover if he ever suggested it. But he never had. Neither had he asked her to be his wife. She was glad of that fact. Although she had lived through her youth and her twenties in the hope that she would meet a man for whom she could care enough to marry him, she was no longer sure she was willing to give up the independence she prized.

But sometimes she thought she would like the experience of being loved—physically loved—by the handsome Duke of Portfrey.

He had been married as a very young man—briefly and tragically. He had been a military officer at the time and a younger son who had not expected ever to succeed to his father's ducal title. He had married secretly before going off with his regiment, first to the Netherlands and then to the West Indies, leaving his bride behind and his marriage undisclosed. She had died before his return. Although it had been years and years ago, Elizabeth often felt that he had never quite recovered from the experience—never forgiven himself, perhaps, for leaving her, for not being with her when she died in a carriage accident, for not being there for her funeral.

It was almost, Elizabeth felt, as if he had never quite accepted her death or let her go—though he never spoke of her. He was a moody man whom she never felt she fully understood. Perhaps, she admitted, that was his fascination.

And now he seemed fascinated with Lily, a young woman whom he had just described— quite accurately—as beautiful. And Elizabeth herself was six-and-thirty. Well. She smiled ruefully.

"Shall we go indoors too?" she suggested. "The breeze is becoming chilly."

He offered her his arm.

Lily tried to re-create in her mind the dream she had held there for longer than a year. How very foolish it seemed now in retrospect. She had pictured herself arriving at that large cottage set in its pretty English garden—her father had always said that English gardens were prettier than any other gardens on earth—and seeing the delight in Neville's face as he opened the door and found her standing on his doorsill. He would enfold her in his arms and squeeze all the breath out of her, and then she would tell him her story and he would forgive her the part that needed forgiveness and they would live happily ever after. She would have a *home*, a permanent place where she belonged and that she could make her own. In her dream there had been no other people—just Neville and herself.

Lily sighed as she opened one of the long windows of her bedchamber and breathed in the cool night air. Had she ever really believed in the dream? Probably not. She was not so naive as to imagine that life could ever be that simple. All her life she had been aware of the insurmountable social gap between the officers and the men—and their women. And her marriage to Neville had been so very sudden and so very brief. But the dream had sustained her through many hardships. And it was better sometimes to have an unrealistic dream, she thought, than to have only the cold truth of reality.

She was the Countess of Kilbourne, mistress of all this—unless he decided after all to divorce her, though she did not think he would. The whole situation was absurd. It was impossible. Teatime had been a nightmare. Dinner had been worse. She had not known what food or drink to accept from the footmen, which knives and forks and spoons to use with which courses. If Neville had not touched her hand almost at the start and murmured to her that she should copy what he did, and if Elizabeth had not caught her eye from across the table, winked, and picked up the utensils that would be needed for the course then being served, she would have disgraced herself utterly.

And in the drawing room afterward there had been all that conversation again. It might have been wonderful indeed to have listened to it if she could have been been invisible, if other people for one reason or another had not tried to draw her in. She had revealed more and more of her ignorance every time she opened her mouth.

She had worn her green muslin again though Dolly had done new things to her hair. Everyone else had changed and made her feel plainer and dowdier than ever. She hated being made aware of such things. What she wore had never particularly mattered before. Clothes had simply been for warmth or coolness or basic decency. But here clothes said something about status.

This was to be her life, she thought, moving from the window toward the bed. She reached down to pull up the sides of her nightgown so that she would not trip over the hem. But she stopped and smiled at her bare toes. Dolly had sat in her dressing room for much of the evening, removing the frill from the bottom, shortening the gown, and sewing the frill back on. How very kind she was when Lily was perfectly capable of doing it for herself. But when she had said so, Dolly had laughed and called her funny again and they had both laughed for no reason at all. The maid had unpacked her bag, she had explained, and noticed that there was no nightgown within. She could not have her ladyship tripping over the frill and breaking her neck.

There was a knock on the dressing room door. Was Dolly *still* up? Did that girl take no time for herself?

"Come in," Lily called.

But it was not Dolly. It was Neville, looking very handsome in a long brocaded blue dressing gown. Lily remembered him saying that he had looked in on her earlier in the day while she was sleeping. She caught her lower lip between her teeth, remembering her wedding night. But almost simultaneously she recalled with a stabbing of pain that this was to have been his wedding night with someone else.

"Lily," he asked her, "do you have everything you need?"

She nodded.

"Are you...all right?" He looked searchingly at her.

She nodded again.

"It has been a difficult day for you," he said. "Perhaps tomorrow will be easier."

"Do you love her?" she couldn't help but blurt out. She stared at him, wishing she could recall the words, wishing she could stop herself from feeling hurt that the answer might be yes. All the time she had been with Manuel and the partisans, clinging to the hope of one day returning to the man who had married her, he had been courting another woman, perhaps falling in love with her. All the time she had been making her difficult journey, with only the thought of reaching him sustaining her, he had been planning a marriage with someone else.

He clasped his hands at his back and regarded her gravely. "We grew up together," he said. "She lived here at the abbey with us. Her mother is married to my uncle, my father's brother, but Lauren was the child of a previous marriage. We were intended for each other from infancy. I have always been very fond of her. After my return from the Peninsula a marriage between us seemed the logical step to take."

"You were promised to someone else when you married me?" she asked him.

"No," he said. "Not really. I was rebelling against my lot in life. Even we privileged aristocrats do that, Lily. I had advised her not to wait for me."

"Was I part of your rebellion, then?" she asked him, realizing that there could surely not be a more magnificent snub to his former life, to his parents, than marrying a sergeant's daughter.

"No, Lily." He was frowning at her. "No, you were not. I married you because there was a need to do so, because I had made a promise to your father. And because I wanted to."

Yes. It was true. She must not start to believe that there had been any cynicism in his choice of her. He had married her because he was a kind and honorable man. And because he had wanted to. What did that mean?

"But all the time you remained fond of her," she said.

"Yes, Lily."

It had not escaped her notice that he had not really answered her original question. Did he *love* the woman called Lauren? Did he realize now what a dreadful mistake he had made in marrying *her* even though he had wanted to in a moment of impulse?

"And today you would have married her," she said.

"Yes." He had not looked away from her. "I have known her all my life, Lily. She waited for me. My father died and I returned to my responsibilities here. One of my duties was to marry so that the abbey would have a countess. And to beget children, in particular an heir. My life of rebellion was over. And you were dead."

"You told no one about me." It was not a question. She turned and touched the silky brocade of the bed hangings. So heavy and so rich. So alien to anything she had ever known in her life. She *wished* she had remained in Portugal. She did not know what she would have done there, but she wished she had not come back. Perhaps she could have clung to part of the dream...

"Lily," he said as if he was reading her thoughts, "I mourned you deep in the privacy of my own heart. I am not sorry you survived. I am *not*, my dear. How could I be?"

No, he was a kind man. He had always

treated her with gentleness and courtesy, even when she had been a girl and must sometimes have seemed an irrelevance at best, a nuisance at worst. Of course he would never wish her dead even though her survival had set an obstacle in the smooth path of his future.

"It was not because I did not care that I never mentioned you here," he said. "It was not because I did not care about you that I was to marry Lauren this morning, only a year and a half after your—your death. Please believe me."

She did. Yes, he had cared. Enough to marry her. Enough to murmur those endearments to her on their wedding night. Enough to mourn her. But if *he* had died, she thought, she would have mourned him for the rest of her life. She would never, could never... But how could she know for sure? Who was she to judge? Meanwhile there was an obstacle even more insuperable than the fact that he was the Earl of Kilbourne while she was the former Lily Doyle.

"I—" She swallowed. "You know what happened to me in Spain, do you not? You *did* understand this morning?"

She could feel him staring at her for a long time as her hands played with the braided fringe of the curtain. "Was it one man, Lily?" he asked. "Or many?"

"One." Manuel, the leader. Small, wiry, darkly handsome Manuel, who ruled his band of partisans through daring and charisma and occasional intimidation. "I have not been true to you."

121

"It was rape," he said harshly.

"I—I never fought," she told him. "I said no a number of times and was quite determined to—to die rather than submit, but when it came to the point I did not fight." It was a burden on her conscience that she had not fought her captor more strenuously.

"Look at me, Lily," he said in the quiet, authoritative voice of the major she had known. She looked unwillingly into his eyes. "Why did you not fight?"

"There were the French prisoners," she began. Her breath was coming in short gasps as she tried not to remember what had happened to them. "Because I was afraid. So afraid. Because I was a coward."

"Lily." He was still using the same voice. His eyes were looking very directly into hers, making it impossible for her to look away. He was her commanding officer again suddenly, not her husband. "It was rape. You were not a coward. It is a soldier's duty to survive any way he can in captivity—and you were a soldier's daughter and a soldier's wife. There is no question of cowardice. It was rape. It was not adultery. Adultery demands consent."

Neville sounded so certain, so sure of what he was saying. Could it possibly be true? She was not a coward? Not an adulteress?

"Let me hold you," he said softly. He was using a different voice now. "You look so very lonely, Lily."

A woman come home to a world that was alien to her and to a husband who had been about to marry someone else. How abject was it possible to feel? Would she never have herself back again, the serene, confident, happy self she remembered, the self who had somehow got lost after her one night of love?

She hunched her shoulders and looked down at her hands. When he came to stand in front of her and took her upper arms in his hands and drew her against him, she relaxed for a while, turning her head to rest against his shoulder, feeling the warmth and the strength of him all along her body. She allowed herself the luxury of feeling safe, of feeling cherished, of feeling that she had come home. He smelled good—of musk and soap and pure masculinity.

Yet she felt like someone who has arrived at the end of the rainbow only to find that there is nothing there after all—no pot of gold, not even the shreds of the rainbow itself. Just...nothing. And no more faith in rainbows. Only the core of herself with which to build a new identity, a new life.

She drew back from him before she could get lost in a dependency that would just not do.

"It would have been better for us both," she said, "if I had died."

"No, Lily." He spoke sharply.

"Can you tell me," she asked him, "that it has not once crossed your mind in the past year and a half that it was better so?"

She paused only briefly, but it did not escape her notice that he did not rush in with any denial.

"I think," she said, "if I had lived—if you

had *known* I lived—you would not have brought me here. You would have found some excuse to keep me far away. You would have been kind about it. You would have explained that it was for my own good, and you would have been right. But you would not have brought me here."

"Lily." He had walked to one of the windows and was standing staring out into the darkness. "You cannot know that. I cannot know it. I do not know what would have happened. You were my wife. You were—dear to me."

Ah, she was *dear* to him. Not the love of his heart he had called her that night? Lily smiled bleakly and sat on the side of the bed, her arms hugging herself against the chill of the evening.

"I believe," she said, "this is an impossibility. To say I am out of place here is so obvious that it is laughable. *She* is not out of place, is she? Lauren? She has been brought up to all this and to being your wife and your countess. Instead she has been made miserable, your future is in ruins, and I... Well."

"Lily." He had come back to her, stooped down on his haunches before her, and taken both her hands in his. "Nothing is impossible. Listen to yourself. Is this Lily Doyle speaking? Lily Doyle, who marched the length and breadth of the Peninsula, undaunted by the heat of summer, the bitter cold of winter, the dangers of battle and ambush, the discomforts and diseases of camp? Lily Doyle, who always had a smile and a cheerful word for everyone? Who saw beauty in the dreariest surroundings? There is nothing impossible that you of all people cannot make possible. And I will help you. We freely joined our lives together on that hillside in Portugal. We must soldier on, Lily. We have no alternative. I am not sure I would even wish for one."

She did not know if she could resurrect that old Lily. But she warmed to his faith in her.

"Perhaps," she said, smiling wanly, "I am just tired and dispirited. Perhaps everything will look brighter in the morning. It has been a difficult day for both of us. Thank you for your kindness. You really have been kind."

"You would rather be alone?" he asked her. "I will stay and hold you through the night if you need the comfort, Lily. I will not press other attentions on you."

It was tempting. It would be so very easy to relax permanently into his kindness and his strength and become as abject in a way as she had been with Manuel. But somehow if she was going to find a way to cope with this new, frightening, impossible life, she must not give in to a need for the comfort of his arms—especially when she did not want more than that from him.

"I would rather be alone," she said.

He squeezed her hands before releasing them and getting to his feet. "Good night, then," he said. "If you should need me, tonight or any other night, my dressing room adjoins yours and my bedchamber is beyond that. If you need anything else, the bell pull is beside your bed. Your maid will answer it."

"Thank you," she said. "Good night."

She wondered suddenly how his intended bride—Lauren—was feeling tonight. Did she love him? Lily felt genuinely sorry for her, caught in a situation in which she was entirely innocent and totally helpless. This was to have been her wedding night, but Lily was in the countess's room instead of her.

Everything was so very *wrong*.

8

Lily had slept too much during the daytime. She dozed fitfully through the night, and two separate times she was awakened by the same dream—the old nightmare. It was always exactly the same in every detail.

Manuel was on top of her while she lay beneath him, and then she opened her eyes to see *him*—Major Newbury, Neville—standing in the doorway of the hut, watching. There was that look on his face that she had seen there sometimes immediately after battle, a hard, cold, battle-mad, almost inhuman look, and his white-knuckled hand was on the hilt of his sword. He was about to kill Manuel and rescue her. Hope soared painfully as she tried to lie still so as not to alert Manuel.

The dream always proceeded the same way. After standing there, white-faced and immobile for endless moments, he turned away and disappeared, and precious minutes were lost to her while Manuel took his pleasure of her.

In the dream she was free to run after Neville as soon as Manuel was finished with her, but her legs were always too weak to carry her at any speed and the air was too thick to move through. She had no voice with which to call to him, and she could never see where he had gone, which direction he had taken. There was always mist swirling about and panic immobilizing her. And then—the cruelest part of the dream—the mist suddenly cleared and there he was, only a few steps away, standing still, his back to her.

In the dream she always stopped too at that moment, afraid to proceed, afraid to reach out to him, afraid of what would be in his eyes if he turned. It was the most dreaded moment of the dream and almost its final moment, when she touched the terrifying depths of despair. For during that second of indecision, the mist swirled again and he disappeared, not to be seen again.

She dreamed the nightmare twice during the first night at Newbury Abbey.

She rose when it was still dark, made up her bed, washed in cold water in the dressing room, and clothed herself in her old blue cotton dress. She had to get outside where she could breathe. She did not stop to pick up a bonnet or to pull on her old shoes. She had to feel the good earth beneath her feet. She had to feel the air against her face and in her hair. She met no one on her way downstairs or while she did battle with the heavy bolts on the front doors.

Eventually she was outside, where there was

the merest suggestion of dawn in the eastern sky. She breathed in deep lungfuls of chilly air. She felt it raise goosebumps on her bare arms and begin to numb her feet. She was immediately calmed and set out for the beach.

She did not stop until she was at the water's edge. At the edge of the land, the edge of place and time. On the brink of infinity and eternity. The wind, blowing off the vast expanses of the unknown, was strong and salt and chill. It flattened her dress against her and sent her hair billowing out behind her. Her feet sank a little into spongy sand. Above her gulls wheeled and cried, like spirits already free of time and space. For a moment she envied them.

But only for a moment. She felt no real desire this morning to escape the bonds of her mortality. Her years with the army had taught her something about the infinite preciousness of the present moment. Life was such an uncertain, such a fleeting thing, so filled with troubles and horrors and miseries— and with wonder and beauty and mystery. Like all persons, she had known her share of troubles. An almost overwhelming abundance of them had begun for her just the day following both the unhappiest and happiest day of her life, when her father had died and Major Newbury had married her. But she had survived.

She had survived!

And now—now at this most precious of moments—she was free and surrounded by such elemental beauty that her chest and her throat ached with the pain of it all. And it seemed to her that the wind blew through her rather than around her, filling her with all the mysterious spirit of life itself.

How could she fail to reach out and accept such a gift?

How could she fail to let go of the suffocating shreds of her dream and of all the misgivings about her new life that had oppressed her yesterday?

At least it was life.

And at least it was new. Ever and always new. Every day.

Lily stretched her arms out to the sides, tipped her face up to the rising sun, and twirled twice about on the sand, overwhelmed by her fleeting glimpse into the very heart of the mystery.

She was alive.

She was!

Filled with new hope, new courage, new exuberance, she set off exploring, picking her way carefully with her bare feet over the rocks at the end of the beach, reveling in the increased seclusion offered by the high cliffs to her left and the ocean to her right. Though the seclusion did not last for long. As soon as she had rounded a bend in the headland, she could see little boats bobbing on the water ahead of her and small houses and other buildings huddled at the base of the cliffs. It must be the lower village, Lower Newbury, she realized, at the bottom of that steep hill she had seen beside the inn.

Lily smiled brightly and continued on her

way. She could see people up and about in the village, early as the hour must still be. Ordinary folk, like herself.

∽

Lily was feeling happy by the time her bare feet finally took her through the gates of Newbury Abbey and onto the long driveway. She had walked up the steep hill to Upper Newbury and across the green, raising a hand in greeting to the few people she had seen. All of them, after some hesitation, had returned her gesture.

It was amazing how a new day could restore one's spirits and one's courage.

But as she was walking past the smaller lane to her left, along which she and Neville had turned the day before on their way from the church, she could see that the path was not deserted. There were two ladies walking toward her along it, not far distant. Lily stopped and smiled. They were very smartly dressed young ladies, probably guests from the house, though she did not recognize either of them.

One of them was tall and slim and darkhaired. The other was smaller and fairer and limped slightly. Both were lovely. The sight of their immaculate elegance reminded Lily of how she must look in her shabby dress and bare feet, her hair loose and curly and tangled by the wind, her complexion doubtless rosy from the air and exercise. She hesitated, about to move on. These ladies were strangers, after all.

But then, with a lurching of her stomach, she recognized the taller of the two, though her face had been veiled the day before.

And they both recognized her. That was very clear. Both stopped walking. Both looked at her with widened eyes and identical expressions of dismay. Then the taller lady came closer.

"You are Lily," she said. Ah, she was very beautiful despite the paleness of her face and the dark shadows beneath her violet eyes.

"Yes." The other lady, Lily noticed, had stiffened with obvious hostility. "And you are Lauren. Major Newbury's bride."

"Major—?" Lauren nodded with understanding. "Ah, yes—Neville. I am pleased to make your acquaintance, Lily. This is Lady Gwendoline, Lady Muir, Neville's sister."

His *sister*. Her own sister-in-law. Lady Gwendoline glared at her with undisguised dislike and said nothing. She stayed where she was.

Lauren's face held no such expression. Or any other either. It was a pale mask.

"I am so very sorry for what happened yesterday," Lily said—oh, the inadequacy of words. "I truly am."

"Well." Lauren's eyes, she noticed, were not quite meeting her own. "Let us look on the bright side. Better yesterday than today or tomorrow. But are you out without a companion or maid, Lily? You ought not to be. Does Neville know?"

Lily felt an overwhelming need to push

past the terrible awkwardness of the meeting and to say something that would lift the blank look from the other woman's face. What a shock she must have suffered. "Oh, I have had *such* a wonderful morning," she told Lauren. "I went down onto the beach to watch the sun rise and then crossed the rocks out of curiosity and came to the village below. Some of the fishermen were getting ready to take their boats out, and their wives were out helping them, and their children were running about, playing. I talked with several of the people and they were *so* kind to me. I had breakfast with Mrs. Fundy—do you know her?—and amused her children while she fed the baby. I do not know how she manages to look after four such young children and keep her house neat all at the same time, but she does. I have made friends with them all and have promised to go back as often as I may." She laughed. "They were all funny at first and wanted to curtsy and bow to me and call me 'my lady,' Can you imagine?"

Lady Gwendoline's silence became almost loud.

Lauren's face stretched for a moment into what might have been a smile.

"But I am keeping you," Lily said, her animation fading. "I really *am* sorry. You are very gracious. He—Major Newbury—told me last night that he was very fond of you. I do not wonder at it. I—Well, I am sorry." She was saying all the wrong things, of course. But were there *right* things to say? "Do you live at Newbury Abbey?"

"At the dower house," Lauren said, nodding in the direction of the trees opposite, through which Lily could see a house just visible when she turned her head to look. "With Gwen and the countess, her mother. Perhaps I will call upon you some time. Tomorrow maybe?"

"Yes." Lily smiled, vastly relived. "I should like that, please. I should like it very much. Will you come too…Gwendoline?" She looked uncertainly at her sister-in-law, who did not answer, but whose nostrils flared with what was clearly barely controlled anger.

Gwendoline loved her cousin, Lily thought. Her anger was understandable. She smiled fleetingly at them both before continuing on her way to the abbey. She felt considerably discomposed. Lauren was beautiful and dignified and far more gracious than she might have been expected to be. How could Neville *not* love her?

Some of the oppressive feeling of the day before weighed down on Lily again.

Lauren and Gwendoline stood gazing after her.

"Well!" Gwendoline expelled her breath audibly and came to stand beside her cousin as Lily moved out of earshot. "I have never been so affronted in my life. How dared she stop and talk to us—to you in particular."

"How dared she, Gwen?" Lauren gazed after the disappearing figure. "She is Neville's *wife*. She is your sister-in-law. She is the Countess of Kilbourne. Besides, I was the first to speak." She laughed, though there was no amusement in the sound. "She is very lovely."

"*Lovely?*" Gwendoline spoke with the utmost scorn. "She would put even a beggar to the blush. Is she deliberately trying to disgrace Neville, or does she simply not know any better? She has appeared in both villages for all to see, looking like that—no bonnet, no shoes, no—" She made a sound of exasperation. "Does she know *nothing* about how to behave?"

"But oh, Gwen," Lauren said so quietly that her cousin almost did not hear the words, "did you not see that she is vivid and original? Something quite out of the ordinary? The sort of woman who would draw a man's eyes and desires? Neville's, for example?"

Gwendoline looked incredulously at her cousin. "Are you mad?" she asked rhetorically. "She is disgusting. She is impossible. And you of all people should hate her, Lauren. You are not defending her, are you?"

Lauren laughed quietly again as she crossed the driveway and strode in the direction of the dower house. "I am merely trying to see her through Neville's eyes," she said. "I am trying to understand why he left me and told me not to wait and then met her and married her. Oh, Gwen, *of course* I hate her." For the first time her voice became impassioned though she did not raise it. "I feel the most intense hatred for her. I wish she were dead. I know I ought not to feel that way. I am horrified by my own feelings. I *wish* she were dead. And so I must try, you see—yes, I really must try to understand. It is not her fault after all, is it? I daresay Neville did not tell her about me any more than he told me about her. And what was there to tell anyway? He had *told* me not to wait. He was under no obligation to me. We were not betrothed. I must try to like her. I *will* try to like her."

Gwendoline limped along beside her, finding it difficult to keep up. "Well, I do not intend even to try," she said. "I will hate her enough for both of us. She has ruined your life and Neville's—though it is entirely his own fault—and you are the two people I love above all others. And do not tell me that Lily is not to blame. *Of course* she is not to blame and of course I am being unfair to her. But she is a loathsome creature for all that, and how can I not hate her when I see you so dreadfully unhappy?"

They had arrived at the house. But Lauren stopped before entering it. "We are going to have to teach her things," she said, her voice flat again as it had been the day before. "How to dress, how to behave, how to be a lady. I *will* call on her tomorrow, Gwen. I will try—to be kind to her."

"And we are going to try learning to play the harp and to balance halos on our heads too," Gwendoline said crossly, "so that we will be ready to become saints or angels when we die."

They both laughed.

"Please, Gwen," Lauren said, taking her

cousin's arm in a tight grip, "help me not to hate her. Help me... Oh, how *could* Neville have married such a—such a wild fairy creature? What is the matter with *me*?"

Gwendoline did not answer. There was no reasonable answer to give.

9

Lily felt suddenly almost as if she were returning to a prison. Her footsteps lagged as the house came into sight. But then they quickened again. She could see that Neville was outside on the terrace, three other gentlemen with him. For so long she had held him steadfastly in her memory and her dreams. But now he was real again. And he was watching her approach, his lips pursed, his eyes crinkled at the corners. They were *all* watching her approach. She had been right earlier, she thought. Things did look brighter this morning after all.

Neville bowed to her when she was close and reached out a hand for hers—and then kissed it.

"Good morning, Lily," he said.

"I have been down on the beach," she told him. "I wanted to watch the sun come up. And then I explored the rocks and found myself in the village." Her purpose and destination would explain her appearance.

"I know." He smiled at her. "I watched you go from my window."

The marquess with the long name bowed to her then. "I am awed into incoherence," he said, but he went on talking anyway. "None of the ladies of my acquaintance ever rise early enough to know that the sun even does anything as peculiar as rise in the morning."

"Then they miss one of the greatest joys of life," Lily assured him. "Please will you tell me your name again, sir? I only remember that it is long."

"Joseph," he said, and laughed, revealing himself to be a very good-looking gentleman indeed. "You are a cousin now, Lily, and do not need to get your tongue around Attingsborough."

"Joseph," she repeated. "I believe I can remember that."

"And James too," one of the other gentlemen said, bowing to her. "Another cousin, Lily. I have a wife, who is Sylvia, and a young son, Patrick. My mother is Nev's Aunt Julia, his father's sister. My father—"

"Devil take it, James." The fourth gentleman tossed his glance at the sky. "Lily's eyes are crossing and her head is spinning on her shoulders. Why do you not add for her edification that Nev's other paternal aunts are Mary and Elizabeth and that his uncle is the famous black sheep, the *lost* sheep, who embarked on a wedding journey more than twenty years ago and never returned? I am Ralph, Lily. Yes, another cousin. If you cannot recall my name the next time we meet, you are welcome to call me 'you.' "

"Thank you," she said, laughing. It was definitely easier this morning. Maybe everything would be easier. But then she had always been comfortable in the company of men, perhaps because she had grown up surrounded by so many of them.

"The exercise has whipped the most lovely roses into your cheeks, Lily," the marquess said. "But however have you managed to walk so far in bare feet?" He was observing them through his quizzing glass.

"Oh." She glanced down at them. "It is so much more comfortable than walking in shoes. If you were to take off your boots and walk in the grass, Joseph, you would discover that I am right."

"Dear me," he commented.

"But you will not do it," she said, smiling sunnily at him. "I know. There were some men in the Peninsula who never removed their boots—ever. I swear they went to bed with them on. Sometimes I wondered if they had feet at all, or if their legs ended just below the knee. They would not wish to admit to such a deformity, of course. Just imagine how short they would have been—and men set great store by their height. They hate to have to look up to other men and feel perfectly shamed to have to look up to a woman."

The gentlemen were all laughing. Lily joined them.

"Good Lord," Joseph said, using his quizzing glass now to look down at his own boots, "my secret is out. When I stopped growing at four foot ten, Lily, I had Hoby make me boots—*tall* boots. So that I could look down on the world from a lofty height."

"He even dances in them, Lily," Ralph said. "You would not wish to risk your toes by tripping a measure with Joe."

"If you knock on them," James added, "they ring hollow."

"This conversation," Lily declared gleefully, "has become absurd. But despite your teasing, I have felt the grass and the dew beneath my feet this morning and the sand between my toes. And I have seen the sun rise over the sea. England is a lovely country, as my papa always said it was."

Neville smiled at her. "You are right, Lily," he said. He offered her his arm. "Let me escort you to your room and summon Dolly to help you tidy up. My mother has come up from the dower house and is awaiting you in the morning room with several of the other ladies."

He did not sound in any way annoyed. He did not utter one word of reproach either then or after they had left the company of his cousins. And yet Lily had not missed the detail about *several* of the ladies.

"Are the others out enjoying the morning?" she asked.

"They are still in bed or in their boudoirs. Ladies generally do not, ah, *enjoy the morning* until their maids have dressed and coiffed them and they have breakfasted, Lily." He smiled down at her as they climbed the grand staircase.

"Oh," she said. Maids—she had not thought of ringing for Dolly when she got up. Besides, she would not have wished to wake the girl so early. And she had no dress suitable for Newbury Abbey except her green muslin, and she had doubts even about that. She might at least, she supposed, have tied back her hair and worn her shoes. "I did not think. I ought not to have gone out as I am, ought I? How embarrassed you must have been when I came back and all your cousins were out there to see me. I am so sorry."

"No, no." He covered her hand on his arm with his free one. "That was not my meaning. I was not *scolding*, for heaven's sake. This is your home, Lily. You must do here whatever you wish."

Lily fell silent, remembering how very elegantly Lauren had been dressed. She had been wearing a bonnet and even gloves. *She* would not have gone dancing off in bare feet and with her hair down her back to watch the sun rise over the sea. *She* would not have embarrassed him out on the terrace.

⁓

Neville took Lily down to the morning room after she had washed and put on stockings and her old shoes and Dolly had dressed her hair in a simple knot at the back of her head with two neat braids wound about it. Dolly had advised against wearing the green muslin as her ladyship would need something into which to change for the afternoon, and so the old cotton would have to do.

Neville stayed with her in the morning room for a short while though there was no other gentleman present, but then he was summoned away to speak with his steward.

The ladies all greeted her pleasantly. The dowager countess even got to her feet to kiss Lily's cheek and seated her beside herself on a love seat. But there was nothing comfortable about the conversation, as there had been out on the terrace. They talked about London and Almack's and lending libraries and rose gardens and the management of servants, none of which topics were within Lily's experience. And when the war was mentioned and the French spoken of as monsters of evil and depravity and Lily spoke up with the opinion that they were people just like the British and shared their capacity for tenderness and loyalty and love and all the finer feelings, the red-haired lady, who Lily remembered was Wilma—Joseph's sister?—declared herself very close to fainting, and someone else scolded young Miranda for introducing such an ungenteel subject into the conversation of ladies.

Lily smiled sympathetically at the young girl, whose numerous ringlets made her appear slightly top heavy, but she was blushing and biting a wobbling lip and gazing downward.

Aunt Sadie tried to turn the awkward moment by asking Lily if she would like some embroidery to work on. Lily had noticed that almost all the ladies were busy with needlework. She was forced to admit that she had never been taught to embroider though she was quite skilled at patching and darning. There was an awkward little silence again before her mother-in-law suggested that Miranda go into the music room and leave the door open while she played for them on the pianoforte.

Lily was finally rescued by the appearance of the butler, who announced that Mrs. and Miss Holyoake had arrived to wait upon the Countess of Kilbourne.

Lily looked at the dowager countess as did all the other ladies present, and that lady raised her eyebrows.

"Whatever can Mrs. Holyoake want with me today?" she asked. "I certainly did not summon her."

"I beg your pardon, my lady," Mr. Forbes said with a discreet clearing of his throat, "but I understand his lordship did—for his wife. I have put them in the blue salon."

Lily felt dreadfully embarrassed at the quickly suppressed look of chagrin on the face of her mother-in-law, who had clearly forgotten that she, Lily, was now the Countess of Kilbourne. This was all going to be quite impossible, Lily thought for the umpteenth time—except that it could not be allowed to be. Somehow she was going to have to live with this situation. They were *all* going to have to live with it.

Lady Elizabeth came hurrying toward her, both hands extended, as she left the morning room.

"Lily," she said, taking her hands and kissing her cheek. "Good morning, my dear.

It is quite all right, Forbes. I shall conduct her ladyship to the Holyoake ladies. They are the village dressmakers, Lily. Neville spoke to me about them earlier and asked if I would see to it that they measure you for as many pretty clothes as they have time to undertake."

It was an enticing prospect, Lily had to admit. The two dresses she possessed were certainly not adequate to the needs of her new life. But more bewilderment was awaiting her in the blue salon. After she had been presented to Mrs. Holyoake and her daughter, black-haired, black-eyed ladies, who looked remarkably alike, and after they had curtsied deeply to her and called her "my lady," she could see that they had brought with them so many bolts of fabric and so many patterns and other tools of their trade that it must have taken several servants to carry everything inside.

"Would it not have been more convenient for *me* to come to *you*?" she asked.

Both ladies looked shocked, and Elizabeth laughed.

"Not when you are the Countess of Kilbourne from Newbury Abbey, Lily," she said.

It seemed that she was not to have just two or three new dresses, which would have seemed an impossible luxury to Lily, but a dozen or more. When she protested, she discovered that she was going to need morning dresses and tea dresses and evening dresses—some for family evenings, some for dinner parties, some for balls—and walking dresses and carriage dresses. And a riding habit too, when it was discovered that she could ride—though perhaps she ought not to have said she could since she had certainly never ridden a great deal.

Different functions of dress called for different fabrics and different designs, she discovered. There were many colors to choose among, but one might not simply choose just what one thought pretty. Apparently there were colors that suited certain people but not others. There were colors that looked good in daylight and others that looked better in candlelight. And there were all sorts of trimmings—suited to different fabrics and functions and occasions. There were trimmings identical in color to the fabrics they were to adorn. There were others that complemented the fabrics—or did not. There were styles that were fashionable and others that were too *avant garde* or too *passé*. There were styles suited to a young girl and others better suited to a young matron or to an older lady. There were measurements to be taken. There were...

For all the kindness of Elizabeth and the respect shown by the two dressmakers, Lily soon felt like a passive doll that lifted its arms when someone pulled the right string and pirouetted when someone pulled another, and smiled constantly with a painted smile. All the joy of having new clothes fled early. She knew nothing and was forced to leave all decisions to those who did. And all the time there was the foolish worry—could he possibly *afford* all this? And she had forgotten to ask him if he would send the money she had borrowed from Captain Harris. How could she have neglected that?

Elizabeth took her arm when the ordeal was finally over and they had left the dressmakers to pack up their things—they had declined Lily's offer of help, looking startled and agitated as they did so.

"Poor Lily," she said. "This is very difficult for you, is it not? Come and have luncheon and relax." She laughed ruefully. "But even a meal is not relaxing for you, is it? It will all get easier as time goes on, I promise you."

Lily would have liked to believe her. But she was not sure she did. If only she could go back, she thought, even just a few days... But what else could she have done but come here? Even if she could go back and decide to wait for Captain Harris to write a letter, she would merely be postponing the inevitable. She could not simply have stayed away. She was Neville's wife. He had a right to know that she was still alive.

What she *really* wished was that she could go all the way back to that day when her father had been killed. She wished she could go back and hear more clearly, more responsibly, what Major Newbury had said to her afterward so that she could summon the courage to say no where she had said yes.

Was that really what she wished? That she had never married him? That there had never been that night? If there had not been that night, that dream of love and perfection, she did not know if she would have been able to survive what had happened to her afterward. Not with her sanity intact, at least.

Lily did not go outside again. Neville watched her with deep concern as she was swept up and borne along by his relatives, most of whom at least were ready enough to do what was proper and accept her into their midst. And she did her best to look cheerful, to learn names and relationships, to answer questions that were put to her, to follow his lead and his mother's and Elizabeth's in matters of etiquette. But the color that had been in her cheeks when she had returned from her morning outing and the brightness in her eyes and the pertness in her manner—all the signs of the old Lily—faded again as the day progressed.

He took her on a tour of the house, and she was interested and seemed impressed. She gazed long and attentively at the family portraits in the long gallery.

"How wonderful it must be," she said when they were halfway down the long room, "to know so much about your ancestors and even to have pictures of them. You look very like your grandfather in this portrait of him. Neither Mama nor Papa ever talked about their families, about my ancestors. Until Papa died, I did not realize how very alone I was. If I had wanted to find his relatives, or Mama's when I came back to England, I would not even have known where to look. I daresay Leicestershire is a large place."

"You were not alone," he told her, his heart aching for her. "You had me and my family." But the day after their wedding he had accepted the unconfirmed evidence of his eyes and the hastily observed evidence of Harris's and had not gone in search of her to bring her home to safety.

She moved on to the next painting.

"Did you not have portraits of your mother and father in your locket, Lily?" he asked her. She had always worn it, he remembered, though she did not do so now.

She touched a hand to her throat as if it were still there. "No," she said. "It was empty."

He did not ask where the locket was. It had probably been taken from her during her captivity, and reminding her further of its loss would be painful to her.

He was disappointed the following morning to find that she had not gone out again to watch the sun rise. It had rained during the night and was still rather cloudy and blustery, but he did not believe it was the weather that had deterred her. He found her, when he peeped into her room, sitting at the window, gazing quietly out. She smiled at him and told him that one of her new dresses was to be delivered early and that she was waiting to wear it. His mother was to introduce her to the housekeeper and include her in the discussion of the day's menu.

It was important, he supposed—certainly

his mother believed it was—that she learn about the running of a great house. But he did not want her new life to sap all the light and joy from her. He wanted her to be Lily, the person he remembered from the Peninsula.

As it turned out, Neville discovered later, Lily had misunderstood and had not realized that the housekeeper was to come to her, not the other way around. She went alone down to the kitchen, expecting to meet her mother-in-law there. By the time, much later, Mrs. Ailsham informed her ladyship, the dowager, that the Countess of Kilbourne was below-stairs and a startled mother-in-law followed her down there, Lily was seated at the large kitchen table, an oversized apron protecting her new dress, peeling potatoes with a kitchen maid and regaling a flustered but delighted kitchen staff with tales of cooking for a regiment on rations that arrived all too irregularly and when they did arrive were often quite inadequate to the men's needs.

After Neville had been told the story and had chuckled over it, though his mother was not amused, he went to find Lily. But by that time she had been safely restored to the respectability of the morning room and the company of his aunts and female cousins. She was looking cheerful and mute and listless all at the same time—and very pretty in her new blue morning gown.

Word had been sent up from the dower house that Lauren and Gwendoline would call during the afternoon.

There was a general air of tension as the family gathered in the drawing room. No one behaved naturally. Everyone smiled a great deal and talked a great deal and laughed more than was necessary. Lily was very quiet.

Neville awaited their arrival with the deepest dread.

But when they came, the moment was almost anticlimactic. They had chosen not to be announced, but entered the room together as soon as a footman had opened the doors, just as they would have done on any other occasion before Lily's arrival. They were both looking their most elegant. Gwen was not smiling. Lauren was—brightly and graciously. And she looked about her, meeting everyone's eyes, apparently perfectly at her ease.

The moment must have cost her enormous effort, Neville guessed as he jumped to his feet and hurried toward them.

"Lauren," he said, resisting the impulse to take both her hands in his. He bowed to her instead. "How are you? Gwen?"

"Hello, Neville." Lauren smiled at him and held out *her* hands to him. "We came to pay our formal respects to your wife, did we not, Gwen? But not to be presented to her. We met her yesterday morning when we were all out for a walk and our paths crossed. Oh, there you are, Lily." She turned away from Neville with a warm smile and held out her hands again. "Looking—tamed." She laughed. "What a very pretty dress. Primrose suits your coloring." She took Lily's hands in hers and leaned forward to kiss her cheek.

It was a stellar performance. But surely it *was* a performance? She went on to greet everyone else with ease and affection before seating herself beside Lily on a love seat.

The contrast between the two of them— between his wife and the woman who had so nearly become his wife two mornings before— could scarcely be more marked. Lily, small, pretty, quiet, slightly flustered when anyone addressed a remark her way, reclining back on the seat, drinking all her tea down without once setting her cup back in its saucer before it was empty, quite without the "presence" his mother considered so important in a countess. Lauren, tall and beautiful and elegant, perfectly at her ease, sitting with erect but graceful posture, her back not touching the love seat, sipping from her cup and setting it down again in its saucer with all the appreciation of a true lady for fine possessions.

It was almost, Neville thought, as if she had seated herself deliberately beside Lily, knowing how the contrasts would be observed and interpreted. But it was an unkind thought. Lauren had never been an unkind woman. But then, of course, she had never found herself in such a situation before.

Gwen was behaving far more as he would

have expected the rejected bride to behave. Although she was perfectly well bred, she pointedly ignored both Lily and himself after the first stiff acknowledgment. She confined her conversation to a group of cousins.

Neville had half expected—and more than half hoped—that Lauren would leave Newbury during the morning with her grandfather and Mr. Calvin Dorsey, who had offered the elderly gentleman quiet comfort since the day of the aborted wedding and had been kind enough to offer his company for the first day of the baron's journey home to Yorkshire. But Lauren had not gone with them. Newbury, after all, had been her home for most of her life. And perhaps, Neville thought, it was important to her not to run away but to stay and face the new conditions of her life.

She was doing magnificently well. Perhaps he should feel relieved—he *was* relieved. But he could not help remembering how Lauren as a child used to prattle happily about what she would do when her mama came home— until she stopped completely one day, never to mention her mother again. And how when she was older she had talked eagerly of writing to her father's family and becoming reacquainted with them and perhaps going to spend a few months with them—until she had stopped talking about them altogether after she had had a reply to her letter. Just the silence on both topics. No loss of cheerfulness. Just total silence.

No stranger appearing in the drawing room now would guess that Lauren had been a bride two mornings before—*his* bride—or that her hopes had been abruptly and cruelly dashed.

Lauren, he thought uneasily, reminded him somewhat of a keg of gunpowder, quite harmless in appearance but awaiting the spark that would ignite it.

Perhaps he was wrong. Perhaps there was just not that much passion in Lauren.

But part of him wished she had raged at him when he had called on her two mornings before. And part of him wished she had stormed into the drawing room this afternoon and made a noisy and scandalous scene.

Pauline Bray, James's sister, finally made a suggestion that broke up the strangely tense normality of the gathering in the drawing room.

"I do believe I am going to take a walk," she announced. "Look. The sun has come out, and the grass must have had sufficient time to dry after last night's rain. Would anyone care to join me?"

It seemed that almost everyone would. The cousins took up the suggestion with some enthusiasm, and even some of the older relatives expressed their willingness to taste the air. There was a brief argument over whether to take the rhododendron walk over the hill behind the house or to go down onto the beach. The beach won even though Wilma protested that sea air was ruinous on the complexion and that sand got everywhere about one's person no matter how carefully one trod.

Before a large party of them set out, the plans had become more elaborate, and urgent directions had been sent belowstairs for a picnic tea to be sent down onto the beach later even though they had just drunk tea in the drawing room.

Neville was glad of the diversion, both for his own sake and for Lily's. She had been confined to the house for a day and a half, and he knew that she was feeling bewildered and oppressed though she had not complained. Lauren's visit in particular must have put a severe strain on her.

But any thought he had to taking her on his arm and leading her, perhaps, a little away from the larger group was squashed even before they left the house. Lauren had not left her side. She took Lily's arm with a smile.

"You and I will walk together, Lily," she said. "We will become better acquainted."

⤚ *10* ⤙

They walked sedately across the terrace and down the lawn. They walked sedately down the steep hillside and sedately along the beach. They walked farther along it than Lily had walked before, past a huge rock that towered above them as they passed beneath it.

Lily was wearing her old shoes though apparently some new pairs were being made for her by the village cobbler. But she was

wearing a new primrose dress and pelisse—
Mrs. and Miss Holyoake must have worked
very hard indeed to complete them within a
day—and the plain straw bonnet she had
picked out from the supply they had brought
to the abbey with them. In the absence of a
milliner in the village, Elizabeth had explained,
Mrs. Holyoake had undertaken to keep a
select supply on hand.

The wide brim of the bonnet shielded
Lily's face from the sun, which shone clear
of the scudding clouds most of the time.
Lauren's parasol, which she insisted on
sharing, prevented even a stray ray of sunlight
from finding her face. They must be very
careful of their complexions, Lauren explained,
especially now that summer was almost upon
them. She had noted that Lily's face was
unfortunately bronzed, probably a casualty
of the voyage home from Portugal. But she
must not despair—the color would fade if she
carried a parasol with her whenever she was
out of doors. Lauren would lend her one.

Wilma would not walk too close to the
water's edge as the salt from the sea would make
her skin rough and coarsen her hair. And
they must stroll very slowly across the sand
for fear of getting some of it inside their
shoes. When they reached a sheltered spot suitable for the picnic tea and servants had
arrived with blankets and baskets, the gentlemen were set the task—by Wilma—of
building what amounted to a tent with the blankets so that they would be shielded from the
wind and the ruinous airs off the sea. When

they sat down, they could not see the water—or even the sand.

They might as well have stayed indoors, Lily thought.

The gentlemen had been having a far better time of it. They had walked briskly to the end of the beach and back before the ladies met them halfway. And they had done their walking down close to the water's edge, where the gulls were flying and the wind was blowing its hardest. There had been much merry laughter from their group. Lily wished she might have walked with them.

They all sat down to tea, but as soon as the edge had been taken from their appetites, some of the younger cousins—Hal and his brothers Richard and William—were eager to be off exploring again. William winked at Miranda, who was about his own age, and beckoned, and Miranda looked anxiously at her mama, who was busy holding two glasses while her son Ralph, Viscount Sterne, filled them with wine. Then Miranda looked uncertainly at Lily.

"I long to escape too," Lily whispered, all her good intentions, which she had kept faithfully for a day and a half, forgotten. Neville, with Elizabeth and the Duke of Portfrey, was listening politely to a monologue that his Aunt Mary had been delivering for the past five minutes or longer.

And so within moments they were off, the two of them, with the young gentlemen, running down the beach until one more step would have soaked their shoes.

"I would wager the water is cold enough to

give one a heart seizure at this time of year," Richard said.

"No," said Lily, who was accustomed to bathing in mountain streams at all seasons of the year except the dead of winter. "It would be refreshing. Oh, the wind feels wonderful." She lifted her face to it and to the sunshine.

"Sea bathing is all the crack in the fashionable resorts," Hal said. "But not here, more is the pity, and not in May. I did it at Brighton last year with the Porters."

"I would die before I would set a toe in sea water," Miranda said. "It would quite shrivel up the skin, I daresay."

Lily laughed. "It is just water, though not to be drunk, of course, because of the salt." And without even thinking of what she did, she shook off her shoes and peeled off her stockings, carried them in one hand while lifting her skirt with the other, and waded into the water until it was halfway to her knees.

Miranda giggled and the young gentlemen hooted with glee.

"It *is* cold," Lily said, laughing even more gaily. "It is lovely. Oh, do try it."

Richard came next and then Hal and then William. Finally even Miranda was persuaded to remove her shoes and stockings and step gingerly into the water almost up to her ankles. She laughed with fear and excitement.

"Oh, Lily," she cried, "you are so much *fun*."

"Wilma is an old fuddy-duddy," Richard remarked with marvelous lack of respect for his elders. "And Lauren and Gwen always have to remember that they are ladies."

They all waded through the water, carrying their shoes and stockings, until they came to the great rock and Lily decided that a rock in just such a position and built in just such a way must have been placed there to be climbed. She scrambled to the top and sat up there, her arms clasped about her knees, her head tipped back. She could feel her hem heavy and wet from the sea water, but it would dry soon enough. It was quite impossible, she thought, to remain for long in low spirits when one could feel the sun and the air on one's face and hear waves rolling their way to shore and gulls screaming overhead. She took off her bonnet and set it down beside her with her shoes and stockings. She felt even better.

The other four had climbed up after her and were seated together a little below her, talking and laughing among themselves. Lily forgot them and enjoyed the familiar feeling of being alone with the universe. She had always had the gift—necessary when there had been so little actual privacy in her life—of being able to shut herself off from crowds.

"Miranda!"

The voice, loud and shocked, made Lily jump and brought her back to her surroundings. Aunt Theodora had appeared at the base of the rock with Elizabeth and Aunt Mary. "Put your shoes and stockings and your bonnet and gloves back on *this instant*. And get down from there! Gracious me, your *hem* is wet. Have you been *wading*? You shocking, vulgar, disobedient girl. A *true lady* would never so much as dream of—" But she had looked upward and spied Lily, who was considerably more disheveled than her daughter.

Elizabeth clucked her tongue and laughed. "How provokingly clever of Lily and Miranda," she said. "They are doing what all of us have been secretly longing to do and are enjoying the sunshine and the sea air—and even the sea."

But her attempt to smooth over the awkwardness of the situation did not quite succeed. The whole party had come into view, Aunt Theodora had turned very red, and Miranda had burst into tears. Aunt Mary was assuring everyone in agitated accents that she dared say her sons were entirely to blame. They were such high-spirited lads. Hal was reminding her indignantly that at the age of one-and-twenty he no longer appreciated being referred to as a lad.

Lily quietly pulled on her stockings and shoes and tied the ribbons of her new bonnet beneath her chin and turned to descend carefully back to the beach. Wilma was loudly complaining about something and Gwendoline was telling her not to be tiresome. The marquess was asking in a deliberately languid voice if anyone had heard about storms in teacups and Pauline choked on a laugh. A pair of strong arms lifted Lily down when she was still carefully picking her footholds.

He turned her and smiled at her, his hands still at her waist. "I had such a vivid memory, seeing you up there," he said, "of watching you sitting on an outcropping of rock, looking about at the hills of Portugal." But his smile faded even before he had finished speaking.

"I am sorry. It was just before your father died."

And just hours before their wedding. How he must regret that any of it had ever happened. How *she* regretted it.

Everyone had begun walking back toward the valley and the path up to the house amid a general atmosphere of discontent and awkwardness. Lily and Neville fell into step a short distance behind.

"I am sorry," she said.

"No," he told her firmly. "No, you must not be, Lily. You must not always be sorry. You must live your life your way."

"But I got Miranda into trouble," she said. "I did not think."

"I will have a word with Aunt Theodora," he told her, chuckling. "It was no very great mischief, you know."

"No," she said, "*I* will have a word with her. You must not always be protecting me. I am not a child."

"Lily," he said softly. "This is not working well, is it? Let us take a little time for ourselves, shall we? Let me show you the cottage."

"The one in the valley?" she asked him.

He nodded. "My private retreat. My haven of peace and tranquility. I'll take you there."

⤳

He took her hand in his and laced his fingers with hers. He did not care that someone ahead of them might look back. They were married, after all.

"The cottage is your own, then?" she asked him. "It is very pretty."

"My grandmother was a painter," he explained. "She liked to be on her own, painting. My grandfather had the cottage built for her on surely the loveliest spot of the whole estate. It is furnished, and it is cleaned and aired once a month. It is there for all of us to use and enjoy, though I believe it has come to be considered my own special place. I like to be alone and quiet too at times."

She smiled at him. Obviously such antisocial needs were quite understandable to her.

"It was the one thing I found hard about military life," he said. "The lack of privacy. You must have felt it too, Lily. And yet there was something about you... I used to notice, you know, that you often went off on your own, though never beyond your father's sight. You used to sit or stand alone, doing nothing except gazing about you. I always used to imagine that you had discovered a world that was closed to me and to almost everyone else. Had you?"

"There are some places," she said, "that seem more specially graced than others. Places where one feels... God, I suppose. I have never been able to feel the presence of God inside a church. Rather, I feel closed in there, oppressed, as I do in many buildings. But there are places of unusual beauty and peace and...holiness. They are rare, though. I did not have a valley like yours when I was growing up, or a waterfall or pool or cottage. And I did not find many of those places with the regiment, though there were some. I learned to—to…"

"To what?" He bent his head closer to hers. He had often talked with Lily in the past, sometimes for an hour or more at a time. They had always been comfortable with each other despite the differences in their gender and stations. He had felt that he knew her well. But he had never asked her about her private world, only observed it. There were depths to her character that were still unknown to him. There was great beauty there, he suspected, and wisdom too despite her youth and lack of formal education. There was nothing shallow about his Lily.

"I do not know how to say it," she said. "I learned to be still and to stop doing and listening and even thinking. I learned to *be*. I learned that almost any place can be one of those special places if I allowed it to be. Perhaps I learned to find the place within myself."

He gazed down at her—pretty, dainty Lily in her new primrose dress and pelisse and straw bonnet. The serenity he had always observed in her had an explanation, then. She had discovered in her short, difficult life what not many people discovered in a whole lifetime, he suspected. He had not progressed as far himself though he knew the value of solitude and silence. He wondered if Lily's ability to find a place within, simply to *be*, as she had put it, had helped her endure her ordeal in Spain. But he would not ask her about that. He could not even bear to think about it.

They had reached the valley and walked up

the path toward the cottage and the pool at the base of the waterfall. Everyone else had already disappeared up the hill and in among the trees. They stopped by unspoken assent when they were a short distance away and feasted their eyes on the beauty of the scene and their ears on the soothing sound of rushing water.

"Ah, yes," she said at last with a sigh, "this is one of those places. I can understand why you come here."

He had noticed that she had not called him by any name since her return even though he had reminded her that she was his wife and might use his given name. He longed to hear it on her lips again. He could remember how it had sounded like the most intimate endearment on their wedding night. But he could not, would not press the point with her. He must give her time.

"Come and see the cottage," he said. It occurred to him suddenly with some surprise that he had never come here with Lauren, or not at least since they were children.

There were just two rooms, both cozily furnished and both possessing fireplaces with logs piled beside them in readiness for a chilly day—or night. He occasionally spent a night here. He had done it sometimes during the past year or so, when he had been remembering his life with the Ninety-fifth and his years in the Peninsula and had been restless with a nameless yearning.

No, not nameless. He had yearned here

for Lily, whom he had grown gradually to love during the years he had known her, though that love had bloomed into sexual passion only a short time before its final glorious flowering the night before he believed she'd died.

He had tried not to think of Lily at Newbury. There he had tried to think only of his new life, the life of duty for which he had been raised and educated, the life that included Lauren. He had come to the cottage to do his remembering and his leftover mourning.

It was still strange to realize that Lily had *not* died. That she was here. Now.

She peered into the bedchamber, but it was the other room that appeared to fascinate her more. There were chairs, a table, books, paper, quill pens and ink—and a view directly over the pool and the waterfall. He liked to sit here, reading or writing. He also liked to sit and merely gaze. Perhaps it was what she called *being*.

"You read here," she said, picking up one of the books after taking off her bonnet and setting it down on one of the chairs. "You learn about other worlds and other minds. And you can go back and read them again and again."

"Yes," he said.

"And sometimes you write down your own thoughts," she said, running a finger along one of the quill pens. "And you can come back and read them and remember what you thought or how you felt about something."

"Yes." She sounded wistful, he noticed.

"It must be the most wonderful feeling in

the whole world," she said, "to be able to read and write."

He took so much for granted, he realized. He had never really considered how privileged he was to have been educated. "Perhaps," he suggested, "you could learn, Lily."

"Perhaps," she agreed. "Though probably I am too old. I daresay I would not be an apt pupil. Papa always said learning to read was the most difficult thing he had ever done in his life. He never did find it easy." She set the book down and went to stand at the window, looking out.

He had not meant to ask her the question whose answer he dreaded to hear—certainly not yet. He did not feel strong enough to know. But somehow the time and the place seemed right and somehow the words just came spilling out.

"Lily," he asked her, "what did you suffer?"

He went to stand beside her, facing her profile. He touched the backs of his fingers to her cheek. She looked so delicate, yet he knew her to be as tough in her own way as even the most hardened of veterans. But how badly had her toughness been tested? "Are you able to talk about it?"

She turned her head and her huge blue eyes gazed back into his. Curiously, they looked both wounded and calm. Whatever she had suffered had hurt her, perhaps permanently, but it had not broken her. Or so her eyes seemed to say.

"It was war," she said. "I saw sufferings far worse than my own. I saw maiming and tor-

164

ture and death. I have not been maimed. I did not die."

"Were you...tortured?"

She shook her head. "Beaten a few times," she said, "when I—when I did not please. But only with the hand. I was never really tortured."

He would have liked a certain Spanish partisan suddenly to materialize before him. He would have liked to break every bone in the man's body with his fists and then pluck him apart limb from limb with his bare hands. He had *beaten* Lily? Somehow it seemed almost as heinous a crime as the rape.

"Not tortured, then," he said. "Only beaten and...used."

"Yes." Her gaze lowered to his cravat.

It hurt to imagine another man using Lily. Not because it made her less desirable to him—he had already considered that possibility the night before and rejected it—but because she had been all innocence and light and goodness and someone had taken her as a slave and thrust darkness and bitterness into her very body with his lust. And perhaps hurt her irreparably.

How was he to know? Perhaps she did not know herself. Perhaps her calm acceptance of what had happened, her sensible explanation about its having been war, was merely a small bandage covering a large and gaping wound. Perhaps in a way her manner of coping was not unlike Lauren's...

He lost his courage suddenly—or what little of it he had found with that first question. Had he asked, she would perhaps have told him the rest. All the atrocious details of what she had suffered and endured and survived. He did not want to know. He could not bear to know. Even though he realized that perhaps she needed to tell.

Ah, Lily, and you spoke of cowardice?

He stroked her cheek and her jaw with the backs of his fingers and then set them beneath her chin to lift it. "You have nothing to be ashamed of, Lily," he said. Did she feel ashamed? But she had fully expected that he might divorce her for adultery. "You did no wrong. I was the one who did wrong. I am the one who should feel shame. I should have protected you better. I should have guessed that they would attack the center of the line. I should have realized that there was a chance you still lived. I should have moved heaven and earth to find you and ransom you."

"No!" Her eyes gazed calmly into his. "Sometimes it is easier to find fault and place the blame—even on oneself—than to accept the fact that war just does not make sense. It was war. That is all."

And yet she blamed herself, as had been apparent the night before last. She blamed herself for cowardice in not fighting for her virtue, in not dying with the French prisoners rather than submit. And he could not accept the excuse of war as absolution for his own guilt.

He had thought himself recovered from his wounds. She looked as if she had none. But perhaps in reality they were two wounded people who must somehow find pardon and peace and healing together.

But to do that they surely needed to have everything in the open between them. Yet he could not bear to know...

He lowered his head and touched his lips to hers. They were soft and warm and yielding. And her eyes, he saw when he drew back his head to look into them, were deep with yearning. He kissed her again, as lightly as before until he felt her lips cling to his own and press back against them—just as they had when he had drawn her beneath his blanket in his tent on their wedding night.

Ah, Lily. He had missed her. Even believing her dead, he had missed her. His life had been empty without her. There had been a void that nothing and no one had filled or would ever have filled. But she was back. Ah, she had come home to him. He set his arms about her and drew her against him. He parted his lips over hers.

And found himself fighting a wild thing, who clawed at him and pushed him away in panic, making mewing noises of distress. She whirled away from him across the room and set a chair between them. When he stared at her in shock, she was staring back, her eyes huge with terror. And then suddenly she shut them tightly, and when he would have spoken, she pressed her hands over her ears and continued with the noises. Shutting him out. Shutting herself in.

He turned to ice inside.

"Lily." He used the only voice he knew

instinctively she would recognize and respond to—his officer's voice. "Lily, you are quite safe. My honor on it. You are *safe*."

She fell silent and after a few moments took her hands from her ears. She opened her eyes, though she did not look at him. They were huge and blank, the terror and everything else erased from them, he saw in some alarm.

"I am sorry," he told her. "My deepest apologies. I did not intend either to hurt or to frighten you. I will never do any-thing...physical to you against your will. I swear it. Please believe me."

"I am afraid," she said, her voice toneless. "So afraid."

"I know." All of his earlier questions had been answered more forcefully than if he had articulated them and she had answered them in words. She was maimed as surely as a soldier who had returned from the wars with missing limbs—more so. He was afraid too—mortally afraid he would never be able to atone. He took a deep breath and used his officer's voice again. "Look at me, Lily."

She looked. All the vibrant color she had gained from her escapade on the beach had fled from her face. She was pale and haggard again.

"Take a good look," he told her. "Whom do you see?"

"You," she said.

"And who am I?"

"Major Lord Newbury."

"Do you trust me, Lily?" he asked her.

She nodded. "With my life."

It was an answer that terrified him—he had betrayed her trust once with appalling, incalculable results—but he could not afford to show his own weakness at the moment. "I will not promise never to kiss you again," he said, "or never to do more than kiss you. But I will never do either without your full, free consent. Do you believe me?"

She nodded again. "Yes."

"Look about you," he commanded her. "Where are you?"

She looked. "In the cottage," she said. "At Newbury Abbey."

"And where is that, Lily?" he asked.

"In England."

"There is no war in England," he told her. "There is peace here. And this little portion of England is mine. You are safe here with me. Do you believe me?"

"Yes," she said.

"Let me see you smile again, then," he said.

Her smile was tremulous. But her terrible fear had gone, he could see, even if his own had not.

"I am sorry," she said.

"Don't be," he told her. He sighed. "We had better not try talking further today. I did not bring you here to upset you. I brought you here because I love this place and instinct told me that you would love it too. It is yours as well as mine, my dear. You are my wife. You must come here whenever you wish. You will always be safe here—even from me. I swear it. And you may be yourself here. You may be exactly the person you choose to be."

She nodded and reached for her bonnet. He watched her tie the ribbons beneath her chin and turn toward the door. He opened it for her and they stepped outside again to make their way down the valley in the direction of the hill path. He walked beside her, his hands clasped at his back. He was afraid to offer even his arm.

The wounds were far deeper than had been apparent, then. Would they ever heal? And was he capable of healing them? Here, where she did not belong, where she was unable to be the woman she had grown up to be, vibrant and spontaneous and free?

But he had no choice except to try to help her heal and cope with the present reality of her life. She was his wife. He had loved her deeply before he married her. He had loved her passionately for that one night of their marriage. He had loved her without ceasing since her apparent death.

And he had loved her again from the moment she had stepped into the nave of the church on his wedding day two mornings ago.

⤳ *11* ⤳

Lily made her apologies to Aunt Theodora, Viscountess Sterne, and took all the blame upon herself for Miranda's wayward behavior. She did it publicly, at dinner, so that everyone would know that the fault had been hers. But Aunt Theodora merely flushed and assured Lily that the incident had really been nothing at all. Hal added hotly that indeed it had not been and his father, Sir Samuel Wollston, told him sharply to hold his tongue. Joseph, the marquess of that long place, sounding decidedly bored, muttered again about storms in teacups. Pauline giggled. And Elizabeth changed the subject.

Lily was left with the conviction that yet again she had done the wrong thing.

It was a feeling with which she became increasingly familiar over the coming days. After she had taken a new dress down to the kitchen one morning and insisted upon ironing it herself and had then helped a kitchen maid carry out an enormous basket of laundry to be pegged on the clothesline, she had been told very gently by her mother-in-law that servants were hired to perform such tasks so that ladies might busy themselves with more important work. But the important work involved a daily meeting with the housekeeper and a perusal of accounts that were written in a ledger Lily could not decipher. Soon enough the dowager countess resumed the task alone.

Ladies—and a few gentlemen—came to call at the abbey, and Lily had to face the ordeal of having them presented to her and of then having to make conversation with them while they all sipped tea. One afternoon Mr. Cannadine, who had accompanied his mother, spoke of the war with Neville and the Duke of Anburey and some other gentlemen, and

Lily enthusiastically joined in the conversation. But after the visitors had left, Lauren drew her to one side and pointed out to her that it was not quite genteel for ladies to discuss such unpleasant subjects. Lily was not to blame, of course, Lauren had added hastily. Mr. Cannadine ought not to have introduced the subject when it was possible the gentlemen's conversation might be overheard by the ladies.

The calls had to be returned. It was common courtesy, the dowager explained, to acknowledge those who had shown such civility. But when the barouche was passing through the village one afternoon on its way to Lady Leigh's, Lily spied Mrs. Fundy and impulsively called to the coachman to stop. She asked Mrs. Fundy how she did, and how her husband and her children did. They were not rhetorical questions. She listened with interest to the answers and reached out her arms for the Fundy baby so that she could hug him and kiss him—even though Mrs. Fundy warned her that he needed his nappy changed and did not smell too sweet. But when the barouche was on its way again and Lily turned a brightly smiling face toward her mother-in-law, she found that she had incurred yet another gentle lecture. One might nod graciously to certain people, but it was quite unnecessary to engage them in conversation.

"Certain people," Lily understood, were those of the lower classes. Of her own class.

Lily escaped out of doors whenever she could. It was not very difficult to do, especially after the house guests had left Newbury. By the end of the week everyone except the Duke and Duchess of Anburey, their daughter, Wilma, Joseph, Elizabeth, and the Duke of Portfrey had returned to their own homes—and the others planned to leave for London within a few days. Lily usually succeeded in leaving the house and returning undetected—she had not forgotten that side door and the servants' stairs by which she had approached her room on the first day.

She explored the whole park—in sunshine and in rain. There was a great deal of the latter in the second half of the week, but adverse weather conditions never deterred Lily. She loved the beach best—though she developed the habit of approaching it with her head averted from the valley and the cottage. She loved also the cultivated lawns and gardens before the house, the dense woods that lay between them and the village and through which the winding driveway passed, and the hill behind the house with its carefully land-scaped walk that formed roughly a horse-shoe shape from just beyond the rock garden up over the hill to emerge in the rose arbor behind the stables. It was called the rhodo-dendron walk.

She climbed it late one afternoon after returning from the tedious visit to Lady Leigh's. She had changed into her old dress and let down her hair, though the chilliness of the day forced her to wear a cloak and shoes. But the climb and the view from the top and the sense of solitude she acquired up there were well worth the discomfort of the weather. She could see the sea and the beach and the cove from where she stood. If she turned, she could see fields and common grazing land stretching away into the distance.

It was not hard, she thought, closing her eyes, to feel a certain sense of belonging. This was England, which her father had so loved, and it was her new home. If only, she thought wistfully, Neville merely owned one of the cottages in the lower village and went out fishing every day with the other men. If only...

But there was no point in if onlys. She looked about her for somewhere to sit so that she could relax and let the beauty of the scene seep into her bones and her soul. And then she spotted the perfect place. It was a good thing Miranda was no longer there to be under her bad influence, she thought ruefully as she climbed the tree, her dress hitched about her knees. A couple of minutes later she was perched on the branch that had looked so perfect from below. Her eyes had not deceived her. It was a broad and sturdy branch. She could wedge her back against the trunk and stretch out her legs and feel perfectly safe.

Now... If she could just let go of everything, even thought, and become a part of the beauty and peace of her surroundings. She drew several deep breaths, smelling leaves and bark and earth and the salt of the sea air. But the old skills would just not work for her this afternoon. She felt lonely. Neville had been very gentle with her since that dreadful scene at the cottage. Very gentle and courteous—and very remote. He seemed to go out of his way to avoid being alone with her. Perhaps he did not want to frighten her again.

He had misunderstood what had happened. He had thought she was afraid of him, afraid that he would force himself on her against her will. It had not been that at all. She had been afraid that there would be more than just the kiss, and she had been afraid to find out what it would be like. She had been afraid that the one sustaining dream of the last year and a half would be destroyed for all time and there would be nothing with which to replace it. What if it had proved no different with him than it had been with Manuel? What if it had left her feeling like a *thing*, an inanimate object, which had been used to bring him physical relief? She knew it would have been different. Memory told her so. And he had been warm and gentle and had smelled clean and musky. She had felt a surge of intense longing.

But what if it *had* turned out to be ugly?

There were birds singing, dozens of them, perhaps hundreds. Yet almost all of them were invisible among the branches of the trees—as perhaps she was. But she was not singing. She set her head back against the trunk of the tree and closed her eyes.

There had been another element to her fear, one she did not want to admit. She had been afraid that it would be ugly for him—that *she* would be ugly for him. She had been afraid that he would find her spoiled, contaminated. She had been with Manuel for seven months. By some miracle she had never conceived—maybe she was barren. But perhaps Neville would have remembered if she had allowed him inside her body that she had belonged, however unwillingly, to another man. And perhaps it would have made a difference. Perhaps despite himself he would have felt disgust.

She would have *known*. And she would have found the knowledge unbearable.

She would have found *herself* unbearable. She could remember after her release, during the long walk back to Lisbon, bathing in a stream and finding suddenly that she could not bring herself to climb out of the water or to stop scrubbing at herself with her folded chemise—scrubbing and scrubbing until she became hysterical. She had felt dirtier than she had ever felt, but she had been unable to wash away the dirt because it had been beneath her skin.

It had not happened again, but she had understood after she'd finally coaxed herself out of the water and lay shivering and frightened on the bank that perhaps she would never feel clean again. It was a secret fear she had learned to live with. But if he should ever come to share the feeling, she would no longer be able to do so.

She should have spoken her fears in the cottage, she thought. She should have told him exactly how she felt. She should have told him about Manuel, about her long trek to Lisbon, about her dreams, her fears, her nightmares—

no, there was only one of those. She should have told him. But she had been unable to.

That, perhaps, had been the worst thing of all. How could they ever grow close again if they did not share everything that was themselves?

Lily, opening her eyes to gaze sightlessly out over the roof of the abbey to the sea in the distance, became aware suddenly of a slight movement to her left. Someone was coming up the path from the direction of the rock garden. Or rather someone was standing off there in the distance close to a tree trunk, scanning the path ahead with one hand shading his eyes. Or hers. It was impossible to tell who it was, but it was someone tallish, wearing a dark cloak. Perhaps it was Neville, come looking for her. Her heart leapt with gladness. Perhaps they could talk after all in a secluded place like this. And he would not care that she had climbed a tree. She waved an arm even as she realized that it was not he. There was something about the way the figure stood that was unfamiliar.

The man—or woman—disappeared. Or ducked out of sight. Embarrassed, perhaps, to see her perched in a tree branch? Or perhaps whoever it was had not seen her at all.

Lily was disappointed. Being alone was obviously not the best idea this afternoon. She would go back home, she decided as she climbed carefully back to the ground and made her way down the path toward the rock garden. Perhaps Elizabeth would care to take a stroll with her.

177

As she rounded a bend halfway down she walked almost headlong into the Duke of Portfrey, who was coming in the opposite direction—wearing a dark cloak.

"Oh," Lily said, "it was you."

"I was in the stables when you passed awhile ago," he told her, "and guessed you were on the rhododendron walk. I just now decided to come to meet you." He offered her his arm.

"That was kind of you," she said, taking it. But why had he stood there so furtively, searching for her, or for someone, and then doubled back only to come onward again and pretend that he was just now coming to meet her?

"Not at all," he said. "You were telling me about your mother some time ago, Lily, when we were interrupted."

They had been interrupted by Elizabeth, who had told him he was being too inquisitive.

"Yes, sir," Lily said.

"Tell me," he asked her. "Was she from Leicestershire too?"

"I believe so, sir," she said.

"And her maiden name?"

Lily had no idea and told him so. But the probing nature of his questions was making her uneasy.

"What did she look like?" he asked. "Like you?"

No. Her mother had been plump and round-faced and rosy-cheeked and dark-eyed. She had been tall—or so she had appeared to a child who was only seven when she died. She had had an ample and comfortable bosom on which to pillow one's head—though Lily did not add that detail to the description she gave the duke.

"How old are you exactly, Lily?" he asked.

"Twenty, sir."

"Ah." He was silent for a few moments. "Twenty. You do not look so old. What is your date of birth?"

"I am twenty years old, sir," she replied firmly, beginning to feel annoyed by the duke's persistent questions.

They had already passed through the rock garden and were approaching the fountain. He looked down at her. "I beg your pardon, Lily," he said. "I have been impertinent. Forgive me, please. It is just that you have reminded me of an old—oh, obsession, I suppose one might call it, from which I thought I had long recovered until you stepped into the nave of the village church."

She was puzzled by him. She was annoyed with him. And she was not sure whether she ought to be a little frightened of him.

"Forgive me." He stopped at the fountain, smiled at her, and raised her hand to his lips.

"Of course, sir," she said graciously, drawing her hand away and turning to run lightly up the steps to the terrace. She forgot that looking the way she did, she ought to have run around to the servants' entrance. But she was fortunate enough not to see anyone except the footman, Mr. Jones, who blushed and responded to her bright greeting with an embarrassed smirk.

The Duke of Portfrey had a handsome, elegant appearance and a pleasant smile, she thought. But it would be foolish indeed to stop being wary of the man.

❧

The following day Neville went out early in the morning on estate business with his steward. It was not quite noon when he returned alone through the village. He decided to stop at the dower house to see how Lauren and Gwen did, though they called most days at the abbey. Lauren insisted on behaving just as if nothing untoward had happened. It might even be said that she had taken Lily under her wing. She sometimes even read and played the pianoforte for her. While it might seem to be a happy turn of events, it had Neville worried.

Gwendoline was alone in the morning room. She set down a book when Neville was shown in and raised her face for his kiss on the cheek. She did not smile at him. Gwen had not done much smiling lately.

"You have missed Lily by only a quarter of an hour," she told him. "She came here after walking on the beach. She returned to the abbey through the forest instead of going by the driveway. She is very unconventional."

"If that is meant as a criticism," he said,

"stow it, Gwen. Lily has my full permission to be as unconventional as she pleases."

She looked assessingly at him. "Then she will never learn to fit in," she said. "It is unwise of you, Nev. But I will tell you something that annoys me more than I can say. In many ways I envy her. I have never waded in the sea water—not since we were children, anyway. I have never climbed that rock and tossed off my bonnet and kicked off my shoes. I have never just…walked off into the forest without taking the path."

They looked at each other gravely for a few moments and then exchanged rueful smiles.

"Don't hate her, Gwen," he said. "She had no intention whatsoever of causing anyone pain. And she is dreadfully lonely. I am not sure my support is enough for her. I need help."

She picked up some tatting from a table beside her and bent over it. "It was such a pleasant dream," she said. "You marrying Lauren and living at the abbey with her. Me here with Mama. All of us together as we always were before I—before I married Vernon. Now it is all spoiled. And Lauren is suffering so much that she will hardly confide even in me. Nev, we have always talked about *every-thing*."

"Where is she?" he asked.

"She went out a few minutes after Lily left," she said. "She said she needed air and exercise, but she did not want me to go with her. I wish she would not insist upon making Lily a—a *project*. She needs to prove some-

181

thing—that she can rise above adversity, that she can refuse to bear a grudge, that she can continue to be the perfect lady, as she has always been. If only she would—"

"Hurl things at my head and hate Lily?" he suggested when she hesitated.

"At least," she said, "it would be healthy, Nev. Or if she would saturate a few towels with bitter tears. She has even spoken of moving back to the abbey so that she can always be available to Lily, to help her cope with her new life."

"No," he said firmly.

"No," she agreed. "I will develop leprosy or something else deadly so that she will have to remain here to nurse me."

They smiled fleetingly at each other again, and then she resumed her work.

"Perhaps," he said, "I should suggest that Lauren go to London for at least a part of the Season. Elizabeth will be returning there within a few days. I am sure she would be delighted to have Lauren's company. Yours too."

"London?" She looked up, startled. "Oh no, Neville. No, I have no wish to go there. Lauren would not either. To find a husband, do you mean? It is too soon. Besides, she must be—our whole family must be rather notorious just now."

He winced. Yes, he had not really thought of that. The events of the past week must be very adequately feeding the *ton*'s insatiable hunger for sensation and scandal. Many of its members had been at Newbury for the wedding. And those who had not been would be avid to learn the details. It would be humiliating to Lauren to appear in London this year.

He sighed and got to his feet. "I suppose," he said, "we all need time. I just wish I could take all the burden of what has happened on my own shoulders and be the only one to suffer. Poor Lily. Poor Lauren. And poor Gwen."

She set her work aside and accompanied him to the stable, where he had left his horse. She took his arm as they walked, and he reduced his stride to accommodate her limp.

"And after we have all been given time," she said, "will you be happy, Nev? Is happiness possible for you now?"

"Yes," he said.

"Then you had better train Lily," she said. "Or better still, you had better allow Mama to train her."

"I will not have Lily made unhappy, Gwen," he said.

"Is she is happy as she is, then?" she cried. "Are *any* of us happy? Oh, what is the use? If we are unhappy, it is not Lily's fault. Or even yours, I suppose. Why is it that we always seek to blame someone for our misery? It is just that I have been determined to dislike Lily quite intensely."

"Gwen," he said, "she is my wife. And it was a love match, you know."

"Oh." She raised her eyebrows. "Was it? Poor Lauren."

She said no more, but raised an arm in farewell as he mounted and rode toward the driveway.

Lily had not yet returned to the abbey, he discovered when he arrived there himself, having left his horse to a groom's care at the stables, though she had left the dower house a good half hour before he had. Where had she gone? It was almost impossible to know, but she had walked into the forest when she left the dower house. Perhaps she was still there. Not that it would be easy to find her. And not that he ought to try.

But perhaps she had lost her way. He strode off past the fountain and across the wide lawn toward the trees.

He might have wandered among them for an hour and not spotted her. It was sheer coincidence that he saw her almost immediately. His eye was caught by the fluttering of the pale blue dress that had been the first of her new clothes. She was standing very still against a tree trunk, her hands flat against it on either side of her body. He did not want to frighten her. He did not attempt to silence his approach as he went to stand in front of her. Even so, he could see the unmistakable fear in her eyes.

"Oh," she said, closing them briefly, "it is just you."

"Who did you think it was?" he asked her curiously. She was not wearing a bonnet—his mother would be scandalized—though her hair was neatly dressed.

She shook her head. "I do not know," she said. "The Duke of Portfrey, perhaps."

"Portfrey?" He frowned. But she had been *afraid*.

"What have you done with your cloak?" she asked.

"I did not wear one today," he replied, looking down at his riding clothes. "It is too warm."

"Oh," she said. "I was mistaken, then."

He would not touch her, but he leaned his head a little closer to hers. "Why were you frightened?"

Her smile was a little wan. "I was not really. It was nothing. I am just jumping at shadows."

His eyes roamed over her face. She looked even now as if she were afraid to abandon the safety of the tree against which she leaned. A new and painful thought struck him.

"I have thought about your captivity," he said, "and I have thought of you in Lisbon, trying to get someone in the army to believe your story. But there is a chunk of missing time I have not considered, is there not? You were somewhere in Spain and walked all the way back to Lisbon in Portugal. Alone, Lily?"

She nodded.

"And every hill and hollow and thicket in both countries might have concealed a band of partisans," he said, "or French troops caught behind their own lines. Or even our own men. You had no papers. I should have given thought to that journey of yours before now, should I not?" What sort of terrors must she have lived through in addition to the physical hardships of such a journey?

"Everyone's life contains suffering," she said. "We each have enough of our own. We do not need to shoulder the burden of other people's too."

"Even when the other person is one's wife?" he asked. She should have been able to look on the partisans as friends, of course—they were all Britain's allies. But her experience with the one group must have given her a healthy fear of meeting another band. And he had not even *thought* of that journey. "Forgive me, Lily."

"For what?" She smiled at him and looked her old sweet beguiling self again. "These woods are beautiful. Old. Secluded. Filled with birds and birdsong."

"Give it time," he told her. "Eventually you will come to believe in the peace and safety of England. And of your home in particular. You are safe here, Lily."

"I am not afraid now," she assured him, and her serene smile seemed to bear out the words. "It was just a—a feeling. It was foolish. Am I late? Is that why you came for me? Are there visitors? I forget that there are always visitors."

"You are not late," he said, "and there are no visitors—though there will be this evening. But even if you *were* late and even if there *were* visitors, it would not matter. You must feel free here, Lily. This is your home."

She nodded, though she did not reply. He held out a hand for hers without thinking. But before he could return his arm to his side, she took his hand and curled her fingers about it as if touching him were the most natural thing in the world to do. It was a warm, smooth hand, which he clasped firmly as they began to walk in the direction of home.

It was the first time he had touched her since that afternoon at the cottage. He looked down at her blond head with its coiled braid at the back and felt curiously like crying.

She was changed. She was no longer Lily Doyle, the carefree young woman who had gladdened the hearts of a hardened, jaded regiment in Portugal. She had lost her innocence. And yet it clung about her still like an almost visible aura.

∾ *12* ∾

The afternoon had turned unseasonably hot. The evening had remained warm and was still comfortably cool at a little before midnight, when Neville saw his guests on their way home from the terrace. His Aunt and Uncle Wollston, with their sons, Hal and Richard; Lauren and Gwen; Charles Cannadine with his mother and sister; Paul Longford; Lord and Lady Leigh with their eldest daughter— all had come to dinner and had stayed for an evening of music and cards.

Lily had found it a difficult evening, Neville knew. She did not play cards—poor Lily, it was yet another absent accomplishment that his friends and neighbors had discovered in her. And while she might have found congenial company with Hal and Richard or even perhaps with Charles or Paul—he had noticed without surprise that she was always more comfortable with men than with women—she

187

had been taken under the wing of Lady Leigh and Mrs. Cannadine, who had proceeded to discover all the other attributes of a lady she simply did not possess. Then she had been borne off by Lauren to the music room, where all the young ladies except Lily had proceeded to display their accomplishments at the pianoforte.

They had been absolutely *fascinated*, Lady Leigh had assured Neville later in the evening, to learn that Lady Kilbourne had often been forced to sleep on the hard ground under the stars in the Peninsula, surrounded by *a thousand men*. His lordship's dear wife simply must be prevailed upon to tell them more about her shocking experiences.

It had often been considerably more than a thousand, Neville thought with inner amusement, and wondered if the ladies, clearly titillated by such scandalous information concerning his countess, realized that sometimes there was safety in numbers.

He was restless after everyone had retired to bed. Being alone again with Lily during the morning, talking and strolling with her, holding her hand, had reawakened the hunger he had been trying to deny for her companionship, for the intimacy of marriage with her. Not just sexual intimacy—though there was that too, he admitted—but emotional closeness, the cleaving of mind to mind and heart to heart. It was something, he realized, that he had never particularly craved with Lauren. With her he would have been content with the comfortable friendship and affection they had always shared. But not with Lily.

He fought the temptation to go into her room to check on her, something he had not done since that day at the cottage. He was afraid he might try to find an excuse to stay.

But suddenly he leaned closer to the window of his bedchamber, through which he had been idly gazing. He braced his hands on the windowsill. Yes, it was Lily down there. Did he even need to doubt the evidence of his own eyes? Who else would be leaving the house at this time of night? Her cloak was billowing out behind her as she hurried in the direction of the valley path—and her hair too. It was loose down her back.

It seemed strange to him at first that she had chosen to go out alone in the middle of the night when she had been frightened in the forest in the middle of the day. But only at first. He understood soon enough that if Lily had demons to fight, she would not cower away from them but would face them head-on. Besides, her peace and serenity had always been drawn from the outdoors and from the solitude she had seemed able to find even in the midst of a teeming army.

He should leave her alone.

He should leave her to find whatever comfort for her unhappiness she was capable of finding on the beach beneath the stars.

Yet he ached for her. He ached to be a part of her life, of her world. He longed to share himself with her as he had never done with any other woman. And he longed for her trust, for her willingness to share herself with him.

He longed for her forgiveness, though he knew that to her there seemed nothing to forgive. He longed to be able to atone.

He should leave her be.

But sometimes selfishness was hard to fight. And perhaps it was not entirely selfishness that drew him to go out after her. Perhaps away from the house, in the beauty of a moonlit night, he could meet her on a different level from any they had yet discovered here at Newbury. Perhaps some of the restraints that had kept them very much apart since her arrival—and especially since that one afternoon—could be brushed aside. Their morning encounter had held out a certain promise. Perhaps...

Perhaps he was merely looking for some excuse—any excuse—for doing what he knew he was going to do anyway. He was already in his dressing room, pulling on the riding clothes his valet had set out for the morning.

He was going out after her.

If nothing else, he could watch out for her safety, make sure that she came to no harm.

∽

Lily had been to the beach since the afternoon of the picnic once in the pouring rain of early morning. She had been scolded roundly on her return by Dolly, who had predicted darkly that her ladyship would catch her

190

death of cold even if she *had* worn a borrowed cloak with the hood up. Lily had been to the beach, but she had never again turned up the valley to the pool and the cottage.

It was definitely one of the beautiful places of this earth, and she had spoiled it by panicking when she had been kissed. She had refused to trust beauty and peace and kindness, and she had been punished as a result. She had found herself unable since that afternoon to forge any of the contentment for herself that she had almost always been able to find in the changing surroundings and conditions in which she had lived her life. She had become fearful. She had started to imagine men—or perhaps women—in dark cloaks stalking her. She did not like such weakness in herself.

The evening had been a great trial to her. It was not that the number of guests had overwhelmed her. Nor was it that anyone had been unkind or even openly disapproving. It was not even that she had felt out of place. It was just that finally, after a week at Newbury Abbey, Lily had come to a terrible realization: that this evening was the pattern of many evenings to come. And the days she had lived through would be repeated over and over down the years.

Perhaps she would adjust. Perhaps no future week would be quite as difficult as this one had been. But something had gone permanently from her life—some hope, some dream.

Fear had taken their place.

Fear of an unknown man. Or perhaps not unknown. The Duke of Portfrey was always watching her indoors. Why not outdoors too when she wished to be alone? Or perhaps it was not the duke. Perhaps it was—Lauren. She came every day to the abbey and invariably attached herself to Lily, being attentive to her, solicitous of her well-being, eager to teach her what she did not know and do for her what she could not do. She was all graciousness and kindness. She was quite the opposite of what she should be, surely. There was something not quite right in her cheerful acceptance of her situation. Just thinking of her gave Lily the shudders. Perhaps it was Lauren who felt it necessary to keep an eye on her even when she was alone. Perhaps in some fiendish way Lauren was trying to make her so uncomfortable in company and so terrified when alone that she would simply go away.

And perhaps, Lily thought, giving herself a mental shake, it was no one at all, male or female, known or unknown.

Fear, she had realized while she stood at the window of her bedchamber gazing longingly out, was the one thing she could not allow to rule her. It would be the ultimate destroyer. She had given in to it once, choosing life and prostitution over torture and death. In many ways she had forgiven herself for that choice. As Neville had said to her—and as her father had taught her—it was a soldier's duty to remain alive in captivity and to escape as soon as he was able. It had been war in which she had been caught up. But the war was over for her now. She was in England. She was at home. She would not allow nameless terrors to consume her.

And so she had come outside—and she was going to face the worst of her fears. The cloaked person whom she had spotted from the rhododendron walk and in the woods this morning was not the worst fear. The cottage was.

The night was still and bright with moonlight and starlight. It was also almost warm. The cloak she had worn seemed unnecessary, though perhaps she would be glad of it in the valley, Lily thought as she hurried down the lawn and found the path through the trees. Especially if she stayed all night. She thought she might do so as she had on that first night, when she had been turned away from the abbey. She thought she might sleep on the beach after she had forced herself to go to the cottage—though not necessarily inside it. Now that she had left the house, some of her fears had already dissipated, and she did not think she would be able to bring herself to go back there. She wished she never had to go back.

She paused when she reached the valley. The beach looked inviting with the moonlit sea at half tide. The sand formed a bright band in the moonlight. It would be soothing to the soul to walk barefoot along it—perhaps to climb the rock again. But it was not what she had come to do. She turned her head reluctantly to look up the valley.

It was an enchanted world, the fern-covered

cliff dark green and mysterious, the waterfall a silver ribbon, the cottage so much a part of its surroundings that it seemed a piece of nature more than a structure built by man. It was a place to which she must return if she was somehow to piece together the fractured shards of her life.

She turned slowly in its direction and approached the pool with lagging footsteps. But she knew as she drew close that she was doing the right thing. There was something about this little part of the valley that was very different from the beach or any other area of the park—or from any other spot on earth. Neville was right and she had been right—it was one of the special places of this world, one of the places in which something broke through. She hesitated to think of that something as God. The God of churches and established religion was such a limiting Being. This was one of the places in which *meaning* broke through and in which she could feel that she might understand everything if she could only find the thoughts or the words with which to grasp it.

But then meaning was not to be grasped. It was a mystery to be trusted.

One needed courage to trust places like this. She had lost her courage the afternoon of the picnic. She needed to restore it.

She went to stand among the thick ferns that overhung the pool. She undid the strings at the neck of her cloak after a couple of minutes and tossed it aside. After a brief hesitation she pulled off her old dress too and kicked off her shoes until she stood there in just her shift. The air was cool, but to someone who had spent most of her life outdoors it was not uncomfortably cold. And she needed to *feel*. She stood very still. After a few minutes she tipped back her head and closed her eyes. The beauty of the moonlit scene threatened to steal everything for the eyes. She wanted to hear the sounds of water and insects and gulls. And she wanted to smell the ferns and the fresh water of the waterfall, the salt of the sea. And to feel the cool night air against her flesh and the ferns and soil beneath her bare feet.

She opened her eyes again once all her senses had become attuned to her surroundings. She looked into the dark, fathomless waters of the pool. The darkness with its suggestion of something to be feared was an illusion. The pool was fed by that bright fall of sparkling waterdrops, and it in its turn fed the shimmering sea. Darkness and light—they were a part of each other, complementary opposites.

"What are you thinking?"

The voice—*his* voice—came from behind her, not very far distant. The words had been softly spoken. She had neither seen nor heard his approach, but she was curiously unstartled, unsurprised. There was none of that terror, that panicked feeling that something menacing was creeping up on her that she had felt on the rhododendron walk and in the forest this morning. It felt right that he had come. It felt as if it were meant to be. What had gone wrong here could not be put right if he were not here with her. She did not turn around.

"That I am not just someone observing this," she said, "but that I am a part of it. People often talk about observing nature. By saying so they set a distance between themselves and what is really a part of them. They miss a part of their very being. I am not just watching this. I *am* this."

She was not thinking out the words, planning them, formulating a philosophy of life. She was merely speaking from her heart to his heart. She had never shared herself so deeply with another human being. But it seemed right to do so with him. He would understand. And he would accept.

He said nothing. Yet his very silence said everything. There was suddenly a feeling of perfect peace, perfect communion.

And then he was beside her, touching the backs of his fingers to the hair at her temples. "Then the one remaining garment has to go too, little water nymph," he said.

There was no element of suggestiveness in the words. They merely showed the understanding and acceptance she had expected. While she crossed her arms and peeled her shift off over her head, he was shrugging out of his coat and waistcoat and shirt.

"You *were* planning to swim, were you not?" he asked her.

Yes. She had not known it consciously, but yes, it would have been the next logical step even if he had not come to put it into words

196

for her. She needed to immerse herself in the waters of the pool, to make herself an inextricable part of the beauty and peace that had been restored to her this night—the perfect gift.

She nodded. He was a part of it too, magnificent in his nakedness after he had stripped away the last of his garments. They looked at each other with frank appreciation and—oh yes, with the stirrings of desire, of hunger, of need. But there was more than just that. There were needs of the soul to be fed, and for now they were of greater importance than the cravings of the body.

Besides, there was all night...

He turned and dived into the pool—and came up gasping and shaking his head like a wet dog. His teeth flashed white in the moonlight. But before he could say anything Lily had dived in too.

The water was cold. Numbingly, breathtakingly cold. And clear and sweet and cleansing. She felt as if it were penetrating beneath the layer of her skin and soothing and cleaning and renewing. Now that she was in the water, she saw after she had surfaced and smoothed her hair back from her face, it was no longer black but shimmering with moving light. Darkness was only a perception, she realized again, dark from one viewpoint but bright from another.

It was not a large pool or even very deep. But they swam side by side for several minutes, saying nothing because nothing needed to be said. And they trod water close to the waterfall and reached out their hands in order to feel the sharp needles of water pounding against fingers and palms. The water was cold even after one had become accustomed to it.

"Wait here," he said eventually, setting his hands on the bank and lifting himself out in one smooth motion.

Lily floated lazily on her back until he came from the cottage with one towel wrapped about himself and others folded over his arm. He reached down a hand and helped her out and then wrapped a large towel about her shivering form. He reached behind her and squeezed the excess water from her hair before giving her the other towel to wrap turban-style about it.

"We could light a fire inside the cottage," he suggested, "if you wish to go inside there again, Lily. You would be in no danger from me. I will not touch you without your consent. Is the prospect of warmth enticing?"

Yes, it was. But more enticing was the thought of prolonging this night of magic, this night in which she could persuade herself that all of life's problems had been solved for all time. She knew life was never that simple, but she knew too that times like this were necessary, a balm for restoring the soul.

On a night like this love could become everything. Love could not always be so, but there were precious times like this that one ought not to deny.

Besides, the cottage was the one niggling fear that remained to be conquered.

She smiled. "Yes," she said. "I am not afraid. How could I be after this?" She gestured with one hand at the scene about them. He would understand, she knew. He had become a part of it with her. "I want to go inside. With you."

⌒

He must know the cottage very well, Lily thought. He had found the towels in darkness, and now it took him only a few seconds to find candles and tinderbox and bring the coziness of candlelight to the sitting room. While Lily pulled on her shift and dress, he knelt and lit the fire that was already laid in the hearth. There was more light then and the pleasant aroma of wood burning. Almost immediately there was a thread of warmth.

The remnants of fear vanished.

He sat in a chair beside the hearth after dressing—though he did not put his waistcoat and coat back on—while Lily sat on the floor close to the flames, her knees drawn up before her, her hair over one shoulder, drying in the heat. She was reminded of the relaxed, informal life of an army camp, though she had never sat thus with him there—there had been too much of a social gap between her father and Major Lord Newbury.

"After your father died, Lily," he said, perfectly in tune with her thoughts, it seemed, "did you have all sorts of regrets about what you might have said to him or done for him if you had only known that he was to die on that day? Or were you always so aware that as a fighting man he could die at any time that you left nothing unsaid, nothing undone?"

"I think the latter," she said after giving the question some thought. "I was fortunate to be able to live all my life with him even to the last day. I was fortunate to have a father who loved me so totally and whom I loved without reserve. I wish, though—I do wish I could have known what he wanted so badly for me to have after his death. He was always so insistent that there was something inside his pack for me. But there was no chance to see what it was— he had left it back at the base. But the important thing is that I know he did love me and did try to provide for my future." She looked up at Neville, sprawled and relaxed and yet elegant too in his chair. "You were not so fortunate?"

"My father was a manager," he said. "He liked to organize the lives of all those he loved. He did it *because* he loved us, of course. He had our lives planned out for us—Gwen's and Lauren's and mine. I rebelled. I wanted my own life. I wanted to make my own choices. Sometimes I was downright spiteful about it. My father opposed my purchasing a commission, but when he finally relented and tried to choose a prestigious cavalry regiment for me, I insisted upon a foot regiment, which he thought beneath the dignity of his son. I loved him, Lily. I would in time have grown past the age of rebellion and have been close to him, I believe. But he died before I had the chance to tell him any of the things he deserved to be told."

"He knew." She hugged her knees. "If he loved you as well as you say he did, then he understood too. He had lived long enough to know about the various stages of life. And I believe that for many people rebellion during youth is normal. You must not blame yourself. You never did anything to disgrace him. I am sure he must have been proud of you."

"And what makes you, at the advanced age of twenty, so wise?" he asked her, a smile on his lips and in his eyes.

"I have seen and listened to many people in those twenty years," she said. "Many different types of people. Everyone is unique, but I have discovered that there are common traits of humanity too."

"I wish I had known your mother," he said. "She was one of the indomitable women who follow the drum even after they have children. It is my good fortune, of course, that she did and that your father was so devoted to you that he kept you with him even after she was gone. They produced a very special daughter."

"Because they were very special people," she said. "I wish I had known Mama better too. I remember her, but more as a sensation than as a person. Endless comfort and security and acceptance and love. I was very fortunate to have her even as long as I did, and to have had Papa. *You* were fortunate to have had such a father too—one who cared even enough to let you go. He did that for you, you know. He purchased your commission and even allowed you to choose a regiment he disapproved of. I am glad for my sake that he did."

They smiled at each other.

They talked for all of an hour while the fire burned down, was rebuilt once, and burned down again. They talked without any deliberate choice of topic, a comfort and ease between them that had not been there during the past week. It was quite like old times.

Eventually their chatter gave place to longer silences, companionable at first, but inevitably more and more charged with something else. Lily was fully aware of the changing atmosphere, but she allowed it to be. Tonight she had chosen to put fear behind her, to relinquish her personal will to the unfolding pattern of her life. She allowed to be what would be.

"Lily," he said finally, still apparently relaxed in his chair, "I want to make love to you. Do you want it too?" he asked her.

"Yes," she whispered.

"Here?" he said. "On the bed in the next room? In this cottage? To erase the memory of what happened the last time we were here?"

"It is why we are here, is it not?" she answered. "To weave ourselves into the magic, to be simply ourselves again, to be together despite all that has happened and is happening. Together as we have been outside in the pool and here by the fire. And together in—in there." She nodded toward the bedroom.

"You must not be frightened," he told her. "Not at any moment. However far advanced in passion I might become, I will stop the instant you tell me to stop. Will you believe that?"

"Yes," she said. "I believe it. But I will not tell you to stop."

She knew that she would want to. Before he came inside her, she would want to stop him. Because once he was in her, she would know. She would know if her dreams of love had been as insubstantial as most dreams are. And she would know if after all he found himself repulsed by the knowledge that another man had known her since their wedding day. But she would not stop him. This— tonight, all of it—was meant to be, and she would let it be, however it turned out.

"Come, then, Lily."

He got to his feet and held out a hand for hers. She stood beside him while he banked the fire, and then took his hand again to go into the bedchamber.

☙ *13* ☙

They undressed without awkwardness or embarrassment, perhaps because they had bathed naked together just an hour or so before. He set his hands on her shoulders and held her away from him before drawing her close. She was small but exquisitely formed. His eyes focused, though, on the purplish, puckered scar on the upper side of her left breast. He traced it lightly with his fingertips and then lowered his head to touch it with his mouth.

"I was this close to losing you forever, Lily?" he said while she ran one hand lightly over the scar that almost circled his left shoulder—the relic of the saber wound that had very nearly hacked off his arm at Talavera.

"Yes," she said, and when he lifted his head she traced the line of his facial scar with one forefinger. "War is cruel. But we both survived it."

He kissed her, merely touching his lips to hers while his hands rested on either side of her small waist, holding her a little away from his own body. She looked and felt, he thought, like a sweet innocent. He could almost imagine that it was her first time even though memory of their wedding night was strong in him. And he thought quite deliberately of the Spaniard, the partisan without a name— a name he did not want to know, though she might at some time in the future need to talk about him, and he would force himself to listen. He thought about the man and what he had done to Lily over and over again for seven months. He did not want to suppress the knowledge that she had been forced to be another man's mistress.

"It matters, does it not?" She was looking into his eyes. "That there has been someone else?"

"It matters," he said, "because it happened to *you*, Lily. Because you suffered it all while I was recuperating in hospital and then was here, beginning a new life or, rather, resuming the old one. It matters because you were totally blameless while I was not. It matters because I do not feel worthy of you."

She set the fingers of one hand lightly to his lips.

"The past is unchangeable," she said. "It was war. This is the present, the only element of time we will ever have in which to create new memories. Better ones."

Ah, Lily. His beautiful, wise, innocent Lily, who could see life as something so incredibly simple that it was profound. He took her hand from his lips with his own, kissed her palm, and then kissed her mouth. He wanted to restore all her lovely innocence. He wanted to restore his honor.

"I am not going to hurt you," he told her. "I am not going to use you for my pleasure and give none in return. I am going to make love to you."

"Yes," she said. "Oh, don't be afraid. I know it. It is what you did the last time."

He brought her against him, slid one arm about her shoulders, the other about her waist, parted his lips over hers, and kissed her more deeply. It was hard to go slowly. The memories of the searing passion of his wedding night were suddenly very vivid—and he had had no woman since. But she set her arms about him, arched her body against his, as she had done on that night, and opened her mouth. He pressed his tongue inside.

"It will be all right," he murmured to her awhile later, forcing his mouth away from hers and feathering kisses at her temples, along her jaw, on her chin. "It is going to be all right."

"Yes," she whispered. "Oh, yes. It *is* all right."

He was as fearful as she—if she *was* fearful. He had to make things right for her. And he *would* make them right. He had heard from Captain Harris by the afternoon post and would surely hear from everyone else soon. Harris had given the answers he had fully expected. The Reverend Parker-Rowe's papers had been abandoned with his body in that Portuguese pass.

He knew what the other answers would be too—what they must be.

"Come and lie down," he whispered to Lily.

He lay on the bed with her, on his side, his head propped on one hand. She gazed back at him without apparent fear. Her eyes were dreamy with desire.

"I want to come on top of you," he said. "It is how I can love you most deeply. But if my weight will make you feel trapped, if you would like it better, I will take you on top. Tell me what you want."

She turned onto her back and lifted one arm. "Come," she said. "I will not feel trapped. I am not afraid. I never was afraid of you, only of myself. I should have explained, told you that. I have always trusted you."

He knelt between her thighs, which she spread as he came over her, but he did not immediately either mount her or lower his weight onto her. He hooked her legs about his own and loved her body slowly with his hands and his mouth, leaning over her but not yet touching his body to hers. She was alive, he thought, his body exulting over her as if the reality of that fact had only just come home to him. She was warm and soft and alive, and she was on the bed with him in the valley cottage, where he had lain many times during the past year, dreaming of her, mourning her.

She was his wife and his love. She was alive.

And ready for love. He slid his hand down over the mound of dark-blond hair at the apex of her thighs. His fingers found her core and caressed her there until he could feel the heat and the slippery wetness of her desire.

"Look at me, Lily," he said, suppressing the urge simply to mount her. Even now he would not take her compliance for granted—he dared not. And she was lying very still.

She opened eyes heavy with unmistakable passion and gazed upward into his face.

"Look at me," he told her again. "I am your husband. I am going to come inside and love you and let you love me. I am not going to use you or hurt you or degrade you."

"I know," she murmured. "I know who you are."

He positioned himself carefully and pressed inward while she watched his face, unflinching. He felt her muscles clench about him and fought for control—she was soft and hot and wet. She searched his eyes with her own, but then they drifted closed and her head tipped back against the pillows and her lips parted. She was experiencing, he could not fail to see with mingled relief and desire, the beginnings of ecstasy.

It was very hard for a man to love unselfishly when desire hummed through his veins and hammered against his temples and was an agony in his groin.

He was still kneeling between her thighs, but he brought his weight down onto her now, careful to take some of it on his forearms. And he began at last to move in her, aroused by her stillness, which was nonetheless not passive, by the small, exquisite body that was unmistakably Lily's, by memory of the last time they had been together, by his long abstinence, by her return from the dead, by the steady squeaking of bedsprings that were noisy even for a single sleeper, by the sighs of pleasure that escaped her with the rhythm of thrust and withdrawal that he held steady for as long as he could.

Lily, he thought as all sensation, all awareness became focused on the exquisite pain of his desire. "Lily," he murmured. "My love. Ah, my love, my love."

She had stopped sighing. Her body had gone slack and he knew that she had moved into the world of release ahead of him with quiet joy rather than with any sudden bursting of passion. He could not have asked for a more precious reward for his patience. She was as far from fear as it was possible to be.

"Beloved." It was a mere whisper of sound.

The endearment she had used on their wedding night.

His own climax came quickly. He bore her downward with all his weight as he pressed hard and deep and allowed the blessed release of all his need, all his pain, all his love into her.

It was a moment of extraordinary oneness.

Everything was going to be all right, he thought as he began to emerge into full awareness again a minute or two later. *Everything*. They were together and they were one. There were some problems—some minor problems that they would solve together over time. There was nothing they could not do together. All was well.

"I am sorry," he murmured, realizing how heavily he was lying on her. He lifted himself away from her, sliding slowly free of her body as he did so, and lay beside her, still warm and breathless and sweaty. He wriggled one arm beneath her neck and turned his head to look at her. But he had only one glimpse before the candle guttered and finally went out. Her eyes were closed. She looked peaceful.

"Thank you," she said, and she turned onto her side to curl against him as one of her hands slid up his damp chest and came to rest near his shoulder.

He felt the pain of tears in his throat. It felt like forgiveness. Like absolution.

The air was cool on his damp body. He hooked the blankets with one foot and drew them up about both of them. "Better?" he asked. He chuckled softly. "And thanks are scarcely necessary unless they are intended as a compliment. In which case I should add my thanks to yours. Thank you, Lily."

She sighed once and fell asleep with a smile on her face.

All was going to be well. He gathered her closer, rubbed his face against her hair, breathing in its fragrance, and shifted into a more comfortable position. If only he could see Lauren as happy. Surely she must be in time. She had so much to offer the right man. And Gwen—her happiness had been cut so short.

But sometimes, he thought sleepily, one could surely be pardoned for indulging in selfish happiness. He felt the deepest sympathy for both his sister and his cousin and former betrothed. But for now, for tonight, he felt so totally happy for himself, for Lily, for *them*, that it was difficult to spare a thought for anyone else.

He slept.

⌒

When Lily awoke, it was to a feeling of yearning so intense that it was painful. There were the first suggestions of dawn beyond the window. She was inside the picturesque little thatched cottage by the pool beneath the waterfall—she could imagine the scene as it appeared when one came down into the valley on the way to the beach. She was there now with Neville, her husband—his arm was slack about her, her head pillowed on his shoulder.

He had made love to her and it had been wonderful beyond imagining. She had felt cleansed from the inside out. And he had not felt disgust—she would have known it if he had.

The yearning was to make this night somehow permanent. If only they could live here together, just the two of them, for the rest of their lives. If only they could forget Newbury Abbey, his responsibilities as the Earl of Kilbourne, her captivity, his family, Lauren. If only they could stay like this forever.

It was without a doubt the happiest night of her life.

But though she had always been a dreamer, she had never confused dreams with reality. Dreams gave one moments of happiness and the strength with which to deal with reality. And sometimes, when dream and reality touched and became one for a brief moment in time, as they had done this night, they were to be accepted as a precious gift, to be lived to the full, and then to be released. Trying to grasp hold of them and retain them would be to destroy them.

The night would be over, and they would return to Newbury Abbey. She would continue to feel—and to be—inadequate, inferior, out of place, and out of her depth. And he, being a gentleman, would continue to make the best of the situation. He would continue to see Lauren almost every day and would continue, perhaps unconsciously, to compare the woman who was his wife with the woman who ought to have been his wife.

Could she draw lasting strength from this dream-come-true? Lily wondered. He could not possibly love someone so unsuited to his station in life despite his endearments while he had been *making* love to her. But he was not averse to her either. He was not repulsed by her. He had wanted her—she had felt it in the growing tension between them as they had sat at the fireside. And he had enjoyed their lovemaking. She had enjoyed it too. All her worst fears—that the act itself would always disgust her, no matter who the lover—had been put to rest. The lover made all the difference to the act. And she loved him.

Perhaps, she thought, something had been gained from this night. They had grown comfortable together, both physically and emotionally. They had talked as friends. They had come together as lovers. She was not so naive as to believe that all their problems were now solved and that they could proceed to live happily ever after. Far from it. But perhaps an impossibility had become just a little more possible tonight.

"I always love waking up here," he said, his voice low against her ear. "I listen to the waterfall and see the edge of the thatch on the roof through the window and smell the vegetation. And I can imagine that the world is very far away."

"Do you sometimes wish it were?" she asked him.

"Frequently." He moved her hair back from her face with one finger and settled it behind her shoulder. "But not forever. Escape is a wonderful thing as long as one can go back again."

He did not, then, feel the yearning to make this night last forever?

He kissed her—softly, lazily. And she kissed him back, feeling the warm, relaxed firmness of his man's body with the soft curves of her own, feeling desire surging through her again like new blood. She could feel the gradual tightening in her breasts and the hardening of her nipples, the aching in her womb and along her inner thighs, the throbbing in the passage between. And she could feel him grow and harden against her abdomen.

They did nothing but kiss for several minutes with softly parted lips. But warmth became heat between them and they were ready without the need for more foreplay.

"Come on top of me," he said, "and take your pleasure as you wish, Lily."

What an unbelievable luxury it was, she thought, to feel desire before a coupling, to know from the throbbing ache that there would be the wonder of completion. And to be invited to take her pleasure in her way— as if she mattered as much as he did. And she believed that with him it was true. He might not love her, but she mattered to him. If he was to couple with her and take pleasure of her, he would take care to give it too.

How very different two men could be— but she did not choose to dwell upon comparisons.

They had done it this way on their wedding night, the second time, she remembered,

213

though he had lifted her over him then and positioned her and held her firm while he took her, her body heavy on his. She had been passive, quite without knowledge. They had had to be very quiet because their tent had been set only a little apart from where a whole company of men slept. She had been sore from the first time and it had hurt and felt wonderful all at the same time.

She came astride him after he had kicked back the blankets and raised his knees to set his feet flat on the bed. She kneeled over him, hugging his sides with her knees while she took hold of him in one hand and placed him at her entrance. She spread her hands on his chest, closed her eyes, and lowered herself onto him.

There could not possibly be a more delightful sensation in the world, she thought, feeling his rigid length stretching her deep, clenching inner muscles about him—this voluntary joining of bodies in preparation for the act's beginning. Unless it was the final moment, when everything dissolved into fulfillment and peace. Or perhaps the act itself was the most beautiful part—the pounding rhythm, the ache spiraling gradually upward through her womb, into her breasts, into every nerve ending in her body, the assurance that this man, this lover, this *husband* would take her to its end. She opened her eyes and looked down into his.

"This feels so very good," she told him.

"Yes," he agreed, "it does."

It had never occurred to her until he had

suggested it that it might be possible to be less than passive in the sexual act. She had always lain very still—in wonder and enjoyment during that first night and this last, in simple endurance for those seven months. She had never thought of the possibility of being a lover—only of being the loved or the used. But she could take her pleasure as she wished, he had told her. And true to his word—though she knew enough now about men to realize that it must be difficult for him—he was lying quite still beneath her, though he was hard and hot inside her.

How did she wish to take it? She braced her hands on his chest, lifted herself almost off him, and brought herself down again. It was possible, she discovered as she repeated the move over and over again, to set the rhythm she had always thought a man's exclusive preserve and to find it intensely exciting.

"Ah, yes," he said, his voice husky, his hands coming to her hips and grasping her lightly there, "ride me, then, Lily. Ride me hard."

It was a startling, erotic comparison. She rode him hard and harder, her eyes squeezed shut to concentrate all the sensation inside her and inside him, inside their joined selves—*there*. She became aware of sound as much as of feeling—their labored breathing, the wet suck and pull of her ride, the squeaking of the bedsprings. And of smell—soap and cologne and a log-dead wood fire and the musk of sex.

But then everything was focused inward on the one spot deep within where she had resisted the deep descent time and time again, tensing against it even as she rode hard onto it, tensing and tensing until fear threatened her concentration.

"Trust it, Lily. Trust me," his voice said. "I will not fail you again."

She always had, always would trust him. And he never had failed her. Never.

But it took a deliberate effort of faith to open, to ride down onto him again without any defense at all against pain, against falling, against death.

She opened—and opened and opened as he clamped his hands hard on her hips at last and held her still while he drove against and through and again through and into and beyond and...

She heard herself cry out.

She did not lose herself completely until after she felt him come deep into the secret place where only she had ever lived, and the two of them met and merged and became one self.

Seconds or minutes or hours passed before she was aware of him bringing her body down onto his and straightening her legs to rest on either side of his own. But she was too close to sleep to respond, except that she tightened her muscles for one moment and could feel him, still warm, still inside. If only they never had to be separate again.

She wondered fleetingly how he could have known, how he could have felt her fear at the very moment she became aware of it herself, how he could have known the very words to use to coax her past it, how he could have controlled his own release so as to let his seed flow into her at the exact moment when she opened to it—she had felt the heat of it deep inside at the moment she had cried out.

She listened to their heartbeats slow to normal and felt filled with well-being from her toes to the crown of her head. She would have drifted completely off to sleep if the air had not felt chilly against her back and her legs. But it also felt good, as did the warmth of his body against her front. Both made her feel alive and tingling with the strangely opposite sensations of exhaustion and energy.

"We can sleep," he said, his fingers playing through her tangled hair and massaging her scalp, "or we can swim. Which will it be?"

They could sleep just like this, all twined together and still joined. He would pull up the blankets again and they would be cocooned in warmth. She was deliciously relaxed and sleepy. Or they could go outside in the chilly dawn and jump into the even chillier water of the pool.

She grimaced. "Is that supposed to be a *choice*?" she asked without opening her eyes. But she grinned suddenly. "The swim, of course. Did you need to ask?"

"Not really," he assured her, chuckling and rolling with her so that they became disengaged and disentangled. "You would not be Lily if you did not prefer a frigid bath to a civilized sleep. The last one in is a brazen coward."

She could not risk incurring that opprobrious

label by stopping to grab any clothes. She had the advantage of being closer to the door of the bedchamber. He had the advantage of longer legs. She had the advantage of thought-lessness. He stopped a moment to grab up their towels. Even so he arrived on the fern-draped bank of the pool a full second ahead of her. But he paused to gloat. They hit the water at the same moment—or so they finally agreed to agree after they had surfaced gasping from the shock of the cold water and had argued the matter, breathless and with chattering teeth.

They swam and they frolicked, alternately sputtering and laughing, for perhaps fifteen minutes before the unrelenting chill of the water and the very definite arrival of day drove them regretfully out again to dry themselves off briskly and to rush for the cottage, where they dressed hastily.

It was the end, Lily realized, of a night when dream and reality had touched and merged. Those two opposites were about to separate again. The night was over and the day must take her and Neville back to Newbury Abbey, where they could not meet as equals in anything at all. And that had been the magic of the night, she understood in a moment of insight. They had been equals through this night, neither of them the other's superior or inferior. They had been equal as lovers. But two persons could not live on love to the exclusion of all else. And there was nothing else in which there was any equality between them. She was by far the inferior in every single regard at Newbury Abbey.

"Would you like to stay here and sleep while I go back to the house?" he asked her when they were both dressed. "You did not have many hours of rest, did you?"

It was tempting. But she knew that she could not bear to watch the dream walk away from her. She must walk away from it. Only in that way could she hope to gain any sort of control over reality.

She shook her head and smiled. "It is time to go home," she said, using the word *home* deliberately though Newbury Abbey did not feel as she had always imagined a home must feel.

"Yes." She did not believe she imagined the look of sadness in his eyes. He felt it too, then— the impossibility that one night of passion had tried to tease them into believing was perhaps possible after all.

He held her hand until they had climbed out of the valley. But though she was unaware of the exact moment when he released it, Lily noticed as they walked side by side up the lawn toward the stables that they were no longer touching. Neither were they talking.

They were going back home.

⤳ *14* ⤳

Lauren had been having trouble sleeping since her ruined wedding day. And eating. And giving the appearance of being patient and cheerful and loving and dutiful. She had never in her life thought of ending it all. But there were moments during the days following that most dreadful one in her life when she had stood at one end of the church aisle and Neville had stood at the other and Lily had stood between them—there were moments when she wished that her life would somehow end itself, that she would simply fall asleep and never wake up again.

There were far more moments when she wished it were Lily who would do the dying.

She had taken to getting up at dawn, sometimes to sit in the morning room reading for an hour or more without ever turning a page, sometimes to wander alone outdoors.

Looking for Lily.

She remembered the morning after the wedding, when Lily had been down on the beach and had then walked across the rocks to the lower village and returned home by the driveway, meeting Lauren and Gwen on the way. She knew that Lily often escaped from the house in order to be alone. Watching Lily, observing all her dreadful inadequacies, trying to deny all her beauty and natural charm, had become something of an obsession with Lauren.

She had never thought of herself as a vain woman. But why had Neville left *her* and then married *Lily*? What was it about herself that caused everyone to leave her or reject her? What was it about Lily that attracted everyone? All the men at the house were half in love with her. And even the women were softening toward her. Even Gwen...

Her wanderings took her in the direction of the beach on that particular morning, as they had done before without any success. The beach had never been her favorite part of the park. She had always preferred the cultivated beauty of the lawns and flower gardens and the rhododendron walk. The wildness of the beach and the sea had seemed too elemental, too frightening to her. They had always reminded her of how close to the edge of security her life had always been lived. She did not belong at Newbury Abbey by right of birth, after all. They could turn her off at any time. If she was not good...

She was partway down the hill when she heard the voices and laughter. At first she did not know exactly where they came from. But as she descended farther—more slowly and cautiously than before—she realized that they came from the pool at the foot of the waterfall. And then she saw them—Neville and Lily—bathing there. If her shocked eyes had not deceived her, she thought as she fled upward after the merest glimpse of them immersed in the water, they were both naked. They were laughing together like carefree children—or like lovers. She could still hear them, even though the sound of her own labored breathing almost drowned out the sound. And she could still see in her mind's eye the door of the cottage standing wide open, as if they had spent the night there.

They were husband and wife, she told herself as her panicked footsteps took her hurrying back along the wood path toward the main gates and the dower house. Of course they were lovers. And of course they had every right...

But Lauren realized something suddenly that froze her heart and almost froze her mind. She would never have been able to do that. She would never have been able to be—to be *naked* with him. And frolicking without any embarrassment. She would never have been able even to laugh with him like that—with all the carefreeness of two people whose happiness was enclosed in the moment spent together. They had laughed when they were children, of course, she and Gwen and Neville. They had surely laughed since then. But not like that.

She would not have been able to satisfy him in the way Lily was clearly doing.

It was a terrifying realization. The idea that she and Neville belonged together, that they were perfect for each other, that they loved each other, had been so much a part of the ordered conception of her world to which she had clung all her life that she was not sure she could live with any sanity if she had to relinquish the idea.

She would *not* relinquish it. She *did* love him. More than Lily did. Lily could love him in that raw, physical way, perhaps, but Lily could not read or write or talk with him on topics that mattered to him. She could not run the abbey for him or entertain his friends or perform the hundred and one duties of his countess. She could not make him proud of her. She could not know him through and through as someone who had grown up with him could do or know unerringly what to do to secure his comfort and happiness.

Lily could never be his soulmate.

But Lily was Neville's wife.

Lauren stopped abruptly on the path and drew her dark cloak tightly about herself for warmth. She was shivering despite her long walk.

It was not fair.

It was not *right*.

How she hated Lily. And how frightened she was of the violence of her own emotions. As a lady she had practiced restraint and kindness and courtesy all her life. If she was good, she had thought as a child, everyone would love her. If she was a perfect lady, she had thought as she grew older, everyone would accept her and depend upon her and love her.

Neville would depend upon her and love her. Finally she would truly *belong*.

But he had gone away and married Lily. *Lily!* The exact antithesis of what she, Lauren, had always thought would win him in the end.

She wished Lily was dead. She *wished* she was dead.

She wished she would *die*.

Lauren stood on the path for a long time, huddled inside her cloak, shivering with the unaccustomed vehemence of her own hatred.

Lily returned to the abbey buoyed by fresh hope. She was not naive enough to imagine that all her problems would magically evaporate, but she felt that she had the strength, and that Neville had the patience, to face and overcome them one at a time.

Dolly was in her dressing room waiting for her when she stepped into it. She looked her mistress over from head to toe and shook her head.

"You will catch your death yet, my lady," she scolded. "Your hair is wet. And your feet are bare. I do not know what I will tell his lordship when you catch a chill."

Lily laughed. "I have been with him, Dolly," she said.

"Oh, my," Dolly said, momentarily confounded. "Here, let me help you out of your dress, my lady." She was always slightly shocked when she observed Lily doing something that she thought of as a maid's preserve—like taking off or putting on a garment.

Lily chuckled again. "And his hair is wet too, Dolly," she said, "though I daresay his valet will not have the problem that you will have getting a comb through this bush. We were swimming."

"Swimming?" Dolly's eyes widened in horror. "At this time of day? In *May*? You and his lordship? I always thought he was—" She remembered to whom she was speaking and turned to pick up the morning gown she had set out for her mistress.

"Sensible?" Lily laughed once more. "He probably *was*, Dolly, until I came here to corrupt him. We have been swimming together in the pool—last night and again this morning. It was wonderful." She allowed Dolly to slip the dress over her head and turned obediently to have it buttoned up the back. "I believe I am going to swim every day of my life from now on. What do you think the dowager countess will say?"

Dolly met her eyes in the looking glass as Lily sat down to have her hair dressed and they dissolved into laughter.

Dolly thought of something else after she had picked up Lily's brush and considered where to start the daunting task of taming her hair. "Why is it that your underthings were not wet, my lady?" she asked.

But she understood the answer even as she spoke and blushed rosily. They both laughed merrily again.

"All I can say," Dolly said, brushing vigorously, "is that it is a very good thing no one came along to see the two of you."

They both snorted with glee.

Lily was determined to cling to the light-heartedness with which she had started the day. After breakfast, when she knew that the ladies as usual would proceed to the morning room to write letters and converse and sit at their embroidery, she went down to the kitchen and helped knead the bread and chop some vegetables while she joined happily in the conversation—the servants, she was glad to find, were becoming accustomed to her appearances and were losing their awkwardness with her. Indeed, the cook even spoke sharply to her after a while.

"Haven't you finished those carrots yet?" she asked briskly. "You have been doing too much talk—" And then she realized to whom *she* was talking, as did everyone else in the kitchen. Everyone froze.

"Oh, dear," Lily said, laughing. "You are quite right, Mrs. Lockhart. I shall not say another word until the carrots are all chopped."

She laughed gaily again after a whole minute of awkward silence had passed, broken only by the sound of her knife against the chopping board.

"At least," she said, "I do not have to fear that Mrs. Ailsham will *sack* me, do I?"

Everyone laughed, perhaps a little too heartily, but then relaxed again. Lily finished the carrots and sat with a cup of tea and the crisp, warm crust of a freshly baked loaf of bread before reluctantly going back upstairs. But she brightened again when her mother-in-law asked if she would like to join her in making a few calls in the village after luncheon and in delivering a couple of baskets to the lower village—one to an elderly man who had been indisposed, and one to a fisherman's wife who was in childbed.

But the delivery of the baskets, Lily discovered later while they were sitting in the parlor of the Misses Taylor, drinking the inevitable cup of tea, was to be done by proxy. The coachman was to carry them down the hill and take them to the relevant cottages.

"Oh, no," Lily protested, jumping to her feet. "I will take them."

"My dear Lady Kilbourne," Miss Amelia said, "what a very kind thought."

"But the hill is too steep for the carriage, Lady Kilbourne," Miss Taylor pointed out.

"Oh, I shall walk." Lily smiled dazzlingly. She had not been down to Lower Newbury since that morning when she had climbed across the rocks to it. She welcomed the chance to return there.

"Lily, my dear." The dowager countess smiled at her and shook her head. "It is quite unnecessary for you to go in person. It will not be expected."

"But I *wish* to go," Lily assured her.

And so after they had left the Misses Taylors' genteel cottage a few minutes later, the dowager proceeded to the vicarage while Lily tripped lightly down the steep hill, one large basket on her arm. The coachman, who had the other, had wanted to carry both, but she had insisted on taking her share of the load. And she would not allow him to walk a few paces behind her. She walked beside him and soon had him talking about his family— he had married one of the chambermaids the year before and they had an infant son.

Mrs. Gish, who had given birth to her seventh child the day before after a long and difficult labor, was attempting to keep her house and her young family in order with the assistance of an elderly neighbor. Lily soon had the main room swept out, the table cleared and wiped, a pile of dirty dishes washed and dried, and one infant knee cleansed of its bloody scrape and bandaged with a clean rag.

Elderly Mr. Howells, who was sitting outside his grandson's cottage, smoking a pipe and looking melancholy, was in dire need of a pair of ears willing to listen to his lengthy reminiscences about his days as a fisherman—and a smuggler. Oh, yes, he assured an interested Lily, they had their fair share of smuggling at Lower Newbury, they did. Why, he could remember...

"My lady," the coachman said eventually after a deferential clearing of his throat—he had been standing some distance away—"her ladyship has sent a servant from the vicarage..."

"Oh, goodness gracious me," Lily said, leaping to her feet. "She will be waiting to return to the abbey."

The dowager countess was indeed waiting—and had been for almost two hours. She was gracious about it in front of the vicar and his wife. Indeed she was gracious about it in the carriage on the way home too.

"Lily, my dear," she said, laying one gloved hand over her daughter-in-law's, "it is like having a breath of fresh air wafted over us to discover your concern for Neville's poorer tenants. And your smiles and your charm are making you friends wherever you go. We have all grown remarkably fond of you."

"But?" Lily said, turning her head away to

look out through the window. "But I am an embarrassment to you all?"

"Oh, my dear." The dowager patted her hand. "No, not that. I daresay you have as much to teach us as we have to teach you. But we *do* have a great deal to teach you, Lily. You are Neville's wife, and he is clearly fond of you. I am glad of that, for I am fond of him, you know. But you are also his *countess*."

"And I am also the daughter of a common soldier," Lily said, some bitterness creeping into her voice. "I am also someone who knows nothing about life in England or in a settled home. And absolutely nothing at all about the life of a lady or of a countess."

"It is never too late to learn," her mother-in-law said briskly but not unkindly.

"While everyone watches my every move to find fault with me?" Lily asked. "Oh, but that is unfair, I know. Everyone has been kind. *You* have been kind. I will try. I really will. But I am not sure I can—give up myself."

"My dear Lily." The dowager sounded genuinely concerned. "No one expects you to give up yourself, as you put it."

"But the part of me that is myself wants to be in Lower Newbury mingling with the fisherfolk," Lily said. "That is where I feel comfortable. That is where I belong. Am I to learn to nod graciously to those people and not speak to them or show personal concern for them or hold their babies?"

"Lily." Her mother-in-law could seem to think of nothing more to say.

"I will try," Lily said again after a minute

or two of silence. "I am not sure I can ever be the person you want me to be. I am not sure I want to stop being myself. And I cannot see how I can be both. But I promise I will try."

"That is all we can ask of you," the dowager said, patting her hand once more.

But Lily, as she raced upstairs to her own apartment after their return to the house, felt like a dismal, hopeless failure who would bring nothing but ridicule upon Neville if she continued as she was.

It had been a happy day for Lily—wondrously happy. With memories of last night and this morning fresh in both her mind and her body and the hope that perhaps he would come to her again tonight, she had lived the day the way she had wished to live it—just as he had told her she might—and she had been happy. But only because she had turned away from reality. The reality was that she was not one of the servants at the abbey—she was the countess. And she was not one of the fisherfolk—they were her husband's tenants. She had avoided the people with whom she ought to have spent the day if she were a good countess. She had made no real effort to learn to be the countess she was in name.

But she was incorrigible, it seemed. Instead of ringing for Dolly and changing into another dress and going down to tea to try somehow to make amends, Lily almost tore off her pretty sprigged muslin dress as soon as she had reached her dressing room, dragged on her old cotton, grabbed her old shawl, and scurried down the back stairs to the side door. She half ran down the lawn and slipped and slid down the hill, grabbing at giant ferns to steady herself. She did not even glance at the valley—she did not want to spoil the memories in her present state of agitation—but ran out onto the beach and along it, her face turned up to the sky, her arms stretched out to the sides so that she would feel the full resistance of the wind.

She grew calm again after a few minutes. She could adjust, she told herself. It would take effort, but she could do it if she tried. She had spent most of her life adjusting to constantly changing circumstances. She forced herself to think about the greatest adjustment of all she had had to make. She had learned docility and obedience—she had even learned the Spanish language—as means to survival. If she could do *that*, she could certainly learn to be a lady and a countess.

The tide was on its way out. The rocks that connected the beach with the cove of Lower Newbury were half exposed. Lily clambered up onto them. Not that she had any intention of going all the way to the village again even if she could, but she needed to use up more energy than a walk or run along the beach would require. And there was a greater sense of wildness and solitude on the rocks, with the sea to one side, an almost sheer cliff wall to the other. She stood still after a while and turned her head to gaze out to sea.

But as she did so, she heard something that was neither the ocean nor the wind nor the gulls. Something unidentifiable that nev-

231

ertheless almost froze her in place while panic crawled up her spine. She looked sharply to either side of her, but there was nothing. No one. She could see a good distance in both directions.

But the feeling would not go away. What was it she had heard, the crunching of stones?

She looked up.

Everything happened within so few seconds that it would have been difficult afterward to give a clear account—even with a clear head. Lily's was far from clear. She saw someone standing at the top of the cliff above her—a figure in a dark cloak. And then the figure turned into a large rock, hurtling down upon her. She twisted away from it, in toward the cliff face, and it crashed onto the very spot where she had been standing—a huge boulder that would without any doubt at all have killed her.

She stood with her back pressed to the cliff face, her hands flat against it on either side of her, clawing for something to grip on to. And she stared at the rock that would have been her death, her heart hammering in her throat and her ears, robbing her of breath and of rationality.

It had been an accident, she told herself with her first coherent thought. The stone had become dislodged through the erosion of time—that was what she had heard—and had fallen. The rocks about her, she saw when she looked, were dotted with similar boulders that must at some time have fallen from above.

No, it was not an accident. The stone had been pushed—by someone in a dark cloak. By the Duke of Portfrey? That was ridiculous. By Lauren? *Ridiculous!* Of course there had not been anyone up there. In that fraction of time she had seen danger to herself in the falling stone and had translated it into the danger she had been imagining ever since that afternoon up on the rhododendron walk.

But there had been someone there!

Was he there now, standing above her, waiting to see if he had succeeded in killing her? Or *she*?

Why would anyone want to kill her?

Was the would-be killer even now coming down the hill path into the valley to circle around onto the rocks and see for himself if he had succeeded? Or *she*?

Lily was mindless with panic again. If she moved a muscle, she thought, she would disintegrate. But if she did not move, she might stand here forever. If she did not move, she could be in no way mistress of her own fate. Memories came flooding back of similar moments during that long, terrifying walk through Spain and Portugal. Several times she had almost lost all nerve, imagining partisans behind every rock, imagining them not believing her story.

She stepped away from the cliff face on shaky legs and drew a slow breath. She looked upward. There was no one there—of course. There was no one down on the beach either—at least not yet. She was tempted to make her way in the opposite direction and hope that the tide was out far enough that she could reach the village and the company of other people. But she would not run from her fear. She would never conquer it if she did that. She clambered carefully back over the rocks to the beach. There was no one there. There was no one in the valley either, or on the hillside.

There was no one at all, she told herself firmly as she climbed resolutely upward. When she reached the top, she forced herself to take the wood path a short distance until she thought she must be close to the spot, and then she made her way through the trees until she came to the open land that ended with the cliff edge. Yes, she was in roughly the right place, though she did not approach the edge to make sure. There was no one there and no sign that anyone had been there.

All she had seen was a rock.

She was satisfied with the explanation until she drew closer to the abbey. Panic returned as the security of its walls drew nearer. Perhaps, she thought, she would have rushed through the front doors, demanded to know where Neville was, and gone hurtling into the safety of his arms if she had not remembered how she was dressed. But she did remember and so she went around to the side entrance and climbed the back stairs to her room. She washed and changed with hands that gradually grew steady again.

There was a knock on the door and it opened halfway before Dolly's head appeared around it.

"Oh, you *are* here, my lady," she said. "His

lordship has been looking for you. He is in the library, my lady."

"Thank you, Dolly."

Lily had to use all her willpower not to rush with unladylike haste. He was in the library, waiting for her. She could not reach him fast enough. More than anything in the world she wanted to feel his arms about her. She wanted to press her body to his and feel his warmth and his strength. She wanted to rest her head against his shoulder and hear the steady beating of his heart.

She wanted to climb right inside him.

15

The afternoon's post had brought the rest of the replies Neville had awaited. But Lily had been nowhere to be found. She had returned from the village with his mother but had not come down for tea. He was not surprised after he had heard his mother's account of the afternoon. Being stranded at the vicarage for two hours had severely embarrassed her. He did not doubt that Lily had been gently scolded on the way home.

He would have found the thought of her lengthy absence in the lower village amusing if he had not been feeling so agitated. He had stayed in the drawing room for a scant half hour and had been pacing in the library ever since. It was impossible to settle to any task.

At last there was a tap on the door, it opened,

and Lily came past the footman in a rush, it seemed, until she came to a sudden stop before him, flushed and smiling. He held out both hands and she set her own in them.

"Lily." He raised both hands to his lips and then leaned forward to kiss her lips. But he paused as he was lifting his head away and searched her eyes with his own. "What is the matter?"

She hesitated and her hands gripped his own more tightly. "Nothing," she said breathlessly. "It was just foolishness."

"More shadows?" he asked. He had hoped last night would have banished them forever. But he must not expect that it would have solved every problem.

She shook her head and smiled. "You wished to see me?"

"Yes. Come and sit down." He kept hold of one of her hands and led her to one of the leather chairs that flanked the fireplace. He took the other chair after she had seated herself. "Did my mother upset you? Is that it? Did she scold you?"

"Oh." She bit her lip. "No, not really. She meant to be kind. She believes I should make more of an effort to behave as the Countess of Kilbourne ought, and of course she is right. I kept her waiting for—oh, for a very long time. I suppose it did not occur to her that I could have walked home."

No, it would not have. "I would wager," he said, "that a couple of my tenants were quite delighted with you this afternoon. You have a gift for delighting people." Himself included.

She gazed at him but did not reply. He felt suddenly nervous and leaned back in his chair. He had not asked her here to discuss the afternoon's events. He just did not know how to broach what he had to say. He must just say it, he supposed.

"We will be leaving for London in the morning," he said. "Just you and I, Lily. I thought at first of going alone, but when I gave the matter more careful consideration, I realized it would be better to take you with me."

"To London?"

He nodded. "I need to procure a special license," he told her. "I could get it in London and bring it back here and we could marry in the village church. It could all be done within a week, I daresay. But it might cause confusion in minds that do not need to be confused."

"A special license." She was looking blankly at him.

"A marriage license. So that we can marry, Lily, without the delay of banns." He really was not explaining this very well at all, he thought uneasily.

"But we *are* married." Blankness was turning to puzzlement.

"Yes." His hands, he noticed, were gripping the arms of his chair. He relaxed them. "Yes, we are, Lily, in every way that matters. But the church and the state are very particular about certain really rather unimportant details. The Reverend Parker-Rowe died in that ambush, and his belongings were abandoned with his body. Captain Harris confirmed that fact in a letter I received yesterday.

Today I have received answers to several other letters I wrote on the day of your arrival. Our marriage papers were lost, Lily, before they could be properly registered. Our marriage, it seems, does not exist in the eyes of either the church or the state. We must go through the ceremony again."

"We are not married?" Her blue eyes had widened and were staring, unblinking, back into his own.

"We *are*, Lily," he hastened to assure her. "But we must satisfy the powers-that-be by making it quite unquestionably legal. No one need know except us. We will go to London—perhaps for a week or two to do some shopping, to see some of the sights, even to take in some of the entertainments of the Season. And while we are there, we will marry by special license. I will not allow this to be an embarrassment to you. No one will know."

He desperately wanted to save her from the shock of feeling utterly alone and abandoned. He was very aware that she had no one but him. He did not want her to believe, even for a single moment, that he would seize upon this small loophole to wriggle out of his obligation to her.

"We are not married." There was nothing in her eyes that suggested she had listened to anything else. They looked dazed. Her face was pale.

"Lily," he said distinctly, "you must not fear. I have no intention of abandoning you. We *are* married. But there is a formality we must observe."

"I am Lily Doyle," she said. "I am still Lily Doyle."

He got to his feet then and closed the distance between them. He reached out a hand for hers. Foolish Lily. After last night how could she doubt for a moment? But he had given all the facts too abruptly. He had not prepared her. Deuce take it, he was a clumsy oaf.

Lily did not take his hand. But when she looked up into his eyes, he could see that the dazed look had gone from hers.

"We are not married," she said. "Oh, thank God."

"Thank God?" He felt as if his stomach had performed a somersault inside him.

"Oh, do you not see?" she asked him, and she gripped the arms of her chair and leaned toward him. "We never should have married, but I was in shock after Papa's death and frightened too, and you were being loyal to him and chivalrous to me. But it was a dreadful mistake on both our parts. Even if we could have spent the rest of our lives with the regiment it would have been a mistake. Even there the gap between an officer and a sergeant's daughter would have been a huge one. I could not easily have been an officer's wife and mixed with the other wives. But here." With one sweep of an arm she seemed to indicate the whole of Newbury Abbey and everyone who lived within its house and park. "Here the gap is quite insurmountable. It is an impossible one. I have dreamed of escape, just as you must have done. And now by some miracle it has been granted us. We are *not married*."

239

It had never, even for one moment, occurred to him that she might be *glad* to hear the truth. He was suddenly overwhelmed by a terror he had had no chance of bracing himself against. He had lost her once, forever he had thought. And then, by some glorious miracle, she had been restored to him. Was he to lose her again even more cruelly than before? Was she going to *leave* him? No, no, no, she did not understand. He went down on his haunches before her chair and possessed himself of both her hands.

"Lily," he said, "there are some things more important than church or state. There is honor, for example. I promised your dying father that I would marry you. At our wedding I vowed before you and before God and witnesses to love and to cherish and keep you until my death. I had your virginity that night. We were together again last night. Even if we never go through the ceremony that will make all legal, I will always consider myself your husband. You are my *wife*."

"No." There was no vestige of color in her face, except for her blue eyes intent on his. She shook her head. "No, I am not. Not if everyone else says it is not so. And not if it *ought* not to be so and if we do not wish it to be so."

"It ought not to be? I have been inside your body, Lily." He squeezed her hands until she winced. Though it was more than just that—far more. He had been...united with her. Last night they had become one.

She looked back directly into his eyes. Her lips moved stiffly when she spoke. "So has

240

Manuel," she said. "But he is not my husband either."

He recoiled almost as if she had slapped him. *Manuel.* Neville shut his eyes tightly and fought a wave of dizziness and nausea. The man now had a name. And she was putting the two of them on the same footing—men who had possessed her but had no marital claim on her. Was there really no difference in her mind? Had last night been nothing to her except sex? Except the exorcism of some of her demons? He would not believe it.

"Lily," he said, "after last night you may be with child. Have you thought of that? You *must* marry me." But that was not the reason. Not practical details like that. She was his *love.* He was hers.

"I am barren, sir," she said, her voice quite flat. "Have you not wondered how I could have been with Manuel for seven months without conceiving? We must *not* marry. You must marry someone who can be the Countess of Kilbourne as well as your wife. You will be able to marry Lauren after all. She is the one for you, I think. She is *right* in every way."

He squeezed her hands again before getting to his feet and running the fingers of one hand through his hair. This was madness. He must be in the throes of some bizarre nightmare. "I *love* you, Lily," he told her, recognizing the frustrating inadequacy of words even as he spoke. "I thought you loved me. I thought that was what last night was all about. And our wedding night too."

She was staring up at him with set, pale face

and eyes brimming with tears. "Love has nothing to do with it," she said. "Can you not *see*? That I could be your mistress but not your wife? Not your countess?" Before he could draw breath to protest his outrage, she spoke again, her voice low and toneless. "But I will not be your mistress."

Lord God!

"What would you do?" He was whispering, he realized. He cleared his throat. He could not believe he was actually asking these questions. "Where would you go?"

Her lips moved without sound for a moment, and he felt a glimmer of hope. She had no alternative but to stay with him. She had no one else, nowhere else. But he had reckoned without Lily's indomitable spirit. Her quiet, sometimes almost childlike demeanor were as illusory now as they had always been.

"I shall go to London," she said, "if you will be so good as to lend me the fare for the stagecoach. I believe Mrs. Harris might be willing to help me find employment. Oh, if *only* I could have returned to Lisbon in time to find my father's pack. There might have been enough money there... But no matter." She stopped talking for a few moments. "You must not worry about me. You have been kind and honorable and would continue to be kind if I would allow it. But you are not responsible for me."

He leaned one arm against the mantel and stared unseeing down into the empty fireplace. "Don't insult me, Lily," he said. "Don't accuse me of acting toward you only out of compassion and honor." He fought panic. "You will not marry me, then? You have hardened your heart? There is nothing I can say to persuade you?"

"No, sir," she said softly.

It was the cruelest blow of all. He wondered if she had deliberately addressed him as if he were still an officer and she still a mere enlisted man's daughter. She had called him "sir."

"Lily." He was on the verge of tears. He closed his eyes and waited until he was sure he had control of his voice. "Lily, promise me that you will not run away. Promise me you will stay here at least for tonight and allow me to send you in my own carriage to someone who may indeed help you. I do not know who yet or how. I had not considered this possibility. Give me until tomorrow morning. Promise me? Please?"

He thought she was going to refuse. There was a lengthy silence. But the tremor in her voice when she spoke proclaimed the reason for it. She was as close to breaking down as he.

"Forgive me," she said at last. "I did not mean an insult. Ah, I did not mean to hurt you. Neville? I did not. But I must go. Surely you understand that. I cannot stay. I promise. I will wait until tomorrow."

⌒

Sir Samuel Wollston and Lady Mary had come the five miles to Newbury Abbey with their four sons in order to dine one more

243

time with the family members who were planning to leave the following day. Lauren and Gwendoline had come from the dower house. The Duke and Duchess of Anburey, Joseph and Wilma, the dowager countess, and Elizabeth were with them in the drawing room when Neville entered and made Lily's excuses. She had a headache, he told them all.

"The poor dear," Aunt Mary said. "I am a martyr to the migraines myself and know how she must suffer."

"It is a dashed shame, Nev," Hal Wollston said. "I was looking forward to seeing Lily again. She is a good sport."

"I am sorry, Neville," Lauren told him. "Will you give her my best wishes for her recovery when you see her later?"

Neville bowed to her.

"She was very sensible not to come down if she has a headache," Elizabeth said.

The dowager was not quite so kind. She spoke in a quiet aside to Neville. "This is the sort of family event," she said, "at which it is important that your countess appear at your side, Neville. Are these headaches to become regular occurrences? I wonder. Lily does not strike me as the type of woman to suffer from nervous indispositions."

"She has a headache, Mama," he said firmly, "and is to be excused."

The truth could not be kept from them for long, of course. It might have been if Lily had fallen in with his plans as he had fully expected her to do. Indeed, his mind could still not quite grasp the reality of the fact that he was not married to Lily and was not going to be. That he had no claim on her. That she was leaving him. That he would not see her again after tomorrow.

Yet there had been last night...

But there was an evening to be lived through. At first he intended to live out to the end of it the charade he had begun with the announcement of Lily's illness. Everyone else appeared to be in a cheerful mood, perhaps because of the presence of several young people. Even young Derek Wollston, who was only fifteen years old, had been allowed to dine with the adults. But Neville changed his mind. There were going to be enough letters of explanation to write as it was. This evening offered the perfect opportunity to break the news to at least a number of those most nearly concerned.

And so when his mother gave the signal after the last cover had been removed from the table for the ladies to adjourn to the drawing room and leave the gentlemen to their port, he spoke up.

"I beg that you will stay for a while, Mama," he said, raising his voice so that it could be heard the length of the table. "And all the ladies, please. I have something to say."

His mother sat down again with a smile and all eyes turned his way. He toyed for a moment with the one spoon left on the table before him. He had not planned what he would say. He had always considered rehearsed speeches an abomination. He raised his eyes and looked about at the various members of his family.

Most were looking at him with polite interest—perhaps they expected a speech of farewell to those who were leaving. A few smiled. Joseph winked. Elizabeth looked at him alertly, as if she read something in his countenance that the others had not yet seen there.

"Lily does not have a headache," he said.

The silence took on a note of decided discomfort. Uncle Samuel cleared his throat. Aunt Sadie fingered her pearls.

"She discovered this afternoon," he said, "that she is not my wife. Not legally, at least."

The silence first became tense and then was lost as everyone, it appeared, tried to question him at once. Neville held up a hand and they all stopped as abruptly as they had started.

"I suspected that it might be so on the day she arrived here," he said, and he proceeded to give them the same explanation he had given Lily earlier. It was not enough that the marriage ceremony really had occurred and that a properly ordained minister had conducted it. It was not enough that he and Lily had made vows to each other and that one of the witnesses was still alive to attest to the fact. There were formalities to be observed before a marriage was valid in the eyes of church and state. And those formalities had not been completed in their case because the Reverend Parker-Rowe had died and the papers had been lost. One of the witnesses had died at Ciudad Rodrigo a month later.

"So Lily is not your wife," the Duke of Anburey said redundantly when Neville had finished speaking. "You never were married to her."

"I say!" Hal exclaimed, sounding dismayed.

"Lily is not the Countess of Kilbourne after all," Aunt Mary said, shaking her head and looking somewhat dazed. "I do not wonder that she has the migraines, the poor dear. *You* still have the title, Clara."

Most of those gathered about the table had something to add—except the countess, who stared at him in silence, and Joseph, who looked at him with knitted brows, and Lauren, who gazed expressionlessly down at the table.

"But, Neville." Elizabeth had leaned forward, and as often happened when she spoke, everyone stopped to listen. "You are surely intending to satisfy the proprieties by marrying Lily again, are you not?"

All eyes turned Neville's way. He tried to smile and failed miserably. "She will not have me," he said. "She has refused me and will not be moved."

"*What?*" The countess spoke for the first time.

"I planned to leave for London with her tomorrow morning, Mama," he told her. "We would have married quietly there by special license and no one but the two of us would have been any the wiser. But she will not do it. She will not marry me."

Unexpectedly Elizabeth smiled as she sat back in her chair. "No, she would not," she said more to herself than to anyone else.

It was Gwendoline who vocalized one of the

implications of what they had all heard. She clasped her hands to her bosom and her eyes lit up.

"Oh, but this is wonderful!" she exclaimed, smiling warmly at her brother. "You and Lauren can marry after all, Nev. You can set a new wedding date and we can begin new plans. A summer wedding will be lovelier than a spring wedding. You can carry roses, Lauren."

Neville's hand closed tightly about the spoon. He drew breath to reply, but Lauren spoke first, her voice breathless.

"No," she said. "No, Gwen. The past nine days cannot simply be erased as if they never were. Nothing can be the same as it was before." She raised her eyes and looked into his. "Can it, Neville?"

He did not know if she wished him to corroborate her words or if she was begging him to disagree with her. He could only give her honesty. He shook his head.

"The truth is," he said, "that I made vows to Lily in all good faith. I fully intended to honor them for a lifetime. Does it make any difference that they are not legally binding? Are they not *morally* binding? And would I wish them not to be? I consider Lily to be my wife. I believe I always will."

Lauren lowered her eyes again. It was impossible to know if she was satisfied or disappointed. One rarely did know with Lauren what her deepest feelings were. Dignity always came first with her. She was dignified now—and pale and beautiful. He felt

248

an ache of deep affection for her. And a yearning to release her from the pain she surely must be feeling. But he was helpless to do anything.

"That is absurd, Neville," his mother said crisply. "Are you above the state? Above the church? If the church says you are not married, then of course you are not. And it is your duty to marry a lady suited to your station and able to give you heirs."

Lily was not a lady; she was not suited to his station; by her own admission, she was incapable of giving him heirs. But Lily was his *wife*.

"The whole thing will be a nine days' wonder, I daresay," the duke said. "The *ton* will be delighted by the story and will forget it as soon as some other sensation or scandal rears its head. Your mother is right, Neville—you must resume your former way of life as soon as possible. Marry someone of your own kind. I do not wish to be unkind to Lily, but—"

"Then do not be, Uncle Webster," Neville said quietly but so firmly that his uncle stopped midsentence and flushed. "If anyone has slurs to cast upon Lily, I beg to inform that person that I will defend her honor in any way I deem necessary—just as surely as if the whole world acknowledged her as my wife."

"Oh, I say," Richard Wollston said. "Bravo, Nev."

"Hold your tongue," his father instructed him sharply.

"Tempers are becoming frayed," Elizabeth said, and proceeded to bring up another pertinent point that no one else seemed to have considered—though it had tormented Neville ever since Lily had left him in the library earlier in the afternoon. "What is to become of Lily, Neville? What will she do? As I understand it, she has no family that she knows of in England."

"She wants to go to London to look for employment," he said. "I dread the thought. I hope she will agree to allow me to make a settlement on her and find her a decent home somewhere. But I am afraid she will not agree. She is a proud woman and a stubborn one, I believe."

Gwendoline's eyes were swimming in tears. "I am so ashamed," she said. "My first thought was for what this could mean for our happiness—Lauren's and Nev's and mine. I did not even wonder what would happen to Lily. I wish—oh yes, I *do* wish—that she had not come into our lives at all. But she has come and I have liked her despite myself. Now I feel dreadfully sorry for her. She will not simply run away, Nev?"

"She has promised not to," he assured her.

"Neville," Elizabeth said, "perhaps I can do something for Lily. I have connections in London and a great liking for her even if she *did* come along to dash the happiness of my poor Lauren. Will you allow me to talk with her?"

"I wish you would, Elizabeth," he said. "Perhaps you could persuade her to change her mind? To marry me after all?"

"Do nothing in haste, Neville," the duke

advised. "You have been given a second chance to choose your countess wisely. You would be well advised to take time to make the decision with your considered judgment rather than with your raw emotions."

Elizabeth got to her feet. "Where is she?" she asked. "In her room?"

"I believe so," he said. One could never be sure with Lily, but that was where she had been when he came down for dinner. She had been curled up on a chair close to the window, gazing out. She had not turned her head to look at him or responded to any of his questions except to shrug her shoulders in a defensive rather than a careless gesture. She had changed, he had noticed, into her old cotton dress.

"I will go up to her now, then," Elizabeth said, "if you will all excuse me."

Forbes, Neville realized belatedly, was standing silently at the sideboard. But it did not matter. Such a truth as the fact that he and Lily were not married could not be kept from the servants anyway. They might as well learn the full story from the butler as be regaled piecemeal with a mixture of truth and rumor over the coming days.

"Perhaps," Neville said, getting to his feet too and pushing back his chair with the backs of his knees, "we should all adjourn to the drawing room. I have no wish to imbibe port for the next half hour or so."

Derek and his brother William, aged seventeen, looked almost comically disappointed. The wave of humor Neville felt in noticing it felt incongruous with his other feelings. But it served to remind him that somehow life went on through even the worst upheavals to which it was subjected.

He was going to find that pack of Doyle's for Lily, he thought suddenly, if it was humanly possible to do so. Whatever it had contained for Lily might well have disappeared, especially if it was money, but perhaps he could retrieve something. She must be quite without a memento of her father, he realized. He remembered some of the things she had said to him when he showed her the gallery. It must be dreadful to have lost all of one's family, to be unacquainted with any who remained, to have lost everything connected with one's parents.

That was what he would do for her. If the pack still existed somewhere in this world, he would find it—even if it took him the rest of his life. He would restore something of her father to her.

It felt soothing to know that there was something, however slight, that he could do.

"Nev." Joseph, Marquess of Attingsborough, set a hand on his shoulder as they were all leaving the dining room. "You don't need drawing room chatter this evening, old chap. You need to get thoroughly foxed. Would you care for sympathetic company while you do it?"

16

Lily was still sitting on the chair she had dragged close to the window, her legs curled up beneath her. She had got up only once since she had come hurrying upstairs from the library, pulled off with frantic haste the pretty new clothes she had so recently donned, and threw on the old cotton dress again instead. She had got up to drag a blanket from the bed and wrap it about herself. The evening had turned chilly, though she would not close the window. She continued to stare out into the darkness.

The soft tap on the door of her bedchamber did not disturb her. She simply ignored it. It would be him, and she could not look at him or speak to him. Her resolve might slip and she might cling to him—for the rest of her life. She would not allow that to happen. Love was not enough. She loved him—she *adored* him— to the depths of her soul, but it simply was not enough. She did not belong in his life. He did not belong in hers—though that thought was potentially frightening. She did not have a life. But she refused to be daunted by the yawning emptiness that lay beyond this final night at Newbury Abbey.

"Lily?" It was Elizabeth's voice. "May I come in, my dear? May I sit here beside you?"

Lily looked up. As usual Elizabeth was the epitome of understated elegance in a dark- green high-waisted gown, her blond hair dressed in a smoothly shining coiffure. She was the quintessential aristocrat, daughter of an earl, educated, accomplished, a woman of immaculate but easy manners. And she was asking to sit beside a sergeant's daughter—Lily Doyle? Well. Lily had always been proud of her father; she cherished fond memories of her mother; she had grown up liking and respecting herself. Her self-respect had faltered during those seven months when she had chosen survival over defiance, but it had recovered. There was nothing in herself or in her life and background of which she was ashamed.

She nodded and returned her gaze to the darkness of the outdoors.

Elizabeth drew a chair close to Lily's and seated herself. She took one of Lily's hands in both her own. They were warm. For the first time Lily realized that she was still cold despite the blanket and the fact that the evening air was not so very cold after all.

"How I honor you, Lily," Elizabeth said.

Lily looked at her in surprise.

"You have done what is right for both Neville and yourself," Elizabeth said. "But it was not easy to do. You have given up a great deal."

"No." Lily shook her head. "It is not difficult to give up Newbury Abbey and all this." She gestured about her with her free arm. "You do not understand. This is the sort of life to which you were born. I grew up in the train of an army."

"What I meant," Elizabeth said gently,

"was that you have given up Neville. You love him." It was not a question.

"It is not enough," Lily said.

"No, it is not, my dear." Elizabeth agreed. They sat together in silence for a while before she spoke again. "Neville says that you wish to find employment."

"Yes," Lily said. "I do not know what I am qualified to do, but I am willing to work hard. I think perhaps Mrs. Harris, with whom I came to England from Lisbon, will help me find something if I ask her."

"I can offer you employment," Elizabeth said.

"You?" Lily stared at her.

Elizabeth smiled. "I am six-and-thirty years old, Lily," she said, "and long past the age of needing chaperones wherever I go. But I am a woman living alone and there are conventions to be observed. I am expected to have a companion in residence and in tow whenever I venture out without male escort. I had Cousin Harriet with me for five years, but she was provoking enough to marry a rector just four months ago and leave me companionless. I was delighted for her, of course—she is older than I and has always believed that a woman is not a complete person until she gives up her personhood in order to marry. And, really, Lily, she was a trial to me. Two women so different in character and temperament it would be difficult to find. I need a replacement. I need a companion. Will you be she? It would be a salaried position, of course."

Lily despised herself for the rush of gladness she felt. But it would not do.

"You are kind," she said. "But I am in no way equipped to offer you companionship. Consider my deficiencies—I cannot read or write; I cannot paint or play the pianoforte; I know nothing about the theater or music or— or *anything*. I am not of your world. If you found your cousin tiresome, you would soon find me impossible."

"Oh, Lily." Elizabeth smiled and squeezed Lily's hand, which she still held. "If you knew how dull life can be for a woman of *ton*, you would not so readily reject my offer. One is cabin'd, cribb'd, and confin'd at every turn, to borrow a phrase. One is subjected to insipid company, insipid entertainments, and insipid conversation, largely because one is a woman. You cannot know, perhaps, what a delight you have been to me in the past week and a half. You think you have nothing to offer by way of companionship because you do not know the things that I know. Well, I know them, my dear. I do not need to be told them by someone else. But I do not know the things *you* know. We could share worlds, Lily. We could entertain each other. Life with you in my home would be great *fun*, I daresay. And you have a lively, intelligent mind, even if you do not realize it—intelligence is *such* an important attribute. Do say you will come— as my friend. For convenience's sake you would be my employee since you will need something on which to live. But to all intents and purposes you would simply be my friend. What do you say?"

She would be an employee, Lily thought.

But within the confines of her employment she would also be a sort of equal. Elizabeth did not believe they were of unequal
mind or intelligence. She believed that
Lily would have as much to offer a friendship as she did. Lily was not quite convinced,
but the temptation to say yes was strong.
Overwhelming, in fact, when the alterna-
tives were so few.

"Perhaps for a short while, then," she said.
"But if you find that I am not what you
expect, then you must tell me so and I will
leave. I will not be anyone's charity case."

Elizabeth raised her eyebrows. "I would not
bring anyone into my own home out of charity,
Lily," she said. "I have far too great a regard
for my own comfort. But I agree to your
terms. And they will work both ways. If you
find after a while that I am impossible to
work for, then you must tell me so and I will
help you find something else. Can you be
ready to leave in the morning?"

"Sooner," Lily said fervently. "But I promised
that I would stay tonight."

"And quite right too," Elizabeth said.
"Neville is not happy with the turn of events,
Lily. Not happy at all. You are not intending
to leave behind all your new clothes by any
chance, are you?"

"I must," Lily said. "They were bought
for his wife. I am not his wife."

"But he would be dreadfully hurt if you did
not take them with you." Elizabeth told her.
"Sometimes pride can be selfish. Will you take
them as a gift from him? It is not wrong, my

dear. It is not greedy. It is the right thing to do. It would be cruel not to."

"Lily bit her lip. But she nodded.

"Splendid!" Elizabeth got to her feet. "We will leave early. Try to sleep?" She bent and kissed Lily's cheek.

Lily nodded. "Thank you," she said. But she stopped Elizabeth before she reached the door. One troubling possibility had occurred to her. "Will the Duke of Portfrey travel with us?"

"No. Provoking man." Elizabeth laughed. "He left this afternoon. He is not going straight to London and may not be there for a few weeks. But he did not abandon me, you know—not that I have any claim on his company anyway. Webster and Sadie will be accompanying us in their own carriage—and Wilma, of course. And Joseph will be leaving at the same time as us, though I expect he will ride on ahead at a pace more suited to his youth and gender. Fortunate man!"

Lily nodded and felt enormous relief. The Duke of Portfrey had gone. He would not be in London for a while. But he had left this afternoon? Suddenly? After he had made his attempt on her life, perhaps? Had he assumed success? But she was horrified by the direction of her thoughts. There had been no man. And even if there had been, there was no proof he had been the Duke of Portfrey. It might as easily have been a woman anyway. But if it had been Lauren, then there would be no more stalking or attempts at creating accidents. Lauren would be free to secure

Neville's affections again. In all probability there had been no one at all. That fallen rock really had been an accident.

She closed her eyes after Elizabeth had left and rested her head against the back of the chair. She thought about her wedding and her wedding night, about the dream of reunion that had kept her sane during her captivity, about the long, lonely, dangerous trek back to Lisbon and the fruitless search for him there and for someone to believe her story, about the long voyage to England and Newbury, about finding him in the church in the village about to marry someone else, about all the events of the past week and a half.

About last night.

Two tears escaped from beneath her eyelashes and ran unchecked down her cheeks to drip onto her dress.

And about this afternoon's disclosures in the library.

She had not yet fully faced the reality of a shattered dream. She dared not look into the future. It appeared brighter now, or at least more secure, than it had an hour ago, it was true. But it was to be a future lived without *him*. Without Neville.

There had always been Neville since she was fourteen, even though for four of those years he had been unattainable and for a year and a half he had been unreachable. But always there had been the dream of him. Dream and reality had touched last night—she had been quite aware even at the time that it was a mere touch that could not last. But she had not realized that so soon they would be completely severed. She had not realized that by tonight she would have reached the end of her dream.

Even though she still loved him and always would.

Even though he loved her.

The end of the impossible dream.

Well, she thought, opening her eyes and getting to her feet in order to prepare for bed, she would survive. That had always been the chief purpose in life of the people with whom she had grown up—simply to survive. She would do it. Perhaps somewhere in the future there was another dream waiting to be dreamed. She could not imagine it now, but she could hope.

She could dream about a dream. She smiled at the absurdity—and the sustaining hope—of the thought.

⌇

Neville did not get drunk. He sat in the library with the Marquess of Attingsborough and toyed with the temptation to seek temporary oblivion while he downed two brandies in quick succession, but he drank no more. Liquor would not cure what ailed him. It would only cloud his mind for what must be faced in the morning.

Lily was leaving him in the morning.

"I wish there were something to say, Nev," the marquess said, setting down his own half-empty glass—his first. "When I was at the church with you nine days ago, I thought there could be no worse disaster than what happened. But there was, damn it. There was this."

"Do you think wringing her neck would help?" Neville chuckled, but the attempt at humor, black as it was, only made him feel worse. He rested his head against the back of his chair and closed his eyes.

"She is a rare one," Joseph said. He chuckled inappropriately. "Who else but Lily would have the deuced nerve to refuse you? Especially when there seems to be nothing else for her. And more especially when she is devilish fond of you."

"Perhaps Elizabeth will persuade her to change her mind," Neville said hopefully. "What will I do if she fails? I promised Lily's father I would look after her. I made her vows. I—Well, all this has little to do with promises and vows. I—You would not under-stand, Joe."

"Being an inanimate block who has never tumbled into love and dreamed that he has found that one and only love he would never tumble out of again?" his cousin said ruefully. "Your feelings for her are pretty obvious, Nev, and look pretty enduring to me. I have envied you. We have all fallen a little under Lily's spell."

But Elizabeth stepped into the room at that moment, and they both scrambled to their feet. She looked significantly at their glasses but made no comment.

"Well?" Neville's hands had formed into tight fists at his sides.

"Lily will be coming to London with me in the morning, Neville," she said. "She has accepted employment with me. As my companion."

"*What?*" Neville could only stare at her incredulously.

The marquess cleared his throat and shuffled his feet awkwardly.

"It is what she has chosen," Elizabeth said calmly. "It will be a respectable position for her, Neville."

"Did you even try to persuade her to stay and marry me?" he asked her. But her expression gave him his answer without the need of words. All his pent-up anxieties exploded in anger. "You did not, did you? You had no intention of doing so. You deliberately misled me. Do you too want to take her out of the way, Elizabeth, so that the stage will be cleared here for a resumption of things as they were? Nothing can be as it was. Lily is my *wife*. I *love* her. Can no one understand that fact just because she is not a *lady*? She is lady enough for me. She is *my* lady. I am going to go up there now and—"

"No, Neville," she said quietly before he could take more than one purposeful step in the direction of the door. "No, my dear. It would be the wrong thing to do. Wrong for you. Wrong for Lily."

"And you know what is right for us?" Neville's eyes blazed at her. "*You*, Elizabeth? The spinster aunt? What do *you* know of love?"

"Watch it, Nev, old boy," Joseph said quietly.

Neville raked the fingers of one hand through his hair. "I am sorry," he said. "Oh, the devil. Forgive me, Elizabeth. I am so sorry."

"I would be worried," she said, quite unruffled, "if you did not react to all this with passion, Neville. But listen to me, please. This may very well prove to be the best thing that could have happened for both of you. You love her—I do not even need to ask if it is so. But you must admit that your marriage stood every chance of turning into a dismally unhappy one. Perhaps the next time you offer Lily marriage there will be more than just love and obligation to bring you together."

"The next time?" His eyebrows snapped together while the marquess strolled to one of the bookcases and examined the spines of the books on a level with his eyes.

"You were never the man to give up without a fight what you most wanted in life, Neville," she said. "And I seriously doubt there is anything you have wanted more than you want Lily. Are you really planning to give her up so easily?"

He gazed at her for several silent moments. His emotions were still raw. He could still not contemplate the prospect of Lily's leaving him on the morrow. He had not really considered the possibility of getting her back once she had left Newbury Abbey. Either she married him now, he had thought, or he would be forced to live all the rest of his life without her.

"When?"

"That is not for me to say," she told him, shaking her head. "Perhaps never. Certainly not within a month at the soonest."

"One month."

"Not one day sooner," she told him. "But we are to make an early start in the morning. I am going to bed. Good night, Neville. Good night, Joseph."

There was silence in the library after she had left, Neville staring at the door, Joseph continuing to peruse the books on the shelf without picking one up.

"It would be a foolish hope," Neville said eventually. "It would, Joe. Would it not?"

"Oh, devil take it." His cousin sighed audibly. "Who can predict female behavior, Nev? Not I, old chap. But I have always had the highest respect for Elizabeth."

"Promise me something," Neville said.

"Anything, Nev." The marquess turned from the bookcase and looked broodingly across the room at his cousin.

"Keep an eye on her," Neville said. "If she shows signs of being desperately unhappy—"

"The devil, Nev," the marquess said. "*If* she is unhappy? The point is, old chap, that she is free and that she will continue to make her own choices. But I will call on Elizabeth a few times. And I will ride beside her carriage all the way to London, which will be a considerable trial to my nerves since my father's carriage will be close by too and travel with my mother and Wilma is never a comfortable business. I'll see that Lily gets safe to London, though. My honor on it."

"Thank you."

"And who knows?" Joseph spoke cheerfully and crossed the room again to clap a friendly hand on Neville's shoulder. "Perhaps Elizabeth is right and Lily will see more clearly what she is missing once she is away from you. Elizabeth knows more about the workings of the female mind than I do. Are you going to get foxed or shall we call it a night and turn in?"

"I don't think I could get drunk if I tried, Joe," Neville told him. "But thanks for the thought."

"What are friends for?" the marquess asked him.

⤿

Neville went to bed buoyed with some faint hope. He even slept in snatches. But in the morning he could hear only the echo of Elizabeth's words *perhaps never*, and the sound of them drowned out hope.

They were all leaving together—Aunt Sadie and Uncle Webster with Wilma, Joe on horseback, Elizabeth with Lily. The terrace was crowded with people saying and hugging their farewells—even Gwen and Lauren had come up from the dower house for the purpose. Lily had her share of hugs, Neville noticed as he took his leave of everyone else; neither Lauren nor Gwen was dry-eyed after

265

saying good-bye to her. She was wearing the pretty blue carriage dress that had recently been made for her—he had been very much afraid that she would refuse to take any of her new clothes.

He turned to her last, and he was aware of everyone else moving tactfully away, giving them a modicum of privacy. He took her gloved right hand in both of his and looked into her eyes. They were huge and calm and clear of the tears that were flowing free among the others.

He reached for something to say to her but could think of nothing. She stared mutely at him. He raised her hand to his lips and kept it there for several moments while he closed his eyes. But when he looked back into her face, there was still nothing to say. No, that was not right. There was everything in the world to say but no words with which to say any of it. And so he said nothing.

Until she did.

"Neville." There was almost no sound, but her lips unmistakably formed his name.

Ah, God! How he had longed to hear her say his name again. She had spoken it yesterday afternoon. She was saying it now. But he felt as if his heart had been pierced by a sharp dagger.

"Lily," he whispered, his head bent close to hers. "Stay. Change your mind. Stay with me. We can make it work."

But she was shaking her head slowly.

"We cannot," she said. "We cannot. Th-that night. I am glad there was that night."

"Lily—"

But she tore her hand from his grasp and hurried toward the open door of Elizabeth's carriage. He watched in wretched despair as a footman handed her inside.

She took her seat beside Elizabeth and stared blankly at the cushions of the seat opposite. The footman put up the steps and closed the door. The carriage jerked slightly on its springs and was in motion.

Neville swallowed once, twice. He fought panic, the urge to lunge forward, to tear open the door, to drag her out into his arms and refuse ever to let her go.

He raised a hand in farewell, but she did not look back.

Perhaps never. The words echoed and reechoed in his brain.

Ah, my love. Once dreams were shattered, there could be no assurance that they could ever be pieced together and dreamed again.

PART IV

The Education of a Lady

"Amuse me, Lily," her new employer commanded her after the first hour of near silence and raw pain had passed, "and answer some questions. You must answer truthfully—that is the one cardinal rule of what-ifs."

Lily turned a determinedly smiling face to her. She still did not know how she could possibly be a competent companion to Elizabeth, but she would try her very best.

"If you had the freedom and the means to do any one thing in the world you wished to do," Elizabeth asked, "what would it be?"

Go back to Neville. But that would be a nonsensical answer. She had the freedom to go back. He had begged her to stay. But going back to him would mean going back to Newbury Abbey too and all it involved. Lily thought hard. But the answer to the question, she found eventually, should have been obvious to her from the first moment.

"I would learn to read and write," she said. "Is that two things?"

"We will consider it one," Elizabeth said, clapping her hands. "What a delightful answer. I can see that you are not going to be a disappointment, Lily. Now something else. Perhaps we will gather five wishes altogether. Proceed."

Yes, there were other things to dream of, Lily thought. Nothing sufficient to replace the dream she had lost, of course, but perhaps enough to give life some purpose. These new dreams would probably prove unattainable, but then that was the nature of dreams. It was their very attraction. But *probably* was the all-important word. It allowed for hope.

"I would learn to play the pianoforte," she said with conviction, "and to know all there is to know about music."

"Now that is definitely more than one thing," Elizabeth protested, laughing. "But since I have made the rules of the game, I will allow its essential unity. Next?"

Lily glanced at Elizabeth, who looked both lovely and elegant in carriage clothes that were coordinated in colors of brown, bronze, and cream, and that were perfectly suited to her age and rank and figure and coloring.

"I would learn how to dress correctly and elegantly and perhaps even fashionably," she said.

"But you already look all those things in that particular ensemble, Lily," Elizabeth told her. "Pale blue is certainly a good color for you."

"You chose everything I am wearing," Lily reminded her, "except my shift and my shoes. I could do nothing alone—I would have no idea. To me a garment has always been something that is comfortable and decent and warm in winter or cool in summer."

"Very well, then." Elizabeth smiled. "It is number three. And numbers four and five? Do you have no wish to travel or to acquire expensive possessions?"

"I have traveled all my life," Lily said. "I

have dreamed of staying in one place long enough for it to feel like home. And possessions..." She shrugged. What else would she choose to make this list complete? She would read and write and learn about music. She would play the pianoforte and dress well and elegantly. She would...

"I would like to be able to figure," Lily said. "Not just on my fingers or in my head, but— oh, but as Mrs. Ailsham and the countess do in the household books. They showed them to me one morning. They could both make sense of what was written there and they could use the figures to know what had been happening at the abbey and to plan what would happen. I *wish* I could do that. I wish I could keep books and know how to run something as big and important as Newbury Abbey."

"And your last wish, Lily?"

"I have always been comfortable with other people," she said after thinking for a while longer. "All kinds of people, even the officers when they were a part of the regiment. But I do not feel comfortable with *your* kind of people. I would like to learn...how to behave, how to converse, how to do what is expected of me. I would like to learn the manners of your class. Not because I aspire to belong to it, but because—oh, I do not know quite why. Because I admire you, perhaps. Because I respect the countess."

Elizabeth said nothing for a while. "I am not sure I should consider your wishes as five, Lily," she said at last. "Really they are all one—the desire for knowledge and the education of a lady. One might add painting and needlework and dancing and the knowledge of languages, perhaps, but they would really be included in one or other of the five things for which you have wished. *Do* you paint or dance or know any languages other than English? I know that you can darn and mend but not embroider."

"I can speak Hindi and Spanish," Lily said. "We used to dance country dances. I have never painted."

But their conversation was interrupted at that point by the carriage's turning into the cobbled yard of a posting inn for a change of horses. It was amazing to Lily to realize that after the first hour her mind had been pleasantly occupied. She had been almost enjoying herself. And it was all Elizabeth's doing—she had set herself to take her companion's mind off the wretched misery of that parting.

The Duke of Anburey had bespoken a private parlor at the inn, and the six of them dined together. Lady Wilma was ecstatic at the prospect of going at last to London, where the Season would already be in progress. Her conversation was all of balls and routs and theaters and court presentations and Vauxhall and Almack's. It was dizzying to Lily, who forced herself to eat at least a small meal and made no attempt to participate in anything that was being said even when Joseph suggested that the discomforts of their journey were probably nothing compared with those of the sort of traveling she had done in the Peninsula. She smiled vaguely at him even as she realized that, like Elizabeth, he was trying to divert her mind from what weighed it down like a ton of lead.

She kept wondering what *he* was doing at that precise moment.

Elizabeth resumed their interrupted conversation after Joseph had handed them back into the carriage and they were on their way again.

"Well, Lily," she said, patting her briskly on the knee, "I can see that the next month or two with you are going to be interesting indeed. Did I use the word *fun* yesterday? The coming months are certainly going to be fun—yes, it is quite the right word. We, my dear, with the help of all the best instructors I can hire, are going to transform you into a lady, with a lady's education and accomplishments—all within a month or two or ten. Obviously some things will take longer than others. What do you say?"

Lily said nothing for several moments. They had been playing a *game* of what-if, had they not? "No," she said, frowning. "Oh, no. Teachers would have to be paid salaries."

"And the best teachers would have to be paid *high* salaries." Elizabeth was smiling. "Lily, my dear, I am almost indecently wealthy."

"But you cannot spend any of it on me," Lily said, aghast. "I am your *servant*."

"Well, yes," Elizabeth agreed. "For your pride's sake I will concede that point, Lily. But servants, you know, have to earn their salaries. And how do they do that? By obeying their employers, by catering to their every whim.

I am one of the most fortunate of women, you know, for any number of reasons. But having everything—*almost* everything—one could possibly need can have its disadvantages, especially when one is a woman. There is a certain boredom with which to contend. I cannot tell you when I last had *fun*. Overseeing your education will be that, Lily. You must not deny me, not when you have confessed that it is what you want more than almost anything else in this world."

It had not been a game, Lily realized suddenly. And she had not been hired to serve—at least, not in any conventional sense. Elizabeth had intended this all along. She had intended to amuse herself and delight Lily by making a lady out of her.

It would be impossible.

It would not!

It would be glorious and wonderful. She could learn to read. She would be able to read *books*. She would be able to fill a room with music—with her very own fingers. She would be able... Oh, there were too many dazzling possibilities crowding her mind.

There was a new dream.

"What are you thinking?" Elizabeth asked.

"I will be able—when I leave you, that is," Lily said, "to find employment as a shop assistant or perhaps even as—as a governess." It was a dizzying prospect. She would acquire knowledge and then she would be able to pass it on to others.

"Of course," Elizabeth said. "Or perhaps you will marry, Lily. I intend to take you with me to meet the *ton* before the Season is over. It is one of the duties of a companion, you know. But you will be more than a companion—you will be a friend and a participant in the social functions we will attend."

Lily sat back in her seat. "Oh, no," she said. "No, no, that would be impossible. I am not a lady."

"Very true," Elizabeth agreed. "And the *beau monde* is very high in the instep about such matters as birth and connections. Behaving like a lady does not, with the highest sticklers, make one into a lady. But there are exceptions to most rules. Remember if you will, Lily, how famous you are. Your story—your arrival in the middle of Neville and Lauren's wedding, his announcement that you were the wife he had long thought dead, his account of your wedding and apparent death—will still be the sensation of London. The rest of the story—the discovery that your marriage is not valid after all, your refusal to make it valid by going through another nuptial service *with the Earl of Kilbourne*—will set the *ton* on its ears. They will be in a frenzy to meet you, even to catch a glimpse of you. When it is known that you are living with me, invitations will pour in. But we will keep everyone waiting for a while. When you do appear, Lily, you will take London by storm. In addition to the story, you see, there are your natural beauty and grace and charm. And by the time you appear, we will have added the refinement of genteel manners and fashionable appearance. I daresay you could marry a duke if you wished—and if there were a suitable one available." She laughed softly. She was clearly enjoying herself.

"I cannot ever marry," Lily said, ignoring the rest of the frightening—and undeniably exciting—picture Elizabeth had just painted for her. She smoothed her hands over the gloves that lay in her lap.

"Why not?" The question was quietly asked, but it demanded an answer.

Lily was quiet for a long time. *Because I am already married. Because I love him. Because I have lain with him and given him, not only my body, but all that is myself. Because... Because, because.*

"I cannot," she said at last. "You must know the reason."

"Yes, my dear." Elizabeth reached along the seat and squeezed one of her hands. "It would be trite for me to assure you that time will heal. I have never experienced anything nearly as intense as what you have suffered and are suffering, and so I cannot know for sure that such wounds as yours will ever heal. But you are a woman of great fortitude and strength of character, Lily. I am sure I am correct in that judgment. You will *live*, my dear. You will not merely drag on an existence. I will give you the benefit of my resources and connections, but I will not be doing anything of substance for you. You will do that for yourself. I have every confidence in you."

Lily was not sure it was well placed. Her spirits, which the game-turned-reality had sent soaring with the excitement of new dreams,

278

were flagging again. With every passing hedgerow and milepost more distance was being set between her and him, and it was a distance that could never again be closed. She was not sure at that precise moment that she wanted even to drag on an existence, let alone make the effort to *live*.

"Thank you," she said.

"Tell me." Elizabeth spoke again after they had traveled some distance in silence. "What happened to you, Lily, during all those months when Neville thought you dead?"

Lily swallowed. "The truth?" she said.

"It has occurred to me," Elizabeth said, "that the French would have informed the British if they had held an officer's wife captive for any length of time. They might have made a very favorable exchange with one or more of their own officers held by the British. That is not what happened, is it?"

"No," Lily said.

"Lily," Elizabeth said before she could say more, "although I believe you are not going to allow me to forget that you are my employee, I would have you know that you will always be at liberty to guard your privacy from me. You are under no compulsion to tell me anything. But you grew up among men, my dear. Perhaps you have not known the joy of having a friend of your own sex, one who can share your perspective on events and experience."

Lily told her everything, all the painful, sordid, humiliating details she had withheld from Neville that day in the cottage, her head back against the cushions, her eyes closed. By the time she had finished, her hand was in Elizabeth's firm clasp again. Her touch was strangely comforting—a woman's touch signifying a woman's sympathy. Elizabeth would understand what it would be like to be a captive, to have one's freedom taken away, and then, as a final indignity, to have one's very body invaded and used for the pleasure of one's captor. Another woman would understand the monumental inner battle that had had to be waged every single day and night to cling to that something at the core of herself that *was* herself, that gave her identity and dignity. That something that even a rapist—even, perhaps, a murderer—could not take away from her.

"Thank you," they said simultaneously after a short silence. They both laughed, though not with amusement.

"You know, Lily," Elizabeth told her, "men have the ridiculous notion that one must maintain a stiff upper lip through all the worst disasters of their lives. Women are not so foolish. It is quite all right to cry, my dear."

Lily cried. She sobbed until she thought the pain must tear her in two. She wept, her face in Elizabeth's lap while the older woman smoothed a hand over her hair and murmured nonsense that Lily did not even hear.

Finally Lily straightened up, dried her eyes, blew her nose, and apologized for the damp patch on Elizabeth's skirt. She laughed shakily. "You will think twice," she said, "before inviting me to cry again."

"Does Neville know?" Elizabeth asked.

"The basic facts," Lily said. "Not the details."

"Ah," Elizabeth said. "Good girl. Now. Let us look ahead, shall we, and plan? Lily, my dear, we are going to have *fun, fun, fun*."

They both laughed again.

⌣

Neville waited for one month.

He tried to resume his normal life. Except that normal life since his return from the Peninsular Wars had included his very close friendship with his sister and his cousin and his gradual, inevitable courtship of Lauren.

The friendship was strained. He did not want to deceive Lauren into believing that he might resume his courtship of her—and she clearly did not wish to give the impression that she expected it. Gwen was just plain uncomfortable. As Lauren herself had said at dinner the evening before Lily's departure, nothing would ever be the same again.

Yet obviously it was expected that he and Lauren would marry. Neighbors who called at the abbey on any flimsy excuse and who issued more than usually frequent invitations to dinners, card parties, informal dances, and picnics were too well bred to mention the subject openly, but there were all sorts of covert and ingenious ways of hinting and of digging for information.

Might they expect the return of Baron

Galton, Miss Edgeworth's grandpapa, to Newbury any time soon? Lady Leigh asked one day. *Such* a distinguished gentleman!

Was the Countess of Kilbourne planning to return her place of residence to the dower house? Miss Amelia Taylor wished to know. She asked only because it would not be at all the thing for her and her sister to call at the abbey one day to find only his lordship in residence. She blushed at the very idea.

Was his lordship still planning a journey to the Lakes this year? Sir Cuthbert Leigh wondered. His cousin's in-laws had just returned from there and pronounced it a remarkably picturesque and genteel destination.

His lordship must be finding Newbury Abbey rather large and lonely with his sister and his cousin no longer living there, Mrs. Cannadine informed him.

Had his lordship quite recovered from his little upset? Mrs. Beckford, the vicar's wife, asked him in the sort of hushed, sympathetic tones her husband used at deathbeds. She and the reverend were hoping—the hope was accompanied by an arch look that ill became her—that *everything* would soon be put to rights again.

It was not just the neighbors. The countess too urged a return to the original plan.

"I liked Lily, Neville," she assured him when they were breakfasting together a week after Lily had left. "Despite myself I liked her. She has a sweet, unaffected charm. I was prepared to give her my affection and support for the rest of my life. And I know you were

282

fond of her and have found the past week difficult. You are my son and I know that about you—and my heart has ached for you."

"But?" He smiled at her rather ruefully.

"But she is not your wife," she reminded him, "and does not wish to be. Lauren has been intended for you from infancy. You know each other well; you have a real fondness for each other; you have an equality of mind and education. She would fit into my role here without any painful period of adjustment. She would give stability to your life and children to the nursery. I long for grandchildren, Neville. You would not understand, perhaps, the disappointment I felt when Gwendoline miscarried as a result of her accident—as well as grief for her. But I stray from the main point. You had decided to marry Lauren. You were happy with the decision. You were literally at the altar awaiting her. Put the turmoil of the past few weeks behind you and pick up the threads of your life where you left them off. For everyone's sake."

He reached across the table and took one of her hands in both his own. "I am truly sorry, Mama," he said. "But no." He tried to think of an explanation that would make sense to her, but he knew that none would. And he could not bare his heart even to his mother. "Let us all give it time," he added lamely.

It seemed that his life these days was made up of waiting, giving himself time. He waited longer than a week for an answer to the letter he had written to regimental headquarters the morning of Lily's departure. But at last it came—he had half expected the problem to be far more difficult, if not impossible, to solve. He had not posted the letter but had sent it, with specific verbal instructions, with his valet, who had once been his batman, a burly, rather morose man who had always served his master's interests well by refusing to budge an inch in the course of duty. The answer gave Neville something to do—and an excuse for leaving the abbey, which had become oppressive to him.

He might have sent another messenger to make further inquiries. But he chose instead to go in person to Leavenscourt in Leicestershire, where Thomas Doyle's belongings had been sent after their return to England. Doyle's father was a groom at the manor of Leavenscourt.

It was a long journey through weather that had turned wet and blustery and chilly. Neville was forced to travel in a closed carriage, something he always found tedious in the extreme. And he expected to find nothing at the end of the journey. But at least, he thought as he kicked his heels in the taproom of the rickety apology for an inn the weather had forced him to put up at one night—at least he was *doing* something. Newbury had become abhorrent to him, and so much there reminded him of Lily. He had even made the mistake of spending one night at the cottage, lying where they had lain on the bed, filled with such a vast emptiness that he had not even been able to force himself to move, to get out of there.

Leavenscourt was a small but prosperous-looking property. He looked about him with some curiosity as he approached the house. This was where Doyle had grown up? The family was not in residence and his appearance threw the housekeeper into consternation. She stared at him when he explained that he had come to speak with Mr. Doyle, one of the grooms, father of the late Sergeant Thomas Doyle of the Ninety-fifth. She even forgot to keep bobbing curtsies.

Henry Doyle, it seemed, had been dead these four years and more.

Neville felt a door slamming in his face. "I understand," he said, "that the regiment returned Sergeant Doyle's belongings here after his death more than eighteen months ago. Would you know anything about those, ma'am?"

"Oh." She curtsied. "I daresay they were given to William Doyle, my lord. Henry Doyle's son, that is."

Ah. "And where may I find William Doyle?" he asked.

"He is dead, my lord," she told him. "He died about a year ago in a nasty accident, my lord."

"I am sorry to hear it," Neville said. And he was too. Two men who would have been perhaps Lily's only surviving relatives were both dead. "Would you know, ma'am, what happened to *his* belongings?"

"I daresay Bessie Doyle has them, my lord," she said. "She is William's widow. She still lives in the cottage. She has two growing lads and the master was too kind of heart to turn them out. She takes in laundry."

Lily's aunt—and her cousins.

"Perhaps," he said, "you would direct me to the cottage, ma'am."

The housekeeper, considerably flustered again, assured his lordship that she could have Bessie summoned to the house, but he declined her offer and was given the directions he needed.

Bessie Doyle was a stout, florid-faced woman of middle years. She kept an untidy home, though it looked clean enough. She greeted the sight of a fashionably dressed earl on her doorstep with an assessing head-to-toe glance and hands firmly planted on ample hips.

"If it is laundry you has for me," she told him, "you have come to the right place. Though I do not answer for fancy boots like them there after they have tramped through the mud. You had better wipe your feet if you intends to come inside."

Neville grinned at her. The tail of the army was full of Bessie Doyles, strong, capable, practical women who would have greeted the whole of Napoleon Bonaparte's army with hands on hips and some tart remark on their lips.

Yes, Bessie remembered the letter that had come to tell them about Thomas's getting killed—Will had taken it to the vicar to read. And yes, this was where his stuff had been sent—useless junk all of it. It had been in a heap over there—she pointed to a corner of the room in which they stood—when she

286

came back from nursing her old mum, who had not died after all, as it happened, though Will had. She had been called back from her mother's a few miles away with the news that he had fallen from his horse and knocked his brains out on a stone when he landed.

"I am very sorry," Neville told her.

"Well," she said philosophically, "at least it proved that he did have brains, didn't it? Sometimes I wondered."

Bessie Doyle, Neville gathered, was not an inconsolably grieving widow.

"I burned the stuff," she told him before he could ask. "The whole bloody lot."

Neville closed his eyes briefly. "Did you look through it carefully first?" he asked her. "Was there no letter, no package, no—no money, perhaps?"

The very idea of money drew a short bark of laughter from Mrs. Doyle. Will, in her wifely opinion, would have drunk it up in a hurry if there had been.

"P'raps that was what made him fall off," she said, but it was not a serious suggestion. "No, course there weren't no money. Tom wouldn't have kept no money for the likes of Will to get his hands on after he croaked, would he now?"

"Thomas Doyle had a daughter," Neville told her.

Well, Bessie Doyle did not know about that and showed no burning desire to learn anything about her long-lost niece. Her lads were going to be home from the stables soon, she told his lordship. They worked there.

And they were going to be hungry enough to eat an ox apiece.

Neville took the remark as a hint to be on his way. But something caught his eye as he turned to leave—a military pack hanging from a nail beside the door.

"Was that Thomas Doyle's?" he asked, pointing at it.

"I daresay it was," she said. "It was the only useful thing out of the whole lot. But filthy? Had to scrub it to a thread, I did, before I could use it." It was stuffed full of rags.

"May I have it?" Neville asked her. "May I buy it from you?" He took his purse out of his pocket and withdrew a ten-pound note from it. He held it out to her.

She eyed it askance. "Are you daft?" she asked his lordship. "That is more than I and the lads earn in a year between us. For *that* old bag?"

"Please." Neville smiled. "If ten pounds are not enough, I will double the amount."

But Bessie Doyle had her pride. His lordship of the expensive muddy boots might be daft, but she was no robber. She emptied the contents of the pack onto the floor, handed it over with one hand, and took the ten pounds with the other.

The clean, misshapen pack that had been his sergeant's lay on the carriage seat opposite the one on which Neville sat all the way back to Newbury. It would be Lily's one memento of her father. He would have paid a hundred pounds for it—a thousand. But he felt disappointment too. Had Mrs. Doyle inadvertently burned a letter or some sort of package that had contained something more personal for Lily?

Neville had given himself a month to remain at Newbury before removing to his town house in London. Two weeks had passed by the time he returned from Leicestershire. Only half of a month with half still to go! And even then, the faint hope that had sustained him might well prove to have been illusory. Lily, he suspected, would not easily be persuaded to change her mind.

But just before the month was over, before he had decided upon an actual date for his departure, a small package arrived from Elizabeth.

"I have procured you this," she had written in a short note, "having let it be known that you are planning to come to town soon. You may wish to be in attendance, Neville."

The accompanying invitation was to a ball at Lady Ashton's on Cavendish Square.

Neville nodded his head to the emptiness of the library. "Yes," he said aloud. "Oh yes, Elizabeth. I'll be there."

❧ 18 ❧

Lady Ashton's annual ball on Cavendish Square was always one of the Season's great squeezes. It was the ball at which Lady Elizabeth Wyatt had decided to introduce her companion to society.

Elizabeth had many friends and acquaintances. A number of them had called upon her during the month since her return to town, and she had done a great deal of visiting herself. She had also attended a number of evening entertainments. But no one had met her new companion, Miss Doyle, or shown any great curiosity about her until Elizabeth let drop, as if by accident, at a dinner one evening shortly before the Ashton ball the information that Lily Doyle and the woman who had caused such a stir at the Earl of Kilborne's wedding at Newbury earlier in the spring were one and the same person.

Everyone knew about Lily. She was perhaps the most famous, or the most notorious, woman in England during that particular spring—among members of the *beau monde*, at least. Even her appearance in the church at Newbury, completely disrupting one of the greatest *ton* weddings of the year, was surely enough to have fed conversations for the whole Season and beyond. But long before that sensation had begun to die, the rest of the deliciously bizarre story was revealed—Lily was not after all the Countess of Kilbourne because her marriage to the earl had never been properly registered.

Lily's story had been told and discussed in every fashionable drawing room and dining room in London. There were so many unanswered questions that there were unending issues for debate: Who was she? Why had Kilbourne married her? Why had he never told anyone? Where exactly had she been during all the time Kilbourne had thought her dead? What had happened when Kilbourne had discovered the truth about the legality of the marriage? Had she begged on bended knee that he marry her again? Was it true that she had threatened to throw herself off a cliff to be dashed on the rocks below? Had anyone heard for sure how large a settlement Kilbourne had been forced to make on her? Was she really as vulgar as everyone said she was? Where had she gone? Was it true that she had run off with half the earl's fortune and one of his grooms to boot? When was Kilbourne to marry Miss Edgeworth? Would they decide upon a quiet wedding this time? Was it true that Miss Edgeworth had spurned the earl's offer? And who *was* this Lily? Was she really just the daughter of a *common soldier*?

And then it became known that the Miss Doyle who was living with Lady Elizabeth Wyatt as her companion was in fact Miss *Lily* Doyle, formerly and briefly the Countess of Kilbourne. And that she was to attend Lady Ashton's ball. It occurred to very few, if any, that as the daughter of a mere infantry sergeant, a member of the lower classes, Lily had no right to appear at a society ball or that Elizabeth was committing a serious breach of etiquette by taking her there.

The fact was that everyone was avidly eager to set eyes upon Lily Doyle, and if that could be done only at the Ashton ball, well then, so be it. Some of those who had already seen her in the church at Newbury remembered the thin, unkempt woman, whom all of them had mistaken for a beggar, and wondered in some fascination how Lady Elizabeth could have the audacity to think of introducing her to society—even if as a paid companion she would be expected to sit quietly in a corner with the chaperones. But most of those same people were glad for their own curiosity's sake that Elizabeth *did* have the audacity—they wanted a second look at the woman they had seen so briefly.

Those who had never seen Lily craved a glimpse of the woman who had somehow snared the Earl of Kilbourne into such an indiscreet marriage in the Peninsula and had then proceeded to set the whole *ton* on its ears. What must a woman be like, everyone asked, who had spent all her life with the riffraff of the army? *Vulgar?* How could she possibly be anything else?

Lady Ashton's ball was always a well-attended event. This year was to be no exception. Indeed the *beau monde*, usually flagging with a certain ennui this far into the Season, buzzed with eager anticipation of an entertainment that was sure to be *different*.

And then two days before the ball the Earl of Kilbourne himself arrived at Kilbourne House on Grosvenor Square. One day before the ball the whole of London knew it—and that he had accepted his own invitation from Lady Ashton.

The Duke of Portfrey had arrived, Lily saw as soon as she entered Elizabeth's drawing room. She had known that he was to escort the two of them to the ball, and so seeing him was no shock. But it was a meeting that played upon her nerves. He had been out of town since her arrival with Elizabeth—not that she would have seen him even if he had been there. She had seen no one except Elizabeth and the servants and the various teachers who had come to give her instruction. She wished the duke had stayed away from town even though she had convinced herself in the month since she last saw him that there was nothing sinister about him.

She stopped not far inside the drawing room door, but not too far into the room— she had been taught the exact distance— and curtsied. It had taken her an absurd amount of time to learn to curtsy correctly. A mere bending of the knee and bobbing of the head was not good enough—it made one look like a servant. The opposite extreme— almost scraping the ground with both her knee and her forehead—was far too lavish except perhaps when being presented to the queen or the prince regent. And it sent Elizabeth into whoops of infectious laughter. Actually, Lily was forced to admit, the learning had been fun—to borrow the word Elizabeth liked to use about the activities of the past month. There had been a great deal of shared laughter.

"Your grace," she said, keeping her eyes modestly lowered while she curtsied, raising them as she rose to look directly at him—not too boldly, but with her chin held just so, and her back and shoulders straight but not as stiff as a soldier on parade would hold them. *Relaxed, dignified grace* was the term Elizabeth used frequently.

"Miss Doyle?"

The duke made her a slight but elegant bow. Everything about him was elegant, from the fashionably disheveled Brutus style of his dark hair on down to his equally fashionable dancing pumps. Lily had learned something of fashion during the past month—both gentlemen's and ladies' fashions—and recognized the distinction between good taste and dandyism. His grace dressed with immaculate good taste. He was really very handsome for an older man, Lily thought. She did not wonder that Elizabeth had accepted him as her beau. But he was looking closely at her too, even using his quizzing glass with which to do so, and she was reminded of the discomfort he had caused her at Newbury.

"Extraordinary. Exquisite," he murmured

"But of course," Elizabeth said, sounding very pleased indeed. "Did you expect otherwise, Lyndon?" She smiled warmly at Lily. "You do indeed look lovely, my dear. More than lovely. You look like—"

"A lady?" Lily said into the pause that

Elizabeth had filled with an expressive hand but no words.

Elizabeth raised her eyebrows. "Oh, that, yes, without a doubt," she said. "But *poised* is the word I was searching for, I believe. You look— oh, to the manner born. Does she not, Lyndon?"

"You will perhaps, Miss Doyle," the duke said, "do me the honor of dancing the first set with me?"

"Thank you, your grace."

Lily stopped herself from either biting her lip or saying what she had been telling Elizabeth for the past week—to no avail. She had argued that though she had the most magnificent ballgown she had ever seen, and though she had learned how to curtsy, how to hold her head and her body and her arms just so, and though she had learned how to address various people and how to do ridiculous things like use her fan correctly—it was not intended, it seemed, merely to cool her off when she felt hot—she really could not possibly think of participating in the ball as a dancer. It was true that she had had dancing lessons three times each week and had been pronounced an apt and graceful pupil by a fussy master who caused her and Elizabeth to explode into merry laughter every time he left, but even so she did not feel even nearly confident enough to perform the steps at a real live *ton* ball. She did not even feel competent enough to stand perfectly still in the darkest shadows at a *ton* ball.

"Shall we be on our way, then?" the duke suggested.

Five minutes later Lily was sitting in his grace's crested town carriage beside Elizabeth, facing the duke, who sat with his back to the horses. They were on their way to Lady Ashton's ball. It was Lily's duty to accompany her there, Elizabeth had said when Lily had first protested in dismay. And of what use was a companion if she could not move in society as an equal of her employer? Elizabeth had no use for another servant—she already had a full complement. She needed a *friend*.

Lily was terrified. Newbury Abbey had given her a taste of what life among the upper classes was like. It was an alien, totally unfamiliar world. That fact had been a large part of her reason for welcoming the knowledge that she was not after all married. And yet now she was to attend a *ton* ball in London during the social Season. Her stomach felt decidedly queasy despite the fact that she had eaten no more than a few bites of her dinner. And if her knees would hold her upright when she was forced to descend from the carriage, she would be very surprised indeed.

She hoped that after the Duke of Portfrey danced with her she would be able to fade into the shadows—but *were* there any shadows into which to fade at a grand ball? She hoped Elizabeth would not force her to dance with anyone else. She hoped no one would know who she was. She was well aware, of course, of the fact that some of tonight's guests must have been in the church at Newbury for the wedding she had interrupted. But she did not believe any of them would recognize her.

Why should they? She certainly looked very different. She *hoped* no one would recognize her. Surely she would be tossed out ignominiously if anyone discovered who she was— or more important, what she was not. She was not a lady.

The Duke of Portfrey was looking at her quite steadily, she saw when she stole a glance at him. He always made her feel breathless—not in the way that Neville did, and not exactly with fear. She could not identify the feeling except that it made her uncomfortable.

"It is really quite remarkable," he murmured.

"Is it not?" Elizabeth said gaily. "Cinderella herself, would you not agree, Lyndon? But not incredible, you must confess. There was a great deal of beauty and natural grace and refinement on which to build. We have not created a new Lily. We have merely polished the old and made her into what she was always meant to be."

"I wonder." His grace raised his eyebrows and kept his eyes on Lily. He spoke softly, leaving Lily with the uncomfortable impression that Elizabeth had misunderstood his earlier remark.

But there was no more time for that particular discomfort. The carriage was slowing and then stopping. They were behind a line of carriages, Lily could see when she looked out through the window. Ahead of them a great deal of light spilled from the open doors of a brilliantly lighted mansion. A red carpet extended from the doors all the way down the steps and across the pavement so that guests alighting from their carriages would not have to set their feet on hard, cold ground.

They had arrived—or very nearly so. They would have to await their turn while the carriages ahead of them drew up one at a time to the carpet, where liveried footmen helped their richly clad passengers to alight.

Lily wished fervently that their turn would never come. And she wished it would come *now*, without any further delay, without any further moment for thought.

"You will be entering the house and the ball-room on my arm, Miss Doyle," his grace said quietly, clearly detecting her agitation, though she had thought she was showing no outer sign of it. "You will be quite perfectly safe. And even without my escort, you look every inch the lady and quite lovely enough to excite the admiration of every other person in attendance."

Lily had no wish to attract such notice, but his words were reassuring, she had to admit. And suddenly he looked perfectly dependable and trustworthy to her. She felt herself grow calmer. Until, that was, the carriage moved forward another few inches and one of the footmen opened the door and set down the steps.

Neville did not arrive early at the ball. He dined with the Marquess of Attingsborough, and they lingered over their port longer than was necessary.

"The fact is I have not set eyes on her," the marquess told him. "Elizabeth has kept her very close. I would not even have known she was in town if I had not been at Newbury when she left there. The word is out now, though. The whole world knows she will be at the ball—and you too, of course."

Neville winced. He thought he knew—he *hoped* he knew—what Elizabeth was up to, but he was not sure he liked her methods. This was going to be an alarmingly public encounter. And at a *ton* squeeze too. He would have preferred to call quietly at Elizabeth's, but she had refused to allow it. He would be willing to wager that Lily did not even know he was in London.

He tried not to imagine how she might react to the knowledge—or how she might react to seeing him unexpectedly tonight.

But poor Lily—she would have far more than that with which to contend tonight. He would have expected Elizabeth to be more sensitive to her feelings of inadequacy than to haul her off to a *ton* ball when even ordinary day-by-day life at Newbury Abbey had been beyond her ability to cope with. She would just not be able to handle such an ordeal, and she would hate it. The nervousness he felt as he finally approached Cavendish Square with his cousin and ascended the stairs to the Ashton ballroom was as much for her as it was for himself.

"The devil," he muttered to the marquess

as the two of them stood in the doorway. "Why am I doing this?"

The dancing was unfortunately between sets, and there was a very definite hush at his appearance, to be followed a mere fraction of a second later by a renewed buzzing of conversation while a ballroomful of people did a poor job of pretending to mind their own business. Lily must indeed be here, then. Neville did not believe his appearance alone would be causing such an obvious stir.

This situation, he supposed, really must be the sensation of the year. Perhaps of the decade. Deuce take it, but he should not have agreed to this. This was all wrong.

"Damn Elizabeth," he said, still muttering.

"My dear Nev," the marquess said languidly, "it was for just such occasions as this that the quizzing glass was invented." He had his own to his eye and was haughtily surveying the gathering through it.

"So that I might see my embarrassment magnified?" Neville asked, clasping his hands at his back and forcing himself to look around. For a whole month he had craved even a single sight of Lily, and yet now he found that he was afraid of seeing her—afraid of seeing her paralyzed by the embarrassment that even he was finding almost intolerable.

"To your far left, Nev," his cousin said.

Portfrey was immediately visible, and beside him, Elizabeth. There was a cluster of people making up their group—almost exclusively male, though there appeared to be a female somewhere in their midst. *Lily?* Being subjected to a mob? Neville felt himself turn cold in much the way he had always done during battle if he saw one of his men beset by a multiple number of the enemy.

The mob had obviously not noticed him. Everyone else had. Everyone else watched him avidly—though he guessed he would not have caught a single one of them at it if he had turned his head to look—as he strode across the ballroom in the direction of the crowd.

"Steady, Nev," the marquess said from the vicinity of his right shoulder. "You look as if you are about to lay about you with both fists. It would not be good *ton*, old chap. The scene would be lapped up, of course, with all the enthusiasm of a cat for cream and would make you notorious for a decade or so. But it would do the same for Lily, you see."

Elizabeth saw them coming and smiled graciously. "Joseph? Neville?" she said. "How delightful to see you both."

Good manners took over. Neville bowed, as did his cousin. They exchanged bows with the Duke of Portfrey, who had also turned to greet them.

"You left your mother well, I trust, Neville?" Elizabeth asked. "And Gwendoline and Lauren too?"

"All three," Neville assured her. "They all send their regards."

"Thank you," she said. "Have you met Miss Doyle? May I present you?"

The gall of the woman, Neville thought. She was enjoying herself. The mob, he was aware, had fallen quieter. Several of them had melted away. And then stupidly, he was afraid to turn his head. It was physically difficult to do so. But he did it—rather jerkily.

He forgot that he was being observed by half the *ton*—and that she was too.

She was all in white—all delicate simplicity. She looked like an angel. She wore a high-waisted, square-necked, short-sleeved satin gown with a netted tunic, and white fan and slippers and long gloves. Even the ribbon threaded through her hair was white—*her hair!* It had been cut short and curled softly about her face, making it look more heart-shaped, making her blues eyes look larger. She looked dainty and innocent and exquisitely alluring.

Lily. Ah, dear God, Lily! He had missed her every minute of every hour since she had left. But he had not realized quite how painfully until he saw her again.

"May I present the Marquess of Attingsborough and the Earl of Kilbourne to you, Lily?" Elizabeth said. "Miss Doyle, gentlemen."

What farce was this? Neville wondered, not taking his eyes from her face. Her own eyes had widened at the sight of him and become fixed on him and she flushed—she had not been warned that he was to be here, then. But she did not lose her composure. Instead, she curtsied prettily.

"My lord," she said, first to Joseph and then to him.

He found himself bowing formally, becoming an actor in the farce. "Miss Doyle?"

He had never called her that, he realized. He had always liked her and always respected her as Sergeant Doyle's daughter, but he had always called her just Lily, as he would surely not have done if she had been the daughter of a fellow officer. He had always treated her, then, as less than a lady. Had he?

"Yes," she was saying in response to some question Joseph had asked her. "Very much, thank you, my lord. Everyone has been most obliging and I have danced all three sets so far. His grace was kind enough to lead me into the first."

How was she different—apart from her hair, which looked very pretty indeed, though Neville felt that he would mourn the loss of the wild mane once he had been given a chance to think about it. She was different in another way—oh, in a thousand other ways. She had always been graceful. But tonight she seemed *elegantly* graceful. There was something too about her speech. It had always been correct—she had never spoken with a vulgar accent. But tonight there was a suggestion of refinement to her voice. The main difference, though, he realized without having to give the matter a great deal of thought, was that she did not look lost or bewildered as she had always looked at Newbury Abbey. She looked poised, at her ease. She looked as if she belonged here.

"Will you dance with me…Miss Doyle?" he asked abruptly. The sets were forming, he could see.

"I am sorry, my lord," she informed him.

"I have already promised this set to Mr. Farnhope."

And sure enough, there was Freddie Farnhope, hovering and looking uncomfortable but determined to stand his ground.

"Perhaps the next," Neville said.

"Thank you," she said, placing her hand on Farnhope's outstretched wrist—where had she learned to do that? "That would be pleasant, my lord."

My lord. It was the first time she had called him that. She was being formal and impersonal, as he had been with her. As if they had just met for the first time. Could Lily dance a quadrille? But it was clear to him from the first measure of music that she could. She danced it with competence and even grace— and with an endearing look of concentration on her face. As if, he thought, she had only recently learned the steps—as was doubtless the case.

Elizabeth and Lily, he understood then, had not been idle during their month in London.

The realization hurt in a strange way. He had carried on with his life at Newbury out of necessity, but he had pictured Elizabeth carrying on with hers while Lily hovered unhappily and awkwardly in the background. All month he had been contriving ways of persuading her to come back to him, ways of making life at Newbury Abbey less daunting to her. Or, failing that, he had been trying to think of what kind of life and environment would suit a young woman who had lived a sort of nomadic existence away from England all her life. He had been determined to settle her happily somewhere. He had dreamed of being her savior, of setting her own happiness above his own, of doing what was right for her.

But all the time Elizabeth and Lily between them had been doing what he had never once considered—indeed, he had resisted his mother's attempts to do so. They had been making her into a *lady*.

Surely she could not be happy, he thought, gazing at her sadly as she danced. Could she? Where was Lily, that happy, dreamy little fairy creature whom he had used to watch in the Peninsula with such a lifting of his spirits long before he fell in love with her? The nymph with the long hair and bare feet who had sat on the rock in Portugal, watching a bird wheeling overhead and dreaming of being borne on the wind? The bewitching woman who had stood in beauty beside the pool at the foot of the waterfall, telling him that she was not just watching the scene but *was* it?

She had become the dainty, elegant, alluring lady who was dancing the quadrille at a *ton* ball in London, smiling at Freddie Farnhope and concentrating on her steps.

"By Jove, Elizabeth," Joseph was saying, using his quizzing glass again, "she has turned into a rare beauty."

"Only to eyes attuned to ballroom beauties, Joe," Neville said, more to himself than to his cousin. "She always has been a rare beauty."

"Neville," Elizabeth said, "you may escort me to the refreshment room, if you please."

He offered her his arm and led her back toward the doors.

"Louisa must be very gratified," she said as soon as they had moved to the relative quietness of the landing beyond the ballroom. "Her ball is even more of a squeeze than it usually is. Or perhaps it is just that most people have been crowding the ballroom itself instead of wandering off to the card room or the salon as they usually do."

"Elizabeth," he asked, "why are you doing this? Why are you trying to change Lily? I liked her just as she was."

"Then you are being selfish," she said. "Yes, the refreshment room is this way. I need a glass of lemonade."

"Selfish?" He frowned.

"Of course," she said. "Perhaps Lily was not happy with herself just the way she was. But there is no question of my *changing* her, Neville. When one learns, one adds knowledge and accomplishments to what one already is. One enriches one's life. One grows. One does not change in fundamentals. I liked Lily as she was too. I like her as she is. She is still Lily and always will be."

"She hated being at Newbury Abbey," he said, "even though everyone tried to be kind to her. Even Mama was kind after she had recovered from the shock. She was quite prepared to take some of the burdens of being my countess off Lily's shoulders. But Lily hated it anyway—you knew that. She must hate this. I will not have her unhappy, Elizabeth, or bullied into doing what she does not want

306

to do or into being who she does not want to be. I will settle her somewhere—in some country village, I believe—where she can live her own quiet life."

"Perhaps it is what she will choose eventually," Elizabeth said. "But perhaps not. Perhaps she will choose employment of some kind—even possibly as my permanent companion. Or perhaps she will marry despite her lack of fortune. There are any number of gentlemen this evening who appear fascinated by her."

"She will not marry," he said between his teeth. "She is *my wife*."

"And you will challenge to pistols at dawn any man who feels inclined to dispute that fact," she said cheerfully as they entered the refreshment room. "Lemonade, if you please, Neville."

She was smiling when he came back to her, glass in hand.

"Thank you," she said before sipping her drink and resuming their conversation. "The point is, Neville, that Lily is twenty years old. In two months time she will be of age. Perhaps you should begin to consider not what you wish for her future but what *she* wishes."

"I want her to be *happy*," he said. "I wish you had known her in the Peninsula, Elizabeth. Despite the conditions of her life she was the happiest, most serene person I have ever known. I want to give back to her that life of simple pleasures."

"But you cannot," she said. "Even apart from the fact that you have no say in what she does, a great deal has happened to her since

those days—the death of her father, marriage to you, captivity, arrival in England, all
that has happened since. She cannot go back.
Allow her to go forward and find her own way."

"Her own way," he said with more bitterness than he had intended. "Without me."

"Her own way," she repeated. "With or
without you, Neville. Ah. We are about to
be joined by Hannah Quisley and George
Carson."

Neville turned with a polite smile.

∽ 19 ∽

The Duke of Portfrey was not in the habit
of gracing fashionable ballrooms during
the Season. He was not by any means a
hermit, but balls, he was fond of remarking
to his friends, were for young sprigs in search
of wives or flirts. At the age of two-and-forty
he was not interested in such public pur-
suits—besides there was Elizabeth, with
whom he certainly had a relationship though
its exact nature had never been defined.

But he was in attendance at the Ashton
ball because of a peculiar fascination with
Lily—and because Elizabeth had asked for his
escort and it would not have occurred to
him to deny her when she made so few
demands on him. He had danced the first set
with Lily, the second with Elizabeth—and had
then been compelled to add an edge of frost
to his habitually impeccable manners in order

to dissuade his hostess from presenting him to a whole host of other young ladies she was sure would be delightful dancing partners.

Two or three of his acquaintances had teased him with threats of matchmaking mamas setting their caps at him once more—their interest had waned a number of years ago as his age and his indifference to feminine wiles and lures had gradually outweighed the attractions of his rank and wealth and enduring good looks.

"They would be better served to keep their caps firmly tied beneath their chins," his grace replied with languid good humor. But good nature deserted him when Mr. Calvin Dorsey wandered up to him after Neville had led Elizabeth away to the refreshment room. The duke ignored him and engaged in a casual perusal of the room through his quizzing glass. Dorsey was his dead wife's first cousin and heir to her father, Baron Onslow. His grace had never liked him, neither had his wife.

"Portfrey? Your servant," Mr. Dorsey said pleasantly, sketching a careless bow. "I arrived late. But can gossip possibly have the right of it? Did the Duke of Portfrey lead the sergeant's daughter into the opening set at the grandest squeeze of the Season?" He shook his head, chuckling. "The lengths to which some men are prepared to go in order to curry favor with their mistr—" But he cut himself off with one finger to his lips. "With their particular *friends*."

"Congratulations, Dorsey," his grace said without deigning to look at his companion. "You still have a talent for avoiding by half a word having a glove slapped in your face."

Mr. Dorsey chuckled good humoredly and said nothing more for a while as he watched the patterns of the dance unfold. He was of an age with the duke, but time had been somewhat less kind to him. His once-auburn hair had grayed and thinned and he looked by far the older of the two. But he was a man of good humor and a certain charm. There were not many people to whom he spoke with a deliberately barbed tongue. The Duke of Portfrey was one of those few.

"I have been told that you called at Nuttall Grange a couple of weeks ago," he said after a while.

"Have you?" His grace bowed to a buxom dowager with gorgeously nodding hair plumes who passed in front of them.

"A little out of the way of anywhere of any importance to you, was it not?" Mr. Dorsey asked.

For the first time the duke turned his glass on his companion before lowering it and regarding him with the naked eye.

"I may not pay my respects to my father-in-law without being quizzed by his nephew?" he asked.

"You upset him," Mr. Dorsey said. "He is in poor health and it is my business to see that he is kept quiet."

"Since you have been waiting for twenty years with barely concealed impatience to succeed to Onslow's title and fortune," his grace said with brutal bluntness, "I would have thought it more in your interest to encourage me to, ah, *upset* him, Dorsey. But you need not fear—or hope. I merely sent up my card as a courtesy since I was in the neighborhood. I neither expected nor wished to be received. There was never any love lost between Onslow's family and my own even before Frances and I defied both with our secret marriage. There was even less after her death and my return from the West Indies."

"Since we are into plain speaking," Mr. Dorsey said, "you might oblige me by explaining why you were snooping around at the Grange when my uncle was too ill to send you packing."

"Snooping?" His grace had his glass to his eye again. "Taking tea with the housekeeper is *snooping*, Dorsey? Dear me, the English language must have different meanings in Leicestershire than anywhere else I have ever been."

"What did you want with Mrs. Ruffles?" Mr. Dorsey demanded.

"My dear fellow," the duke said faintly. "I wished to know—I felt a burning desire to discover, in fact—how many sets of bed linen she keeps in the linen closet."

Mr. Dorsey flushed with annoyance. "I do not like your levity, Portfrey," he said. "And I would warn you to stay away from my uncle in future if you know what is good for you."

"Oh, I certainly know what is good for me," his grace said, the languidness back in his voice. "You will excuse me, Dorsey? A pleasure to converse with one of my wife's relatives again. It has been a long time, has it not, given the fact that we rather pointedly ignored each other at Newbury Abbey a month or so ago. One can only hope it will be at least as long again before the next time." And he strolled away to exchange civilities with the dowager who had passed them a few minutes before.

What Mrs. Ruffles had been able to do was answer the Duke of Portfrey's questions rather satisfactorily. She had had to think very carefully because the events about which he inquired were twenty years and more in the past. But yes, there had been a Beatrice employed at the Grange. The housekeeper particularly remembered, now she thought about it, because the girl had been dismissed for impertinence, though not to Miss Frances, if she recalled correctly. Why had she thought it might have been Frances, the duke asked. Well, Mrs. Ruffles told him, remembering clearly then, because Beatrice had been Miss Frances's personal maid and Miss Frances had been fond of her and very annoyed with her cousin. The housekeeper had frowned in thought, Yes, that was it. It was Mr. Dorsey to whom Beatrice had been insolent, though she did not remember, probably had never known, exactly what the girl had said to him or done.

Beatrice had left Nuttall Grange a year or more—oh yes, surely more—before Miss Frances's death, Mrs. Ruffles believed. She did not know where the maid had gone. But she had a sister still living in the village, she had added almost as an afterthought.

His grace had called upon the sister, who, once she had recovered from the flusters and the almost incoherent babble that had succeeded them, had been able to inform him that Beatrice had gone away to stay with their aunt and had then married Private Thomas Doyle of the army, whose father had been head groom at Mr. Craddock's estate of Leavenscourt six miles away. The Doyles had gone to India, where Beatrice had died years ago. She thought Thomas Doyle must be dead by now too. She had never heard of his coming back. Not that he would go to Leavenscourt anyway, she supposed. His dad and his brother were both dead, she had heard.

She had not heard of there having been any children born to Beatrice and Thomas.

She knew nothing of Lily Doyle, whom the Duke of Portfrey now watched intently as she danced a quadrille at the Ashton ball with Freddie Farnhope.

❦

Lily was in a daze. She smiled and even conversed. She danced the intricate, newly learned steps without faltering. She coped with all the frightening, dizzying newness of being at a *ton* ball and of being a full participant. It had not taken her long to realize that she was not merely the anonymous companion of

Lady Elizabeth Wyatt, but that everyone knew exactly who she was and had probably known even before her arrival. It had not taken her long, either, to realize that she was not going to be treated with hostility but with an indulgent, avid curiosity.

It was all a challenge, she realized, that Elizabeth had deliberately set her in the belief that she would rise to the occasion. She had not disappointed either Elizabeth or herself, she believed. She had remembered everything she had been taught, and somehow it had all worked. If she had not felt exactly at her ease, she had at least felt in command of herself.

Until she had turned her head to meet yet another gentleman who had applied to Elizabeth for an introduction—and had found herself looking at Neville.

She had been in a daze since. She was not even sure she remembered quite what had happened. He had bowed; she had curtsied. He had called her Miss Doyle—*had he?* He had never called her that before. And it had been a formal bow. He had not been smiling. She had remembered—she *believed* she had—to call him "my lord."

They had both behaved as if they had not met before. And yet...

Mr. Farnhope said something to her, and she smiled at him and replied without giving her answer thought.

And yet there had been that night at the pool and in the cottage—that night she had relived over and over again during the past month.

The memories had become more and more painful as time passed. It was all very well to steel oneself to doing what one knew must be done, she had found. One somehow assumed that the pain would pass, that time would heal. Time did not heal—not some wounds, at least.

She had dreamed the dream—the nightmare—a number of times during the past month.

She danced with Mr. Farnhope and knew that the eyes of the *ton* were on her even more intently than they had been at the start of the ball. She danced and smiled and all the while felt raw pain. Why had he come? He could not have expected to find her at tonight's ball, of course. But why had he come to London? To acquire a special license, perhaps? For Lauren this time?

She did not wish to know. It was none of her business.

And then she remembered that she was to dance the next set with him. For the first time all evening she felt the sort of panic she had felt often at Newbury Abbey and the urge to run away. But there was no park beyond the doors of Lady Ashton's mansion into which to run and no forest and no beach. Besides, running away would serve no purpose except to make it impossible to come back. A lady did not run away. Neither, for that matter, did Lily Doyle. Not any longer.

He was standing with Elizabeth, she saw as the quadrille came to an end. Mr. Farnhope led her in their direction. Neville was looking extremely elegant and handsome all in black and cream and white. He was looking at her with an unsmiling, almost haughty expression. Perhaps he too was feeling the embarrassment of knowing them to be the focus of attention, though everyone was far too well bred to stare openly. He looked unfamiliar. It was hard to believe that he was the man who had once married her—Major Lord Newbury. And the same man who had made love to her in the cottage by the waterfall.

He bowed to her again and she curtsied again.

"I hope the Countess of Kilbourne is well, my lord?" she asked him.

"I thank you, yes," he said.

"And Lauren and Gwendoline too?"

"Both well, thank you."

She smiled and wished fervently that Elizabeth would step into the breach—she remained silent.

"I trust you are enjoying yourself...Miss Doyle?" he asked.

"Oh, exceedingly well, thank you, my lord." Lily remembered her smile and her fan and made use of both.

"And I trust you have been seeing something of London?"

"Not a great deal yet, my lord," she said. "I have been very busy."

If Elizabeth only had a knife, Lily thought without a glimmering of amusement, she would surely be able to slice the air between them. Would no one come to the rescue? And then someone did.

"Lady Elizabeth? Would you do me the honor of presenting me—again?" It was a pleasant man's voice, and Lily turned with a grateful smile toward its owner. But she recognized him. He had been at Newbury Abbey for a few days after her arrival. He was a friend of Baron Galton, Lauren's grandfather.

"Mr. Dorsey?" Elizabeth said. She turned to Lily. "Lily, do you remember Mr. Dorsey? Miss Doyle, sir."

"I am pleased to make your acquaintance, sir," Lily said, curtsying and hoping fervently that he would stay awhile and make conversation, though she was fully aware that at any moment the next sets would be forming.

"Charmed, Miss Doyle," he said. "And charming too if I may be allowed to say so. Would you honor me with your hand for the next set?"

"It is promised to his lordship," Lily said.

"Ah, of course." He smiled at Neville. "How do you do, Kilbourne. Then perhaps the next?"

"The next is promised to me, Dorsey."

Lily turned in some surprise to see that the Duke of Portfrey had come up behind her. His words had been clipped and none too politely spoken.

"And every set after that is also promised," his grace went on to say, quite erroneously. He had not even reserved the next set but one with her.

"Lyndon—" Elizabeth began.

"Good evening, Dorsey," the duke said in quite decisively dismissive accents.

Mr. Dorsey smiled, bowed to them all, and strolled away without another word.

"Lyndon," Elizabeth said, "whatever possessed you to be so ill-mannered?"

"Ill-mannered, ma'am?" he said coldly. "To keep rogues away from young innocents? I am amazed that you would deem it unexceptionable to present to Miss Doyle any scoundrel who asks for the favor."

Elizabeth was tight-lipped and pale. "And I am amazed, your grace," she said, "that you would presume to instruct me in proper behavior. Mr. Dorsey, I recollect, was your wife's cousin. If you have a quarrel with him, you can scarce expect that I will make it mine."

It had been a short, sharp exchange conducted in lowered voices. It shocked and upset Lily, who felt that she had been the cause of the unexpected quarrel. It also helped quench her own indignation over the Duke of Portfrey's presuming to speak and act on her behalf.

"Lily," Neville said, extending his arm for hers, "the sets are forming. Shall we join one?"

For a few moments she had forgotten him. But the sets were indeed forming, and she had agreed to spend all of half an hour in his company. It was not an enticing thought. The prospect of half an hour with him when there must be a whole lifetime and a whole eternity beyond it without him was a mortal agony to her.

She raised her hand, hoping it was not trembling quite noticeably, and set it, as she had been taught to do, on the cuff of his black evening coat. She felt his strength and his warmth. She smelled his familiar cologne. And she well-nigh forgot her surroundings and lost her awareness that this was the moment for which the gathered members of the *beau monde* must have waited ever since he entered the ballroom. She wanted to grip his wrist tightly and turn in to his body and burrow safely and warmly there. She wanted to sob out her grief and her loneliness.

A moment later she was horrified both by the wave of forgetfulness and by her own weakness. A month had passed, a month of hard work and fun. A month of living and preparing herself to live an independent and productive life. She had set a whole month between herself and him. A mighty bulwark, she had thought. But one sight of him, one touch, and everything had come crashing down again. The pain, she was sure, was worse than it had ever been.

She took her place in the line of ladies facing the line of gentlemen. She smiled—and he smiled back at her.

Elizabeth was still tight-lipped. She was looking about her for some friend whom she might join. The Duke of Portfrey gazed at her coldly.

"Take my arm," he commanded. "We will go to the refreshment room."

"I have just come from there," she said. "And I do not answer to that tone, your grace."

He sighed audibly. "Elizabeth," he said, "will you please accompany me to the refreshment room? It will be quieter there. Experience has taught me that a quarrel that is not resolved in the immediate aftermath of a heated moment is likely never to be resolved."

"Perhaps," she said, "it would be as well if this one never were."

"Do you mean that?" he asked her, the coldness all gone from his voice.

She looked at him—a long, measuring look—and then took his arm.

"Do you know Dorsey well?" he asked her as they walked.

"Scarcely at all," she admitted. "I do not believe we exchanged more than a dozen words at Newbury this spring. I was surprised when he applied to me for a formal introduction to Lily since he had seen her there. But it was hardly an unusual request this evening, and I knew of no reason to decline his request. Is there one?"

"He forced his attentions on Frances— my wife," he said. "Unwelcome attentions even after he knew that they were so. Is that reason enough?"

"Oh, heavens!" she exclaimed. "Oh, I am so sorry, Lyndon. I will not excuse him by saying that it was all of twenty or more years ago and he must have been young and headstrong. To you the offense must seem very fresh."

"He was desperate to marry her," he said.

"Apart from the title, everything of Onslow's is unentailed, including Nuttall Grange. He had willed it all to Frances. When she would not accept Dorsey, he tried to—to force her into matrimony. It was one reason for our rushing into a secret marriage the day before I was to leave for the Netherlands with my regiment. There was the family feud, which made it difficult for us to marry openly. We both thought that when I returned we would be better able to persuade both families that our attachment had been of a long enough duration that it must be accepted. We were young—though both of age—and foolish. But at least the fact of our marriage could have been her trump card against Dorsey's insistence."

He had never before spoken of his wife, Elizabeth thought as they entered the refreshment room, which was deserted apart from a couple of servants who were doing something at a sideboard, their backs to the room. She had never liked to ask about his marriage.

"I can understand," she said, "why you dislike him so. He may, of course, have changed in twenty years, and there can certainly be nothing about Lily to attract his greed. But I will discourage any future attempt he may make to extend his acquaintance with her."

"Thank you," he said. "Keep her from him, Elizabeth."

She frowned suddenly and regarded him closely, her head tipped to one side. She did not care for the feelings she was experiencing. Jealousy? "What is your particular interest in Lily?" she asked him.

He did not answer in words. He did what he had never done before despite a close acquaintance of several years. He leaned toward her and kissed her fiercely on the lips.

"This must be the supper dance," he said, "the reason this room is so empty. Shall we go early to the dining room?"

Elizabeth fought to set her thoughts into working order as she took his arm. She felt, she thought with self-mockery, like a young girl fresh from the schoolroom who had just experienced her first kiss—all breathless and weak-kneed and eager for more. And hopelessly in love, of course. She was usually well disciplined enough to disguise that fact even from herself.

~

It was a slow and stately country dance in which they engaged. Since the patterns had them several times dancing about each other or joining hands, there were opportunities for some conversation. But Neville availed himself of none of them, and Lily for her part made no attempt to talk to him, though she smiled all the time they danced. Short snatches of conversation could deal with only trivial topics. Besides, any conversation under such circumstances might have been overheard. They danced in silence.

He knew they were watched. He knew that every look and gesture, every touch and word would be noted and commented upon tomorrow in many drawing rooms and that significance would be read into every detail. He found that he did not care.

She danced lightly and gracefully. She held herself proudly and elegantly. She looked as if she had always belonged in such surroundings. She was a beauty, a diamond of the first water. He could not—he *would* not—take his eyes from her.

He had come to London with hopes, albeit anxious ones. He had expected to find her miserable. He had hoped to be able to gather her—both figuratively and literally, perhaps—into his arms and assure her that he would protect her for the rest of his life even if she would not marry him. But she looked as if she belonged in Lady Ashton's ballroom. She looked poised and relaxed.

He felt almost as if he were seeing her for the first time. She had recovered the weight she had lost before coming to Newbury, weight she had never regained there. She was still small and slender, but she was all pleasing, enticing curves now. There were no traces left of the coltish, carefree girl he remembered so well. And none either of the beautiful, rather gaunt woman who had stepped into the church at Newbury. She looked now—

There were no words adequate to the task. She was femininity personified. No, too tame. She was everything he had ever wanted, *could* even want. Not just a companion, a wife, a soulmate. She was everything his body craved. She was—she was *woman*.

If this were only a waltz, he thought, he would maneuver her close to the French windows, twirl her through them, dance her into the shadows beyond the candlelight, and kiss both her and himself senseless.

It was not a waltz. They danced toward each other, moved about each other back to back, and returned to their respective lines without once touching, though he felt her body heat curl about him like a warm blanket. She held the smile she had worn from the start, but her eyes surely smoldered with an answering awareness to his own.

Thank God it was not a waltz. Her eyes merely smiled. Honor dictated that he not even try to take advantage of her without her full and free consent.

Ah, Lily.

It was the supper dance, Neville realized as the set drew to an end, and she clearly knew what that meant. She took his arm without protest and allowed him to lead her into the dining room, where he was fortunate enough to procure them two places at a table slightly apart from any other guests. He seated her and brought her a plate of food and a cup of tea.

"Lily," he asked her, taking the seat beside her and resisting the impulse to take her hand in his, "how *are* you?"

"I am very well, I thank you, my lord," she said. Her eyes, which had smiled into his throughout the dance, were focused somewhere in the region of his chin.

"You look lovely," he told her. "But I could weep for your hair."

That drew her eyes to his, and he saw the old Lily in the amusement that lit them. "Dolly *did* weep, the silly girl," she said, "until I promised that I would still need her services. She used to spend hours on my hair. She is still always busy, though. I no longer iron my own clothes or do any alterations or mending."

"Or make your own bed or help peel potatoes or chop onions?" he asked her.

"Or those things," she agreed. "Ladies do not do such things."

"Unless they choose to," he said, smiling.

"They are too busy with other things," she told him.

"Are they, Lily?" he asked her. "Such as?"

But she would not tell him what had kept her so busy during the past month—apart from having her hair cut and learning to dance and behave like a lady. She changed the subject.

"I thank you for repaying the money I borrowed from Captain Harris, my lord," she said, "even though you were under no obligation to do so. I have called on them a number of times. Elizabeth said she would willingly spare me to visit *them*."

"Is she a hard taskmaster in general, then?" he asked.

"Of course not," she said. "Would I offend you, my lord, if I offered to repay what you sent to Captain Harris as soon as I am able?"

"I would be offended, Lily," he said. He added a further truth. "I would be hurt, my dear."

She nodded. "Yes," she said. "I thought you would. So I will not insist."

"Thank you," he said.

She had been toying with her food, he noticed. But then he had not even touched his own.

"May I call upon you, Lily?" he asked her. "Tomorrow afternoon?"

"Why?" Her eyes looked fully into his again. He was jolted by the question. Was she going to say no?

"I have something for you," he said. "Something in the nature of a gift."

"I may not accept gifts from you, my lord," she said.

"This is different," he assured her. "It is not personal. It is something you will certainly accept and delight in. May I bring it myself and put it into your hands? Please?"

Her eyes brightened for a moment with what might have been tears, but she looked down before he could be sure. "Very well, then," she said, "if Elizabeth will permit your call. You must remember, my lord, that I am her paid companion."

"I will apply to her for permission," he said. And after all he could not resist the self-indulgence of possessing himself of one of her hands and raising it briefly to his lips. "Lily, my dear…"

Her eyelids came down faster this time, but not before he was quite sure of the tears she hid from him. He forced himself to stop what he had been about to say. Even if her feelings were still engaged, he knew she would not easily capitulate to his wooing. Love, or lack of love, had had little if anything to do with her rejection of him. If they could not find a common world in which to live together, and if they could not live somehow as equals, she would reject him even if he asked her weekly for the next fifty years.

But her feelings *were* still engaged. He was certain of it. It was both a painful and an encouraging discovery. At least there was something still to hope for, something to live for.

✑ *20* ✑

Lily had reached a frustrating point in her education. At first everything had been bewildering and exhausting but really rather easy—and definitely exciting. Every day there had been something new to learn, and every day she had been able to see her progress. Within the month, she had thought, she would know everything—or at least she would have a thorough grasp of the basic skills that would enable her to know as much as she would ever wish to know.

But inevitably the time came when the lessons became repetitious and tedious, when progress seemed slow and sometimes nonexistent, when it seemed to her that she would never achieve anything resembling even a tolerably basic education.

She had learned all the letters of the

alphabet—she could recognize them in both their upper and lower cases, and she could write them all. She could decipher a number of words, particularly those that looked the way they sounded and those that occurred in almost every sentence. Sometimes she persuaded herself that she could read, but whenever she picked up a book from a shelf in Elizabeth's book room, she found that every page was still a mystery to her. The few words she could read did not enable her to master the meaning of the whole, and the slowness with which she read even what she could decipher killed interest and continuity of meaning. When she picked up an invitation from the desk one day and discovered that the appearance of the writing was so different from what she had been taught from books that she could scarcely recognize a single letter, she felt close to despair.

Sheer stubbornness kept her going. She *would not* admit defeat. She even insisted upon sitting at her lessons all through the morning following the ball even though it had been almost dawn when they arrived home and Elizabeth had suggested sending a note to stop the tutor from coming.

And she sat at her music lesson immediately after luncheon. The pianoforte was proving equally frustrating. At first it had been wonderful just to be able to depress the keys and learn their names. She had felt that she had somehow begun to unravel the mystery of music. It had been exhilarating to learn scales, to practice playing them smoothly and with the correct fingering and the fingers correctly arched, her spine and her feet and her head held just so. It had been sheer magic to play an actual melody with her right hand and to be able to tell herself that she could *play the pianoforte*. But then had come the demon of the left hand, which played something simultaneously with the right hand but different from it. How could she divide her attention between the two and play both correctly? It was akin to the old game the army children had used to laugh over—of trying to rub one's stomach and pat one's head both at the same time.

But she persevered. She *would* learn to play. She would never be a great musician. She probably would never be good enough even to play to a drawing room audience, as most ladies seemed able to do. But she was determined to be able to play correctly and somewhat musically for her own satisfaction.

She had been playing the same Bach finger exercise over and over for half an hour. Every time her teacher stopped her to point out an error or commented adversely on what she had done when she played through it without interruption she felt ready to indulge in a tantrum, to hurl the music and some abuse at his head, to declare that she never wanted to touch a pianoforte keyboard ever again, to yell that she just *did not care*. But every time she listened and tried one more time. She recognized her tiredness—not only had the night been short, but she had lain awake thinking about *him*—and her anxiety. He was to call later. He had a gift for her. How could she see him again without crumbling, without showing him how very weak she was?

But she played on. And finally she succeeded in playing, not only without interruption, but with what she considered more competence than ever before. She lowered her hands to her lap when she was finished and waited for the verdict.

"Wonderful!" he exclaimed.

Her head whipped back over her shoulder. He was standing in the open doorway of the drawing room with Elizabeth, looking both astonished and pleased.

"This is what you have been doing with your time, Lily?" he asked.

She got to her feet and curtsied to him. If there had been a deep black hole at her feet, she would gladly have jumped into it. She had been caught practicing an exercise that a five-year-old would surely be able to play with twice the competence. She glanced reproachfully at Elizabeth.

"I believe, Mr. Stanwick," Elizabeth said to the music teacher, "Miss Doyle will agree to release you early today. Lily?"

Lily nodded. "Yes," she said. "Thank you, Mr. Stanwick."

Elizabeth went, quite unnecessarily, to see him on his way, and did not come back immediately.

"That sounded very pretty," Neville said.

"It was a very elementary exercise," she said, "which I played indifferently well, my lord."

"Yes," he agreed gravely, "it was and you did."

And so he had taken argument away from her as a weapon. She felt indignant then. Had he paid her a compliment only to withdraw it?

"And all within one month," he continued. "It is an extraordinary achievement, Lily. And you have learned how to mingle with high society with grace and ease—as well as how to dance. What else have you been doing?"

"I have been learning to read and write," she said, lifting her chin. "I can do neither even indifferently well—yet."

He smiled at her. "I remember your saying— it was at the cottage," he said, "that you thought it must be the most wonderful feeling in the world to be able to read and write. I missed my cue then. It was no idle dream, was it? I thought all you needed was freedom and the soothing balm of wild nature."

She half turned from him and sat down on the edge of the pianoforte bench. She did not want to be reminded of the cottage. Those memories were her greatest weakness.

"How is Lauren?" she asked—had she asked him that last night?

"Well," he said.

She was examining the backs of her hands. "Are you—is there to be a summer wedding?" she asked without ever intending to.

"Between Lauren and me?" he said. "No, Lily."

She had not realized how much she had feared it until she heard his answer, though of course he had not said there would not be an autumn wedding or a winter one or...

"Why not?" she asked him.

"Because I am already married," he said quietly.

Lily felt as if her insides had somersaulted. But it was exactly the way he had talked at Newbury. Nothing had changed. If he were to ask her again what he had asked there, her answer would be the same. It could not change.

"I have brought you the gift I mentioned last evening," he said, walking a little closer to her. Glancing at him she could see that he carried a package. He held it out to her.

He had said it was nothing personal. If it were, she must refuse it. He had bought her clothes and shoes when she was at Newbury Abbey, and she had kept them. But that was different. She had thought herself to be his legal wife at that time. Now she was a single woman in company with a single gentleman and could not accept gifts from him. But she lifted one arm and took the package.

She knew what it was as soon as she opened the wrapping, even though it was faded and misshapen and unnaturally clean. But she asked the question anyway as she set her hand flat on top of it.

"Papa's?" she whispered.

"Yes," he said. "I am afraid the contents are all gone, Lily. This is all I could retrieve for you. But I thought you would wish to have it anyway."

"Yes." There was a painful aching in her throat. "Yes. Thank you. Oh, thank you." She watched a dark wet spot spreading on the pack and blotted it with one finger. "Thank you." She stumbled to her feet and had her arms about his neck and her face among the folds of his cravat before she realized what she was doing. His arms came firmly about her. She clutched the pack tightly in one hand and felt the link of security there had been during those years in the Peninsula—her father, Major Lord Newbury, and herself. They had not been carefree years—war could never be anything but horrifying—but nostalgia washed over her nonetheless. She had her eyes tightly shut almost as if she were willing herself to be back there in that life when she opened them.

He let her go when she had recovered herself, and she sat on the stool again.

"I am sorry about the contents," he said. "I am sorry you will never know what your father kept there for you."

"Where did you find it?" she asked.

"It had been sent to your grandfather at Leavenscourt in Leicestershire," he told her. "He was a groom there. He died before your father, I am afraid, and his son, your father's brother, died soon after. But you have an aunt still living there, Lily, and two cousins. Your aunt had the pack."

She had relatives of her own—an aunt and two cousins. The thought should excite her, Lily supposed. Perhaps in time it would. But she was too full of grief for her father at the moment. She had never properly grieved for him, she realized. She had married a mere three hours after his death, and a few hours after that the long, long nightmare had begun when she had been shot above the heart. She had never had a chance fully to realize the enormity of her loss.

"I miss him," she said.

"I do too, Lily." He had gone to lean against the far end of the pianoforte. "But you have at least something now by which to remember him. What happened to your locket? Did the French take it—or the Spanish?"

"Manuel," she said. "But he returned it to me when I was released. It is broken, though. The chain snapped when he tore it from my neck."

She heard him suck in his breath. "You always wore it," he said. "Was it a gift from your father or mother?"

"From both, I suppose," she said. "I have always had it, for as far back as I can remember. Papa used to say I must always wear it, that I must never take it off or lose it."

"But the chain is broken," he said. "You must wear the locket again, Lily, as a more personal remembrance of both your parents. Will you allow me to take it to a jeweler to have the chain mended?"

She hesitated. She would trust him even with her life, but she could not bear the thought of allowing the locket out of her possession again. She had been stripped of clothes when she was first taken by the Spanish, but she had felt most naked when Manuel had torn the locket from her neck. She had felt that part of herself had been ripped away.

"Better still," Neville said, reading her

hesitation correctly, "will you allow me to escort you to a jeweler's, Lily, to have the chain mended? I would not doubt it can be done on the spot while you watch."

She looked at him and trusted him and forgot for the moment the barrier that must forever be kept between them. "Yes," she said. "Thank you, Neville." And she sucked her lower lip between her teeth as their eyes met and held. She felt as if she had spoken an endearment; he looked as if he had heard one.

But the door opened at that opportune moment and Elizabeth came into the room, smiling cheerfully. "Oh, dear," she said, "Mr. Stanwick does like to talk when one gives him the opportunity. Do forgive me for abandoning you, Neville. But I daresay Lily has kept you entertained. She has become adept at social conversation."

"I am not complaining," Neville told her.

"Let us all go to my sitting room for tea," Elizabeth suggested. "There is a fire burning there. It is a rather chilly day for summer, is it not? Damp too."

Lily's eyes went to the drawing room window. It was indeed a gray, cloudy day. There were raindrops on the glass though it appeared that it was not raining at that moment. The weather had depressed her all morning, she remembered. Yet she had had the distinct impression that the sun had been shining this afternoon. She had been mistaken.

Elizabeth had always openly admitted to Neville that he was her favorite nephew. She wished for his happiness, he knew. He knew too that she was aware of the depth of his feelings for Lily. But she would not press Lily to come back to him. She had too great an integrity for that. She had set herself to giving Lily the opportunity to learn skills and acquire confidence so that she could choose her future for herself. If Lily chose to marry him, Elizabeth would be pleased. If she chose not to do so, Elizabeth would support her.

Women, when they banded together, Neville thought ruefully, could be as easily moved as the Rock of Gibraltar.

He was eager to take Lily to a jeweler's. He knew that the locket was precious to her and he wanted to help restore it to her whole so that she could wear it again. That *was* his main motive, he was quite sure. There was also, of course, the excuse the expedition would give him to spend some time with Lily again.

But the following day would not do at all, Elizabeth informed him during tea on the afternoon he had brought Doyle's pack. Lily would be busy all morning with her lessons, and there was the Fogles' garden party in the afternoon. She would need Lily to attend her for that occasion. And the following day there were the morning lessons *and* a dancing lesson during the afternoon. It was also to be the day of the week on which Elizabeth was regularly at home to callers, and this week she would have Lily sit with her and help her entertain.

The best Neville could do, since he had not received an invitation to the garden party, was call at Elizabeth's the following afternoon and sit drinking tea and conversing with a group of visitors that did not include Lily. It was not until the next afternoon that she was finally declared free to go with him to a jeweler's. And even then Elizabeth would have accompanied them if he had not been able to assure her that he would be taking an open carriage with his groom up behind.

Elizabeth, of course, had always been a high stickler. But she was treating Lily more like a treasured ward than a paid companion. It was frustrating, but Neville found himself glad of it too. All too many young blades had called for tea at Elizabeth's with no other apparent reason for doing so than a wish to ogle Lily.

The sun was shining again at last on the appointed afternoon, and Lily was wearing an attractive and extremely fashionable green dress with a straw bonnet. Neville handed her into his phaeton and took his seat beside her before taking the ribbons from his groom's hand and waiting for the boy to clamber up behind.

"Tell me the truth, Lily," he said as they drove in the direction of Bond Street. "Are you enjoying yourself?"

She considered her answer. "I feel...at ease," she said. "I feel that I can now mingle with almost any company in which I happen to find myself during the rest of my life. It is a good feeling, my lord."

"And are you learning all you wished to learn?" he asked her.

"By no means," she said. "I doubt one can ever learn or even be in the process of learning all the fascinating facts and mysteries of life. I am learning far more slowly than I expected. I can barely read and yet I have been having lessons for over a month. Yet every day when I become frustrated and unhappy with myself I remember how I have always yearned for knowledge and skills. And I remember how very fortunate I am to be able to satisfy my yearning at last."

He sighed. "I did not want you to change, Lily," he said. "I liked you just as you were. But when I told Elizabeth that, she pointed out to me how selfish I was being. And I must admit that it is a delight to see you at your ease, as you put it." He smiled across at her. "And I *do* like your hair that way."

"So do I." She smiled gaily and raised one gloved hand in greeting to two ladies who were emerging from a milliner's shop. At the same moment George Brigham, who was passing on the street, touched the brim of his hat with his cane and inclined his head to Lily.

She was looking like and she was being treated like a young lady of *ton*, Neville realized. Her own courage and Elizabeth's encouragement had brought her out of hiding and she was at ease. He would have sheltered and protected her and made her forever uncomfortable and unhappy. It was not a pleasant admission to make to himself.

He escorted her into the shop of the jeweler he had selected as the best and explained that Miss Doyle would rather not leave her locket to be collected later, but would like to watch as the chain was mended. And so they were given seats, and the precious piece did not leave her sight.

The locket was gold. So was the chain. It was not the sort of trinket one would expect to have been within the means of a soldier who had not even had a sergeant's pay when it had been purchased. Neville had seen it dozens of times about Lily's neck. It had seemed a part of her. It had never occurred to him to wonder about it. There was some sort of intricate design on the outside of the locket, but he did not attempt to lean close enough to examine it. For some reason Lily guarded its privacy. He would respect her wishes.

He paid for the work when it was finished, and she put the locket carefully back inside her reticule.

"You are not going to wear it?" he asked her as they left the shop.

"I have not worn it for so long," she said, "that I wish to choose some special occasion on which to wear it for the first time again. I do not know when. I will think of the right time."

"Let me take you to Gunter's for an ice?" he asked.

She bit her lip, but she nodded. "Yes," she said. "Thank you, my lord. And thank you for having my locket mended. You are very kind."

He stopped on the pavement with her and bent his head closer to hers so that he could look into her eyes.

"Lily," he said, "do not deceive yourself into thinking I acted from kindness. I have been selfish again. When you wear the locket once more, I hope—indeed, I believe—that you will remember not only your mama and papa but also the man who will always consider himself your husband."

"Oh, don't," she said quickly, gazing back at him with wide blue eyes.

"But you *will* remember that, will you not?" he said.

She did not answer him, but she nodded almost imperceptibly after a few moments.

⌒

Lily had been dreading the afternoon. She had prayed that Elizabeth would go with them. After the question of the carriage had been settled, she had prayed for rain so that he would be forced to bring a closed carriage and Elizabeth would have to accompany them after all.

She was so very weak. It was so difficult to see him, to speak with him, to be alone with him and not reveal her true feelings to him. It was an agony to know that these memories of him would cling about her with almost unbearable pain once he had gone home again. She did not need more memories. She already had far too many.

But in the event she was finding the afternoon quite magical. The weather had turned summery again after several days of gloom and intermittent rain. Riding in an open phaeton and feeling the warmth of the sun and seeing its brightness gave a wonderful lift to her spirits. So did his company.

But it was something else that created the magic. An idea had struck her and excited her, and she could not help but be buoyed up by it even though she knew she must return home and think carefully about it before in any way acting upon it.

She had refused to marry Neville because she was uncomfortable in his world and could never fit the role of countess. She had refused for her own sake and for his too—eventually he would have been made intensely unhappy by her inadequacy.

But the realization had come that she would no longer be uncomfortable or unfit in his world. Oh, she had not been transformed in little over a month. She still had a vast long way to go before she could function like a lady who had been born and raised to the life. But she was on the way. And slow and difficult as some of the lessons were, she knew that she could master them. She would never be a lady by birth, and there were those in the *beau monde* who would always hold that against her, but she would be a lady by training. And there were plenty of people—people she liked and respected—who would accept her.

What was to stop her, then, from marrying Neville again?

She would not allow him to marry her out of a sense of obligation, she told herself at first. But she knew that was ridiculous. She knew that he still loved her even before he stopped her outside the jeweler's shop and said what he did about her locket. And she certainly knew that she loved him. She had not stopped adoring him since she was fourteen and first set eyes on him.

She must think carefully, though. She must be very sure that she was not rationalizing. She must be certain that no lingering sense of inferiority would prevent her from seeing herself as his equal. She would *not* be his equal in birth or fortune. She must know for sure that that fact would never be a stumbling block for either of them—even after the first bright bloom had worn off their love, as it inevitably would in the course of their lives.

But she would think when she was alone again. For this afternoon she would allow herself to relax into the magic and simply enjoy herself. And so she went to Gunter's with him, and she ate her ice and talked to him about all the lessons she had learned in the past month. She chose to amuse him with all the comical details she could think of—most of them at her own expense. They laughed merrily together, and she knew, perhaps with a twinge of unease, that the magic had taken hold of him too.

It was something of a disappointment to have

their tête-à-tête interrupted, but Lily smiled politely at the gentleman who stopped at their table to have a word with them. It was difficult to remember the names of all the people to whom she had been introduced since the evening of the Ashton ball, but she remembered Mr. Dorsey immediately, partly because he had been at Newbury Abbey for a day or two after her arrival, but mainly because it was over him that Elizabeth and the Duke of Portfrey had quarreled.

"Ah, Miss Doyle. Good afternoon," he said, smiling and bowing and looking surprised, as if he had just spotted her. "Kilbourne?"

They both answered politely but without any great enthusiasm. Neville wanted to be alone with her as much as she wished to be alone with him, Lily guessed. She was remembering Elizabeth's brief reference to the incident at the ball the morning after. She could not break a confidence to give a full explanation, Elizabeth had said, but she believed there was indeed good reason for Lily to avoid furthering an acquaintance with Mr. Dorsey.

But he was an amiable gentleman and surely harmless, Lily thought over the coming five minutes, during which he sat uninvited at their table and chatted with them. He had heard that the Earl of Kilbourne had recently been at Leavenscourt in Leicestershire. He wished he had known. He was heir to the ailing Baron Onslow, who lived at Nuttall Grange a mere five or six miles away. He would have been delighted to go there himself to show the earl the countryside. Or perhaps his lordship had been there on business?

It was a rather embarrassing coincidence, Lily thought, that the Duke of Portfrey himself should happen to walk past Gunter's during those five minutes and, glancing in, see the three of them there. He paused for a moment and then walked on after touching his hat to Lily. Well, she thought, at least she would be able to assure Elizabeth that she and Neville had been given no choice beyond being rude.

A minute or two later Mr. Dorsey took his leave.

"A curiously amiable fellow," Neville said. "He would have gone all the way to Leicestershire merely to show me the countryside if he had known I was five miles away from his uncle's estate? And yet I scarcely know him. Perhaps he believes he owes me a courtesy because he was a guest at Newbury in May. But he came as an acquaintance of Lauren's grandfather. At least he has gone out of his way to show that he bears me no grudge."

They smiled at each other.

"You have not, I suppose," he said, leaning toward her, the interruption forgotten, "been to Vauxhall Gardens yet, have you, Lily?"

"No." She shook her head. "But I have heard of them. They are said to be enchanted at night."

"Will you go there with me," he asked her, "if I can get up a party?"

It might well be a most dangerous place to go if upon careful consideration she decided that she could not after all change her mind about him. She should perhaps refuse outright now. Or at least she should say no more than that she would think about it and talk with Elizabeth about it.

But she found herself leaning eagerly toward him until their faces were only inches apart.

"Oh, yes," she said. "Yes, please, my lord."

⤴ *21* ⤴

"I wonder," the Duke of Portfrey said, "what Mr. Calvin Dorsey's interest in you might be, Miss Doyle."

Elizabeth and Lily were members of a party of guests the duke had invited to share his box at the theater. Lily had been enthralled by the whole experience so far—by the sumptuous elegance of the theater, by the audience in the other boxes, the pit, and the galleries, by the first act of the play. She had been swept away into another world as soon as the performance had begun and had lost all sense of her separate identity—she had become the characters on stage and had lived their lives with them. But now there was an interval, and the box had filled with visitors come to greet Elizabeth or other members of the party—and to get a closer look at the famous Lily Doyle.

His grace had wasted no time on idle chatter. He had suggested that Lily stroll outside the box with him for a while.

"What is *anyone's* interest in me, your

grace?" she said in answer to his remark. "By *ton* standards I am a nobody."

"He has never been in the petticoat line," his grace said, "or into any particular gallantries to the ladies. But he has deliberately sought you out on two separate occasions that I am aware of."

"I believe, your grace," Lily said, "it is none of your concern."

"Ah, that flashing of the eye and jerking upward of the chin," he said, shaking his head. "Lily, what does one do when... Well, no matter."

"Besides," Lily said, "Mr. Dorsey was more interested in the Earl of Kilbourne than in me at Gunter's. He would have gone to Leicestershire himself a few weeks ago, he said, if he had known his lordship was there."

"Kilbourne was in Leicestershire?" the duke asked.

"At Leavenscourt," Lily said, "where my father grew up—my grandfather was a groom there."

"He is still alive?" his grace asked.

"No," Lily said. "He died before my father did, and my father's brother has died since then too."

"Ah," the duke said, "so there is no one left. I am sorry."

"Only an aunt," Lily said, "and two cousins."

"My wife was from Leicestershire," the duke said. "Did you know I was once married, Lily? She grew up at Nuttall Grange a few miles from Leavenscourt. Calvin Dorsey was her cousin. And your mother was once her personal maid."

Lily stopped walking abruptly. She stared at him, not even noticing other strollers, who almost collided with them and were obliged to circle about them. Suddenly, for no reason she could name, she felt very afraid.

"How do you know?" she asked almost in a whisper.

"I have spoken with her sister," he said. "Another aunt."

During the past week Lily had discovered certain facts about her parents' roots. And she had just discovered that both had surviving family. She was not quite as alone in the world as she had thought. But instead of exulting, her mind was churning with unease—worse than unease. She could get no grip on the feeling, though. Of what exactly—or of *whom* exactly—was she afraid?

"I believe," his grace said, "it is time we returned to the box, Lily. The second act will be beginning soon."

༺

Lily was extremely fond of Elizabeth, who exemplified for her all the finer qualities of a true lady. Lily respected and admired her. She was also aware of the fact that she was Elizabeth's employee, who did almost no work for her very generous salary. All Elizabeth required by way of service was that Lily apply herself to the lessons she herself had dreamed of and that she display as much as possible of her newly acquired knowledge and skills by attending certain social functions with her employer.

Lily had worked very hard, both for her own sake and for that of her employer. And she was pleased with the results, if a little impatient with the slowness by which some of them were being achieved. But sometimes a nostalgia for the old way of life became almost overwhelming. Sometimes the need to be outdoors, to be in communion with nature, to disappear into her own world of inner tranquility could not be denied. Hyde Park was no real substitute for the countryside, surrounded as it was by the largest, busiest city in the world. And through most of the day it was a fashionable resort for the *beau monde*, who liked to parade there to see and be seen, to exchange the latest *on dits* of gossip. But Lily had rarely known idyllic conditions in which to enjoy the natural world. She was accustomed to seeing what she wished to see while shutting out the world around her for precious moments of time. And Hyde Park in the early mornings came close to being idyllic.

A few times since her arrival in London Lily had stolen out of the house alone soon after dawn in order to enjoy a quiet hour by herself before the lessons and the busy round of activities began. She never told Elizabeth, and if Elizabeth knew, she gave no indication. If she had admitted to knowing, of course, she would have felt obliged to insist that Lily take a maid or a footman with her. And that would have ruined the whole thing.

Lily went to the park the morning after the play. It was a cool morning, a little misty, but with the promise of another lovely day ahead. There was scarcely anyone about. Lily avoided the paths and walked on the dew-wet grass. She was tempted to remove her shoes and stockings, but she did not do so. There were, alas, proprieties to be observed. The park was not *quite* deserted, after all. There were a few tradesmen hurrying about their early-morning business, and the occasional rider cantered along the paths.

Lily tipped back her head to gaze at the tree-tops while she drew in deep lungfuls of air. She tried to clear her mind, in which unease and exhilaration mingled to such a disturbing degree that she had been waking and sleeping and waking and sleeping all night long—and there had been the old nightmare again.

She could not understand quite why she had been frightened by what she had learned last evening. Perhaps it was just that she was accustomed to believing that she was without close connections. Since she was seven there had been only her father—a rock of security while he lived, but the only rock. Yet now suddenly there was a whole crowding of con-nections—two aunts, two cousins, and two acquaintances who had close ties with the place where her mother had been a maid. Lily had not even known that her mother had been in service. But she had been a personal maid to Mr. Dorsey's cousin, the Duke of Portfrey's wife.

What made her vaguely uneasy about those

facts? Lily could still not find an answer this morning. She tried to shake off the feeling.

She knew very well why she was exhilarated. Neville had indeed got together a party to go to Vauxhall Gardens three evenings hence. She would have been excited just at the prospect of going to the famous pleasure gardens, Lily thought. But... Well, it was not just the idea of going there that had her so excited she could hardly sleep. Vauxhall Gardens was the place for romance, she had heard, with its tree-lined, lantern-lighted avenues and more private paths, with its private boxes and concerts and dances and fireworks displays.

And she would be going there within a few evenings with Neville. The party was to consist of eight persons, but that fact meant nothing to Lily. She knew that he had invited the other six only because he could not invite her alone.

She wondered if he planned an evening of romance—and if she would allow it. She still had not quite made up her mind.

She tried not to mull over the old arguments as she walked in the park. She kept her face lifted and listened to the birds, which were singing in full chorus. She tried to focus her mind on the precious present moment.

She would wear her locket to Vauxhall, she decided. He would notice and remember her telling him that she would wear it for some special occasion.

But was she prepared to give him such a signal?

She breathed in the slightly damp air with

its strong smell of vegetation and listened to the distant sounds of a horse's cantering hooves.

If the Duke of Portfrey had talked with her mother's sister, he too must have been in Leicestershire recently. But why not? He had been married to a woman who had grown up there. Perhaps he was still on terms of intimacy with her family.

The horse was coming closer from behind her. Its pace had quickened almost to a gallop. The few times Lily had been on horseback, she had found riding a most wonderful sensation. She thought she would rather like to fly along the paths of Hyde Park on a horse's back.

And then three things happened simultaneously—the sound of the horse's hooves became muffled, as if they were riding now on grass; someone screamed; and Lily had that feeling again—that feeling of bone-chilling, mind-numbing terror. When she turned her head, horse and rider were almost upon her. By sheer instinct she twisted away and fell heavily to the grass. The horse thundered past and continued on its way at full gallop.

The scream was repeated and a young serving girl came rushing across the grass, dropping a large basket as she did so. Two men, one in the dress of a laborer, the other looking more like a prosperous merchant, also appeared as if from nowhere. Lily lay dazed on the wet grass, gazing up at them.

"Oh, miss." The girl came down on her knees beside Lily. "Oh, miss, are you dead?"

"She's shocked, not dead, you daft girl," the laborer said. "Are you 'urt, miss?"

"No," Lily said. "I think not. I do not know."

"Best not to move, ma'am," the merchant said briskly, "until you are sure. Get your breath back and then see how your legs feel."

"The brute!" the maid exclaimed, glaring after the fast-disappearing horse and rider. " 'E did not even look where 'e was going, 'e didn't. Prob'ly don't even know 'e almost killed someone."

" 'E wouldn't care," the laborer added cynically. "The quality don't care about 'urting a bloke or a wench provided they don't damage the 'orseflesh under 'em. 'Ere, miss, do you want an 'and up?"

"Leave her for a moment," the merchant said. "You do not have your maid with you, ma'am?"

Lily's mind was just beginning to inform her that she had escaped death by a whisker—again. It had not yet drawn her attention to the various bruises she had sustained in her awkward fall.

"I am quite all right," she said. "Thank you."

" 'E looked like the devil from 'ell, 'e did," the maid was informing them all, "with that black cloak flying out be'ind 'im. I didn't see 'is face. P'raps there *was* no face. Oooh, p'raps 'e really were the devil."

"Don't be daft, girl," the laborer told her. "Though why 'e were wearing an 'ood over 'is 'ead on a morning like this, I don't know—unless 'e were a woman, that is, and she didn't want anyone seeing 'er riding astride and recognizing 'er. The quality is all queer in the upper works if you arsk me."

The merchant was more practically engaged in helping Lily to her feet and allowing her to cling to his arm for a few moments until she could be sure that her legs would hold her upright.

"Will you allow me to see you home, ma'am?" he asked her.

"Oh, thank you," she said. "But no. I am quite all right, if a little damp. Thank you all. I am very grateful to you."

"Well, if you are sure," the merchant said, ruining his gesture of gallantry by withdrawing a watch from an upper pocket, frowning, and remarking that it was just as well as he was late for an appointment.

Lily walked home alone and succeeded in getting into the house and up to her room without being seen by either Elizabeth or any of the servants. She stripped off her wet clothes before ringing for Dolly and then smiled beguilingly at her maid and told her that she had been to the park and slipped on the grass—but she would prefer that her escapade not be discovered by anyone else. Dolly entered gleefully into the conspiracy and promised that her lips would be tightly sealed—and then she proceeded, as she tended to Lily, to give an enthusiastic progress report on her budding relationship with Elizabeth's handsome coachman.

It had been an accident, Lily told herself, beginning to feel the painful effects of her bruises. A careless rider had strayed from the path and had not even noticed her.

He had been wearing a dark cloak—*with the hood up*.

Probably every gentleman in the nation owned at least one dark cloak. And the morning had been cool, even if not exactly cold.

And it was certainly possible that the *he* really had been a *she*.

It had been an accident.

But she feared it had not been.

Any more than the rock falling from the top of the cliff at Newbury had been.

～

Matters were progressing slowly—if at all. Neville had not even seen Lily every day since his arrival in town. And when he did see her, it was usually at some entertainment when she stayed close to Elizabeth's side and good manners kept him from trying to spend too much time with her.

They were still watched avidly wherever they appeared together. Joseph had told him that drawing room conversation was thriving on the topic. There were even said to be two items relating to them recorded in the betting book at White's Club. There were gentlemen who had placed their bets on the likelihood or otherwise of his marrying Lily again within the year. And there were others—or possibly the same ones—who had bet on the possibility of his marrying Lauren within the same time frame.

354

Joseph was privately amused by the whole business. Publicly he considered it all a crashing bore—there was no one better able to show ennui than the Marquess of Attingsborough.

But Neville intended to throw caution to the wind during the Vauxhall evening. He intended to take full advantage of the setting. While he had reserved a private box and invited guests and made it his own party, he nevertheless planned to spend some time alone with Lily. He had been wooing her very gently and cautiously for almost two weeks. He intended to woo her in earnest at Vauxhall. He was not without hope of success. He remembered the afternoon at the jeweler's and Gunter's almost with bated breath. She had been relaxed and happy on that afternoon—happy to be with him.

He prayed for good weather.

And his prayers were granted. The day had been hot and sunny, if a little windy. The wind dropped as evening fell to create conditions that could not have been more favorable for Vauxhall if Neville had had the ordering of them.

They crossed the River Thames by boat—the slower but by far more picturesque way of approaching Vauxhall Gardens. Neville took a seat in the boat beside Lily while Elizabeth sat in front of them—Portfrey, who had been out of town for a few days, had been expected back today but had not yet put in an appearance. Joseph was sitting behind, flirting discreetly with Lady Selina Rawlings, his current lady love and present for the evening under Elizabeth's chaperonage. Captain Harris and his wife were seated in the stern of the boat. Colored lights from the gardens shivered across the water. Darkness had all but fallen.

"Well, Lily?" Neville bent his head closer to hers so that he could see her expression.

"It is magic," she said.

And it was too—magic to weave its spell about the two of them and not release them until the night was over, and perhaps not even then.

He took Lily on one arm, Elizabeth on the other as they entered Vauxhall Gardens and made their way to the box he had reserved, in an area with all the other boxes and the place where the orchestra members were tuning their instruments. It was one of the nights when there was to be dancing.

"Have you danced beneath the stars before, Lily?" he asked her after he had seated everyone in the box and ordered food and drinks.

"Of course I have," she said. "Do you not remember all the dancing we used to do?"

In the army? Yes, there had been a great deal of it. The officers had had dances of their own, better organized, more formal, not nearly as enjoyable, Neville had always thought, as the ones that took place about the campfires or in some rude barn. He had used to stand and watch sometimes. He had never dampened the spirits of his men by trying to join in and claim a partner when there were not nearly enough women to go around.

"Yes, I do." He smiled at her. "But have you *waltzed* beneath the stars? Do you know the steps of the waltz?"

"I am not allowed to dance it," she told him. "I have to be approved by one of the patronesses of Almack's first—though I daresay that will never happen."

He moved his head a little closer and spoke for her ears only. "But this is not a formal ball, Lily. The rules do not apply here. Tonight you will waltz—with me."

Her eyes told him that she wanted to do so. And her eyes told him other things too. There was a certain depth of yearning in them—he was sure he did not mistake the expression.

And then he noticed her locket.

"Is this the first time you have worn it?" he asked, touching it briefly.

"Yes," she said.

"Is this the special occasion, then, Lily?" He looked up into her eyes.

"Yes, Neville."

Strange, he thought, how his name on her lips became the most intimate of endearments.

There was no more chance for personal discourse for a while. The food and drink had arrived, the orchestra had begun playing, and conversation became general.

When the dancing began, Neville led Elizabeth out onto the dancing area and then Mrs. Harris. But the third dance was a waltz, and the time for general socializing was at an end. The time for romance had begun.

"You cannot know," Lily said, placing one

hand on his shoulder and the other in his as the orchestra started to play, "how I have longed to waltz—perhaps because I thought I never would."

"With me, Lily?" he murmured. "Have you dreamed of waltzing with me?"

Her eyes widened. "Yes," she said. "Oh, yes. With you."

He did not attempt to converse after that. There was a time for words and there was a time for simply experiencing. The air was cool and the moon and stars above them were bright. But nature at Vauxhall was in happy communion with the man-made beauty of the sounds of the orchestra and the colors of the lanterns nodding gently in the trees.

And there was the woman in his arms, small and shapely and dainty, and smiling into his eyes through the whole dance without embarrassment and without any pretense of indifference.

"Well?" he asked when the waltz was almost at an end. "Is it as wicked a dance as it is said to be, Lily?"

"Oh," she said. "Wickeder."

He laughed softly and she joined him.

"Come walking?" he asked.

She nodded.

"We must take everyone with us," he said, leading her back to the box. "But with a little ingenuity, Lily, I believe we can lose them before we have gone too far."

She did not voice any objection.

She had not been mistaken. Oh, she had *not*. He had married her out of a sense of obligation. He had treated her with kindness after her arrival in England because he was a kind man. He had made love to her because he would make the best of any situation in which he found himself. He had offered for her again even after he knew they were not legally married because he had felt obligated, honor-bound to do so. There had been some love too, of course—he had said so, and she had not doubted him.

But now it was love pure and simple. There was no obligation left. She had freed him, and since then she had made a life for herself and learned the skills that would help her to live independently of anyone's charity and earn her own living.

He was wooing her now—simply because he loved her.

She would no longer entertain even a vestige of doubt. And she would no longer erect obstacles between them that just did not need to be there. She might never be his equal in the eyes of the world, but she knew now that she could live in his world with some comfort and with a good deal of self-respect. The thought of Newbury Abbey no longer filled her with despair.

She was going to allow it to happen.

And so when they strolled along the tree-lined, lantern-lighted avenue with the marquess and Lady Selina, she made no protest at the almost comical maneuverings of both gentlemen to arrange matters that the two couples part company. Neither did Lady Selina.

"You see, Lily," Neville said after the two of them had turned down one of the narrower, darker, quieter paths, "there are these areas that were made for lovers."

"Yes," she said. "How wonderfully convenient."

"And they were made narrow enough," he said, "that two people must walk single file or else with their arms about each other."

"We cannot talk if we walk single file," she said, smiling at the darkness ahead.

"Precisely." He set an arm about her shoulders and drew her close to his side. There was nowhere to put her arm then except about his waist. And then she found that her head was most comfortable against his shoulder.

There was a strange feeling of seclusion even while the sounds of the orchestra and of voices shouting and laughing were still quite audible. There was an occasional lantern in a tree, but in the main the path was lighted by moonlight. If it was romance she had been hoping for, Lily thought, then she had surely found it in abundance.

Their footsteps inevitably lagged when they had walked a distance along the path, and then they stopped altogether. He turned her, and she found her back resting comfortably against the broad trunk of a tree.

"Lily," he said, bracketing her head with his

hands pressed against the trunk, "you must say no now, my dear, if you want this to go no farther."

She reached up one hand and traced his facial scar with one fingertip. "I am not saying no," she whispered to him.

He kissed her, touching her at first only with his mouth. It was a kiss of love, she thought before setting her hands on his shoulders and then sliding her arms about his neck. There could be no other motive on either side. Just love. She parted her lips and kissed him back with love.

He lifted his head as his arms came about her and arched her in against him. She could scarcely see his face with the moonlight behind him, but she thought he was smiling.

"This," he said, his lips brushing hers as he spoke, "was meant to be, Lily, from the very first moment."

She did not ask to what first moment he referred—the moment they had first met? The moment she had walked into the church at Newbury? The first moment of time at the dawn of the world? Perhaps he meant all those moments. And he was right. This had always been meant to be.

He kissed her mouth, her eyes, her temples. He feathered kisses along her jaw to her chin. He kissed her throat. And he kissed her mouth again, murmuring endearments.

The sense of romance faded. She could feel the familiar hard planes of his body pressed against her own. She could smell his cologne and the male essence of him. She could taste the wine he had drunk earlier on his lips and his tongue, inside his mouth. She could hear his breath quicken and could feel his growingly urgent desire pressing against her abdomen. Her own body responded—had done since the first touch of his lips. There was a throbbing ache in her womb and down along her inner thighs as she pressed herself to him in a blind urge to be close—closer. Neville. She wanted him. She wanted him *there. Here. Now.*

But suddenly he lifted his head and his arms about her stiffened. He held his head in a listening attitude. Even in the darkness she could see the frown on his face.

Lily was never sure afterward if she heard a sound herself—a sound other than the distant noise of revelry. But certainly she was suddenly awash in that terrible dread again as he turned away from her to gaze into the trees at the other side of the path. She was not even sure afterward if she saw anything. She was not quite sure she had seen a figure in a dark cloak with a pointed pistol. Everything happened too fast.

Neville suddenly spun back toward her and whisked her around behind the tree, his own body between her and danger. The sound seemed to come after. The bullet had missed her, she thought as he pressed her painfully against the other side of the tree, his back against her, shielding her. But the noise of it still rang in her ears.

She felt suffocated. His hands were spread behind him, on either side of her body. She could scarcely breathe. Even so she welcomed the shield he had provided for her. Without it, she would disintegrate into mindless terror.

She could hear him breathing in heavy gasps that she knew he was trying to silence so that he would not betray their whereabouts. And she knew that she was an impediment to him. Without the necessity of protecting her, he could move, go in search of their assailant instead of waiting for him to find them.

It seemed that they stood there in unbearable tension for five minutes, even ten—probably, she thought afterward, it had been no longer than a minute or two. And then there was the sound of laughter fairly close and drawing closer and she knew with knee-weakening relief that someone was coming along the path—more than one person, in fact.

Actually it was four. As they came up to the tree and then passed it, Neville took her firmly by the hand and drew her out onto the path. They walked down it behind the two couples, who were so merrily foxed that they did not appear to notice that their numbers had been swelled.

"I am taking you back to Elizabeth," Neville said, setting one arm about her when they reached the main avenue. "And then I am going back to find the bast—" He cut off the word in time. He was breathing noisily.

But Lily, setting an arm firmly about his waist, fearing that she would collapse, suddenly became aware of something—something warm and wet and sticky.

"You have been hit," she said. And then in utter panic: "Neville, you have been *shot*!"

"It is nothing," he said through teeth she knew he had gritted together. And he increased their pace.

But as they approached the box, he released his hold on her and half pushed her into a startled Elizabeth, who was standing outside the box with the Duke of Portfrey.

"Take her," Neville said harshly. "Get her out of here. Take her home."

And he collapsed on the ground at their feet.

⤳ *22* ⤳

When Neville came to himself, he was lying facedown on a bed that was not his own. His arms were spread to the sides and someone was hanging on tightly to each of his wrists. He was naked, he realized, at least from the waist up. And his right shoulder was hurting like a thousand devils.

He knew from past experience what was happening.

"The devil!" It was Joseph's voice—he was hanging on to the right wrist with a grip of steel. "You could not have slept a few minutes longer, Nev? Enjoyed dreamland and all that?"

"You can let go your infernal grip on me," Neville said. "I am not going to struggle. Who is the sawbones?"

"Dr. Nightingale is my personal physician,

Neville." Elizabeth's voice, as he might have expected, was cool and sensible—no hysterics from her. "The bullet is still in your shoulder."

And Dr. Nightingale had already made a pass at removing it. That was what had brought him to, Neville realized, taking a firm grip on the edges of the mattress. He opened his eyes at the same moment. His head was turned to the left—it was Lily who was clinging to his left wrist.

"Get out of here," he told her.

"No."

"Wives are supposed to obey their husbands," he said.

"You are not my husband."

"And of course," he said, "you have seen far worse than this on the battlefield. This is nothing at all to you. Foolish of me to try to protect you from a massive fit of the vapors."

"Yes," she agreed.

The physician, far less deft at such a task than the army surgeons, came at him again then, trying to probe gently and causing prolonged and excruciating agony. Neville kept his eyes on Lily's until the pain threatened to get beyond him, and then he clenched his eyes shut and gritted his teeth hard.

"Ah," Dr. Nightingale said at last, a note of satisfaction in the sound.

"Got it!" Joseph sounded breathless, as if he had just run a mile with a wild bull in hot pursuit. "It is out, Nev."

"And no damage to the bone or sinews from what I can see," the doctor added. "We will have you patched up in no time, my lord."

The pain did not subside to any substantial degree. He felt submerged in it, peering out at reality from a long distance within it. But he knew as he opened his eyes again that Lily's hand had gone from his wrist and was somehow clasped in his own—*crushed* in his own. For a few moments longer his hand seemed locked in place, but gradually he relaxed it and set hers free. He saw with a curious detachment from deep inside himself that her fingers appeared white and tightly welded together, that for a short while she could neither move nor separate them. It was amazing he had not broken all of them, but she had not made a sound.

She turned away and then back again and he felt a cool, damp cloth against his hot face.

Joe was talking—Neville did not know what about. The doctor was still busy with his shoulder and apparently Elizabeth was assisting him. Neville watched Lily as she worked quietly and efficiently, as she had always done after a battle or skirmish, dipping the cloth, squeezing out the excess water, pressing it lightly to his face or his neck. He made a cocoon of his pain and hid deep inside it.

"Was he caught?" he asked finally. He had suddenly remembered being at Vauxhall, kissing Lily in one of the darker alleys, considering the very indiscreet act of moving her back father into the trees so that they could take their embrace farther, and then recognizing the strange prickling feeling along his spine as the type of sixth-sense warning of danger he had developed during his years as an officer. He had heard the snapping of a twig, perhaps, without even realizing it. He remembered seeing a cloaked figure lurking in the trees at the other side of the path, aiming a pistol at them. He remembered leaping sideways to shield Lily and taking the bullet that would surely have killed her. "Did someone catch the bastard?" He remembered Elizabeth's and Lily's presence too late.

"Harris and Portfrey went charging off in pursuit," the marquess said, "as did a small army of other men, Nev. I would wager Vauxhall emptied out faster of ladies and everyone else than in its whole history. I doubt anyone found the gunman, though. A man in a dark cloak, Lily said. There were probably fifty men there to answer the description, Portfrey and myself among them."

"You were in the wrong place at the wrong time, Neville," Elizabeth said coolly. "There, Dr. Nightingale is finished. Perhaps you would see him on his way, Lily, while Joseph and I get Neville out of the rest of his clothes and into a nightshirt."

"No," Lily said, "I am staying."

"Lily, my dear—"

"I am staying," she said.

Neville gathered that it was Elizabeth who saw the physician out. For him there followed a nightmarish few minutes—which felt more like a few hours—while Lily and his cousin undressed him and somehow got him, wounded shoulder and all, inside someone's nightshirt, and hauled him off the bed so that the towels on which he had been lying could be removed and the bedclothes properly turned back. Then there was all the difficulty of lying down again. He had suffered his share of wounds during his war years. Every time he found that he had not quite remembered the full extent of the physical agony.

He could hear the rasping of his own breathing. If he concentrated on the rhythm of it, he thought, he could impose some sort of control over the situation.

"We should not have put him on his back." That was Joseph.

"No." That was Lily. "He will be better thus. Neville, you must take this laudanum that the doctor left."

"Go to hell," he said, and his eyes snapped open. "I do beg your pardon."

Her lips were quirking into a smile. "I will support your head," she said.

He had always fought against taking medicines of any sort. But he meekly downed the whole dose of laudanum as punishment for what he had said to her.

After that everything became a blur of pain and gradual, blessed fuzziness. He thought Elizabeth and Portfrey were in the room, though he did not open his eyes to see or take any particular notice of the report that no trace had been found of any suspicious character with a pistol. And then there were just Elizabeth and Lily in the room, arguing over who would stay with him during the night. At least, Elizabeth was arguing—she would take the first watch, the housekeeper the second. It was unseemly for Lily to be alone with him in his bedchamber—if only he could climb out of the depths of himself, he would find something decidedly funny in that argument. She would tire herself out. She was too emotionally involved to make a good nurse—they could expect a fever, and then calmness and a certain detachment would be essential.

Lily put up no argument at all; she simply refused to leave.

He was sinking fast into lethargy by the time they were alone together, but he opened his eyes to confirm his impression that they were. She was standing beside the bed, gazing down at him. She was still wearing the elegant gold silk and gauze evening dress she had worn to Vauxhall.

"You are not going to sit beside the bed all night while I sleep," he told her—it sounded to his own ears as if his words were slurring. "If you are intending to stay, take off that dress and lie down beside me. You are my wife, after all."

"Yes," she said, but his mind was not focused enough to understand to what she was agreeing.

The pain had localized and became a dull pulsing in his shoulder. His tongue felt thick. His breathing was deepening. There was a new warmth along his left side and someone's small hand was in his.

Lily awoke when the predawn light was graying the room—an unfamiliar room. She felt as if a fire was burning close to her right side. Someone was talking.

Neville was apologizing to Lauren. Then he was telling Sergeant Doyle in marvelously profane language what a damned foolish thing he had done by throwing his body in the path of a bullet intended for someone else. Then he was instructing a whole company of men to stay where they were in the pass, to ignore the murderous French fire from the hills to either side—to search for the marriage papers until they had found them. Then he was telling someone that he was by thunder going to get Lily alone at Vauxhall and just let Elizabeth try to stop him.

He was in a raging fever, with the accompanying delirium.

Lily had opened his nightshirt down the front and was bathing him with cool water when Elizabeth arrived. But apart from raising her eyebrows as she observed Lily clad only in her shift and then glancing at the left side of the bed, which had obviously been slept in, she made no comment. She quietly set about sharing the nursing. She had, she told Lily, made arrangements to cancel all lessons until further notice.

Lily steadfastly refused to leave the room until late in the afternoon. She knew from experience that many more men died from the fever that succeeded surgery than ever died from the wounds themselves. A bullet in the shoulder ought not to be a mortal wound, but the fever might well kill. She would not leave him. She would nurse him back to health or she would be by his side when he died.

But Elizabeth had been right—it was hard to nurse a man when one had an emotional involvement with him. When one loved him so deeply that one knew his death would leave a yawning emptiness in one's own life that could never again be filled. When one knew that he had taken the bullet intended for her. And when one did not understand why it had happened.

She had never told him that she loved him—or not since her wedding night. Now it might be too late. She could tell him so a dozen times during the course of the day—and she did so—but he could not understand.

She had never told him that to her dying day she would consider him to be her husband no matter what the church and the state had to say to the contrary—that she had never wavered in her fidelity to their marriage.

He caught her wrist in a hot, bruising grip late in the morning. "I should have kept her with me at the head of the line, should I not?" he asked her, his eyes bright with fever. "I should not have entrusted her safety to other men at the center. I should never have done that. I should have died protecting her."

"You did your very best, Neville," she told

371

him, leaning close to him. "That is all anyone can ever do."

"I might have saved her," he said, "from—Is it true that it is a fate worse than death, do you suppose? I wish I could have died to save her from that."

"Nothing is worse than death," she said. "There is always hope this side of the grave. As long as I was alive, I could dream of coming back to you. I loved you. I have always loved you."

"You must not say that, Lauren," he said. "Please do not say that, dear."

Elizabeth finally persuaded her late in the afternoon to return to her own room—with the promise that she would not argue about Lily's keeping the night watch again. Dolly was waiting for Lily, she said, and was threatening to come and drag her mistress away by force. There was a hot bath awaiting her and a bed.

"I will have you woken if there is any change," she promised. "He is tough, Lily. He will come through this."

Lily would have known very well that Elizabeth spoke the truth if he had been anyone but Neville. But she was too desperate for him to live to believe that he would.

She surprised herself by sleeping deeply and dreamlessly for four hours. When she rang for Dolly, her maid informed her that his grace, the Duke of Portfrey, begged a few minutes of her time in the drawing room before she returned to the sickroom.

Lily had very firmly pushed from her mind

all thoughts of what had happened at Vaux-hall. It was easier said than done, of course, but she had refused to dwell upon the terri-fying mystery. She could not afford to do so now. She needed all her emotional strength for Neville. But the terror came rushing back when she learned that the duke was below-stairs—and with it the memory that he had suddenly appeared at Vauxhall between the time she and the others had left for their walk and the time of their return. *And he had been wearing a long black opera cloak.*

She went down to the drawing room anyway.

He came hurrying across the room toward her, both his hands outstretched. "Lily, my dear," he said. His handsome face was all frowning concern.

Lily leaned back against the door and clutched the doorknob with both hands behind her.

He dropped his hands and stopped a few feet away from her. "We were unable to catch him," he said. "I am so sorry. Did you see him, Lily? Did you have a good look at him? Can you remember anything in addition to the dark cloak and the pistol?"

"Was it you?" She was whispering.

He stared at her in seeming incompre-hension. "What?" he said.

"Was it you who shot Neville?" She was speaking aloud now.

He said nothing for what seemed a long while. "Why would you think it was me?" he asked her.

"It was you on the rhodondendron walk,"

she said. "Was it you in the woods? And you who pushed the stone over the cliff and tried to kill me on the rocks below? Was it you who tried to run me down with your horse in Hyde Park? I know I was the target at Vauxhall, not Neville. Was it you?" Curiously she felt very calm. His face, she noticed, was drained of all color.

"Someone tried to kill you at *Newbury*?" he asked her. "And in Hyde Park?"

"I saw a figure on the rhododendron walk," she said, "standing still and looking for me— I was in a tree. And then I came down the path and there you were. Why do you want me dead?"

His hand was over his eyes, which he had closed. "There is only one explanation," he muttered. He opened his eyes and looked at her. "But how the devil am I going to prove it?" He blinked and looked at her with more awareness in his eyes. "Lily, it was not I. I swear it. I do not wish you any harm. On the contrary. If you but knew..." He shook his head. "I have no proof... of anything. Please believe that it was not I."

And suddenly her suspicions seemed ridiculous to her. She could not imagine why she had ever entertained them. But then the idea that someone wanted her dead was ridiculous too. And one could hardly expect a prospective murderer to confess to the victim he had stalked for well over a month.

"For your own peace of mind," he said, "please believe me. Oh, Lily, if you just knew how I love you."

She recoiled in horror and pressed herself against the door so that the knob to which she clung dug painfully into her back. What did he mean? He *loved* her? In what way? But there was only one way, surely. Yet he was old enough to be her father. And he was dangling after Elizabeth—was he not?

His grace ran the fingers of one hand through his silvering hair and blew out his breath from puffed cheeks. "Forgive me," he said. "I have never been so inept. Go up to Kilbourne, Lily, and ask Elizabeth to join me here, if you will. And do me the honor of trusting me, I beg you."

She did not answer him. She turned and opened the door and fled through it. She had every reason to distrust him—now more than ever. What had he meant by saying that he loved her? And yet, when he had asked her to trust him, she had felt inclined to do just that.

~

The room was dark when he opened his eyes. He was not sure if it was the same night as the one during which a bullet had been dug out of his shoulder. He rather thought it was not. He was feeling weak—and his shoulder was stiff and as sore as hell. He turned his head and winced from the pain. She was lying beside him, her head turned toward him, her eyes open.

"If I am dreaming," he said, smiling at her, "don't tell me."

"Your fever broke two hours ago," she said. "You have been sleeping. But you are awake now. Are you hungry?"

"Thirsty," he said.

She was wearing only a thin shift, he could see when she got out of bed and crossed the room to pour him a glass of water. She held it while he sat up. It took him awhile to do so—he had refused her help. But she set a bank of pillows behind him after he had taken the glass. He leaned gingerly back against them after he had finished drinking.

"Civilian life makes one soft, Lily," he said. "If this had happened in the Peninsula, I would have been back on the battlefield by now."

"I know," she said.

He patted the bed beside him and took one of her hands in his when she sat down. "I suppose," he said, "no one was caught."

She shook her head.

"You must not fear," he told her—not that he could really imagine Lily cowering with prolonged terror. "It was one of those senseless and random acts of violence that always seem to happen to other people. He was some sort of madman, or else something had happened on that night to give him a grudge against the world and we happened to be there in his line of fire. It will not happen again."

"It has happened before," she said.

He did not for a moment misunderstand her. He felt himself turn cold. He had not, he realized, believed his own explanation—

except that he had nothing to offer in its place. Why would anyone wish to shoot at either him or Lily?

"Someone has shot at you before?" It was too bizarre even to think about.

She shook her head. "Not shot," she said, and proceeded to tell him about the distant glimpse she had had on the rhododendron walk of a figure in a black cloak and the feeling she had had in the woods that she had spotted someone in a cloak again. She told him about the stone falling from the cliff as she had been scrambling on the rocks below. She told him about her near encounter with death in Hyde Park.

"Someone wants me dead," she said.

"Why?" He frowned. He wished he did not feel so damnably weak. He wished his brain was not working so sluggishly.

She shook her head and shrugged her shoulders.

Someone wanted Lily dead and had almost got his wish on three separate occasions—*once at Newbury.*

He reached for her suddenly, hardly even noticing the screaming pain in his shoulder. He brought her down half across him and wrapped his arms about her, her head cradled on his left shoulder.

"No," he said, almost as if by his very will he could protect her, "it is not going to happen, Lily. I swear it is not. I failed once to save you. It will not happen again."

"You must forget about that ambush in

Portugal," she said, her hand smoothing over the side of his face. "You saved my life at Vauxhall. The slate is wiped clean."

"No one is going to harm you," he said. "My word on it." Ridiculous word of a man who had not even known that her life had been threatened and almost lost on his own property.

She kissed the underside of his jaw. "You must rest again," she said, "or the fever will come back."

"Lie down with me, then," he said. "I do not want to let you out of my sight."

She came around the bed and lay down beside him beneath the covers. "Rest," she said. "I should not have said anything until you were strong again."

He took her hand in his and turned his head to look at her. "Let me make love to you?"

She hesitated, but she shook her head. "No," she said. "Not yet, Neville. It is not the right time."

She was calling him Neville again, he noticed. And although she had said no, she had added *not yet*. He closed his eyes and smiled. Where the devil would he have found the energy if she had said yes?

"Besides," she said, "you are still too weak."

"Grrr," he said without opening his eyes.

She laughed softly.

She must have used up a great deal of energy nursing him. And for all her calm manner, she must have been exhausted by anxiety. She was fast asleep within minutes.

Neville lay beside her, staring upward.

Someone wanted Lily dead. It made no sense. Why? What possible motive could anyone have? Who could possibly have any reason to resent her? Try as he would, he could think only of Lauren or Gwen. And the sort of resentment either of them might feel was certainly not the stuff from which murder came. Besides, they were far away, Gwen at Newbury, Lauren at her grandfather's. She had decided to go there quite on the spur of the moment soon after his departure for London, his mother had written, but had refused company for the journey.

Who else?

There was no one else.

What did Lily have that anyone could want, then? Lily had nothing. Her locket was the only thing of any value that she possessed, and no one would want to kill her for the sake of a gold locket when almost every mansion in Mayfair must be loaded down with far costlier jewels. Besides, until the evening of Vauxhall, she had not worn the locket since the Peninsula. There might have been money for her in Doyle's pack, but it would not have been a sum for which to kill. Besides, whatever it was had been burned.

His mind for some reason stuck on that idea. Perhaps because there *were* no other ideas.

Was it likely that Bessie Doyle would have burned the contents of that pack without sifting through them first? If there had been anything of value, would she not have kept it? *Had* she kept something apart from the bag itself? She seemed a woman of open enough honesty, though. He had not been given the impression that she was hiding anything—he still did not believe it.

She had been away from home when the pack arrived. Presumably her husband had received it. He had died in an accident before she returned home, leaving the pack and its contents spilled all over the floor in one corner of the cottage.

Almost as if he—*or someone else*—had been searching for something.

Without understanding the reason, Neville felt chilled and uneasy.

Sergeant Doyle had been trying to tell him something before his death. Something he ought to have told Lily and someone else. Something about the pack he had left back at the base. He had repeatedly told Lily that there was something inside it for her. Was it possible that William Doyle had found whatever it was?

And had been killed as a result?

But there was no way now of discovering the answers.

This was ridiculous, Neville thought impatiently. He would be writing Gothic novels before he was finished. But then the idea of three attempts being made on Lily's life was ridiculous too.

And then a memory popped into his head as if from nowhere—a detail he had not paid much attention to at the time. A letter had come, Bessie Doyle had told him, informing them of Sergeant Doyle's death. And William, who could not read, had taken the letter to the vicar to read to him. If the pack itself had contained a letter or a package with some writing, *would he have taken that too to the vicar?*

This was ridiculous stuff, Neville thought again.

Someone wanted Lily dead. Nothing was more senseless than that. But somehow, somewhere, there must be a reason for it.

He knew then what he was going to have to do.

He closed his hand more protectively about Lily's.

He was going to save her. If it cost him his life, if it cost him *her*, he would save her from terror and death. He would not stop looking until he found and destroyed whatever—or *whoever*—was threatening her.

∽ *23* ∽

Lily was feeling depressed. Neville had made a quick recovery after coming out of his fever, as might have been expected of a seasoned soldier, and had returned to Kilbourne House two days later. He had called the day after that, but only briefly to announce that he was leaving town for a few days. He had not explained either where he was going or when he expected to return—if he ever did. His manner had been abrupt and impersonal, though he had taken Lily's hands in his when he took his leave. Elizabeth had been in the room too.

"Lily," he had said, "you will promise me, if you please, not to leave this house alone and not to leave any room in a house other than this without company."

He had waited for her answer. It had not seemed an appropriate moment to assert her independence. Anyway, she would have done as he suggested even if he had not asked it of her.

"I promise."

He had squeezed her hands, hesitated a moment, and then said more. "When you *do* leave this house," he had told her, "you may sense that you are being watched and followed. You must not be alarmed even though you will be right. There will be more than one of them—watching out for your safety."

Her eyes had widened, but she had not argued. It was no longer possible to persuade herself that she had been imagining any of the attacks on her life. And he had earned the right—with a bullet in his shoulder—to show an active concern for her safety.

She had nodded again and he had left after squeezing her hands once more and bending toward her to place one light kiss on her cheek.

Since then she had gone driving in the park twice at the fashionable hour with Elizabeth and the Duke of Portfrey, and she had been to one private dinner at the Duke of Anburey's and one select soirée at the home of one of Elizabeth's friends—a lady with a reputation as a bluestocking. And her lessons had resumed.

She had thrown herself into her studies with a frenzy of energy and determination. At last she seemed to have passed a frustrating plateau and could see progress again in almost all skills except embroidery.

But she was depressed. No progress had been made in apprehending the man who had tried on three separate occasions to kill her. She had kept quiet about her own groundless suspicions. There were no clues, no leads. But in the meantime she felt as if she lived in a cage. She could go nowhere alone even though the weather had been uniformly glorious and the early mornings had beckoned her with an almost irresistible invitation. And even when she was from home she felt the presence of her guards.

Her nerves were feeling frayed. Elizabeth had mentioned quite casually that she was glad to have learned that Lauren was going to her grandfather's in Yorkshire. A change of scene would be good for her.

When had she left?

"Did Gwendoline go with her?" Lily had asked.

But Lauren had intended going alone. *Had she really gone to Yorkshire?* Lily could not help asking herself. But it was absurd. Lauren, though she rode, was not the type to gallop astride across the open stretches of Hyde Park. And one could not somehow imagine her aiming and firing a pistol. Or thrusting a rock from its moorings on top of a cliff. But even so...

Worst of all, Neville was gone—just at the

time when Lily had thought there was a new courtship between them and he was on the verge of declaring himself. She tried not to think about him. She had a life to live. But that life was so very dreary at present. She looked forward to the evening party Elizabeth had been planning for several weeks. It was expected to be a large gathering. Lily's fame had reached new heights after the incident at Vauxhall. Besides, invitations to Elizabeth's select parties were always coveted.

Lily dressed carefully for the occasion. She intended to enjoy herself and to acquit herself well. She was to be in the nature of a hostess since she lived here, and that was an entirely new venture for her.

"What do you think, Dolly?" she asked her maid before going downstairs. "Am I beautiful or am I beautiful?" She pirouetted, her arms held gracefully to the sides.

"Well, I don't know as how either word would describe you exactly, my lady," Dolly said, her head tipped to one side, one finger against her chin—Dolly had never stopped addressing her as if she were a countess. "If you was to ask me—which you *are doing*—I would say you look beautiful."

They both laughed, tickled at the sorry joke.

"You always look lovely in white," Dolly continued. "And lots of ladies would kill for all that fine lace. You need some jewelry, though."

"Shall I wear the diamonds or the rubies?"

They chuckled together again, and Lily fetched her locket from the drawer beside her bed. She had not worn it since Vauxhall—that very special occasion that had gone all awry. But she would not be superstitious. She touched a hand to it after Dolly had clasped it about her neck. Oh yes, he had been right, she thought, closing her eyes briefly. The locket made her papa seem closer and reminded her of her mama. But most of all it made her think of *him* taking her to the jeweler's to have the chain mended so that she could wear it again.

"He will come back, my lady," Dolly said.

Lily looked at her, startled. Her maid was nodding sagely.

"Gracious," Lily lied, "I was not even thinking of him, Dolly."

"Then how do you know which him I was talking about?" Dolly asked saucily, and went off into peals of laughter again.

Lily was still smiling as she went downstairs. The guests began arriving almost immediately, and she had no time for further thought or brooding. She concentrated on her posture and smiles, on listening and on saying the right things. It was not so very difficult after all, she was finding, to mingle with the *ton*. And most people were kind to her.

She was in the book room about an hour later with Elizabeth, the Marquess of Attingsborough, and two other gentlemen. Mr. Wylie had asked her in the drawing room if she had taken out a subscription to any of the libraries, and the marquess had informed him that Miss Doyle could not read but they would not hold that against her as she was certainly one of the loveliest young ladies in town. Lily had been unwise enough to protest indignantly that indeed she could read.

Joseph had grinned at her. "People who tell fibs, you know, Lily," he had said, "go straight to hell when they die."

"Then I shall prove it to you," she had told him.

That was why they were in the book room. Lily had challenged the marquess to withdraw any book from any shelf and she would read the first sentence aloud.

"Are there any books of sermons here, Elizabeth?" he asked, looking along the shelves.

"I say," Mr. Wylie told Lily, "I would take your word for it, Miss Doyle. I am sure you read very prettily indeed. And I cannot see that it matters if you don't. I was merely making conversation."

Lily smiled at him.

"Gallantry to ladies," Elizabeth said, "was never Joseph's strongest point, Mr. Wylie. There *are* no sermons, Joseph. I hear enough at church on Sundays."

"A shame," he muttered. "Ah, here, this will do—*The Pilgrim's Progress.*" He made a great to-do about drawing the leather-bound volume from the shelf and opening it to the first page before handing the book to Lily.

She was laughing and feeling horribly flustered at the same time. She felt even more embarrassed when someone else appeared in the doorway and she saw that it was the Duke of Portfrey. He must have just arrived and had come to greet Elizabeth.

"Ah, Lyndon," she said, "Joseph has insulted Lily by claiming that she is illiterate. She is about to prove him wrong."

The duke smiled and stood where he was in the doorway, his hands clasped behind him. "We should have had a wager on it, Attingsborough," he said. "I would be about to relieve you of a fortune."

"Oh, dear," Lily said. "I do not read very well yet. I may not be able to decipher every word." She bent her head and saw with some relief that the first sentence was not very long; neither did it appear to contain many long words.

" 'As I walked through the wild-er-ness of this world,' " she read in a halting monotone, " 'I l-lighted on a certain place where was a den, and I laid me down in that place to sleep; and, as I slept, I drrr-eamed a dream.' " She looked up with a triumphant smile and lowered the book.

The gentlemen applauded and the marquess whistled.

"Bravo, Lily," he said. "Perhaps you are bound for heaven after all. My humblest, most abject apologies." He took the book from her hands and closed it with a flourish.

Lily glanced toward the Duke of Portfrey, who had taken a couple of steps closer to her. But her smile died. He was staring at her, all color drained from his face. Everyone seemed to notice at the same time. An unnatural hush fell on the room.

"Lily," he said in a strange half whisper, "where did you get that locket?"

Her hand lifted to it and covered it protectively. "It is mine," she said. "My mother
and father gave it to me."

"When?" he asked.

"I have always had it," she told him, "for
as long as I can remember. It *is* mine." She
was frightened again. She curled her fingers
around the locket.

"Let me see it," he commanded her. He had
come within arm's length of her.

She tightened her hold of the locket.

"Lyndon—" Elizabeth began.

"Let me see it!"

Lily took her hand away and he stared at
the locket, his face paler if that were possible—
he looked as if he might well faint.

"It has the entwined F and L," he said.
"Open it for me. What is inside?"

"Lyndon, what *is* this?" Elizabeth sounded
annoyed.

"Open it!" His grace had taken no notice
of her.

Lily shook her head, sick with terror even
though there were four other people in the
room besides the two of them. The Duke of
Portfrey seemed unaware of them—until he
withdrew his eyes from the locket suddenly
and passed one hand over his face. Then
while they all watched silently he loosened his
neckcloth sufficiently that he could reach
inside his shirt to pull out a gold chain that
bore a locket identical to the one Lily wore.

"There were only two of them," he said. "I
had them specially made. Is there anything
inside yours, Lily?"

She was shaking her head. "My papa gave it to me," she said. "He was not a thief."

"No, no," he said. "No, I am quite sure he was not. Is there anything inside?"

She shook her head again and took one step back from him. "It is empty," she said. "The locket is mine. You are not going to take it from me. I will not let you."

Elizabeth had come to stand beside her. "Lyndon," she said, "you are frightening Lily. But what is the meaning of this? You had two such identical lockets specially made?"

"The L stands for Lyndon," he said. "The F is for Frances. My wife. Your mother, Lily."

Lily stared at him blankly.

"You are Lily Montague," he said, gazing back at her. "My daughter."

Lily shook her head. There was a buzzing in her ears.

"Lyndon." It was Elizabeth's voice. "You cannot just assume that. Perhaps—"

"I have known it," he said, "since the moment I set eyes on her in the church at Newbury. Apart from the blue eyes, Lily bears a quite uncanny resemblance to Frances—to her mother."

"I say! Look to Miss Doyle," one of the gentlemen was saying, but his words were unnecessary. The Duke of Portfrey had lunged for her and caught her up in his arms. Lily, only half conscious, was aware of her locket—no, *his*—swinging from his neck just before her eyes.

He set her down on a sofa and chafed her hands while Elizabeth placed a cushion behind her head.

"I had no proof, Lily," his grace said, "until now. I *knew* you must exist, though I had little evidence for that either. But I could not find you. I have never quite stopped searching for you. I have never been quite able to proceed with my life. And then you stepped into that church."

Lily was turning her head from side to side on the cushion. She was trying not to listen.

"Lyndon," Elizabeth said quietly, "go slowly. I am well-nigh fainting myself. Imagine how Lily must be feeling."

He looked up at Elizabeth then and about the room.

"Yes," she said, "the other gentlemen have tactfully withdrawn. Lily, my dear, do not fear. No one is going to take anything—or anyone— away from you."

"Mama and Papa are my mother and father," Lily whispered.

Elizabeth kissed her forehead.

"What is going on in here?" a new voice asked briskly from the doorway. "Joseph told me as I was walking through the door that I had better get in here fast. Lily?"

She gave a little cry and stumbled to her feet. She was in his arms before she could take even one step away from the sofa—tightly enfolded in them, her face against his neckcloth.

"I am the one who has upset her, Kilbourne," the Duke of Portfrey said. "I have just told her that she is my daughter."

Lily burrowed closer into warmth and safety.

"Ah, yes," Neville said quietly. "Yes, she is."

"The letter was addressed to Lady Frances Lilian Montague," Neville said. "But someone had written beneath it in a different hand—or so the vicar assured me—'Lily Doyle.' "

He was sitting on the sofa beside Lily, her hand in his, her shoulder leaning against his arm. She was gazing down at her other hand in her lap. She was showing no apparent interest in the conversation. The Duke of Portfrey had crossed the room and come back with a glass of brandy, which he had held out silently to her. She had shaken her head. He had set it down and pulled up a chair so that he could sit facing her. He was gazing at her now, his eyes devouring her. Elizabeth was pacing the room.

"If only we could know what was in the letter," his grace said wistfully.

"But we do." Neville drew the duke's eyes from Lily for a moment. "The letter was addressed to Lily Doyle. William Doyle was her next of kin though he had not known of her existence. The vicar opened the letter and read it to him."

"And the vicar remembers its contents?" his grace asked sharply.

"Better yet," Neville said. "He made a copy of the letter. After reading it, he advised William Doyle to take it over to Nuttall Grange, to Baron Onslow, Lily's grandfather. But he believed that William had a right to a copy of it too. He seemed to feel that the Doyles might wish to claim some sort of compensation for the years of care Thomas Doyle had given Lily."

Lily was pleating the expensive lace of her overdress between her fingers. She was like a child sitting quietly and listlessly while the adults talked.

"You have this copy?" the duke asked, his voice tight.

Neville drew it out of a pocket and handed it over without a word. His grace read silently.

"Lady Lyndon Montague informed her father that she was going to stay with an ailing school friend for a couple of months," Neville said after a few minutes. Elizabeth had come to sit close by. "In reality she went to stay with her former maid and the girl's new husband—Beatrice and Private Thomas Doyle—in order to give birth to a child."

Lily smoothed out the creases she had created and then proceeded to pleat the lace again.

"Her marriage to Lord Lyndon Montague had been a secret one," Neville said, "and both had pledged not to reveal it until his return from his posting to the Netherlands. But he was sent on to the West Indies with his regiment and she discovered she was with child. She was afraid of her own father's wrath as well as his. Worse, she was afraid of her cousin, who was pressing her to marry him so that he would inherit the fortune and the estate as well as the title after Onslow's death. She was afraid of what he would do to her—and the child—if he discovered the truth."

"Mr. Dorsey?" Elizabeth asked.

"None other." His grace had folded the letter and held it in his lap. His gaze had returned to Lily. "We were foolish enough to believe that our marriage would protect her from him. The opposite was, of course, true."

"She was afraid to go home and take the baby with her," Neville said. "She was waiting for her husband to return from the West Indies— she had written to him there to tell him of her condition. In the meantime she left the baby with the Doyles. She must have intended to write to her husband again after she returned home. But he was an officer and therefore always in danger of death. And she must have been very fearful for her own safety. And so she left her locket with the baby and a letter to be given to her husband on his return or to her daughter in the event that neither of them ever came for her."

"I always suspected," his grace said, "that her death was no accident. I suspected too that Dorsey had killed her. She had indeed written to tell me there was to be a child—but if she wrote another letter, I certainly did not receive it. When she died there was no child within her, and no one knew of any recently born to her. She might have been mistaken when she wrote that first letter, I realized, or she might have miscarried. But somehow I have always known that there *was* a child, that there was someone in this world who was my son or my daughter. I explored every possibility I could think of—but I did not know about Beatrice Doyle."

"Lyndon," Elizabeth asked, "is it Mr. Dorsey who has tried to kill Lily, then? But surely not. I cannot believe such a thing of him."

"Onslow is bedridden," Neville said. "Probably it was into Dorsey's hands that William Doyle placed the letter. He would have discovered the truth then, though it would not have appeared very awful to him because Lily was dead. I do wonder, though, if William Doyle's death was accidental. He might have made some awkward claims on Onslow for the years of support given his granddaughter. The vicar at Leavenscourt is perhaps fortunate to be still alive. But then, of course, came Lily's sudden appearance at Newbury. Dorsey was there in the church too. He saw what Portfrey saw and must have realized the truth immediately."

"Lily." The Duke of Portfrey leaned forward in his chair suddenly and possessed himself of her free hand with both his own. The letter slipped unheeded to the floor. "Beatrice and Thomas Doyle were your mama and papa. They gave you a family and security and a good upbringing and an unusually deep love, I believe. No one—least of all me—is ever going to try to take them away from you. They will always be your parents."

She nestled her head against Neville's arm, but he could see that she had raised her eyes to look at Portfrey.

"We loved each other, Lily," Portfrey said, "your m—Frances and I. You were conceived in love. We would have lavished all our affec-

394

tion on you if..." He drew a deep breath and let it out slowly. "She loved you enough to give you up temporarily for your safety. In twenty years I have never been quite able to lay her to rest or to let go of the possibility of you. We did not abandon you. If you can possibly think of her—of Frances, my wife—as your mother, Lily, if not your mama... If you could possibly think of me as your father... I do not set myself up as a rival to your papa. Never that. But allow me..." He lifted her hand to his lips and then released it and got abruptly to his feet.

"Where are you going?" Elizabeth asked.

"She is in shock," he said, "and I am pressing my own selfish claims on her. I have to leave, Elizabeth. Excuse me? I will call tomorrow if I may. But you must not try forcing Lily to receive me. Look after her."

"Your grace." Lily spoke for the first time since Neville had come into the room. Portfrey and Elizabeth spun around to look at her. "I will receive you—tomorrow."

"Thank you." He did not smile, but he looked at her again as if he would devour her. He made a formal bow and turned toward the door.

"Wait for me, Portfrey, will you?" Neville asked. "I will be with you in a minute."

His grace nodded and left the book room with Elizabeth.

Neville got to his feet and drew Lily to hers. He set his arms about her and drew her close. What must it feel like, he wondered, suddenly to discover that one's dearly loved parents were not one's real mother and father after all? He tried to imagine discovering it of his own parents. He would feel without roots, without anchor. He would feel...fear.

"I want you to forget about the party," he told her, "and go up to your room. Ring for Dolly and then go to bed. Try to sleep. Will you?"

"Yes," she said.

It hurt him to see her so listless, so willing to obey, just like an obedient child. So unlike Lily. But Portfrey was right. She was in deep shock. He was reminded of the way she had been in the hours following Doyle's death.

"Try not to think too much tonight," he said. "Tomorrow you will better be able to adjust to the new realities. I believe you will eventually realize that you have lost nothing. It is one thing, Lily, to care for the child of one's own seed or womb. It is another to love and cherish someone else's child for whom one really has no responsibility at all. That is what your mama and papa did for you. I did not know your mama, but I always marveled that a father could feel such devoted, tender love for his daughter as your papa felt for you. You have not lost them. You have merely gained people who will love and cherish you in the future and not be jealous of the past."

"I am so very tired," she said, and she lifted her face to him—her pale, large-eyed face. "I cannot think straight—or even in crooked lines."

"I know." He lowered his head and kissed

her, and she sighed and pushed her lips back against his own and raised her arms to twine about his neck.

He had missed her dreadfully during his journey into Leicestershire. And he had been sick with worry for her safety—especially after reading the letter. Feeling her small, shapely body against his own again, feeling her arms about his neck and her lips cleaving to his awoke hungers that threatened to over-whelm him. But she was in no condition for passion. Besides, there was a matter of grave importance to be attended to tonight—and Portfrey would be waiting for him.

"Go to bed now, my love," he said, lifting his head and framing her face with both hands. "I will see you tomorrow."

"Yes," she said. "Tomorrow. Maybe my brain will work tomorrow."

⤞ 24 ⤝

Lily awoke from a deep sleep when the early-morning sun was already shining in at her window. She threw back the covers and leaped out of bed as she often did, and stretched. What a strange dream she had been having! She could not even remember it yet, but she knew it had been bizarre.

She stopped midstretch.

And remembered. It had not been a dream.

She was not Lily Doyle. Papa had not been her father. She was not even Lily Wyatt,

Countess of Kilbourne. She was Lady Frances Lilian Montague, a total stranger. She was the daughter of the Duke of Portfrey. Her grandfather was Baron Onslow.

For one moment her mind threatened to take refuge in last evening's daze again, but there was nothing to be served by doing that. She fought panic.

Who was she?

All through those seven months in Spain she had fought to retain her identity. It had not been easy. Everything had been taken from her—her own clothes, her locket, her freedom, her very body. And yet she had clung to the basic knowledge of who she was—she had refused to give up that.

Now, this morning, she no longer knew herself. Who was Frances Lilian Montague? How could that austere, handsome man—*with blue eyes like hers*—be her father? How could the woman whose initial was twined with his on her locket be her mother?

They had been separated, the duke who was her father and the woman who was her mother, very soon after their marriage. Lily knew what *that* felt like. She knew the ache of longing and loneliness the woman must have felt. And they had loved each other. Lily had been conceived in love, the duke had told her last evening. They had loved each other and been separated forever. Their child had been left for what had been intended to be a short spell with the people who had become Lily's parents.

Mama and Papa, who had loved her as

dearly as any parents could possibly love their child.

The woman, her mother, must have loved her too. Lily pictured to herself how she would have felt if she had had a child of Neville's after their separation. Oh, yes, her mother had loved her. And for over twenty years the duke, her father, had been unable to let go of either his wife or his conviction that somewhere she, Lily, existed.

She did not want to be Lady Frances Lilian Montague. She did not want the Duke of Portfrey to be her father. She wanted her papa to be the man who had begotten her. But it was all true whether she wanted it to be or not. And she could not stop herself from thinking that while for eighteen years she had had the best papa in the world and for the three years since his death had had her memories of him, the Duke of Portfrey for all that time had been without his own child. All those years, so filled with love for her, had been empty for him.

He was her father. She tested the idea in her mind without shying away from it. The Duke of Portfrey was her father. And Papa had always intended that she know it eventually. He and Mama had given her the locket to wear all her life, and Papa had always insisted that she must take his pack to an officer if he should die in battle. She did not know why he had kept the truth from her for so long or why he had not tried to contact the Duke of Portfrey. Oh, yes, she did. She could remember how her mama had doted on her, how her papa had acted as if the sun rose and set on her.

They had found themselves unable to give her up and had doubtless found all sorts of good reasons for not doing so. Papa had intended to tell her when she reached adulthood. She was sure he must have intended that.

She would never know for sure what his intentions or motives had been, Lily decided. But she did know two things. Papa had not intended to keep the truth a secret from her forever. And Papa had loved her.

It was not, she thought suddenly, a bad thing to be the daughter of a duke and the granddaughter of a baron. She had dreamed of equality with Neville and had believed that perhaps she would achieve it in everything except birth and fortune.

She smiled rather wanly.

Elizabeth was dressed and in the breakfast room before Lily—an unusual occurrence. She got to her feet, took Lily's hands in hers, and kissed her on both cheeks before looking searchingly into her face.

"Lily," she said, "how *are* you, my dear?"

"Awake," Lily said. "Fully awake."

"You will receive him this morning?" Elizabeth sounded rather anxious. "You need not if you do not feel quite ready to do so."

"I will receive him," Lily said.

He came an hour later, when they were sitting in the drawing room, working at their embroidery—or at least pretending to. He came striding into the room close on the butler's heels, made his bow, and then hovered close to the door as if he had suddenly lost all his confidence.

"Gracious, Lyndon," Elizabeth said, hurrying toward him, "whatever happened?"

"An unfortunate encounter with a door?" he said, phrasing the words as a question, as if asking if they would be willing to accept a patently ridiculous lie. His face was shiny with bruises. His left eye was bloodshot and purplish at the outer corner.

"You have been fighting Mr. Dorsey," Lily said quietly.

He came a few paces closer to her. "You have not been in grave danger from him for some time, Lily," he said. "Kilbourne, I gather, has had a close watch put on you, and I have had a close watch put on Dorsey. I knew it was he, you see, but did not have proof of it until last evening. He will not be bothering you ever again."

Lily supposed that she had known last night why the duke and Neville left the party so early. But her mind had not been able to cope with the knowledge, or with anything else for that matter.

"He is dead?" she asked.

He inclined his head.

"You killed him?"

He hesitated. "I knocked him insensible," he said, "in a fist fight. Kilbourne and I had agreed with considerable regret that we could not reconcile it with our consciences to kill him in cold blood or even in a duel to the death, but we did agree that we would punish him severely before turning him over to a constable and a magistrate for trial. But we were careless. He snatched up a gun before he could be taken away and would have killed me if Kilbourne had not first shot him."

Elizabeth had both hands to her mouth. Lily merely looked calmly into the duke's eyes and knew that she had heard everything that he was prepared to tell. She knew that although Mr. Dorsey had probably killed her mother and Mr. William Doyle, that although he had tried three separate times to kill her and had almost killed Neville, it might have been difficult to prove any one of those murders or attempted murders in a court of law. She was not sure if it was carelessness that had left a gun within Mr. Dorsey's reach. Perhaps they had wanted him to have that gun. Perhaps they had wanted him to try to use it so that there would be a perfectly good excuse to shoot him in self-defense.

The duke himself would never say, of course. Neither would Neville. And she would never ask. She did not really wish to know.

"I am glad he is dead," she said, almost shocked to realize that she spoke the truth. "Thank you."

"And that is all we need say on the topic of Calvin Dorsey," he said. "You are safe, Lily. Free."

She nodded.

"Well," Elizabeth said briskly, "I am due to meet with my housekeeper. It is our day for going over the accounts. You will excuse me for half an hour, Lyndon? Lily?"

Lily nodded and the duke bowed.

He looked wary when he turned back from

seeing Elizabeth out of the room, but Lily smiled at him.

"Will you have a seat, your grace?" she asked.

He took a chair quite close to hers and looked at her silently for several moments.

"I will understand," he said at last, sounding as if he were delivering a well-rehearsed speech, "if you feel yourself unable to acknowledge the relationship, Lily. Kilbourne told me a good deal last night about Sergeant Thomas Doyle. I can understand your pride in him and your affection for him. But I beg you— please!—to allow me to settle a considerable portion of my fortune on you so that you may live in comfortable independence for the rest of your life. At the very least allow me to do that for you."

"What would you wish to do," she asked him, "if I said I was willing to accept more than the very least?"

He leaned back in his chair and drew a deep breath, looking at her consideringly as he did so. "I would acknowledge you publicly," he said. "I would take you home to Rutland Park in Warwickshire and spend every available minute of every day getting to know you and allowing you to get to know me. I would clothe you and deck you with jewels. I would encourage you to continue with your education. I would take you to Nuttall Grange in Leicestershire to meet your grandfather. I would... What is left? I would try in every way available to me to make up for the lost years." He smiled slowly. "And I would have you tell me every single thing you can remember about Thomas and Beatrice Doyle and your growing years. That is what I would wish to do, Lily."

"You must do it, then, your grace," she said.

They stared at each other for a long time, it seemed, before he got to his feet, came closer to her, and extended a hand for hers. She stood up, gave him her hand, and watched as he raised it to his lips.

"Lily," he said. "Oh, my dear. My very, very dear."

She withdrew her hand, set her arms about his waist, and rested her cheek against his shoulder. "He will always be my papa," she said. "But from this day on you will be my father. Shall I call you that? Father?"

His arms were like iron bands about her. She was a little alarmed when she heard the first painful-sounding sob, but she closed her arms more tightly about him when he would have pulled away.

"No, no," she said. "It is all right. It is quite all right."

He did not weep for long. Men did not. She knew that from experience. They saw it as a sign of horribly embarrassing weakness, even if they had just watched a close friend smashed to a thousand pieces by a cannonball or had just had a limb sawn off by the surgeons—or had just discovered a daughter after almost twenty-one years. He drew away from her after a couple of minutes and moved off to the window, where he stood with his back to the room, blowing his nose in a large handkerchief.

"I am so very sorry to have subjected you to that," he said. "It will not happen again. You will find me strong and dependable, I believe, Lily—a good provider and a good protector."

"Yes, I know, Father," she said, smiling at his back.

She heard him draw an inward breath and hold it for a few moments. "I could, I suppose," he said, "have remarried any time during the past twenty years. I could have had a nurseryful of children and been called that a thousand times and more before now. I believe, Lily, it has been worth waiting to hear it first from your lips."

"When will we leave for Rutland Park?" she asked. "Is it a large house? Will I like it...Father?"

He turned to look at her. "As soon as possible," he said. "It is larger than Newbury Abbey. You will love it. It has been waiting for you all these years. We had better see if Elizabeth will come with you. Today is Thursday. Shall we say Monday?"

Lily nodded.

He smiled at her and strode to the bell pull. He told the servant who answered the summons to ask Lady Elizabeth to return to the drawing room at her convenience. Then they both sat down again and gazed at each other.

It would be more accurate, Lily thought, to say that he was beaming at her. Despite the battered look of his face, he appeared very happy. She deliberately kept her own expression bright—not that it was all pretense. But a part of it was. She was stepping into the unknown again as she had done so many times, it seemed, during the past couple of years.

She remembered traveling down to Newbury Abbey from London and hoping that the long journey was almost ended. She remembered seeing Neville for the first time in almost a year and a half and experiencing, despite the difficulty of the circumstances, a feeling of final homecoming. But she had not been home. And she still was not. She wondered if she ever would be. Would the time ever come when she would feel at last that she had arrived, that she could settle in peace to live out the rest of her life?

Or was life always a journey along an unknown path?

"Kilbourne," the duke said to her just before Elizabeth came back into the room, "asked me to inform you of his intention to call this afternoon, Lily—if you are willing to receive him."

Killing another human being was not something one did with any relish, Neville thought during the night and the morning following the death of Calvin Dorsey. Certainly not in battle—one was too aware of the fact that the men one killed were no more evil or deserving of death than one was oneself. But not even when the man one killed was a murderer and had killed one's wife's mother and had tried on a number of occasions to kill her too. There had been a certain satisfaction, perhaps, in watching Dorsey take the bait of that carelessly abandoned pistol and in being given then little choice but to kill him—especially when Portfrey had won the argument about which of them was to punish Dorsey before he was turned over to the law. But certainly no relish.

Was there pleasure in having discovered the truth about Lily's birth? In having learned that she outranked him? That he had nothing to offer her that she did not now have in overabudance herself? And was that how he had hoped to win Lily—with his position and his wealth and the hope that her own near destitution would force her back to him? Surely not. He wanted her to be his equal, to *feel* his equal. The fact that she had felt herself to be by far his inferior had wrecked any chance they might have had for happiness when she had come to Newbury.

He should be rejoicing, then, in this turn of events. Why was he not? It was because of Lily herself, he concluded finally. Poor Lily had suffered so much turmoil in the past year and a half. How could she sustain the loss of her very roots? Would he find her all broken up when he called at Elizabeth's during the afternoon? Worse, would he find her still quite unlike her indomitable self, dazed and passive as she had been last evening?

He approached Elizabeth's with a great deal of trepidation. He even found himself half hoping as he entered the house and asked if Miss Doyle would receive him that she would send down a refusal. But she did not. The butler showed him up to the drawing room. Both Lily and Elizabeth were there.

"Neville," Elizabeth said, coming across the room toward him after he had made his bow and exchanged greetings with them. She kissed his cheek. "I will allow you a private word with Lily." And she left the room without further ado.

Lily was not looking crushed—or dazed. Indeed, she looked remarkably vibrant in a fashionable sprigged muslin dress with her hair softly curling about her face.

"You killed Mr. Dorsey," she said. "My father told me this morning. I am not sorry that he is dead though I have never before wished for anyone's death. But I am sorry you were forced to do it. I know it is not easy to kill."

Yes, Lily would know that, having grown up with an army whose business it was to kill.

But—*my father?*

"This one," he said, "was almost easy."

"We will say no more of it," she said firmly. She had risen from her chair and came across the room toward him. "Neville, I am going to go to Rutland Park on Monday with my father and Elizabeth. There is to be a notice in the papers tomorrow. I am going to spend some time with him, learning to be his daughter, letting him learn to be my father.

I am going to see my grandfather and my mother's grave. I am going to...go."

"Yes." His heart felt as if it somersaulted and then sank all the way to the soles of his boots—even as he told himself that he was glad for her.

She half smiled at him. "I was Lily Doyle," she said. "Then I was Lily Wyatt—and then not. Now I am Lily Montague. I have to discover who I really am. I thought I was discovering the answer after I came here to London, but today it feels as far away as ever."

"You are Lily." He tried to smile back at her.

She nodded and her eyes brightened with tears.

"How long?" he asked her.

She shook her head.

He could not press her on the point, he realized. She did not need one more burden to carry. And he knew the question to be unanswerable.

He had begun to believe that there was a future for them after all. He had been on the brink of putting the matter to the test at Vauxhall. He hated to remember that night, which had started with such magical promise. Now he would have to wait an indefinite length of time again with no certainties to make the wait easy.

He reached out both hands for hers, and she set her own in them.

"You will like him, Lily," he said. "You will even love him, I daresay. He is a good man and he is your father. Go then and find yourself. And be happy. Promise me?"

She was biting on her upper lip, he could see.

He squeezed her hands and raised them one at a time to his lips. "I am not overfond of London," he said. "I shall be glad to return to Newbury for the summer. I daresay I will go tomorrow or the next day. Perhaps, if you think it appropriate, you will write me a letter there?"

"I cannot...write well enough," she said.

"But you will." He smiled at her. "And you will be able to read my reply too."

"Will I?" she asked him. "Sometimes I wish—oh, *how* I wish I were Lily Doyle again and you were Major Lord Newbury and Papa..."

"But we are not," he said sadly. "I want you to know something, though, Lily. Not so that you will have one more burden to shoulder, but so that you will know that some things are unchanged and unchangeable. I loved you when I married you. I love you today. I will love you with my dying breath. I have loved you and will love you during every moment between those time spans."

"Oh. But it is not the right moment," she said, her eyes clouding with some emotion he was unable to enter into. Poor Lily. So much had happened to her recently and she had borne it all with dignity and integrity.

"I will not prolong this visit," he told her. "I will take my leave, Lily. Make my excuses to Elizabeth?"

She nodded.

They clung to each other's hands for a few

moments longer. But she was correct. It was not the right time. If she came back to him— *when* she came back to him—there must be no other need in her except to be with him for the rest of their lives.

He withdrew his hands gently, keeping the smile in his eyes, and left her without another word.

He was halfway back to Kilbourne House, striding unseeing along the streets, before he remembered that he had driven his curricle to Elizabeth's.

PART V

A Wedding

25

Lily gazed eagerly from the carriage window, not even trying to appear properly genteel. The village of Upper Newbury looked so very familiar. There was the inn, where she had descended from the stagecoach, and the steep lane leading down to the lower village. And there—

"Oh, *may* the carriage be stopped?" she asked.

The Duke of Portfrey, from his seat opposite, rapped on the front panel, and the carriage drew to an abrupt halt. Lily had the window down in a trice despite the coolness of the day and leaned her head through it.

"Mrs. Fundy," she called. "How are you? And how are the children? Oh, the baby *has* grown."

While the duke and Elizabeth exchanged glances of silent amusement, Mrs. Fundy, who had been gawking at the grand carriage with its ducal crest, smiled broadly, looked suddenly flustered, and bobbed a curtsy.

"We are all very well, thank you, my lady," she said. "It is good to see you back again."

"Oh, and it is good to *be* back again," Lily said. "I shall call on you one day if I may."

She beamed at Mrs. Fundy while the carriage lurched into motion again. She was not coming home, she reminded herself. Newbury Abbey was not home. Oh, but she *felt* as if it were. She had come to love Rutland Park, as her father had predicted she would. She had come to love him too, as she had been determined to do, though it had not proved difficult at all. She had even enjoyed their extended visit to Nuttall Grange, where she had won the affection of her bedridden grandpapa and of her two aunts who were not really aunts at all—Bessie Doyle and her mama's sister. She had even come to feel happy and settled and at peace with herself and the world. She had not once, since leaving London, dreamed the nightmare.

But Newbury Abbey, though she had not seen either the park or the house yet, felt like home.

"Oh, look!" she exclaimed in awe after the carriage had turned through the gates and was proceeding along the driveway through the forest. The trees were all glorious shades of reds and yellows and browns. A few of the leaves had fallen already and lay in a colorful carpet along the drive. "Have you ever seen anything more splendid than England in autumn, Father? Have you, Elizabeth?"

"No," her father said.

"Only England in the springtime," Elizabeth said. "And that is not *more* splendid, I declare, only *as* splendid."

It had been springtime when Lily had come here first. It was autumn now—October. How much had happened in the months between, Lily thought. She could remember trudging along this driveway at night, her bag clutched in her hand...

She had written to him at the beginning of

September, as he had asked her to do. She had asked Elizabeth if it was unexceptionable to do so—for her to write to a single gentleman. Elizabeth had answered, with a twinkle in her eye, that it was really not the thing at all. But Father, who had also been present at the time, had reminded them all that she was Lily and was quite adept at stretching every rule almost to the breaking point without ever doing anything shockingly improper— that was her chief charm, he had added with the smiling indulgence that had surprised her about him at first. And so she had written— with laborious care and round, childish handwriting. She was working on her penmanship but it was going to take time.

She was happy with her father, she had written. She was happy with Elizabeth's company. She had been to Nuttall Grange and met her grandfather. She had put flowers on her mother's grave. She hoped Lady Kilbourne was well and Lauren and Gwendoline too. She hoped he was well. She was his obedient servant.

He had written back to invite her and her father to come as guests to Newbury Abbey for the celebration of his mother's fiftieth birthday in October. Elizabeth had already made arrangements to attend.

And so here they were. They were merely guests. But it felt like a homecoming. And Lily, looking suddenly with shining eyes at her father as the house came into view, saw that he understood and was a little saddened, though he smiled at her.

"Father." She leaned forward impulsively and took his hand. "Thank you for agreeing that we might come. I do love you so."

He patted her hand with his free one. "Lily," he said, "you are one-and-twenty, my dear. Shockingly old to be still at home with your father. I do not expect to have you all to myself for much longer."

But that was far too explicit a thing to say. She sat back, her smile fading a little. She would take nothing for granted. Several months had passed. A great deal had changed in her life and might have changed in his also. He had invited them out of courtesy. Doubtless there were to be many other guests too. She would not set great store by the fact that he had invited *her*.

If she told herself those foolish things often enough, perhaps she would come to believe them in the end.

Their carriage had been spotted. The great double doors opened as it approached, and people spilled out of the house—Gwendoline, Joseph, the countess, and...*him*.

It was the marquess who opened the carriage door and set down the steps. The duke was out almost before they had been lowered and turned to hand Elizabeth down. The countess came forward to hug her. Everyone was trying to talk at once.

Then someone leaned inside the carriage and reached out a hand toward Lily—and they might as easily have been alone. Everything else faded from sight and sound. He was gazing at her with shining eyes and tightly compressed lips. She was beaming foolishly back at him.

"Lily," he said.

"Yes." And suddenly she knew that all her anxieties had been very foolish indeed. "Hello, Neville."

She set her hand in his.

⌒

There were a number of guests already at the house even though the birthday party was still one day away. Dinner was a crowded and noisy affair. His mother, Neville was pleased to note, had seated Portfrey at her right hand, Lily at her left. They were far distant from his place at the head of the table. Apart from those moments on the terrace during the afternoon, there had been scarcely a chance to exchange a word with her.

He did not really mind. He was content for the moment to observe, to watch her, to note the changes a few months had wrought in her. He remembered Elizabeth telling him at one time that new knowledge and skills did not change a person but merely added to what was already there. It was true of Lily. She was fashionable and poised and animated. Gone was the terrible sense of inadequacy that had tongue-tied her in genteel company—in female company, at least—when she was last at Newbury Abbey. She talked as much as anyone and more than many. She smiled and laughed.

But she was still Lily. She was Lily as she had been created to be—but free now to find joy in any company and in any surroundings.

He caught snippets of her conversation for the simple reason that she seemed somehow to be the focus of attention with everyone and there was often near silence along the length of the table as everyone leaned forward to hear her—when Joseph asked her how her reading skills were coming along, for example.

"Oh, you would lose a very large wager if you were foolish enough to make one now, I do assure you," she told him. "I read very well indeed. Do I not, Elizabeth? I can read a whole page in half an hour, I daresay, if there are no distractions and no very long words. And I do not have to say the words aloud or even mouth them silently. What do you think of *that*, Joseph?" She laughed merrily at her own expense, a sound that was echoed along the table.

"I think I would fall asleep long before you reached the end of the page, Lily," Joseph said, yawning, the fingers of one hand delicately patting his mouth.

She was delightful, Neville thought, trying to take his eyes off her occasionally so that he could keep up a conversation with the relatives who sat closer to him. It was not easy to do.

Oh, yes, she was still Lily, he thought a few minutes later. One of the footmen leaned across the table beside her to remove a dish, and she looked up at him, her face brightening with recognition.

"Mr. Jones!" she exclaimed. "How do you do?"

Poor Jones almost dropped the dish. He blushed scarlet and mumbled something that Neville did not catch.

"Oh, I know," Lily said, instantly contrite. "I do apologize for embarrassing you. I shall come down to the kitchen tomorrow morning if I may and chat with everyone. It seems an age since I saw you all."

His mother, Neville noticed, was smiling at Lily with what looked to be genuine affection.

"If you do not mind, that is, ma'am," Lily said, turning to her. "I forget that I am not at home. I often go down to the kitchen at home, do I not, Father? It is the coziest room in the house, and I can always be sure of finding something useful to do there. Father does not mind."

"And neither do I, child," the countess said, patting her hand on the table.

"One quickly learns, ma'am," the Duke of Portfrey said with a sigh, "that daughters were created for the express purpose of wrapping their fathers about their little fingers."

He looked like a different man, Neville had noticed almost from the moment of his arrival. There was a glow of happiness about him, and he did little if anything to disguise the enormous pride he felt in his daughter.

Later, in the drawing room, Lily made herself charming to everyone, sitting and talking with each of his aunts and with his mother. After the tea tray had been removed and some of the cousins had gone into the music room to entertain themselves with music, she sat for a while with Lauren and talked earnestly to her, holding her hand as she did so. And then Gwen was bending over her, saying something, and they smiled at each other before going into the music room arm in arm.

It must be a difficult evening for Lauren, Neville thought sadly. There had been a certain awkwardness between them since his return from London—she had not after all gone to Yorkshire—for though nothing had been said in their hearing, they both knew that speculation was rife in the neighborhood about his future plans. Did he intend to offer for Lady Lilian Montague, or did he intend to renew his plans to marry Lauren?

He and Lauren both knew the answer. But it had never been put into words between them. How could it be? How could he tell her that he had no intention of renewing his addresses to her without implying that she expected such a thing? And how could she tell him that she understood there could be nothing more between them than friendship without implying that she expected him to marry her?

But as always she behaved with outer poise and dignity. There was no knowing what went on in her mind.

He had loved Lily for a long time. He had not thought it possible back in the spring to love her more. But he did. He had tried to live his old life without brooding constantly about her. He had tried not to be too certain that she would in her own time come back to him.

But one sight of her had banished all pretense from his mind. Without Lily life would have very little meaning for him. She was sunshine and warmth and laughter. She was... Well, she was simply his love.

He kept his distance from her. He would not rush her even though there was an inevitability to the way this visit was developing. She had come with her father to celebrate a birthday party. He would allow her to enjoy it, then— tomorrow. But after tomorrow...

All his dreams rested upon what would surely happen after tomorrow. He refused to doubt, to fear.

Lauren and Gwendoline did not go immediately to bed when they returned to the dower house even though the hour was late. They sat together in the sitting room, in which a fire had been lit. It was a smaller, cozier room than the drawing room. They both gazed into the depths of the crackling flames for a while without talking.

"Do you know what she told me?" Lauren said at last.

"What?" Gwendoline asked. There was no need to clarify about whom they were talking.

"She told me that she knows I must resent her," Lauren said. "She told me that she resented me too last spring because I was so perfect, the model of what all ladies should be, so much more suited to being Neville's countess than she was. She told me that she admires my restraint, my dignity, my unfailing kindness to her despite what my real feelings must be. She asked me to forgive her for ever doubting my motives."

"She is right to have spoken so openly of what is between you," Gwendoline said. "She does speak her mind, does she not?"

"She is—" Lauren closed her eyes. "She is the woman Neville wants. Did you notice the way he looked at her all evening? Did you see his *eyes*?"

"She told me," Gwendoline said quietly, "that she knew she had hurt me by stepping all unbidden into the midst of my family when I had not finished grieving for Vernon or adjusting to all the upheavals of my life. She asked me to forgive her. She was not being obsequious, Lauren. She meant it. I still wish it were possible to hate her, but it is not, is it? She is so very likable."

Lauren smiled into the fire.

"When I said that," Gwendoline added hastily, "I did not mean—"

"That you do not therefore like me?" Lauren said, looking at her. "No, of course not, Gwen. Why should it mean that? She is not my rival. Neville and I would have married if she had not come, but it is a good thing she did. Ours would not have been a love match."

"Oh, Lauren, of course it would!" Gwendoline cried.

"No." Lauren shook her head. "You must have felt this evening what everyone else was feeling, Gwen. The air fairly crackled with the tension of their passion for each other. They were meant for each other. There was never that between Neville and me."

"Perhaps—" Gwendoline began, but Lauren was gazing into the fire again and something in her face silenced her cousin.

"I saw them once, you know," Lauren said, "when I ought not to have done so. They were down at the pool together, early one morning. They were bathing and laughing and entirely happy. The door of the cottage was open—they had spent the night together there. That is what love should be like, Gwen. It is what you had with Lord Muir."

Gwendoline's hands tightened about the arms of her chair and she drew a sharp breath, but she said nothing.

"It is the sort of love I will never know," Lauren said.

"Of course you will," Gwendoline assured her. "You are young and lovely and—"

"And incapable of passion," Lauren said. "Have you noted the contrast between Lily and me, Gwen? After the—the wedding, I could have left here. I could have gone home with Grandpapa. I daresay he would have done something for me. I could have begun a new life. I stayed here instead, hoping that she would die. And even after I decided later that I would go after all, I changed my mind. I was afraid to go lest I—miss something here. But Lily, who had far less to go to than

I and far more to leave behind, went away to make a new life for herself rather than cling to what was not satisfactory for her at the time. I do not have that sort of courage."

"You are tired," Gwendoline said briskly, "and a little dispirited. Everything will look better in the morning."

"But there is one thing I *do* have the courage to do," Lauren said, getting to her feet. She stretched up with great care to remove a costly porcelain shepherdess from the mantel and held it in her hands, smiling at it. "Oh, yes, indeed I do."

She dashed the ornament onto the hearth, where it smashed into a thousand pieces.

The main celebrations for the countess's birthday party were to occur during the evening, but with so many house guests at New-bury Abbey, even tea was a crowded, noisy affair. It was a raw, autumn day outside. Everyone was quite happy to be indoors.

Except Elizabeth. Oh, she was delighted to be home again, to see all her relatives again, to join in a family celebration. And she was more than delighted to see that what she had hoped for since the spring was about to happen. Although the occasion was nominally Clara's birthday, everyone understood quite clearly that there was something far more significant than that afoot. The sort of love that Neville and

Lily obviously shared was rare and wonderful to behold.

It gladdened the unselfish part of Elizabeth's heart.

And saddened the selfish part.

She would no longer be needed, either by Lily or by—or by Lily's father.

She withdrew quietly from the drawing room sooner than most of the other guests, fetched a warm cloak and bonnet and gloves from her rooms, and stepped outside for a solitary stroll to the rock garden. It looked rather bleak and colorless at this time of the year, she found. She remembered coming here on the day of Lily's first arrival at Newbury Abbey, the day that was to have seen Neville and Lauren's nuptials. Lyndon had questioned Lily closely on that occasion, and she, Elizabeth, had chided him, not knowing that even then he had suspected the truth. Such a long time ago...

"Is company permitted?" a voice asked from behind her. "Or would you prefer to be alone?"

He had come after her. She turned to smile at him. She wished she had the strength to tell him that yes, indeed she did prefer to be alone, but it would have been a lie. She had the rest of a lifetime in which to be alone. There was no point in beginning before it was necessary.

"Lyndon," she said as he walked closer to her, "does it make you just a little sad? You have had so little time with her." She had watched the transformation of her friend since his discovery of Lily with amazement and gladness—and an unwilling chill at her heart.

"That she is going to desert me for Kilbourne?" he said. "Yes, a little. The past few months have been the happiest of my life. Shall we take the rhododendron walk? Or will you be too cold?"

She shook her head. But he did not offer his arm, she noticed, perhaps because she clasped her hands so determinedly behind her. She had never felt awkward with him. She felt awkward now.

"But there is also a certain feeling of satisfaction," he said. "Lily will be happy—*if* she accepts him. But I feel little doubt that it will happen. Neither does the countess or anyone else here at Newbury for that matter. There is a certain satisfaction, Elizabeth, in the knowledge that finally I will be able to proceed with my own life."

"When you wept at Frances's grave last summer," she said, "as Lily did too, you were finally able to accept that she had gone, were you not? You must have loved her very dearly."

"Yes, I did," he said. "A long, long time ago. I used to think of remarrying, you know, and fathering a son and bringing him up as my heir. And then I used to imagine discovering Frances's child and my own—and finding that it was a son. I pictured the enmity and bitterness that would develop between those two brothers—both children of my own loins but only one of them able to be my heir."

There was more beauty on the hill path than

there had been in the garden. The leaves were multicolored above their heads and beneath their feet. The year was not yet quite dead.

"It is not too late, Lyndon," she forced herself to say, her heart cold and heavy, in tune with the chill breeze that blew in their faces. "To father a son and heir, I mean. You are not so very old, after all. And you are extremely eligible. If you were to marry a young woman, you might yet have several more children. You might have a family to comfort you for Lily's absence."

"It is what you would advise then, my friend?" he asked her.

"Yes," she said, hoping that her voice was as cool and as firm as she intended it to be.

She had always loved the way the path had been constructed to bring one above the level of the treetops at its highest point so that one suddenly had a vast view over the abbey and the park to the sea in the distance. She concentrated her mind on the beauty of her surroundings while the silence stretched between them. They had stopped walking, she realized.

"Do you consider yourself young, Elizabeth?" he asked her at last.

Something lurched inside her. She gazed ahead to the leaden gray sea, refusing to pay attention to the fact that he was unclasping her hands from her back and taking one of them in his own.

"Not young enough," she said. "I am not young enough, Lyndon. I am six-and-thirty.

I have remained single from choice, you know. I have always chosen not to marry where I cannot love. But now I am too old."

"Do you love me?" he asked her.

He was not himself looking at the view, which seemed absurd in light of the fact that they had walked all this way in order to do so. He was turned toward her and looking at her. It was not a fair question that he had asked. Her heart pounded so hard that it threatened to rob her of breath.

"As a very dear friend," she told him.

"Ah," he said softly. "That is a pity, Elizabeth. I might have said the same of my feelings for you until a few months ago. But no longer. There is little point in broaching the subject of marriage with you, then? You do not love me as you would wish to love a husband?"

"Lyndon," she whispered, "it is too late for me to bear you a son."

"Is it?" he asked her, lifting her hand to his lips and holding it there after pulling back her glove. "But you are *only* six-and-thirty, my dear."

He was laughing. Oh, not out loud, but there was laughter in his voice, wretched man. She tried to draw her hand away, but his own closed more tightly about it.

"Lyndon," she pleaded, "be sensible. You owe me nothing. You owe much to your name and your position."

"I owe something to myself," he told her. "I owe it to myself to marry where I love, Elizabeth. I love you. Will you marry me?"

"Oh," she said—and could think of nothing

else to say for several moments while he turned her hand and found her bare wrist with his lips. "You will regret this in a few days' time after everything is settled with Lily and you realize you will soon be free to do whatever you wish with your life. You will be relieved that I have said no."

"Are you saying no, then, my dear?" He sounded suddenly sad, the laughter all gone from his voice. "Will you look at me now and tell me that it is because you do not love me and choose rather to live the rest of your life alone than with me? Into my eyes, if you please."

She turned her head and looked at his chin—and then into his very blue eyes. Ah, could such a look be intended for her? The sort of look with which Neville regarded Lily and which she had so envied? But the Duke of Portfrey was looking unwaveringly into her eyes.

"Promise me you will never regret it." Hope and terror all mingled together were doing painful and peculiar things to her insides. "Promise me you will not be sorry in a year's time or two years' time if there are no children. Promise me—"

He kissed her hard.

"I have never known you to babble nonsense before today, Elizabeth," he said well over a minute later.

"Lyndon." She blinked her eyes to clear her vision. Somehow her hands had found their way to his shoulders. "Oh, Lyndon, are you quite, quite s—"

He kissed her again, open-mouthed this time, and pressed his tongue past her startled lips and teeth right into her mouth. It was such a shockingly intimate embrace that she lost both her breath and her knees and was forced to lock her arms about his neck and cling for dear life. And then she kissed him back, touching his tongue with her own, sucking on it, listening with exhultation to the soft murmurs of appreciation with which he responded.

He was smiling when he lifted his head again. "I do beg your pardon," he said. "I interrupted you. What were you saying?"

"I have the feeling," she said severely, "that you will not allow me to complete any sentence you do not wish to hear."

"You learn fast," he said, rubbing his nose against hers and then trailing soft kisses across one cheek to her ear before nibbling on her earlobe and startling a cry of pure pleasure from her. "But then you are an intelligent woman. You must understand now how I intend to enforce wifely obedience."

"I never realized how absurd you can be," she said. "Or how unscrupulous. Lyndon?"

"Mmm?" He feathered kisses along her jaw toward her chin.

"I do love you, you know," she said, closing her eyes. "As a dear friend and so very much more than just that. If I marry you, I will try my very hardest to give you a son."

He threw back his head and laughed aloud before hugging her very tightly to him. "Will you indeed?" he said. "Those are provocative words, my dear—*very* provocative. I will test your resolve on our wedding night, I promise you, and every night following it. Perhaps on the occasional morning or afternoon too. When, Elizabeth? Soon? Sooner? By special license? I have no patience with banns, have you? I am forty-two years old. You are six-and-thirty. I want us to spend every day, every moment, of the rest of our lives together."

"We are not so very old," she protested.

"Certainly not too old," he agreed, kissing her on the lips again. He grinned. "Let us see what those children decide to do during the next day or two, shall we? I shall certainly insist upon a proper wedding at Rutland for my beloved Lily—nowhere else will do. But I would dearly like her to have a stepmother to help me organize it."

"Ah," she cried, "*now* we come to the real point of all this. *Now* we come to the truth of why you are going to such pains to persuade me—"

He kissed her long and hard.

∽ 26 ∽

Newbury Abbey, Lily had discovered, looked much the same and yet so very different. She had been oppressed by it, dwarfed by it, overwhelmed by it when she had last been here. Now she could admire its magnificence and love the light elegance of its design. Now it felt like home. Because it was *his* home, and surely would be hers too.

During the day and a half since her arrival she had talked with everyone and enjoyed everyone's company—including that of the kitchen staff with whom she had taken coffee at midmorning while she peeled potatoes. She had been in Neville's company too, though she had not been alone with him even once. The most private they had been was that minute—no, not even so long—when he had leaned into her father's carriage.

It did not matter. There was a way of being alone with someone even in the midst of crowds. She had grown up surrounded by a regiment of soldiers and its women and children and had learned that lesson early.

They conversed with each other—in company with others. They looked at each other and smiled at each other—in full view of everyone else. But all the time there was really just the two of them, and the shared understanding that at last the time was right. That at last she was home to stay. For the rest of their lives. Lily was sure she was not wrong.

It had not yet been spoken in words, for although the time was right, the exact, perfect moment had not yet arrived. And they would not rush it—it was as if they had a tacit agreement on that. They had waited a long time; they had endured a great deal. The moment of their final commitment would reveal itself. They would not try to force it.

The carpet in the drawing room was rolled back during the evening so that there could be dancing for the countess's birthday party. Lady Wollston, Neville's Aunt Mary, took her place at the pianoforte. Neville danced with his mother and then with Gwendoline, who liked to dance despite her injured leg. He danced with Elizabeth and Miranda.

And of course he danced with Lily—the last dance of the evening, a waltz.

"I am selfish, you see, Lily," he told her with a smile. "If it were a country set, I would have to relinquish you to other partners with every new pattern of the dance. With a waltz, I have you all to myself."

Lily laughed. She had danced with her father, with Joseph, with Ralph, with Hal. She had thoroughly enjoyed the evening. But only because she had known that finally, at last, she would dance with Neville.

"I knew it would be a waltz," she told him.

"Lily." He leaned his head a little closer. "You are a single woman, daughter of a duke, bound by all the proprieties that apply to a lady of the *beau monde*."

Lily's eyes danced with merriment.

"I have already spoken with Portfrey and have won his consent," he said. "I could speak with you formally in the library tomorrow. Your father or Elizabeth would bring you there and then tactfully leave us alone together for fifteen minutes. No longer than fifteen—it would be improper."

"Or?" Lily laughed again. "I hear an alternative in your voice and see it in your face. If the prospect of fifteen minutes alone in the library makes you wince, as it does me, what then?"

He grinned at her. "Portfrey would challenge me to pistols at dawn for even thinking it," he said.

"Neville." She leaned a little closer. Their proximity would have scandalized the *beau monde* at a *ton* ball. But they were among family, who watched them with affectionate indulgence while pretending not to watch at all. "What is the alternative to the library? Oh. Shall *I* say it? You mean the valley, don't you? And the waterfall and pool. The cottage."

He nodded and smiled slowly.

"Tomorrow morning?" she asked. "No, that would not provoke a challenge from any irate father. You mean tonight, don't you?"

His smile lingered, as did her own. But they were gazing deep into each other's eyes, performing the steps of the waltz almost without realizing that they still danced. And Lily, feeling a tightening in her breasts and a weakening in her knees, knew that the moment had found itself. The perfect moment. He spoke again only when the music came to an end.

"You will go there with me, Lily?"

"Of course," she said.

"After everyone has settled for the night? I will knock on your door."

"I will be ready."

Yes, Lily thought as she made her way to her room a short while later, having hugged the countess, Elizabeth, and her father, and said a decorous good night to Neville. Yes, it was entirely right that they go to the cottage. Tonight. She was a lady now, daughter of a duke, and she was single, and she was bound by all the rules by which polite society regulated itself. But deeper than those realities was the fact that she was *Lily*, that in her heart she was married and had been for almost two years, that she was bound by something far stronger than mere man-made rules.

⤳

An almost full moon beamed down from a clear, star-studded sky. It was autumn and it was cold. But Lily, her hand clasped in Neville's, saw and felt only the beauty of this moment to which they had come. They hurried past the stables, down over the lawn, through the trees, through the ferns, down the steep slope to the valley. They did not speak even when they were far enough from the house not to disturb anyone with the sound of their voices. There was no need of speech. Something far deeper than words pulsed between them as they went.

They turned up the valley together at last, making their way toward the waterfall and the pool and the cottage. It was there they had lived through another moment—a tantalizingly brief moment—of total, utter happiness before being torn apart by a series of events that did not need to be remembered just now. They were back where they had been happy together. And where they would be happy again.

They were back where they belonged.

He spoke before opening the cottage door.

"Lily," he said, bending his head toward hers, cupping her face with gentle hands, "we will make love before we talk, will we? Even though church and state do not recognize our right to do so?"

"I recognize it," she told him. "And you do. It is all that matters. I am your wife. You are my husband." It had always been true, from that moment on the hillside in Portugal, when she had been dazed with shock and grief. Even then she had known that he was everything in the world that she would ever need or want. No one—least of all the impersonal forces of church and state—could destroy the sanctity of that ceremony.

"Yes." He touched his forehead briefly to hers and closed his eyes. "Yes, you are my wife."

He lighted two candles inside the cottage. She carried one of them through to the bed-chamber while he knelt at the fireplace there, lighting the fire. The air was frigidly cold.

"It will take awhile to warm up in here," he said, getting to his feet and opening back his cloak before drawing her against him and wrapping it about both of them. He rested his cheek against the top of her head. "Let me hold you and kiss you until it is warm enough to undress and lie down on the bed."

But she laughed and tipped back her head to look up into his face. "It was cold," she reminded him, "on our wedding night."

"Oh, Lord, yes," he said, grinning. "Only cloaks and blankets and a tent to keep out the December chill."

"And passion," she said.

He brushed his lips against hers. "I must have crushed you horribly. It is not the introduction to passion I would have chosen for you if I had had the planning of it."

"It was one of the two most beautiful nights in my life," she told him. "The other was here. The air is already warm by the fire."

"But the floor is hard."

She smiled dazzlingly at him. "Not harder than the ground inside your tent in Portugal."

They used the pillows and all the blankets from the bed. They used their cloaks. They did not remove all their clothes. The floor was indeed hard and cold, and the air was not comfortably warm despite the crackling fire that was catching hold in the hearth.

Their passion knew none of the discomforts. For each there was only the other, warm and alive and eager. After a while, after they had caressed each other with hands and mouths and murmured endearments and he had raised her dress and adjusted his own clothing and pressed himself deep inside her, there was not even each other, but the two of them seemed one body, one heart, one being. And, after he had moved in her and with her for long minutes of shared passion and pleasure, there was not even the one left but only a mindless bliss.

Oh, yes, they were married.

He was still inside her. He had been sleeping, all his relaxed weight bearing down on her. And her back was to the hard floor of the cottage. He disengaged himself and rolled off her, keeping his arms about her. But she moaned her protest at the loss of him and turned against him with sleepy murmurings.

The fire, he saw over her shoulder, was blazing healthily. He could not have been sleeping for long, then.

"You must have a bodyful of squashed bones," he said.

"Mmm." She sighed. Then she moved her head and kissed him with soft languor on the lips. "Are you going to make an honest woman of me?"

"Lily." He hugged her to him tightly. "Oh, Lily, my love. As if you could ever be *dis*honest. You are my *wife*. You can say no a thousand times over, you can say it for the rest of our lives and never make me waver in that conviction."

"I do not intend to say no a thousand times," she said. "Or even once. I said yes the first time you asked. I married you an hour later. I have been married to you ever since even though I could not agree to make it legal back in the spring. I am not saying no now. I am married to you and I want the world to acknowledge the fact—Father, your mother, everyone. But only to acknowledge what already is."

He kissed her.

"Father will want a grand wedding," she said, "even though the only wedding that will really matter to me is the one in Portugal. He will want us to get married at Rutland Park. We must give him what he wants, Neville. He is very special to me. He is... I love him."

"Of course. And Mama will expect it too," he said, kissing her again. "Society will expect it. Of course we will get married again—in the grand manner. When, Lily?"

"Whenever Father and your mother want it," she said.

"No." He smiled at her suddenly. "No, Lily. We will decide. How does the second anniversary of our first, our *real* wedding sound to you? December—at Rutland Park."

"Oh, yes." She smiled back with obvious delight. "Yes, that would be perfect."

Everything was perfect—for the present. It would not remain so throughout the rest of their lives, of course. Life did not work that way. But now, this night, all was well. The future looked bright and the past...

Ah, the past. The past that Lily had endured and he had never found the courage to share completely with her. It did not matter, perhaps. The past was best left just where it was. But then the past could never remain there. It encroached on the present and could blight the future if the issues it had raised were never dealt with. Lily's past would always be something he tiptoed about, something she deliberately never spoke about to him.

"What are you thinking?" She touched her lips to his. "Why do you look so sad?"

"Lily." He spoke quietly, looking into her shadowed eyes though he would rather have looked anywhere else in the world. "Tell me about those months. There was more to tell, was there not? But I did not have the courage or fortitude to listen to the whole of it back in the spring. The pain of those we love is always harder to bear than our own, especially when there is guilt involved. But I need to know. I need to share it all so that there are no shadows left between us. And perhaps you need to tell. I need to help you let go of it, if I can. I need—"

"Forgiveness?" she said when he did not complete the thought. Her finger was tracing the line of his facial scar. "You did all you could, Neville, both for me and for the men who died in the pass. It was war. And it was Papa who took me on that scouting mission. I knew the risk; he knew it. You must not blame yourself. You *must not*. But yes, I will tell you. And then we will *both* let go of the pain. Together. It will be finally in the past, where it belongs."

Even now he wished he had left it alone. He wished he had held on to their perfect night without allowing the intrusion of the one piece of ugliness they had never confronted together.

"His name was Manuel," he said quietly.

She drew a slow and audible breath. "Yes. His name was Manuel," she said. "He was small and wiry of build and handsome and charismatic. He was the leader of the band of partisans and a fanatical nationalist. He was fiercely loyal to his countrymen, terrifyingly cruel to his enemies. I was his woman for seven months. I believe he grew fond of me. He wept when he let me go."

He held her while she continued. And after she had finished talking. She had cried at the end. She was crying now. So was he.

"It does not need to be said," he murmured against one of her ears when he had control of his voice, "because there was no guilt, Lily. But I know you blame yourself for living when those French captives died. And for allowing that man to use your body instead of fighting to the death. So I will say it, my love, and you must believe me. You are forgiven. I forgive you."

Her tears stopped eventually, and she blew her nose on the handkerchief he had somehow found in the pocket of his cloak.

"Thank you," she said. She smiled tremulously. "It does not need to be said, because there was no guilt, Neville. But I know you need to hear it. I forgive you for failing to protect me, for neglecting to come in search of me, for coming home to England and proceeding with your life. You are forgiven."

He drew her head beneath his chin and massaged her scalp through her hair with light fingers. He gazed into the fire.

Strange night, he thought. Almost like the first night they spent together, ugliness and grief on the one hand, love and bliss of physical passion on the other, weaving themselves into some fabric called life. Something that despite everything was worth living and fighting for. As long as there was love—that indefinable element that gave it all a meaning and a value deeper than words.

It had been strangely right to confront the final painful barrier tonight of all nights. To recognize openly together that the path to this night and this cottage had been a long and a difficult one. But to understand that together they could ease each other's burdens and offer each other pardon and peace as well as love and passion.

"Lily." He kissed her on the mouth. "Lily—"

She pressed herself to him and clung tightly.

It was a fierce loving, without foreplay, without any great gentleness. It was the yearning of two bodies to reach beyond desire, beyond pleasure, beyond simple sexual passion to the very core of love. And blessedly they found it there in the cottage beside the pool and the waterfall, their final cries wordless, their sated bodies tangled together on the hard floor among blankets and cloaks and other garments.

They slept.

⌒

Neville was still fast asleep and awkwardly tangled up in the blankets after Lily had risen to her feet, straightened her clothes, fluffed up her hair as best she could, and drawn on her

444

cloak. She was tempted to leave him there, but the fire had died down and soon enough the cold would wake him anyway. She nudged him with one foot.

He grunted.

"Neville," she said, and watched, unsurprised, as he came fully awake and sat up all in one moment—he had been an army officer, after all. "Neville, in another few hours we are going to have to go back to the house and look fresh and tidy and innocent enough to face Father and your mother and everyone else. We are going to have to tell them our news and allow them to take everything else out of our hands. Are we going to waste these precious few hours?"

He grinned and reached out an arm for her. "Now that you mention it—" he began.

But she clucked her tongue. "I did think of bathing," she admitted, "but I suppose the water would be rather chilly."

He grimaced.

"So we will go walking on the beach instead," she told him. "No, running."

"We will?" He stretched. "When we could be making love instead?"

"We will go running on the beach," she said firmly. "In fact"—she grinned cheekily at him—"the last one to the rock and up to the very top of it is a shameful slug-a-bed."

"A *what*?" he said, shouting with laughter.

But she was gone, into the other room, out through the door, leaving it wide open, leaving behind her only an echo of answering laughter.

Neville grimaced again, sighed, cast one longing look at the dying fire, chuckled, jumped to his feet, gathering his clothes about him as he did so, and went in pursuit.

∽ 27 ∽

Lily had not judged the Duke of Portfrey quite correctly. He wanted a wedding for her at Rutland Park, it was true. She was his daughter, and he had finally found her and brought her home where she belonged. It was from home that he would give her away to the man who had won his blessing to be her husband.

But he left the choice to the size of wedding to Lily herself. If she wanted the whole *ton* there, then he would coerce every last member to come. If, on the other hand, she preferred something more intimate, with only family and friends in attendance, then so be it.

"The whole *ton* would not fit into the church," she told him. It was an ancient Norman church, set on a hill above the village, a narrow path winding upward through the churchyard to its arched doorway. It was not a large church.

"They will be squeezed in," he assured her, "if it is what you wish."

"Are you *sure* you would not mind," she asked him, "if I were to choose a wedding with just relatives and some friends?"

"Not at all." He shook his head. "I know,

Lily, that this wedding will take second place to your first. But I want it to be a *precious* second place. Something you will remember fondly for the rest of your life."

She threw her arms about his neck and hugged him tightly. "It will be," she said. "It will be, Father. *You* will be there this time, and Elizabeth will be there, and all of Neville's family. Oh, it will not take second place, I promise you, but an *equal* place."

"A smaller, more intimate wedding it will be then," he told her. "It is what I hoped you would choose, anyway."

It was not as small or as intimate as his own wedding to Elizabeth, though, which took place at Rutland at the beginning of November, with only Lily and the duke's steward in attendance. And yet nothing, he said afterward, could possibly have made the day happier for him or his bride.

Elizabeth, always beautiful, elegant, dignified, serene, glowed with a new happiness that put the bloom of youth back into her cheeks. She threw herself with eager energy into the plans for the wedding of her stepdaughter and her favorite nephew.

⁓

And so on a crisp, frosty, sunny morning in December, Neville waited before the altar of the church in Rutland for his bride to make her appearance. The church was not quite full, but everyone who was important in his life and

Lily's was there, with the exception of Lauren, who had insisted despite all their protests on staying at home. His mother was there, sitting in the front pew with his uncle and aunt, the Duke and Duchess of Anburey. Elizabeth, the Duchess of Portfrey, was there in the pew across the aisle from them. All the uncles and aunts and cousins were there. Captain and Mrs. Harris had come as well as a number of Portfrey's relatives. Baron Onslow had got up from his sickbed in Leicestershire in order to attend his granddaughter's wedding.

And Joseph, Marquess of Attingsborough, was at Neville's side as his best man.

There was a stirring of movement at the back of the church and a brief glimpse of Gwen as she stooped to straighten the hem of the bride's gown. The bride herself stayed tantalizingly out of sight.

But not for long. Portfrey stepped into view, immaculate in black and silver and white, and then the bride herself stepped up beside him and took his arm. The bride, in a white gown of classically simple design that shimmered in the dim light of the church interior, her short blond curls entwined with tiny white flowers and green leaves.

There was a sigh of satisfaction from those gathered in the pews.

But Neville did not see a bride dressed with elegance and taste and at vast expense. He saw Lily. Lily in her faded blue cotton dress, draped in on old army cloak that was still voluminous even though she had cut it down to size. Lily with bare feet despite the December chill, and unfettered hair in a wild mane down her back to her waist.

His bride.

His love.

His life.

He watched her coming toward him, her blue eyes steady on his and looking deep into him. And he knew in that moment that she was not seeing a bridegroom in wine velvet coat with silver brocaded waistcoat and gray knee breeches and crisp white linen. He knew she was seeing on officer of the Ninety-fifth, shabby and dusty in his green and black regimentals, his boots unpolished, his hair cropped short.

She smiled at him and he realized that he was smiling back. Portfrey was placing her hand in his and turning to take his seat beside Elizabeth.

Neville was back in the church at Rutland Park with his elegantly, expensively dressed bride. His beautiful Lily. Beautiful in her wildness, beautiful in her elegance.

"Dearly beloved, we are gathered..."

He turned his attention to the service that would join them together in the eyes of church and state, just as that service in the hills of central Portugal had joined them forever in their own hearts.

❧

Cold air met them when they stepped out of the church. But it was the coldness of a perfect winter's day, the sort of coldness that whipped color into cheeks and a sparkle into eyes and energy into muscles.

Lily laughed. "Oh, dear," she said.

She really had not noticed as they had walked up the aisle after signing the church register, smiling to right and to left at relatives and friends, who beamed back at them, that a significant number of the congregation, especially its younger members, had disappeared. It was obvious now. There they were on either side of the winding churchyard path, their hands loaded with ammunition.

Neville was laughing too. "Where the devil," he asked irreverently, "did they come by all those live flowers in December?"

"Father's hothouses," Lily guessed. "But they are no longer flowers. They are *petals*."

Hundreds of them. Thousands of them. All in the clutches of cousins who waited gleefully to pelt the bride and groom with them.

"Well," Neville said, eyeing the open carriage that was to take them back to the house for the wedding breakfast, "we must not disappoint them and walk sedately as if we did not mind being covered with debris, Lily. We had better run for it."

He grasped her hand tightly, and laughing gaily they ran the gauntlet down the winding path while the cousins cheered and whooped and had the air raining multicolored petals on their hair and their bridal clothes.

"Sanctuary," Neville said, still laughing when they reached the carriage. He handed Lily inside and reached out to wrap about her shoulders the white, fur-trimmed cloak that awaited her there. "Uh-oh."

Lily snuggled into her petal-lined cloak while Neville stood up in the carriage and shook one fist at the merry wedding guests. They were all there now, sober adults as well as riotous youngsters. The countess had been weeping, Lily saw, and she stretched out a hand to her mother-in-law and kissed her when she came closer. She kissed Elizabeth, who was also dewy-eyed, and hugged her father, who was pretending that the cold had set his eyes to watering.

Neville, still standing in the carriage, was hurling a shower of coins in the direction of a large group of villagers gathered to observe the spectacle. The children among them shrieked and scampered to pick up the treasure.

And then the carriage was in motion, and both Lily and Neville became aware that it was dragging a whole arsenal of ribbons and bows and bells behind it.

"One would think," Neville said, settling beside Lily, "that the cousins had nothing better to do with their time."

"You have a petal on your nose," she said, laughing gleefully and reaching out to remove it.

But he captured her hand as soon as she had done so and carried it to his lips. His own laughter had faded. She gazed into his eyes, her own glowing.

"Lily," he said. "My wife. My countess."

"Yes." She opened her hand to cup his

cheek. They had turned a bend in the country lane that would take them back to the house. Church and wedding guests and villagers had disappeared from sight. "I have changed identity so many times in the past two years that I have not known quite who I am or who I ought to be."

"I know." He set his hand over the back of hers. "And now you have found yourself at last? Who are you, Lily?"

"I am Lily Doyle," she said, "and Lady Frances Lilian Montague. And Lily Wyatt, Countess of Kilbourne. I am all three."

"You sound confused still," he said wistfully.

But she shook her head and smiled at him, all her happiness shining from her eyes.

"I am all the persons I have ever been," she said, "and all the experiences I have ever lived. I do not have to make choices. I do not have to deny one identity in order to claim another. I am who I am. I am Lily." Her smile became gay. "Also known as your wife."

He turned his head, closed his eyes, and pressed his lips to her wrist. "Yes," he said. "That is exactly who you are. You are Lily. The woman I love. I *do* love you, Lily."

"I know." She bent her head closer to his. "You loved me enough to let me go in order that I might find myself."

"And you have come back to me."

"Yes," she said. "Because I did not have to, Neville. Because I could come freely and offer myself freely. And because I love you. I always have. From the first moment I saw you talking to Papa. You were my hero then. You became my friend after that. And then my love. And now you are even more than that. You are the person I can meet as an equal and love as an equal."

"Have I told you," he asked her, smiling slowly at her, "what a beautiful bride you make, Lily?"

"Oh," she said, "you have Elizabeth to thank for that. She is the one who convinced me that this gown was the one and that I would look better with just flowers in my hair than with a bonnet and veil."

"I meant," he said, "in your blue cotton dress with your army cloak and nothing in your hair at all. Not even a hairpin."

"Oh." She bit her lip. "What a lovely thing to say. And you were never more handsome than in your well-worn regimentals. Neville, how *fortunate* we are to have two such wedding days to remember."

"Uh-oh," he said suddenly. He was looking ahead along the lane while Lily was still looking into his face. She turned her head sharply.

"Oh, dear," she said.

Every servant from Rutland Park, she would swear, from the butler on down to the lowliest undergardener, was out on the terrace. They were neatly lined up in order of rank to greet the newlyweds. They were also— every last one of them—armed to the teeth with flower petals.

Neville set an arm about Lily's shoulders and bent his head to look into her face. She gazed back at him. Their lovely interlude of privacy was over, it seemed. At least for now.

"Until tonight, my love," he said.

"Yes," she said wistfully. "Until tonight."

They turned laughing faces toward the servants and the floral ambush awaiting them.

JRW